The Madonna *of* Bolton

MATT CAIN

First published in 2018
This paperback edition first published in 2019

Unbound
6th Floor Mutual House,
70 Conduit Street,
London W1S 2GF

www.unbound.com

Text Design by Ellipsis, Glasgow

A CIP record for this book is available from the British Library

ISBN 978-1-78352-800-4 (B-format paperback)
ISBN 978-1-78352-618-5 (trade hbk)
ISBN 978-1-78352-729-8 (trade paperback)
ISBN 978-1-78352-620-8 (ebook)
ISBN 978-1-78352-619-2 (limited edition)

Printed and bound in Great Britain by Clays Ltd, Elcograf S.p.A.

For Mum and Dad, my original idols and still the best.

And for Ruth and Andrew, my first ever teammates
and still on my side.

And for Marie, who'll always remember.

Contents

Prologue

I put the phone down and sit up straight, staring into the darkness. By the side of my bed the alarm clock flashes 02.45.

People always say that when the phone rings in the middle of the night you know it's going to be bad news. But the funny thing is, when I was woken up by the sound of my mobile, the first thing I thought was that a friend was out drinking and wanted to know if I was in town – either that or they wanted to share a drunken 'I love you' experience. God knows I've put my friends through enough of those myself.

'You know what,' I'll slur to whoever I'm with at the end of a night out, 'I think you're brilliant. I really *really* love you.'

But I shake the words out of my head. No, this time it isn't that. It isn't that at all. Although right now I wish more than anything else that it was.

I stand up and pull on my dressing gown. If I quickly pack my things and leave London now I can be back in Bolton by the start of the day.

I pad into the kitchen and fill the kettle. As I take out a mug and drop in a teaspoon of instant coffee, I feel a twist of frustration. It's been months and months since I was last home; there are so many unhappy memories there and so many relationships I'm finding it difficult to deal with. But yesterday, as if from nowhere, I finally found myself *wanting* to go back. I suddenly felt homesick and wanted to reconnect with my family. I wanted to see the very people I've been running away from.

Then this happened, one of the things I've been dreading most for my whole life. And now I'm being called home for a completely different reason, a reason that makes me feel sick with fear – fear that, after all this time staying away, I might just have left it too late to go back.

Part One

Lucky Star

My love story begins during a time when little boys want to grow up to be Michael Jackson and little girls want to be just like Princess Diana. I'm at an age when the most important thing in life is remembering my Green Cross Code, never trusting strangers and making it through the mental arithmetic test my teacher sets every Friday – because, as she's so fond of saying, when we're grown-ups we won't be able to carry a calculator around *all* the time.

It's my ninth birthday and we're having a special tea to celebrate. Only my close family are there as we're having it at home, in our box-shaped 1960s pebble-dashed semi in a suburb of Bolton. I sit at the kitchen table with Mum, Dad, Grandma and my brother Joe and can feel the happiness warming me up from within as Mum leans over to light the candles on my cake. She's made me a Victoria sandwich with my name iced on the top in big letters – Charlie. She's particularly proud of it as baking isn't her forte and she's never attempted anything as complicated as piping a name onto a cake before, even if she has misjudged the spacing so that the 'i' and the 'e' are both squashed up at the edge. I don't care, though, because I know how hard she must have tried.

'What do you think, love?' she asks, brightly.

'I love it, Mum,' I chirp. 'It's the best cake I've ever had.'

Her face breaks into a broad grin and, as she finishes lighting the candles, I notice that she's being careful to keep her hair tucked away from the matches. Although I've always thought my mum's pretty, there's one thing that really makes her stand out from the crowd – her naturally blonde hair. It's something she spends a lot of money looking after and a lot of time talking about; I've lost track of the number of occasions I've overheard her asking her friends if they think its exact shade is closer to baby, honey or California blonde. She never tires of telling me and Joe that we don't know how lucky we are to have 'hit the jackpot' by inheriting her hair colour, something she always refers to as her 'trump card'. 'Although I wasted it on your dad,' she'll sometimes add if Dad's in earshot and has done something to annoy her. 'I threw it all away on a man who doesn't appreciate it.'

If Dad doesn't immediately rise to the bait, Mum will go on to tell him about a handsome customer she's served at work in Bolton Market Hall who's told her she looks like Farrah Fawcett in *Charlie's Angels* or Goldie Hawn in *Private Benjamin*.

'Maggie, you work on a women's underwear stall,' Dad will pipe back at her. 'So I wouldn't get too excited about some bloke who comes in to buy frilly knickers.'

At this point Mum usually huffs loudly and tells Dad that it's always nice to be complimented, after which he'll reassure her that she's 'a beltin' looking woman' and whatever he's done will be promptly forgiven.

I guess it's fair to say my dad isn't what you'd call romantic; in fact, he's fond of describing himself as a 'man's man', which for some reason he thinks excuses him from any effort at romance. He's bald with a thick brown moustache and muscles that strain at his shirt sleeves; his job involves lifting around heavy loads all day as he delivers lard and cooking fat to chip shops and food vans all over Bolton. When he comes home from work at five o'clock in the evening, he sometimes makes me and Joe laugh by flexing his muscles, kissing them and saying, 'Eat your heart out, Popeye!'

Right now Dad stands up from the kitchen table to turn the lights out so that everyone can sing 'Happy Birthday'. As I listen with glee, my feet jiggling away under the table, I try to decide what to wish for. The problem is there are far too many things I want. I'm very pleased when I eventually work out how to narrow everything down to just one wish – to get *loads and loads* of presents. And then I blow out all nine candles.

'Hurray!' everyone choruses. 'Hip, hip, hurray!'

After we've demolished the cake, we go through to the front room so that I can unwrap my presents. The main living space of our home has a heavily patterned shag carpet, walls that are painted bright orange, and a stripy purple three-piece suite; even though we're a good few years into the 1980s, in Bolton the new decade is only just beginning and the 1970s still cling on to most areas of life, especially interior design. In front of the fire stands an enormous Bell's Whisky bottle that's been emptied of booze and is now filled with so much of Mum and Dad's loose change that it reminds me of a pirate's treasure chest. And finishing off the room are several of Mum's much-loved houseplants, including a huge cheese plant and an overgrown ivy that trails around the skirting boards on all four walls.

At the moment, however, our front room is dominated by a massive stack of presents that stand piled up in the centre. I bowl in and begin to unwrap them with the crazed desperation of a starving animal hunting for food. I'm delighted to find boxes of felt tip pens and art materials as well as several *Star Wars* figures and an elaborate Ewok Village from *The Return of the Jedi*. Joe looks on, wide-eyed – he's two years older than me and obsessed with *Star Wars*. I'm chuffed with the presents I've got but even more chuffed that for once I've managed to impress my big brother.

As tends to happen when it's my birthday, I also get a few presents I don't really want; this year these include two packets of plastic soldiers, a Bolton Wanderers football kit, and an electric boardgame called Computer Battleship. I always feel like this kind of present has been bought for a different boy to me, or the boy some people want me to be, but I can't bear the idea of upsetting anyone on my birthday so pretend to be pleased. Besides, I don't want to appear ungrateful; as Mum's fond of saying, some children at my school don't get any presents at all, such as Steven Spriggs, whose dad has just lost his job in one of the town's last cotton mills, or the Pickup sisters, who don't celebrate birthdays or Christmas because they're Jehovah's Witnesses.

And anyway, I'm being bombarded with far too many brilliant presents for me to feel even remotely disappointed. My favourite of all has to be a brand new Soda Stream. Ever since I saw this advertised on telly I've desperately wanted one. It looks so modern and so much fun that for months I've fantasized about concocting colourful cocktails as the kids from school look on with envy.

'*Get busy with the fizzy – Soda Stream!*'

For children like me growing up in Bolton, the back pages of the Argos catalogue are like an encyclopaedia of toys. If there's anything we want for Christmas or birthdays we'll look it up first in what's become our Bible. Every day for weeks I've left the catalogue lying around the house, strategically opened on the page with the coveted Soda Stream. In the kitchen, in Dad's tool shed, even on the toilet seat. I'm thrilled to see now that my persistence has paid off.

'Oh thanks a lot!' I say as I unwrap it. 'This is the best present *ever*!'

Once my excitement has died down, Dad helps me set it up behind the minibar. 'It's just like being down The Flat Iron,' he approves, in his strong Lancashire accent.

'Very snazzy, love,' agrees Mum, her accent equally broad. 'You look like a proper little barman.'

I can't quite believe I've been given such a grown-up present. Until now, the most grown-up I've ever felt is when Mum gives me a new twenty-pence piece and sends me to the shop on my own to buy her a Walnut Whip. I'm overjoyed and make a big show of reading out the different flavours and then serving everyone a drink.

'I'nt it marvellous?' Grandma coos as she looks on. 'And to think that in my day we had to make do with Corporation pop.'

'Hey Charlie,' yaps Joe, 'can I have a go?'

I pretend to think it over. 'Oh go on then. But only if you let me play with your Millennium Falcon.'

'Deal!'

'How about trying on that Wanderers strip?' chips in Dad. 'Or you and me having a game of Computer Battleship?'

I've no idea how to reply; I'm not remotely interested in playing war games and surely my birthday's the one day in the year when I don't have to worry about liking things in order to impress my dad?

'Urm, do you mind if we do it later, Dad?' I attempt. I watch his smile wilt and my heart sinks like a knackered lift.

Thankfully at that moment our attention is distracted by the sound of the front door opening and the arrival of my Auntie Jan.

'Coo-ee! Where's the birthday boy?'

I jump up and bounce over to greet her. Auntie Jan is Mum's younger sister and I think she's ace. When she babysits she lets me and Joe stay up late to watch *Magnum P.I.* and, if we're really lucky, *Cagney and Lacey*. She listens to music by Duran Duran and Culture Club and everyone says she looks like the blonde one out of Bananarama. All the kids in the street think she's dead trendy – today she's wearing a cerise pink rara skirt with a banana-yellow off-the-shoulder top, electric-blue leg warmers and white stiletto heels. Auntie Jan's *well* ace.

'Hiya!' I squeak.

'Hello, sunshine!' She gives me a kiss and as usual smells of Wrigley's Juicy Fruit. 'Many Happy Returns!'

'Thanks. Have you brought me a present?'

'By 'eck, Charlie, let me get through the door first!'

Once she's settled and has been served a Sarsaparilla from the Soda Stream, Auntie Jan takes my present out of her bag. I rip off the paper and find two pairs of towelling socks – one luminous green and one luminous pink.

'That way you can wear them on odd feet,' she says.

'Oh mega, thanks!'

Underneath the socks I notice that there's something else. I tug away the wrapping paper and pull it out. It's a 7" single, the first one I've ever owned. I wipe the smudged fingerprints off my glasses so I can take a proper look. On the cover there's a bare-shouldered woman wearing bright pink lipstick and a big crucifix in her ear. She has black rags tied through her bleached blonde hair and her arms are almost entirely covered in plastic bangles. The look on her face is one of arrogance and a defiant sexiness. I'm too young to understand any of it but am intrigued and want to know more.

'She's called Madonna,' explains Auntie Jan, as I read the name on the front of the record sleeve. 'And the song's called "Lucky Star". I heard it at Ritzy's last week and thought it was dead good.'

Dad isn't so keen. 'Flamin' 'eck, Jan,' he says, 'I don't know who this bird is but she looks like one of them girls down Shifnall Street!'

''Ey Frank, you be quiet in front of the kids,' says Mum.

'Dad,' I say, 'where's Shifnall Street?'

Mum rolls her eyes. '*Now* look what you've done!'

'Oh please tell me where it is. Please, please, please!'

'It's nowhere, love,' she replies. 'It's just some place naughty girls go to play kissy kissy with bad boys.'

I'm fascinated. 'Have you ever been, Auntie Jan?'

'No I have *not*!' she huffs.

'But Mum said you always play kissy kissy with bad boys.'

'*Did* she now?'

Mum's neck starts to flush red. 'Honestly, Frank, I wish you'd keep your trap shut sometimes.'

Jan folds her arms. 'Anyway,' she says, 'your dad's talking rubbish – this woman's American and I reckon she's going to be a big star.'

I look again at the picture on the front cover. I may be too young to appreciate what goes on in Bolton's red light district but I can tell there's something a bit naughty about this Madonna. For some reason, though, I really like it.

'Mum, please can we play my new record?'

She looks relieved that I've changed the subject. 'Course we can, love.'

There's an excited silence as we all gather round the record player and wait for the song to begin. As I hear the opening notes I can honestly say it's love at first sound. By the time the vocal comes in I can feel the edges of my mouth brighten into a big grin. Madonna starts singing about a man she calls her lucky star, someone who'll shine on her all the time and be there to guide her through life, whatever happens. Straight away I think this is a lovely idea.

And Auntie Jan's right; the song *is* dead good. In fact, it's dead, *dead* good. And it has the added bonus of making Dad forget all about that game of Computer Battleship. Unfortunately the rest of my family don't see the appeal.

'Are you sure it's on at the right speed?' asks Dad. 'Her voice sounds a bit high.'

'God, Frank,' sighs Jan, 'that's what she's supposed to sound like!'

'By 'eck,' says Mum, 'you'd think she'd got hold of one of them balloons and swallowed a gobful of helium.'

I pay no attention and listen away. As Madonna's vocals bounce around our front room, I become aware of something stirring inside me. Somehow I understand that I've just found my own lucky star. And I feel energized. I feel uplifted. I feel happy.

If only the rest of my family could feel the same.

'She sounds like she's got a peg on her nose,' says Joe. Everyone falls about laughing.

I hate it when Joe sides with Mum and Dad; it makes me feel like the odd one out in my own family.

'Eeh, she's not a patch on Gracie Fields,' says Grandma. 'Now there were a *proper* singer.'

Dad agrees. 'You mark my words, lad, this Madonna's nothing but a flash-in-the-pan. She'll be a has-been by Christmas.'

I take no notice. My foot's tapping and I'm hooked already. As soon as the song finishes I ask to listen to it again. We have a rule in our house that if it's your birthday you can choose whatever telly or music you want all day. Needless to say, I drive everyone mad with repeated plays of 'Lucky Star' for the rest of the evening.

A couple of hours later, Auntie Jan and Grandma have both left, as have a few other friends and members of the family who arrived later in the evening. I've had my bath, brushed my teeth and put on my pyjamas. I've even managed to sneak in another piece of cake Mum saved, after which I had to brush my teeth again. And at the end of all this, Madonna's *still* playing – and, as I've learnt the lyrics, I've started singing along. Mum announces that she just can't take it anymore. 'Come on, Charlie – it's past your bedtime and you've got school tomorrow.'

'But Mum, I'm not even tired yet!'

'Your Mam's right,' booms Dad. 'Get up them dancers before Wee Willie Winkie gets you.'

I give a big sigh but decide not to argue. I don't actually mind that the day's over. It's been brilliant and I couldn't feel happier. I say my goodnights and thank Mum and Dad once again for their presents. All in all, it's been my best birthday yet.

I lie in bed gazing up at the luminous stars Dad's stuck onto my ceiling. I don't feel sleepy at all and in my head I can still hear the lyrics to 'Lucky Star'. I'm nine years old and I've just fallen in love. Little do I know it's a love that will influence the rest of my life.

Dress You Up

'Charlie Matthews and Shanaz Gulati – you're on next!'

I can feel my heart thumping in my chest. Flippin' 'eck I'm nervous!

I'm in my final year of primary school and about to take to the stage for the first time. To me, my school's enormous, even though it only consists of one dirty redbrick building, a concrete playground with a football pitch, and a 1960s prefab where we all go for parties on Pancake Tuesday and St George's Day. At the centre of the school is the main hall, a room so important that we use it for loads of different things – assembly, dinnertime and even games of rounders when it's too wet to do PE outside.

Right now the hall's full of schoolchildren and their families, all their eyes trained on the stage. I peek through the curtains and look at them. Sitting on the front row is the headmistress Miss Leach – or Miss Bleach as everyone calls her because she's so strict. Miss Bleach's favourite expression is 'Woe betide' and whenever she gets cross, she screams and shouts until the veins stick out on her neck like the Incredible Hulk or Deirdre Barlow on *Coronation Street*.

Sitting just a few seats away is Vince Hargreaves, someone who terrifies me even more than Miss Bleach. Like me, Vince is in the top class and everyone knows he's the cock of the school. For some reason he's taken a particular dislike to me – he'll steal my glasses so I can't see anything at playtime, give me Chinese burns whenever he feels like it and, if he's in a really bad mood, throw my satchel onto the railway line next to the playground. Right now he looks in my direction and I'm pretty sure he catches my eye. I quickly shut the curtains and fart with fear.

Every Christmas in my school, the top class put on a show for their parents and the rest of the children, singing and dancing along to their favourite pop songs. So far this year, Marina Broadbent and Lucy Drury, who both have fringes so long you can't see their eyes, have bounced their way through Wham!'s 'Wake Me Up Before You Go Go', and Steven Spriggs, who always seems to have a hole in his trousers and a cold sore on his top lip, has pulled off an uncannily accurate impression of Shakin' Stevens. Right now, Damian Bradley and his girlfriend Bev Adams, who caused a stir when they were caught timing themselves necking with a stopwatch behind the caretaker's room, are finishing off their version of 'Take on Me' by a-ha. The stakes are high – so far each performance has been a huge success. Shanaz and I have something different planned and, even though I let her convince me it was a good idea when we were hidden away in the safety of her bedroom, now that it's come down to it I'm not sure what I've let myself in for. From the look on her face, Shanaz isn't either.

'Good luck, Shanaz,' I stammer.

'Don't say that!' she yelps. 'Don't you know it's *bad* luck?'

'Really? What are you supposed to say then?'

'Break a leg. Honestly – it's what all the stars say. I saw it on *Fame* last week.'

Shanaz is so clever and my best friend in the whole world. We first met in reception class and bonded by painting a big picture of Wonder Woman together on our first day. To me Shanaz is brave and fearless; she can climb to the top of the tree behind the headmistress's office and pick leaves off the thistles near the kitchens without being stung. She tells really great stories, like the one about her grandma, who grew up in a Maharajah's palace in India but escaped to England so that she could marry a stable boy she'd been forbidden from seeing by her parents. And at dinnertimes she always has exotic things like chapattis and bhajis in her butty box, which I think look much more exciting than my dull salmon-paste sarnies and Trio or Penguin biscuit. For some reason, though, the other kids at school aren't so impressed. They complain loudly about the smell of her food, pulling faces and holding their noses as if it's disgusting. If there are no dinner ladies around they even spit at Shanaz and call her a 'Paki'. Whenever they do, she just smiles and says, 'Actually, my family are from India and my grandma's a *princess*!'

I never really understand why the other kids don't like Shanaz but the truth is they don't like me much either. Not only do I have no interest in the war games the boys like to play but I'm no good at football and always come last in every event on sports day, which makes everyone think I'm weird and not a proper boy – at least that's what they never tire of telling me. Maybe that's why Shanaz and I have become such good friends, because I'm the only one who doesn't mind what the other kids say about her and she's the only one who doesn't mind what they all say about me. Not that we ever talk about that; the last thing we want to do when we're together is to go over things that make us unhappy. No, as soon as we're together we play games that make us believe nothing bad ever happens to us at all.

When we were little, this mainly consisted of re-enacting scenes from films like *Bugsy Malone* and TV shows like *Rentaghost*. Or we'd dress up Shanaz's pet cat in doll's clothes, brush its hair into bunches and play Mummies and Daddies, pushing it around in her sister's pram. Once we were a bit older we left behind those kinds of silly, childish games and instead devoured every volume of *The Chronicles of Narnia*, chatting endlessly through each book and painting pictures of the castle of Cair Paravel and the Battle of Beruna that we'd stick up on Shanaz's bedroom wall. Shortly after that we moved on to the *Choose Your Own Adventure* books, which we thought were ace as at the end of each chapter you got to decide what happened next. We'd never read anything like it and couldn't get enough of them – we'd borrow one each from the local library, race through them in a day or two and then swap books with each other.

But recently we've decided that we've outgrown *Choose Your Own Adventure* books too. Now that we're ten it's time for us to find a more mature way to spend our time. And that's how we became obsessed with Madonna.

These days it's not difficult for us to feed our obsession as Madonna's everywhere; this is the year of Live Aid, the increasing success of the *Like a Virgin* album and the film *Desperately Seeking Susan*. Every week Shanaz and I buy *Smash Hits* or *Look-In* magazine, cut out the posters and song lyrics and stick them up on our bedroom walls. We use my mum and dad's new VHS recorder to tape her videos on *Top of the Pops*, playing them back repeatedly to study their every frame. And we devise elaborate dance routines to her music, performing imaginary concerts to audiences of thousands in my backyard. Madonna's our idol and we want to be just like her. The way we look at it, this year's Christmas show has given us our opportunity.

'How are you feeling?' asks Shanaz.

'Terrified,' I bleat.

'Well, try not to be. I bet Madonna doesn't get nervous when she goes on stage.'

I make a big effort to relax and tell myself I'm doing nothing wrong; all I'm doing is trying to be like Madonna and she's so famous that loads of people are doing that at the moment. The only thing is, all the people you see dressing up like her are girls. I look down at my outfit and feel my heart slam into my throat. I wonder whether it will work if I actually say a prayer to Madonna. Oh please make this go well, Madonna!

We're about to perform a routine to 'Dress You Up', using a big coat stand and a screen that we'll disappear behind to change costumes, adding hats, fingerless gloves and other Madonna-themed accessories as we go along. We've adapted the dance routine from a performance we saw her do in the video of *The Virgin Tour* and have spent months rehearsing it in Shanaz's bedroom. We found two long blonde wigs in the school dressing-up box and Auntie Jan helped us put together our costumes using her sewing machine at home, agreeing to keep the whole thing secret from Mum and Dad. She's made us blue and yellow jackets to wear like the one Madonna had on tour, with blue miniskirts and matching lacy tights. Shanaz has a BOY TOY belt buckle tied around her waist and I'm wearing a huge crucifix around my neck. I've never dressed up like a girl before and think it's ace fun. The only thing that slightly spoils it is having to wear my big plastic NHS glasses on the end of my nose. But I try not to worry about it too much – if I don't wear them I won't be able to see what I'm doing. And it's important that I get the routine absolutely right. This is my chance to impress everyone. This is my chance to make the other kids like me.

'Now Ladies and Gentlemen,' announces Mr Fletcher in his broad Bolton accent, 'please welcome Shanaz Gulati and Charlie Matthews to sing 'Dress You Up' by Maradona!'

The audience chuckle at his mistake although he doesn't seem to notice. By now my heart's pounding so violently that I'm worried it might burst through my ribcage. We stand to one side to make way for Bev Adams and Damian Bradley, who are just leaving the stage and come barging past. They take one look at us and burst out laughing.

'Freaks!' hisses Bev.

'Weirdos!' adds Damian, elbowing me in the ribs.

I try to take no notice and look at Shanaz and smile feebly.

As the four beats of the introduction sound, we take to the stage in darkness. When the lights come up we launch into the routine and straight away begin to relax. We're singing along to the instrumental version on the B-side of the 12" single and so far I'm amazed to find that things are going well. For those first few moments on stage we understand what it must feel like to be Madonna performing a gig in front of thousands of fans. And the feeling's mega.

For the first verse and chorus I sing with so much joy I don't even notice the reactions of people in the audience – and forget to worry about what people think of me. In fact, I'm so carried away with my performance that for once I forget to feel any kind of fear at all. I've never experienced such a powerful sensation and feel as if I've enough energy to take on the world.

But then I pause so that Shanaz can sing a few lines on her own and that's when I notice everyone's faces; most of the kids and their families are looking at us with a mixture of fascination and, for some reason, distaste. I can just about make out my own family watching by the door – Mum's pawing her neck as it flushes redder than ever and Dad's mouth is gaping so wide that even from this distance I can see his tonsils. When I catch sight of Joe, his eyes are bulging in their sockets and his chin plummeting slowly, his Jawbreaker gobstopper eventually falling to the floor and rolling halfway across the room.

A few rows in front of them, I spot Miss Bleach glaring up at us disapprovingly, all steely expression and pursed lips. Just a few seats away from her, Vince Hargreaves glowers at me and punches his fist into his palm. I tell myself not to pay any attention but to concentrate on my performance.

Miraculously, we're working our way through the rather complicated dance routine without a hitch. The problems only start during the bridge in the middle of the song, when the record skips and we lose where we're up to. We just about manage to catch up with the music when it skips again and leaves us really lost. We freeze and look at each other in panic. I hear a few kids snigger in the audience and am suddenly paralysed by fear. I recognize Vince Hargreaves laughing like Muttley the dog and see him pointing right at me.

What do we do?

What would Madonna do if she were us?

And what will all the kids think if we mess up now?

Shanaz gives me a determined glare and nods at me to carry on.

We throw ourselves back into it, determined to give it our all and make up for the hiccup. I move forward with a twist and hand Shanaz a fur stole and rosary beads, which she wraps around her neck as she carries on singing. As she leaps forward to launch into the next move, it's obvious that her rosary beads have become attached to my crucifix. By the time we realize what's wrong, we're all tangled up and it's too late. I lose my balance and collapse into her, propelling her forward and over the edge of the stage. Before I know it, I'm lying in a heap on the floor of the auditorium, my blonde wig in Miss Bleach's lap and my eyes held by the gaze of a snorting Vince Hargreaves.

The music's still playing loudly and no one can hear me scream. As I hit the floor I must have crashed down onto my leg and done myself an injury. The pain's almost unbearable. I can't tell what's going on but there's a big kerfuffle and lots of adults fussing around me. And then I black out.

When I eventually come round, I'm sitting in the back of an ambulance on my way to hospital. My costume has been hacked off and the music to 'Dress You Up' has been replaced by the sound of a blaring siren. Mum and Dad are asking lots of questions and a sweaty paramedic with eyebrows as thick as Dad's moustache is prodding me in various places. He eventually announces that I've broken my leg.

'Waaaaah!' Mum starts wailing. 'Is he going to be like that Joey Deacon?'

'Shut up, you daft bat!' says Dad. 'It's only a broken leg. I bet you can hardly feel a thing, can you, lad?'

But I *can* feel it. I can feel it a lot. I tell myself to be brave but the pain is so bad that I start to feel dizzy. I black out again.

The next thing I know, I'm lying in a hospital bed with my leg in plaster and a sombre-looking Mum, Dad and Joe huddled around me. Mum's trying to get me to drink a cup of hot OXO, which she always makes when Joe and I have anything wrong with us.

'Come on, love,' she coos, 'a nice beef tea will do you good.'

Joe holds his head in his hands. 'You're so embarrassing, Charlie,' he moans, 'I hope none of my mates from footie find out you dressed up like a girl.'

Dad grumbles away under his breath. 'Well, all I can say is, let that be a lesson to you, lad. That's what you get for parading round the stage tarted up like a woman.'

I wait for Mum to defend me but she doesn't. In the past she's sometimes been an ally, such as when Dad found out I liked skipping and confiscated my skipping ropes and she let me know where they were hidden. Or the time I wanted a length of elastic to try out the new craze for what the girls at school called 'Chinese skipping' and she secretly bought me some from a gypsy who came knocking on the door. But then Dad started calling me a 'Mummy's boy' and all that stopped. It doesn't look like it's going to be starting again now.

'Oh maybe it *was* a mistake, love,' says Mum. 'This is only Bolton, after all.'

'What are you on about, woman?' Dad bellows. 'There's nowt wrong with Bolton!'

'I never said there was, Frank.'

'Yeah, well, that kind of carry-on would be embarrassing anywhere. I don't know, Charlie, what were you thinking?'

As I listen to his words, a deep shame about what I've done sits in me like a boulder. I can feel hot, frustrated tears beginning to leak from my eyes and sniff them back quickly. If I start to cry I'll only make things a lot worse.

As the event keeps replaying itself in my mind I feel overwhelmed by a sickening sense of humiliation. I might have had my doubts about the performance we were planning beforehand but I enjoyed myself so much during rehearsals that I couldn't see how going ahead with it would be a bad idea at all. I never for one second dreamed it would end up like this. But when I close my eyes now all I can see is Vince Hargreaves, sniggering as he looks at me lying in a heap on the floor. The whole thing has been a disaster and I've made an utter fool of myself in front of the entire school. I don't know how I can ever face anyone again. They didn't think much of me before – now they'll think I'm *really* rubbish!

'Flamin' 'eck!' sighs Dad. 'I reckon I'll take you to watch the football next week.'

'Yeah,' agrees Mum, 'that might be a good idea, love.'

As I listen to their words, I feel hollowed out. If Mum and Dad don't like me the way I am, what hope do I have with anyone else?

I groan aloud. I try to be like my idol and this is where it gets me.

Maybe this love story is going to be a bit more complicated than I thought.

Holiday

While Dad lights the barbecue Mum fills up her wine glass. 'This is the life!' she croons.

'You're right there, Maggie,' says Dad. 'What a beltin' holiday!'

The four of us are sitting outside our tent getting ready for tea. Everyone feels rested and relaxed after another long day in the sun. The Matthews family are abroad for the first time and, as far as I'm concerned, France is the best place in the whole world.

''Ere, do you lads want some Orangina?' asks Dad.

I love Orangina – to me it tastes like bottled sunshine.

'Oh *mega*!'

This has easily been my favourite holiday yet. Until this year the furthest we ever travelled was to Tenby and once to Scotland, when it was so cold and wet that I got really ill and we had to come home early. But being in France is totally different. I keep telling myself that we're in a foreign country and that Bolton's hundreds of miles away. I feel like I've discovered a real-life Narnia and don't want the fairytale to end. Looking around me now, I'm so pleased to see that the others feel the same way too.

'Well,' grins Dad. 'I'm as happy as a pig in muck.'

'If the girls at work could see me now,' breathes Mum. 'I feel just like Krystle Carrington!'

The funny thing is, the holiday didn't start particularly well. Two weeks ago, we drove all the way to Dover in our pea-green Austin Allegro. On the back seat, Joe and I played endless games of I Spy, which descended into bickering when the competitiveness kicked in and we started coming up with two, three and even four-word answers. Dad said we had to stick to answers that began with one letter but this still didn't stop us breaking into a full-on fight. As Mum tried to keep the peace, she unfortunately forgot that she was supposed to be in charge of navigating and we soon realized that we were lost. When Dad accused Mum of not being able to read a map properly, a full-scale row erupted. It continued as we raced through Dover to catch the ferry, and then all the way through France, where Dad struggled to get used to driving on the other side of the road and kept bumping into the kerb and swearing crossly.

Several hours later, when we finally arrived at our destination, we were all frazzled and fed up. But as soon as Dad parked up, everything changed. The sun winked at us from behind the clouds and as it gradually broke through it brightened up everyone's mood. Joe and I took our BMXs off the back of the car and pedalled off to explore the campsite. We were fascinated to find that it had its own little shops, playgrounds, a launderette and an area for a game French men like to play called boules. And the best thing was, we were free to roam around this whole new world on our own.

Every morning for the past two weeks I've woken up brimming with excitement about the day ahead. The first thing I do is bounce out of bed and zip open the tent door to see the bright blue sky; I just can't get over the contrast with Bolton, where it rains all the time and the sky's always a dull grey. We have a quick breakfast of croissants and *pains au chocolat* that Dad buys from the bakery, which taste so much better than the Ready Brek and hard-boiled egg I have at home. And then Joe and I rush out of the tent, eager to meet up with the new friends we've made. There's a French boy called Cyril who speaks like a character from *'Allo 'Allo*, and an Irish girl called Ciara who has a face full of freckles and says 'grand' a lot. In fact, there are all kinds of children on the campsite and they all seem to come from different countries – Sweden, the Netherlands, Belgium . . . I've been delighted to discover that none of them do impressions of my girlie voice or laugh at me when I skip around. Maybe because we're all so different to start off with, for once I don't feel like the odd one out and really enjoy the sensation of being one of the gang.

Mum and Dad seem to love being on holiday just as much as I do. Dad spends his time sitting in the shade reading a book about the role played by Lancashire soldiers in the Second World War, or drinking beer and playing boules with the other British dads. Mum spends most of her days sunbathing, gradually reducing the factor of her suncream from the hardcore eight she started with to some kind of oil that smells of coconuts, which as far as I can tell doesn't offer any protection from the sun at all. She's delighted with her tan but even more delighted with the colour of her hair, which she announces repeatedly is now 'definitely platinum'.

Mum's so busy working on her tan and lightening her hair, she doesn't mind if Joe and I disappear to the other side of the campsite to play around the pool, jumping in and out of the water in different formations and throwing a ten-franc coin into the deep end which we race each other to find. The agreement is that once an hour we report back to the tent so that she can slather us with suncream and squeeze lemon juice onto our hair.

'You'll look like little angels by the time we get back to Bolton,' she gushes, holding out a wet towel so we can dab the lemon out of our eyes.

'More like Hitler Youth if you ask me,' Dad smirks, although neither Joe nor I understand the joke.

After hours in the water we're always starving and today's no exception. As Dad prods the charcoal on the barbecue, I can hear my tummy rumble. I glance around and see that we all look tanned and healthy, although Mum and Dad have black teeth and tongues from the big carton of *vin de table* they've been steadily emptying all evening. But they don't seem to mind and I don't want to spoil things so keep quiet.

'I tell you what,' says Mum, 'I'm going to have to watch out – this wine's going straight to my head!'

'Aye,' says Dad, 'it's crackin' stuff, i'nt it?'

Mum drains her glass and hauls herself out of her chair. ''Ey Frank,' she slurs, 'come here and gizza kiss.'

Dad usually shies away from Mum's affection but ever since we arrived at the campsite he hasn't been able to keep his hands off her. Right now he happily trots over and kisses her fully on the lips. She starts to giggle flirtatiously.

'Eurgh!' complains Joe. 'Will you two stop necking?'

'Oh belt up, Joe! You're next – come here and give your mum a squeeze.'

Joe bats her away. 'Get off, Mum, you're *embarrassing*!'

'What're you on about? Nobody's looking!'

'I know but I'm not a kid anymore, am I?'

'Well, what about my baby then?' She staggers over and starts to nuzzle me. 'Come and give your mum a nice cuddle, Charlie.'

Even though she likes a glass of wine when she's doing the ironing and will sometimes polish off a bottle with Auntie Jan while she listens to her moan about her latest boyfriend, I've never seen Mum drunk before and think it's hilarious. I put my arms round her but struggle to breathe under the weight of her grip. Even so, it's lovely feeling her squeeze me so tight.

'Aw, little Charlie!'

I watch as Dad pours himself another glass of wine and spills half of it onto the table. 'Whoops-a-daisy!'

''Ey I tell you what, Frank,' says Mum, 'I think I'd better lay off the booze from now on – I don't want a thick head tomorrow.'

The very mention of tomorrow makes me feel heavy with dread. I can't bear to think of us having to pack up our luggage and drive home.

'Dad,' I say, 'I've just thought of something.'

'Oh yeah, what's that?'

'Well, don't you think it'd be mega if we came and lived here forever? I mean it's so much better than home.'

He looks at me and smiles. 'It's not as simple as that, lad. When you grow up you have to work to earn money. Life can be tough, you know.'

Mum puts her hand on my shoulder. 'We're on holiday now, love, and nobody can be on holiday *all* the time.'

'But our friend Cyril lives in France all the time. I don't understand why we can't move here too.'

'But Cyril was born here, love. He isn't on holiday and his family live here with him.'

'Well, why can't we all move here then? We could bring Grandma too.'

Dad laughs. 'Can you really imagine your grandma abroad? The furthest she's ever been is Blackpool!'

'Yeah, Charlie,' Joe agrees. 'Think about it properly – she'd miss dancing in the club, going to bingo and smoking fags with her mates.'

I can't believe Joe's siding with the adults just like he always does at home. We've been getting on so well on holiday and it's been great that for once he doesn't seem embarrassed by me. 'But Joe,' I stammer, 'how can you possibly want to go home?'

'Actually,' he says, trying his best to sound grown-up, 'I *like* it in Bolton. I'm looking forward to going to the Lads' Club after school and having a chippy tea on Fridays.'

'Eeh, that reminds me,' says Mum, 'I hope your Auntie Jan remembered to tape *Coronation Street* – I'm dying to see the fire in the Rovers.'

''Ey and don't forget the football season's starting in a few weeks,' says Dad. 'Now that I think of it, I'm really looking forward to getting home myself.'

As I listen to them speak I can feel the sense of frustration rising within me. I really don't want to go back to miserable Bolton, where the older I get the more the other children pick on me and call me names. But how can I tell Mum and Dad about that? How can I tell them the other kids have started to call me poof and queer, names I don't really understand but know from the way they say them they have to be the worst things ever. One time, Mr Fletcher overheard Vince Hargreaves and his mates chanting the words at me in the playground and he looked so disgusted he pretended not to notice and scurried off with his head down. What if Mum and Dad react in the same way? What if they even believe what the other kids say?

No, there's no way I can risk telling them. I remember how Dad carried on about me dressing up as Madonna in the school show and how disappointed in me he looked. Yet the funny thing is, while we've been on holiday he's stopped looking at me like that. It's as if we've left all our troubles behind and forgotten about the bad times – and to me that's something to celebrate. But now we're about to go home and everyone else is saying they *want* to go.

I fold my arms and sit down with a sulk. 'Well, I don't care,' I announce. 'When *I* grow up *I'm* going to live in France!'

Dad ignores me and begins serving out the meat. He plonks a burger onto my plate and I bite into it stroppily.

One day I'll show them. From now on my mind's made up. As soon as I'm old enough, I'm getting out of Bolton and coming right back here – and every day will be like one long holiday.

La Isla Bonita

'*¡Hola chicos!*' warbles the teacher. 'Welcome to your first Spanish lesson.'

Less than a month later and my summer holiday feels like a remote, misty memory. It's coming to the end of my first week at secondary school and I'm sitting in a chilly classroom as outside the rain's coming down sideways, lashing away at the rusty old windows so that they rattle on their hinges. I try to stay positive. Ever since discovering a new country on holiday I've been looking forward to learning a foreign language and now I'm doing just that. It doesn't matter that the language isn't French but Spanish. In fact, with Madonna singing the odd line in Spanish in 'La Isla Bonita', it seems entirely appropriate.

'Now, my name is Miss Wiggins,' says the teacher, a middle-aged woman who looks remarkably like a Womble and has applied her make-up so badly that her face is a different colour to her neck. 'But as we're here to learn Spanish I'd like you to call me *Señorita* Wiggins.'

Somebody at the back of the class sniggers and Señorita Wiggins begins to flush. Earlier today I heard some of the kids in my form saying her lessons are a doss as she can't control the class and sneaks into the storeroom to binge on Mars bars in between setting exercises. I hope the class I'm in aren't too hard on her, and flash her a supportive smile.

As she picks up some chalk and writes the word *señorita* on the blackboard, I take out my new vocab book and copy it down on the first page. One of the big changes that comes with moving up to secondary school is being allowed to write in pen rather than pencil. We've all been told to buy some Tipp-Ex to correct our mistakes, but even so, I take great care not to make any as I write my first word in Spanish.

Although this is only my fifth day at my new school, I've already discovered that it can be a hostile, bleak place. From the outside it doesn't look particularly welcoming; it's housed in a series of dour, characterless buildings that are surrounded by dull concrete yards and flat fields. But on the inside it's much worse; it's teeming with hundreds of kids all dressed in the uniform of rat-grey and pond-scum green, most of whom are much older than me and all of whom seem to talk about sex and swear constantly. Many of them are prone to violence and fights break out on a daily basis, which means there's a permanently tense atmosphere and just walking from one classroom to another can be terrifying.

Of course there are teachers around to keep the peace during break time, which is what everyone calls playtime now we're at secondary school, but nobody seems to have any respect for them. Admittedly, it's easy to see why; most of the teachers are pale, stale and male, with yellow sweat patches under their arms and breath that smells as if they've gargled with diarrhoea. There are the odd exceptions, such as the young music teacher Miss Whitehouse, who's popular with the boys because of her short skirts and low-cut tops, which have earned her the nickname Miss Whorehouse. And there's the athletic PE teacher

Mr Dobbs, who's a big hit with the girls because of the noticeably large bulge in his trousers; perhaps unsurprisingly, they call him Dobbin. But other than that, the teachers are only ever addressed with disdain and they're often openly disobeyed. I glance around the room and can tell from the looks on several faces that the kids in my new Spanish class aren't going to go easy on Señorita Wiggins; some of them are looking at her with all the mercilessness of a rattlesnake eyeing up a mouse.

'Now, has anyone ever been to Spain?' she asks, brightly.

After much coaxing, five or six children eventually put their hands up and admit that they've been on holiday to Majorca, Benidorm and the Costa del Sol. As Señorita Wiggins asks them questions and they reply in a series of mumbles and grunts, she points out the places they've been to on a map of Spain.

'*¡Muy bien!*' she says, with an enthusiasm that's already starting to border on desperate. 'I've been to several places in Spain but my boyfriend Roberto is from Torremolinos.'

As she draws out the sound of the word *Torremolinos* I marvel at the way she rolls her 'r's but most of the class scoff and snort.

'What, you mean *you've* got a boyfriend, Miss?' asks Sally Swallow, a hatchet-faced girl with chipped nails and an attitude you could break your teeth on.

Señorita Wiggins's neck stains a deeper shade of red. 'I do, actually, yes,' she quips. 'Now who knows how to say "boyfriend" in Spanish?'

She looks out at the sea of faces but is met with an insolent silence.

'The word you're looking for is *novio*,' she announces, forcing out a shaky smile. 'You never know, some of you girls might find it useful one day.'

'And don't forget Charlie Matthews, Miss!' shouts Vince Hargreaves, who's sitting splayed out on the back row. 'I bet he'd like a Spanish boyfriend!'

As the entire class bursts out laughing, I can feel my stomach falling away. Thankfully, Señorita Wiggins pretends she hasn't heard and moves quickly on. I suck in my breath and try to stay calm.

When I was preparing to move from primary to secondary school I hoped above all else that the other kids would stop terrorizing me, that the ones who were moving up with me would forget about the names they called me and there'd be a whole load of new kids who'd want to make friends. But if anything, the situation has got worse. Vince Hargreaves has been joined by the cocks of several other primary schools in Bolton, all of them desperate to prove to their peers that they're the toughest in their new school year – and the way they do this often involves picking on kids who are easy targets. Of course I'm not alone; anyone with red hair is laughed at for being ginger, some overweight kids are called 'fatsos', and anyone from a poor family is ridiculed for being a 'scrubber'. But the insults levelled at me always sound much worse and I can't seem to walk down a corridor without someone spitting out the word 'poof' or 'queer'.

I assume Shanaz is still being called a 'Paki' but once we're inside the school gates I hardly see her. She's in a different form to me and the way that the forms are grouped together for classes means we don't have any lessons together. Not only that but in break times boys and girls are kept in separate playgrounds, which we now call yards, so in between lessons I'm not allowed to see her and often don't speak to anyone at all. Part of me thinks I should try to make friends with some of the other boys who are bullied but I don't dare approach them, sensing that the association might taint me even further.

From time to time I'll spot Joe in the boys' yard but he'll just ignore me and pretend we've never met. I've no idea whether this is because he's by now so ashamed of me he doesn't want people to know we're related, or whether it's just in keeping with some secondary school etiquette I haven't yet grasped. Whatever the reason, it comes as a relief; I'd hate for Joe to hear what the other kids say about me and report it back to Mum and Dad.

As of yesterday I've decided to keep as low a profile as possible and have started eating my packed lunch in a toilet cubicle, chewing every mouthful as quietly as I can so that no one will notice I'm there. And every time I start a new class I've stopped asking the other kids if they want to sit next to me because I can't bear to hear their refusal on the grounds that they 'might catch AIDS'. I gaze at the empty seat beside me now and try not to look up at any of the kids who've just been laughing at me. I find an ink stain on the desk and stare at it intently, hoping it will somehow take me away from where I am. But it's no use; even though Señorita Wiggins is now teaching the class the word for 'girlfriend', I can still hear everyone's nasty laughter ringing in my ears. When I finally dare to look up, I can see Vince Hargreaves passing some kind of note to a boy called Carl Ashworth, who has a face full of angry spots and I've noticed in PE already has huge clumps of hair under his arms. I watch in terror as he looks up at me, nods at Vince and then writes something on the note and passes it on.

'Now, who in the class can tell me what Spain is famous for?' continues Señorita Wiggins, trying to remain unruffled. There's a sudden burst of enthusiasm.

'Real Madrid,' shouts Vince.

'Sangria,' adds Sally Swallow.

'Bullfighting,' chips in Carl Ashworth.

'*Muy bien*,' says Señorita Wiggins, writing the words down on the board. 'And who can tell me what people in Spain like to eat?'

This time there's an uninterested silence.

'Has anyone heard of paella?' she asks, pronouncing the double 'l' like a 'y'.

'Say that again, Miss!' crows Marina Broadbent, whose long fringe has by now been replaced by big hair, fluffed up as high as possible using countless cans of Silvikrin hairspray.

'Paella,' repeats Señorita Wiggins, her composure starting to waver. 'In Spanish a double "l" is pronounced as a "y". Paella is a typical dish in Spain – it's made with rice, saffron and seafood.'

Someone on the back row yawns loudly and Señorita Wiggins tucks an imaginary strand of hair behind her ear. I see that the note everyone was signing has now made it halfway around the room.

'And how about chorizo?' Señorita Wiggins presses on. 'Has anyone heard of chorizo?'

She looks out onto row upon row of bored faces. I think I know the answer but am too frightened to put my hand up.

'Chorizo is a type of spicy Spanish sausage,' Señorita Wiggins explains. 'If you haven't tried it, it's very very tasty.'

'Does your boyfriend have a spicy Spanish sausage, Miss?' asks Carl Ashworth, provoking another wave of laughter.

'Is it very very tasty?' adds Vince Hargreaves, anxious not to be outdone.

Señorita Wiggins's eyebrows shoot up to her hairline and she gives an unsteady smile. I feel sorry for her; why does everyone have to be so horrible when all she's trying to do is teach us Spanish? She gamely struggles on for a few more minutes and then tells everyone to make a list of all the Spanish words we already know in our exercise books while she pops into the storeroom to 'look for her textbook'. As soon as she's gone, the laughter resurfaces and everyone starts joking about her stuffing her face on chocolate.

'Greedy cow!'

'Flabby porker!'

'Fat fucking bitch!'

I keep my head down and say nothing; I stare at the ink stain again, hoping everyone will forget I'm here. But no such luck. After a few seconds the note that's been passed around the class finally lands on my desk. The communal laughter drops to an expectant hush.

'Go on, Charlie, open it!' orders Vince Hargreaves.

I pretend I haven't heard him but he begins chanting, 'Open it, open it, open it!' and soon the entire class is joining in.

Knowing I have no choice, I take a deep breath and unfold the piece of paper. At the top someone has written, 'Sign here if you think Charlie Matthews is queer' and underneath the entire class has written their names. Seeing the list staring out at me knocks the air from my chest and I find myself struggling to breathe. As I become aware of a volley of verbal insults being added to the onslaught, I can hear the blood singing loudly in my ears.

I look down at my exercise book, which I've covered with a poster of Madonna in the video for 'La Isla Bonita'; at the start of term we were all instructed to protect our books with an extra layer of paper and I thought the image of my idol wearing a flamenco dress would be the perfect accompaniment to a course of Spanish. I focus on the image now to transport myself out of the classroom, picturing Madonna in the video as she walks down from her home to the street, where a long-haired Latin man is sitting on an old sofa playing the guitar and everyone's dancing around him without a care in the world.

'How are you getting on, *chicos*?' asks Señorita Wiggins as she walks back into the room with no pretence at having picked up her textbook, dabbing at the sides of her mouth with a tissue. 'Have you made a list of all the Spanish you know?'

'*¡Cojones!*'

'*¡Hijo de puta!*'

'*¡Chúpame la polla!*'

As the kids around me bombard her with every swear word or sexual suggestion anyone ever taught them on a Spanish holiday, I look again at the note I've been sent. I have to admit that, now I'm at secondary school surrounded by everyone talking about sex, I've noticed that when it comes down to it I do fancy boys rather than girls. I feel an excited little rumble in my tummy when I flick through *Smash Hits* and see pictures of Morten Harket or Nick Kamen that I simply don't feel when it comes to The Bangles or Mel and Kim. But it's such a terrible thing there's no way I could ever tell anyone about it. I tuck the note under my exercise book and can feel the shame burning a hole inside me.

Once again I picture Madonna in the video to 'La Isla Bonita' and imagine how wonderful it would feel to be one of the kids at the street party when she enters the throng and joins in. I tell myself that Madonna wouldn't hate me if she knew I fancied boys. How could she when she's said in so many interviews that it was her gay dance teacher who first inspired her to follow her dream?

I realize then that what I need isn't to move to another country like France or Spain or anywhere else for that matter. No, the place I need to get to is the wider world Madonna sings about in her songs. But how can I get there for real and not just in my imagination? No matter how much I think about it, I still have no idea. And in the meantime I'm stuck here in this horrible school. How on earth am I going to make it through?

Open Your Heart

Don't look at it. Whatever you do, don't look at it . . .

It's a warm Saturday in spring and I'm walking into Bolton town centre, wearing the purple and gold Kappa shell suit Mum bought me from someone she knows who can apparently get hold of clothes that 'fell off the back of a lorry', although I don't really understand what that means. The walk takes me about forty-five minutes in total and begins at the top of Tonge Moor Road, taking me past Tom Ashton's petrol station and the new Kwik Save supermarket, then Tonge Moor Library, Dave's Aquarium and the LADA dealership on Folds Road. But I know what's coming up next and the very thought of it makes my heart start racing.

I'm going into town to buy the 12" single of Madonna's 'Open Your Heart'. I did buy a copy when it first came out but it hasn't played properly since Dad spilt a cup of hot tea over it and damaged the vinyl, something I can't help suspecting he did on purpose. When I told him I needed to replace it as I couldn't possibly have any gaps in my collection, he said he'd give me £2 if I cleaned his van for him, which is what I've been doing all morning. Now I've got the £2 and, combined with my £1 spending money, I have just enough to buy the 12" – but not enough for my bus fare into town, which is why I'm walking.

I pass under the bridge and make my way up Bow Street, which leads right up to the Market Hall, where Mum works. I'm nearly there but all I can think about is the building I'm about to pass, the building I desperately don't want to look at.

I keep my head down as I sense it coming up on my right. I already know exactly what it looks like from the outside. And I know just what the sign says too – The Star and Garter.

The Star and Garter is Bolton's only pub for queers, not that there's any way you'd know this by looking at it as it's hardly the kind of thing you'd advertise. I only know because the kids at school are always making jokes about it; rumours will sometimes spread that someone's dad was spotted going in there and every Monday I'm asked if I've been in over the weekend. I've no idea what it's like inside and there'd be no way of finding out even if I wanted to; the pub only has very small windows with bars over them, frosted glass *and* net curtains. Clearly no one who goes in there wants to be seen. I remember reading an article in the *Bolton Evening News* once about some lads who tried setting fire to the pub; the police actually caught them but they were let off with a caution, which makes me think that most people in Bolton probably want the place to burn down. The last thing I need is for anyone to see me near it. I can feel the beads of sweat breaking out on my forehead as I dart past, my eyes trained feverishly on the ground.

Once I emerge onto Bridge Street I can feel myself starting to relax. With a new bounce in my step, I walk up the street and past Woolworths and the turning that leads to Churchgate and Ye Olde Pastie Shoppe, where they sell the most amazing meat and potato pasties that you can only get in Bolton. I continue up Mealhouse Lane, past the entrance to the Arndale Centre, which has a huge cage full of brightly coloured budgies in the middle. I cross Victoria Square, with its fountains frothing away and the stone lions looking down grandly from the town hall steps. In the distance I can see the entrance to the museum, which has dinosaur skeletons, a mummy of an Egyptian princess, and, best of all, tanks of tropical fish, including real-life piranhas, in the basement. And then I arrive at Newport Street and my final destination – Virgin Records.

I go inside and walk straight over to the section marked 'Rock and Pop – M'. I called in last Saturday to check they still had copies of the 12" as the single came out ages ago. I slide one out of the rack and hold it up to check it's in mint condition then take it over to the counter and pay. I hug my new record to me and head out of the shop.

I don't want to linger around town as cleaning Dad's van took me all morning and I know I'll be tired by the time I've walked all the way home. I cross the town hall square and thread my way through the streets until I arrive back at the turning into Bow Street. And I know what's waiting for me – The Star and Garter.

As I round the corner, I try not to look at the pub but the sound of the door slamming attracts my attention. Instinctively, I glance across the road and there it is, I can't avoid it anymore. The exterior is darker than I remember and someone has painted graffiti on the walls that says 'QUEERS OUT' and 'NO AIDS HERE'. Almost instantly my heart rate soars and I start sweating.

Because the truth is I know I'm queer – and I absolutely hate it. According to the other kids at school, queers have to wear Tampax up their bums to stop them crapping themselves and if you have sex with another man you catch AIDS and die. More than anything else I don't want to be queer and the knowledge that I am feels like a poison corroding me from within. I wonder if it would be possible to identify the poison and somehow cut it out of me.

I don't see how else I'm supposed to feel about it. The thing is, I've never met any queers – and nobody in my world ever says anything nice about them. There's the odd camp person like John Inman or Larry Grayson on the telly but they always deny they're queer, which only confirms that it has to be the worst thing anyone could ever admit to. Other than Erasure's Andy Bell, who everyone at school calls a pervert, the only queers I ever come across are Colin and Barry in *EastEnders* but Dad always switches the channel over whenever they come on. Or I'll see the odd picture in the paper of men in handcuffs and gimp masks marching at Gay Pride in London, or shots of people dying of AIDS on the news – but the last time that happened Dad switched off the telly and left the room.

All I have to hold on to are the occasional gay men I see in Madonna videos, like the sailors holding hands in 'Open Your Heart', and the interviews in which my idol talks about her gay friends. But, as far as I can make out, all these live in America, which might as well be on another planet to Bolton. All there is here is The Star and Garter, which looks like the dirtiest, dingiest pub in the world. I can only imagine what kind of people go in there.

Just then, I hear the sound of the door closing again and a young man walks out of the pub and into the street. I'm shocked but there he is, right in front of me; a young man with a blond quiff wearing snow-wash jeans and a matching jacket. He pulls his collar up, presumably so that no one will recognize him. There are plenty of people on the street and I hope no one can spot me watching. I carry on walking but I can't help following the man out of the corner of my eye. Who is he? And where's he going?

'Oi!' shouts an aggressive-sounding voice.

I stop and see that three lads wearing Bolton Wanderers shirts are walking from the bus stop towards the man from the pub. Their leader has a thick neck and a bullet head and is the kind of lad Mum would call 'dog rough'.

'All right, nancy boy!' he calls out menacingly.

But the man from the pub ignores him and carries on walking.

When the three lads reach him, the one with the thick neck shoulder-barges him so hard he almost knocks him into the wall. 'Hey, I'm talking to you!' he booms.

The man from the pub goes white in the face and freezes. 'Listen, I don't want any trouble,' he stammers.

The lad with the thick neck stands over him and shouts into his face, 'Well, you should have thought about that before you went in there then, shouldn't you?'

By now my heart's pounding so violently I can feel it at the back of my throat. There are several people on the street but none of them is saying anything or trying to intervene; people are just pretending they haven't noticed and are looking away. But I can't stop myself from standing staring. Without realizing it, I'm holding my 12" in front of me, like a shield.

'Leave it, Daz,' says one of the leader's mates.

'Yeah,' agrees the other, 'he's not worth it. He's only a dirty queer.'

There's a tense silence while the one called Daz stares at the man from the pub and considers what his mates are saying. The man from the pub looks at him, petrified. Then Daz backs away and, with a look of wretched relief, the man scurries off and around the corner.

'Just don't ever let us see you here again!' Daz shouts after him, spitting for good measure.

I suddenly realize I haven't breathed in all this time and gulp in some air. I have to stop staring and move on before anyone notices me. What if the lads in the football shirts can tell I'm queer and start having a go at me too?

I force myself to set off and start walking again. I tell myself that I'm not queer, I can't be. This is what happens to queers in Bolton. They get sneered at and pushed around in the street. If I accept being queer then this is what I've got to look forward to.

The problem is, however hard I try, I can't stop myself fancying boys. However much I try to suppress these feelings, they always resurface; it's like trying to hold an inflatable ball under water only for it to bob up over and over again. Well, I'll just have to keep trying to hold it down – being queer is a dirty secret I have no choice but to keep to myself forever.

I quicken my pace and start walking home, all the way clinging onto Madonna.

Papa Don't Preach

'Go on, my son!'

Joe weaves his way through the defenders, curls the ball to the left and then whacks it straight into the back of the net. The crowd goes wild.

'*Goal!*'

Dad's jumping up and down and hollering at the top of his voice – I don't think I've ever seen him so excited. We're watching Joe play centre forward for the school football team and today's the final to decide which school will come top of the whole Bolton league.

'By 'eck, he's doing well, our Joe. One more and he'll have his hat-trick.'

I know how important today is but for some reason I can't concentrate and find myself fidgeting the whole time. On the other side of the pitch I spot Vince Hargreaves and a group of boys from my year and I'm terrified they'll come over and start calling me queer in front of Dad.

'What's up with you, lad?' he booms. 'Why aren't you cheering for your brother?'

'Oh yeah, sorry.'

I stand next to Dad on the touchline and do my best to be supportive. My eyes follow Joe as he zigzags across the pitch but all I can feel is envy. I hate watching Joe play football. I know it's bad of me but however hard I try I can't stop myself. Dad gets so fired up and proud but I always come home feeling utterly miserable. I wish I didn't have to come at all but for some reason Dad thinks it's 'good for me' and Mum hasn't raised any objections.

'Look at that!' Dad boasts to the man on his other side as he points to Joe on the pitch. 'That's my lad, that is.'

I feel the envy grow till it lodges in my throat. Hoping Dad won't notice, I slope a little way off and fish my shiny blue Walkman out of my pocket. Mum and Dad gave it to me for Christmas, probably because they're now resigned to my love of Madonna but sick of me playing her songs on their music centre. The cassette inside is the *True Blue* album and I rewind it and press Play. As I hear the orchestral opening of 'Papa Don't Preach' I immediately feel better.

In my mind I see images from the video, with Madonna playing a rebellious teenager who falls out with her dad. I picture her bouncing through New York with a leather jacket slung over her shoulder and a T-shirt emblazoned with the slogan 'Italians Do It Better'. I imagine myself bouncing along with her and soon I forget all about the football match. I've no idea that by the chorus I've begun to sing along at the top of my voice.

'Switch that thing off!' snaps Dad.

Several people are staring at me and I flush bright red. 'Sorry, Dad – I didn't realize I was so loud.'

He lets out a long sigh. 'How are you ever going to learn how to appreciate football if you can't even concentrate on the game?'

I take off the headphones and press Stop.

Dad still can't get his head around the fact that I don't like football. The problem is, in Bolton in the 1980s, as a male who isn't into football I'm in a tiny minority. There are times when the whole town seems to revolve around the game; the fortunes of Bolton Wanderers are regularly documented on the front page of the local paper and whenever a group of men or boys get together it seems like that's all they can talk about. All right, the town has two cinemas, an art gallery and a small theatre called the Octagon, where Auntie Jan takes us to watch the Christmas show every year. But, although most people living in Bolton go to the pictures, very few of them have ever visited the Octagon and some don't even know the art gallery exists. Whereas no one could ever doubt Bolton Wanderers exists; the club is the town's beating heart. And it seems to get everyone else's pulse racing except mine.

Desperate to find some kind of intelligent comment to make, I turn to the pitch and locate the ball. The other team have possession and are preparing to attack. I can feel the tension mounting all around me. Just in time, Joe delivers a killer tackle and our team regain control. Everyone breathes a sigh of relief. But before they've had time to cheer, Joe turns around and pounds forward to the opposition's goal. Excitement spreads like lightning along the touchline.

'Go on, lad!' bellows Dad.

'Go on, Joe!' I shout, careful to deepen my voice so it won't attract the attention of Vince and his mates.

As I watch my brother hammer forward, I feel a familiar knot of admiration, resentment and shame tighten in my stomach.

'*Goal!*'

Thankfully I don't have to endure much more before the whistle blows for half-time.

Dad suggests nipping to the food stall for a pie and I briefly perk up. I love going to takeaways with Dad as the people behind the counter always give him a hero's welcome. Everyone we meet seems to appreciate how hard he works on their deliveries and not only that but they revel in his presence; Dad's the kind of man people cuff on the shoulder and call 'a real character'. He's the kind of man I can't imagine I'll ever be.

'All right, Frank?' asks the man on the stall, who has a bull neck and a chest so flabby he could do with a bra.

'How do,' replies Dad.

I'm proud of the fact that so many people know and like my dad, and wonder if one day I'll be able to do something to make him proud of me too. After all, he's the same man who carried me on his shoulders when I was little, the same man who chased me around the house pretending to be a monster, the same man who snuggled up in bed between me and Joe so he could sing 'Two Little Boys' – and he looked at both of us as he sang it, not just Joe. I bite into my meat and potato pie and tell myself there's still a chance to make him look at me like that again.

After half-time, the rest of the match goes brilliantly and our team wins the game *and* the championship. Joe scores a fourth goal and is made Man of the Match. Everyone starts making comparisons with Gary Lineker in the last World Cup and Dad looks like he's going to burst with joy. Once again I step quietly away from the crowd and try not to let jealousy get the better of me. But there's no chance; I can feel it stinging like acid at the back of my throat.

After a few minutes, Joe spots that I've slipped off and comes trotting over to me.

'All right, Charlie?' he says, still panting from his exertions on the pitch.

'All right, Joe?' I manage to mumble. An awkward silence sets in between us. 'Well done,' I offer after a while. 'You were ace, as usual.'

'Thanks,' he says. 'And thanks for coming. I know this really isn't your thing.'

I straighten up defensively. 'What are you on about? I really like football.'

He gives me a look. 'Charlie, you don't have to pretend with me. I know you'd rather be with Shanaz dressing up or reading magazines or something.'

I suddenly feel judged and under attack; it's like he knows what's wrong with me and is honing in on it to make me feel bad. 'Joe,' I say, 'stop having a go at me! I'm here, aren't I? What more do you want?'

'All right, all right,' he says, backing away as if he's been stung. 'I was only trying to be nice.'

'Yeah, well, don't,' I find myself almost spitting. 'Everything's fine. *I'm* fine, honestly.'

'OK, OK, if you insist.'

As he turns around and runs back to Dad, I feel my anger rising. How dare he come over here and remind me I don't fit in? The last person I want pointing it out is him. How can he possibly understand how I'm feeling when he's everything Dad wants in a son, when he's the chip off the old block who'll grow up to be exactly the kind of man Dad is now, exactly the kind of man everyone loves?

Besides, Joe never makes the slightest effort to support me when we're at school, when the occasional sign of solidarity from an older boy as popular as him might go some way to persuading all the other kids to lay off me. But no, when we're at school he can't get far enough away from me, even though he must have heard the insults everyone throws my way. And now I'm expected to let him offload his guilt by being nice to me after his football match. Well, I'm not going to.

I kick a stone around the touchline for a few minutes until I've calmed down and feel brave enough to rejoin the crowd. Once I get there, I discover that the other dads' admiration of Joe's performance is making my dad even more jubilant. He tells the two of us that a celebration's in order and before we know it he's whisking us off to The Flat Iron. The Flat Iron is our local pub and by the age of twelve I already know it well. The walls are panelled with wood, the tables topped with Formica and the air filled with smoke. Serving behind the bar is Babs Flitcroft, a barmaid so sour-faced that Mum says she always looks like she's chewing a gobful of wasps. On the wall behind her are football scarves, a picture of the Queen, and photos of girls with their boobs out advertising Big D peanuts.

As I walk in today, I immediately recognize some of the regulars dotted around the place. Sitting in the snug is Gabby Annie, who always fascinates me because she's lost all of her teeth and can't be bothered to wear false ones. Unfortunately, she also has an incontinence problem and whenever she stands up leaves a damp patch on the seat behind her. Leaning against the bar is a man who's changed his name by deed poll to John Wayne, dresses in a cowboy hat and boots and insists on speaking in a totally unconvincing American accent. He'll walk into the pub as if it's a western saloon and always keeps one hand on his belt, as if about to draw an imaginary gun. And the final regular I recognize is standing in his usual position between the pinball machine and the dartboard. It's Dad's brother, my Uncle Les.

Dad and Uncle Les are particularly close as they had another brother who moved away from Bolton and died when I was little and they always say the experience brought them together. Uncle Les still lives with Grandma, works as a builder and people always describe him as 'handy'; when anything breaks in our house, he comes round to fix it straight away. Joe and I think he's like a real-life James Bond; although he looks very much like Dad, he has even bigger muscles, a full head of hair and leaves his shirt collars open to show off his chunky gold chain and hairy chest. At Christmas he usually forgets to buy us a present but will pull a wad of notes out of his back pocket and peel some off for us instead. He can perform magic tricks and make a ten-pence piece disappear from his hand and then miraculously reappear behind his ear. But what I like best of all about Uncle Les are his two pet ferrets, Slap and Tickle. In the summer he lets us chase them around Grandma's garden and, if we're good, feed them Liquorice Allsorts, which for some reason they love.

At weekends Uncle Les spends a lot of his time in The Flat Iron and today's no exception. When we arrive, Dad sits down with him, sips at his pint and recounts every single move and manoeuvre of Joe's game.

'It sounds like he's turning into a proper little Nat Lofthouse,' says Uncle Les. He ruffles Joe's hair and Joe smiles bashfully. I look away, repulsed by the force of my own jealousy.

I don't really know what to say so ask Dad for some money for the jukebox. Thankfully, he's in such a good mood that he says yes. As Madonna launches into 'Papa Don't Preach' once again, somebody suggests having a kickabout in the beer garden – Joe and Uncle Les on one side and me and Dad on the other. I feel sick with panic at the idea but know there's no way out. At least at school there are enough players for me to hang around the nets and sing to myself without anyone noticing. All I can do now is join in and hope it'll be over with soon.

From the moment we start there's no disguising my lack of interest in the game and consequent lack of ability. I miss a goal in an open net, trip over every time I'm tackled and duck to avoid the ball whenever it comes towards me.

'What's wrong with you, lad? Get stuck in!'

I summon up all my energy and can feel the determination hardening inside me. The next time the ball approaches I decide to be brave and confront it head-on. I bounce into the air to deliver a cracking header but miss and take the full force of the ball straight in my face. It's surprisingly painful and knocks me back onto the ground. When I look up I realize that my nose is bleeding and my glasses are lying next to me, broken.

'By 'eck, lad!'

I pick them up and see that one of the lenses has fallen out. I'm gutted. The last time this happened, Dad stuck them together with Sellotape and gave everyone at school yet another excuse to lay into me. The thought of it happening again fills me with dread. I can't help feeling angry at myself. Oh why do I have to be so *crap*?

'Please try and fix them, Uncle Les!'

He comes over and sits down next to me. 'Let's have a look, cocker,' he says soothingly.

Dad gives me a hanky for my nose and pats my shoulder sympathetically. 'You know we can always have another go with footie lessons if you want, son. You never know – you might even turn out to be as good as your brother.'

It's as if I've been hit in the face a second time and I try my best to avoid looking at Joe. Out of the corner of my eye I'm sure I can see him frowning at me in sympathy again – or, even worse, is he smirking? Either way, I feel like a total fool and press the hanky to my nose. I'm ashamed to think it but in that second I'm pretty sure I don't just hate watching Joe play football, I hate *him* too.

'I think we might need a screwdriver for these,' says Uncle Les.

I feel a flutter of hope. 'So you reckon you can fix them?'

'Well, that and a bit of Sellotape.'

My stomach hits the floor.

'Come on then,' says Dad, 'we should be heading back anyway – your mam's making a big pan of corned beef hash for tea.'

I stagger up and onto my feet. It's such a relief to be finally going home.

I tell myself that as soon as I've finished eating I'm heading upstairs to my bedroom; all I want to do is put on my earphones, listen to Madonna, and blast away all memories of the day.

Who's That Girl

I see a sign for Leeds and tremble with excitement. I shake myself as a surge of adrenalin races around my body. I can't quite believe I'm actually about to see my idol in the flesh for the first time.

Shanaz and I are on our way to the opening British date of Madonna's *Who's That Girl* tour. We're so excited we haven't slept properly for days. Ever since we heard Madonna was coming to the UK, we saved up our pocket money until we eventually had enough for a £15 ticket each. When they finally arrived in the post we looked at them in awe and examined every inch to check they weren't fake. I felt like Charlie Bucket holding up his golden ticket to Willy Wonka's chocolate factory. Only this is much better because it's happening for real.

Mum and Dad weren't thrilled about the idea of me going to the concert and did their best to put me off, but after weeks of pestering they finally gave in and granted their permission. The only thing is, as Shanaz and I are twelve, Mum said we could only go if an adult went with us – and this turned into more of a problem than I thought. Mum wasn't interested in coming as it meant she'd miss *Coronation Street*, Dad grunted and said he'd rather watch Bolton Wanderers lose to Man United, and Grandma muttered something about her varicose veins giving her gyp. Thankfully, Auntie Jan stepped in to volunteer, which is why the three of us are driving across the Pennines in her shiny gold Ford Fiesta Turbo. These days Auntie Jan has spiky peroxide blonde hair and today she's wearing electric blue cycling shorts with a matching boob tube and a silver bolero jacket over the top. I think she looks *mega*.

'Auntie Jan,' I ask, 'why don't you become a pop star like Madonna?'

She looks at me and smiles. 'Don't be daft, Charlie! I'm a hairdresser – why would I want to be a pop star?'

'Because you get to see the world!' says Shanaz.

'Because it's dead glamorous!' I add.

'Yeah, well, I hate to disappoint you but Klassy Kutz is just about glamorous enough for me.'

'But don't you ever get bored cutting people's hair?' asks Shanaz.

Auntie Jan starts to look exasperated. 'Well, it's not quite as simple as that, is it?'

'Why not?'

'Well, for a start, if I didn't cut people's hair then I wouldn't have enough money to go to Ritzy's on a Saturday night. And then how would I ever find myself a fella?'

Shanaz isn't convinced. 'But if you were a pop star you'd have even more money.'

'Yeah,' I add, 'and you could have any fella you wanted!'

At this point Auntie Jan loses her patience. 'Bloomin' 'eck, you two! I'm a hairdresser from Bolton – we can't all be Madonna you know!'

She leans forward to switch on the music. Shanaz and I shake our heads and frown.

Half an hour later we arrive in Roundhay Park – and it really is an incredible sight. The audience area is huge and I'm stunned by how many people are filing through the gates. Shanaz and I want to get a good view so start working our way towards the front. When we reach the hotdog stand, Auntie Jan stops and pretends to be refastening her shoe. Shanaz nudges me and points to a man hovering nearby. He has blond highlighted hair that he's grown long at the back and is wearing a suit jacket with the sleeves rolled up and white leather slip-on shoes. He must have caught Auntie Jan's eye because before I know it the two of them are having a conversation.

'Has anyone ever told you you look like Brigitte Nielsen?' he asks.

'Has anyone ever told *you* you look like Don Johnson?' she giggles.

It doesn't take long for Shanaz and I to sense we're in the way.

''Ere sunshine,' Auntie Jan says to me, 'I've just thought of something – why don't we split up and meet back here at the end of the show?'

I feel slightly nervous. 'But Mum said we had to stay with you all the time.'

'Oh don't worry about *that*! Have this pound note and go and buy yourselves some sweets.' As soon as our backs are turned, she skips off into the distance, laughing away with the Don Johnson lookalike.

Shanaz and I shrug and decide to continue heading towards the stage. We soon find that, as we're smaller than most people, we can weave our way in and out of the crowd until we're almost on the front row. It's unbelievable – we're actually standing just a few metres away from the very spot where Madonna will soon be making her entrance.

'Charlie, this is ace!' squeaks Shanaz.

'I know – we're that close she might even look us in the eye!'

By now our obsession with Madonna has reached a new peak. Every Saturday morning we sit glued to *The Chart Show* to catch a glimpse of her latest video and every Sunday at five o'clock we listen to the Top Forty on the radio to see if she's number one. Most evenings after school we sit around in Shanaz's bedroom going over and over the story of our idol leaving the hometown where she never fitted in to start a new life in New York with nothing but a teddy bear and $35 in her pocket. We've joined the official fan club, which includes receiving regular magazines that open with a personal letter Madonna herself has written. Even better, our gift on joining was a photo she actually signed, and we spent ages tracing the grooves her pen made, knowing that at the moment she wrote her name she was thinking of us. One day we copied out her autograph over and over again then adapted it to devise grown-up signatures for ourselves, convinced that in doing so some of Madonna's spirit was somehow passing into us.

We're hoping that will happen again today, as we wait for Madonna to make her entrance in Roundhay Park. Her band take to the stage and we can feel the bass reverberating through us as they begin blasting their way into the opening number. The audience roars and rushes forward towards them, sweeping along me and Shanaz in the momentum. Then we see a silhouette of our idol at the top of the stairs, masked by a screen. All of a sudden the screen lifts and, as if it's the most natural thing in the world, Madonna appears on stage and is standing there right in front of us.

I can hardly believe it – she's at a distance of no more than the length of our back garden. I blink to check I'm not dreaming but when I open my eyes there she is in her black basque and fishnets, lit by a spotlight and glowing like a goddess. She launches into her routine and begins dancing around a chair, slowly removing her black gloves in time to the music. I'm mesmerized and see that Shanaz is too – her mouth falls open so wide that a fly disappears inside.

At the end of her first number Madonna looks out to the audience and says, 'I've finally made it to England and it looks like all of it's here!' For a split second her eyes flit past us and we squeeze each other's hands excitedly. We're awestruck – it's as if we're standing in the park alone and she's talking only to us.

For the next hour and a half, we watch Madonna bounce around the stage in various costumes, singing and dancing with perfect discipline and smiling as if she's enjoying every second. The fact that she looks so happy is amazing as we've read in interviews that she's still haunted by her mum's death when she was five and, according to the newspapers, at the moment her private life is in crisis; not only is her marriage to Sean Penn supposed to be on the verge of divorce but he's in the middle of serving a prison sentence for punching a photographer. Not that you'd be able to tell Madonna has any kind of worries on her mind from the smile on her face. And as she skips her way through the show, her happiness transmits to the audience. It's the most incredible thing I've ever experienced, to be among tens of thousands of people all going through exactly the same emotion. I can feel it somehow transforming me and making me feel whole.

As Madonna comes to the end of her set and begins performing her encore, I can feel a new drive and motivation taking hold of me. Seeing my idol live has made me feel for the first time that I'm capable of achieving anything. I realize at this moment that I don't want to be normal and go through the motions of the same life as everyone else – I want to be superhuman like Madonna. Who cares whether or not I can play football? Who cares about Bolton when there's a whole universe out there? Didn't Madonna once say that her ambition was 'to conquer the world'? I feel now like I can do just the same. All I have to do is work out how I'm going to do it.

As my idol throws herself into another perfectly executed dance routine, I begin casting my mind around to figure out what I might be able to do as well as her. Unfortunately, I can't sing, I enjoy dancing but don't really have any talent for it, and, ever since my turn on stage at primary school, I haven't had anywhere near enough confidence to act in any kind of school play. All I can do is work hard in class – and whenever I do that I always get good results, particularly in English. And that's when it hits me; one of the things I enjoy most at school is writing. So why don't I become a writer? Yes, I'd love to write a book. I've no idea what it would be about yet but I have plenty of time to decide. And in the meantime I can always start practising. Now that I think about it, as soon as I get home I'm going to make a start by writing about tonight's concert – and how it's been the most incredible experience of my life.

But just then the experience comes to an end. As the encore thunders to its finish, Madonna bows to the audience and bounds upstairs and out of sight. The lights go out and the crowd of nearly 75,000 people gives an almost deafening cheer.

As the final notes of music start receding into my memory, I blink myself out of a daze. I notice that all around me, people are beginning to leave. I turn to Shanaz and, as we start heading towards the exit, we're eager to relive every second of the show, talking through it so fast we can hardly understand what each other's saying. By the time we reach the hotdog stand we realize there are more urgent things to think about – if we're ever going to make it home tonight, we have to find Auntie Jan. After a rather anxious ten minutes, we eventually spot her leaning against the Portaloos, necking with the bloke who looks like Don Johnson. He has a cigarette in one hand and a can of lager in the other and Auntie Jan's arms are clasped around his neck, pulling him towards her.

'Auntie Jan,' I stammer, 'the concert's finished now.'

'Oh Charlie, oh right,' she splutters, prising herself away and straightening out her clothes. 'Me and Kev were just saying goodbye, weren't we, Kev?'

'Aye, we were.' Kev's clearly drunk and has pink lipstick smeared all over his face. Auntie Jan wipes it off with a tissue and then generously re-coats her own lips.

She says her final goodbye and we set off back to the car. On the way I notice that she's smiling to herself.

'Well, you two,' she gushes, 'what a brill night!'

'Yeah!' I agree. 'Madonna was amazing! How mega was "Who's That Girl"?'

'Oh it was my favourite too!' says Shanaz. 'How about you, Jan? Which song was your favourite?'

'Oh, probably "Angel". I love that one.'

'"Angel"? But she didn't do that.'

We watch as Auntie Jan blushes the same colour as her lipstick. 'Oh, did she not? I must have, urm . . . I must have misheard or something. Anyway, we've all had a good time, haven't we?'

'Good time? I think this has been the best day of my life!'

She gives me a big grin and puts her arm round me. 'Come on then, sunshine, let's get home.'

My heart sags.

I try telling myself that today may be over and my idol may have disappeared from my life for the time being, but she's left me with something that, without realizing it, I've been in search of for a long time; she's left me with a dream.

Crazy For You

All around me hundreds of teenagers are waving their arms in the air to the sound of The Farm's 'All Together Now'. As I watch from the sidelines, it feels like the Madonna concert is a million miles away.

I'm fifteen years old and making my debut at the all-important school disco. I look around and can see that *everyone's* here, which is no surprise considering the entire school has been talking about it for weeks, endlessly discussing who'll be wearing what and who'll be copping off with who. The doors only opened an hour ago but it looks like the snogging's started already. I spot Carl Ashworth and Sally Swallow going at it hell for leather in the middle of the dance floor.

Everywhere I look, people are swigging from bottles of pop secretly laced with alcohol and those over sixteen are openly smoking cigarettes with a carefree defiance. I feel awkward and out of place. I don't want to snog anyone and am certainly not going to start smoking – the very idea repulses me. I'm frightened of turning into Grandma, who laughs like she's swallowed a bag of gravel and has a mouth that reminds me of a cat's bum. I wonder why I'm so different to everyone else my age – the rest of the school seems to be having such a good time.

All the action's taking place in the main hall, where a DJ's playing music from some decks set up on the stage. The chairs have been cleared to create a dance floor and, standing around the edges, the teachers are looking on with wry smiles. I spot Mr Beveridge, who started at the school in my second year and teaches me English. Some of the kids call him Beverley because he speaks a bit like a woman and they affect a limp wrist and mimic his camp voice, sometimes to his face. Last term, someone said their dad saw him going into The Star and Garter and everyone was disgusted and said that if he really is queer he shouldn't be allowed to teach kids. I wasn't brave enough to defend him but secretly he's my favourite teacher; he's vibrant and enthusiastic and I love how passionate he gets when he talks about books by Charles Dickens and Thomas Hardy. There's something special about his lessons and I love losing myself in the stories he teaches us – it's as if I can feel the whole world opening up before me.

'All Together Now' comes to an end and the DJ plays 'Fool's Gold' by The Stone Roses. Half of the room goes wild and stampedes onto the dance floor and the other half snorts and skulks away. By this stage, most of the kids at my school can roughly be split into two opposing groups. In one there are the indies; this year the Madchester movement is in full swing and bands like The Stone Roses and The Inspiral Carpets are the ultimate in cool. Indies are vegetarian, watch *Twin Peaks* and have an extensive collection of hooded tops. They carry their exercise books around in green rucksacks they bought from the Army and Navy store and then covered with the names of their favourite bands in black felt tip pen. They read *Melody Maker* and the *NME* and catch the train to Manchester at the weekend to mooch around Affleck's Palace. Everyone wants to be part of the indie crowd – if you're fifteen and living in Bolton, indie is what you aspire to be.

In the other group, there are the townies. Townies watch *Baywatch* and listen to Technotronic, Snap! and Vanilla Ice. If they're girls they have a spiral perm and read *Just Seventeen* and if they're boys they use too much hair gel and don't read anything. Townies carry their schoolbooks in Head bags and shop at Mark One, River Island and Topshop. On Saturday afternoons they go into Bolton to hang around the bus station or on the benches in the Arndale. Female townies tend to have either a baby in a pram or a boyfriend who'll pick them up in his Escort XR3i outside the school gates. Male townies boast about fighting and fingering their girlfriends and usually have a problem either with shoplifting or glue-sniffing. Even if you are one, being a townie is something nobody admits to. The word 'townie' is the ultimate insult.

Thankfully, Shanaz and I aren't townies. The only problem is, we aren't indies either. And we might be clever and hard-working but we don't even fit in with the stiffs because they've no interest in TV or pop music. No, we don't really slot into any recognizable category of teenager; it's almost as if we're outcasts. Although at least now we have each other, as the older children at our school have their own mixed-sex common room and yard. Also, now we're studying for our GCSEs, the top sets of children from the whole year group have lessons together – so in the subjects we're both taking we always sit together. Unfortunately, the name-calling directed at both of us hasn't eased off. In my case the words 'queer' and 'poof' have morphed into more graphic insults like 'arse bandit', 'shit stabber' and 'Marmite miner'. In Shanaz's case, she's regularly told that she reeks of curry, even though she now only eats sandwiches at lunchtime, and is often ordered to 'fuck off back to Paki-land'. It's been a long time since she's bothered correcting anyone that her family is actually from India. But it's a comfort to both of us that we can now form a team of two and, even though I know allying myself with someone just as despised as me can only make me more of a target for the bullies, when it comes to Shanaz I don't care. Besides, we've got used to what people think about us and have come to expect that whatever we do they'll hate us. Although there are times when I'm starting to feel angry at the injustice of it all.

Tonight is one of those times and I can feel the urge to fight back slowly uncoiling inside me. After years of persecution, I'm mightily sick of my rock-bottom social status and know that Shanaz is too. Well, tonight we're going to try and get ourselves an upgrade.

Shanaz hands me a plastic Coke bottle filled with booze and I take a swig. Unfortunately for us, nobody has invented an alcoholic drink that tastes like pop and we've no idea what indies drink. Earlier this evening I raided my mum's drinks cabinet and found a bottle of Hock hidden at the back that she must have forgotten about, half a bottle of Tia Maria and the fag end of some out-of-date Cinzano. Shanaz mixed it all together in a washing-up bowl and then added some Coke she pilfered from the shop so the teachers won't notice the booze. The resulting taste reminds me of the time I was rushed to hospital when I was seven because I'd drunk a whole bottle of Mr Muscle thinking it would make me as strong as Dad. We pass the cocktail between us, desperately trying to smile as we swig it down.

Shanaz is pulling it off. 'Mmm, it's well top this, i'nt it?'

'Yeah!' I strain. 'Buzzin'!'

Earlier this week, we overheard a group of indies arranging to meet behind the sports hall, where apparently they've hidden a stash of booze in the bushes. We know it's a long shot but we decide to go and find them and see if they'll let us join in. It's cold outside but neither of us has brought a coat – everyone knows only stiffs wear coats. And if we're ever going to be accepted as indies, we can't run the slightest risk of being mistaken for stiffs.

We turn the corner, chatting between ourselves, and the indies turn to look at us expectantly. When they see who it is, they turn away uninterested. Desperate to brazen it out, Shanaz sidles over and I shuffle along behind her.

'Hiya,' she says to Matt McGregor. 'How's it going?'

Matt has to be the most popular boy in our year and all the girls fancy him. He has long hair in a bob and a part-time job in the Eastern Bloc record shop in Manchester. To our astonishment, he actually smiles at us and says hello. And then he starts talking. All right, he's drunk and slurring his words and keeps calling us Colin and Shiraz – but he's still talking to us. He talks for ten minutes about learning to play the guitar and the band he's forming with his brothers. We look at him wide-eyed, exploding with laughter at even the slightest gag. We can't believe it – we're standing with a crowd of indies and Matt McGregor's talking to *us*!

'Would you two like some of this?' He holds out a bottle of what looks like fizzy orange juice and explains that he's drinking Blastaway. We must look puzzled.

'It's Castaway mixed with Diamond White,' he explains.

I've never heard of either.

'Oh, *Blastaway*!' I say, feigning recognition. 'Sorted!'

I take a swig and it tastes like sweat. I can feel the bile rise to the top of my throat but try my best to swallow it and force out a smile. 'Cheers,' I manage, 'thanks a lot.'

Once Shanaz has had a taste, Matt takes out a cigarette and lights it. 'Do either of you fancy a drag?'

There's a nervous pause. My first reaction is to say no but I tell myself that that'll put paid to any chance I have of being accepted as an indie. For weeks now I've been hobbling around in a new pair of Doc Martens, pretending not to notice that the backs of my ankles are red raw. And I've been trying to grow my hair into curtains, frustrated at how long it's taking and spending ages in front of the mirror every morning trying to comb out the kinks, wishing someone would design some kind of machine to straighten them. But here's my chance to gain the upgrade I so desperately want – all the indies smoke and being offered a drag on one of their fags is tantamount to full acceptance.

I look at the cigarette and wonder what harm it can do. The booze I've drunk has given me a new kind of confidence and I can feel my willpower crumbling.

Shanaz gives in first, even though smoking is one of the things her parents hate most. 'Too right!' she chirps.

I watch as she takes hold of the fag, breathes in the smoke and exhales with surprising panache.

I can hardly say no now.

Trying not to think about the wrinkles around my grandma's mouth, I lean forward and take the cigarette. 'Buzzin', thanks.'

I lift it to my lips and suck on the end. I inhale as deeply as possible and can hardly believe it when I manage not to cough. I casually breathe out the smoke and hand it back to Matt, ecstatic that I've actually pulled it off. I'm just about to congratulate myself when I start to feel dizzy and can sense the colour draining from my face.

'Is everything all right?'

I hold onto the wall to steady myself and feel my stomach lurch. 'Yeah, yeah, s-s-sorted, honestly.'

All the indies are looking at me and I try my best to remain calm. My head's spinning all over the place but I have to get a grip. I take a deep breath and down another swig of booze.

Luckily, at that moment someone recognizes 'Step On' by the Happy Mondays coming from the main hall.

'Top one!' they all chorus.

'Nice one!' I agree.

'Sorted!' adds Shanaz.

'Just a minute,' says Matt, 'I thought you two liked Madonna?'

Shanaz looks flummoxed. 'Urm, yeah, urm, yeah . . .'

' . . .But we like indie music too!'

Everyone gathers around with suspicion. 'OK then,' asks one, 'who are your favourite bands?'

I feel a bolt of panic shoot through me but Shanaz rises to the challenge. 'Oh you know, the Roses, the Mondays, the Inspirals . . .'

'What about The Kerbs?' asks Matt.

'Oh *The Kerbs*!' I gush. 'I *love* The Kerbs!'

'Really?' He seems surprised.

'Yeah, they're well bangin'.'

'Hmm.' I can sense their hostility harden and Matt strokes his chin. 'The funny thing is,' he says, 'The Kerbs don't exist – I just made them up.'

I'm stumped.

'Oh really . . . Did you say . . . Did you say *The Kerbs*? I urm, I, I thought you said, urm . . . Cud – I thought you said *Cud*!'

It's no use – I've made an utter fool of myself and there's no turning back. I suddenly realize just how cold it is outside without a coat.

Shanaz comes to my rescue and mumbles an excuse. The two of us begin backing away and I watch the indies huddle together, muttering and sniggering to each other. I'm pretty sure I hear one of them say the words 'poof' and 'Paki' and I flinch. There's no denying it – we've been totally humiliated. Now we'll *never* be indies!

I down a huge swig of our booze and begin plodding my way back to the hall. Everyone must have had lots to drink by now because the atmosphere in there is much rowdier than before. Shanaz and I slip in quietly and hover sheepishly in an empty corner. On the dance floor I can see Joe, who by now is in the sixth form and a fully fledged indie. *He'll* know The Kerbs don't exist. I try my best not to feel my jealousy of Joe come surging back but it's difficult – everyone says Joe's well top. He has long hair in a ponytail, an earring through his eyebrow and smokes Embassy Number 1 cigarettes. As I watch him being fawned over by the most popular indies in the school, not only do I realize I hate him more than ever but I also hate myself for not being like him.

To cap it all, Joe's girlfriend is Becky Eccleston and everyone knows she's the fittest girl in the school. She's an indie too and has a Saturday job in a shop that sells joss sticks in the Corn Exchange in Manchester. Once or twice I've stolen her love letters from his bedroom and read them out loud to Shanaz. There's lots of talk about 'johnnies' and where they can get together to 'do it' – in her mum's car, my parents' garage, the school toilets . . .

At the moment it seems like everyone at school is obsessed with 'doing it'. If you haven't at least felt someone else's private parts then you're in danger of being publicly denounced as a V-Reg and treated like a leper. If you're really unlucky, rumours will start that you're frigid and everyone will call you a fridge-freezer. Of course I haven't done anything at all but the upside to being a social outcast is that nobody cares. Everyone cares about Joe, though. Joe's the kind of sixth-former the younger boys look up to and idolize.

I remind myself that I have to be careful that he doesn't spot me standing there watching him. Joe's continued to distance himself from me at school and by this stage has made it quite clear he doesn't want his friends to be reminded we're related; over the last few years we've grown further and further apart so presumably he's decided that he no longer has to avoid hurting my feelings. I look at him and see that he's busy snogging Becky – I'm in the clear.

It's ten o'clock and I feel what I realize must be drunk. My mouth tastes like an ashtray and I have a headache starting. It suddenly dawns on me how little I'm enjoying myself but I daren't say anything. Shanaz pulls a face and looks at her watch.

'You know what,' she says, 'I wish we could sack this off – I'd much rather be at home watching *Blind Date* with a tin of pineapple chunks.'

'Sssh,' I hiss, 'someone might hear you! If we're ever going to be indies we've got to get into this kind of thing.'

I recognize the first notes of 'Sit Down' by James and watch as Joe sits cross-legged on the dance floor. Everyone takes his lead and sits around him, closing their eyes and swaying their upper bodies as if they're going through some kind of spiritual communion.

Shanaz tells me that she's going to the loo and I instantly feel vulnerable and self-conscious standing on my own. I step back into the shadows so that no one will see me.

'You skulking here on your own, Charlie?' Mr Beveridge is coming towards me with a smile on his face.

'Oh hi, sir, I – I didn't see you.' I'm embarrassed he might think I don't have anyone to hang around with and can feel my cheeks flush. 'I'm just waiting for Shanaz – she's only just left, honest.'

'Ah, I see.' He gives me a knowing chuckle. 'And are you enjoying yourself?'

'Yeah!' I bleat, a little too enthusiastically. 'I *love* indie music!'

'Hmmm.' He doesn't look too convinced. 'I thought you liked Madonna? You know, that essay you wrote about her was brilliant.'

One of the first things I wrote for Mr Beveridge was an essay about what I'd done over the summer when he started teaching me English at the beginning of my second year. I focused on going to the Madonna concert and how I'd felt completely transformed by the experience. It was the most honest thing I've ever written and he was impressed, telling me that the best writing comes when a writer reveals himself – and he encouraged me to share more of my feelings in my essays. But there's only so much I want to open up and, as the school year progressed and once again I became the target for everyone's hatred, I lost confidence in what I'd written. Once I completed the exercise book, I hid it away in the bottom of a drawer. And I haven't dared tell anyone about my dream of becoming a writer, not even Shanaz. I'm not sure I want to share that with Mr Beveridge.

I stick to safer ground. 'Yeah, sir, I do like Madonna. It's just . . .'

'You want to fit in?' he suggests. 'You want to like the same music as everyone else?'

I've never heard a teacher talk like this before and don't know how to respond. 'Yeah, maybe.'

'Well, don't, Charlie. Have the courage to be yourself. You know, when I was your age I used to like David Bowie.' He smiles fondly. 'Funnily enough, your essay made me think about the first time I went to see him live.'

'Did it?' I ask, feeling drawn in. 'What was he like?'

'Oh he was amazing,' he says, 'completely and utterly amazing. I can't tell you how exciting David Bowie was in those days. He was like nothing anyone had ever seen.'

'Really?' I ask. 'What kind of thing did he do then, sir?'

'Well, let's just say he liked breaking boundaries and challenging conventions. Put it this way, when some of the other kids found out I liked him they weren't very impressed. But looking back now, David Bowie got me through some difficult times. And he helped me stay true to myself when there was so much pressure to try to be someone else.'

I suddenly wonder if it's true Mr Beveridge is queer and if he's trying to tell me that he can spot it in me too. Then I remember that there's no way that could be true because of that new law called Clause 28, which has been all over the news; apparently teachers can't tell anyone they're queer in case it corrupts the kids and encourages them to turn the same way. Mind you, the kids at my school don't need any confirmation that Mr Beveridge is queer and if anyone sees me talking to him they'll read it as more evidence that I am. I look around nervously, but thankfully we're not being watched. I hope Mr Beveridge can't sense my discomfort.

'Charlie,' he goes on, gently, 'have you ever heard the saying, "The nail that sticks out gets hammered in"?'

'No, sir,' I reply, 'I don't think so.'

'Well, unfortunately it's true. And when I was your age I had to fight really hard not to let myself get hammered in.'

I nod, thoughtfully. 'But isn't it nice to be the same as everyone else, sir? Doesn't that make life easier?'

'Well, by the time you get to my age you realize that a person's difference can actually be what makes them special. So don't let yourself get hammered in, Charlie. Don't let that happen to you.'

I'm just about to reply when Miss Whorehouse comes running over huffing and puffing. Apparently a fight has broken out between two female townies after one called the other a slag and the other retaliated by saying she had a bucket fanny. It seems that Mr Beveridge is needed to break it up.

He trots away from me but calls back over his shoulder. 'Don't forget what I said, Charlie. And if you need reminding, remember what you loved about the Madonna concert and hold on to it. That'll get you through!'

He winks at me and disappears out of the hall. I step back into the shadows.

I take another swig of my drink and scan the room for Shanaz. In the distance I spot Vince Hargreaves lurking around with a few of his mates but he's too busy eyeing up some townie girls from the third year to notice me. By this time, Vince's grown into a huge dump-truck of a boy who loves nothing more than throwing his weight around to get what he wants. He knows that he terrifies me more than ever and uses this to make me hand over my bus fare at the end of the day so that he can buy cigarettes. Every evening after school I have to walk all the way home with my heavy rucksack, hurrying along as fast as I can so Mum won't ask why I'm arriving so late. Sometimes he'll kick or punch me just for fun and if he leaves any bruises I have to make up elaborate excuses to explain why I look such a mess. My blood boils at how unfair it all is but I don't see how I can make him like me when nobody else does. No, the best thing is to avoid him, which is exactly what I intend to do now. I breathe a sigh of relief as he stomps away from me and follows the girls out of the room.

Just then the music changes and I recognize the introduction to Madonna's 'Crazy for You'. The DJ must have decided to wind down the tempo and I watch what's been a mob of people suddenly become a sea of couples. Evidently, the indies have forgotten their dislike of Madonna and everyone's hitting the dance floor with their partners.

As my idol begins singing one of her most famous ballads, there's a tap on my shoulder and I turn around expecting to see Shanaz. Instead, I'm surprised to find Geraldine Hoggett, a redhead with glasses and a blotchy complexion like corned beef. Geraldine always smells of vanilla essence, walks around school with a briefcase and is obsessed with collecting different sections for her Filofax. I don't need reminding that Geraldine's a stiff – and one of the biggest stiffs in the school.

'Hi Charlie, would you like to dance?'

I wonder which is worse – having no one to dance with or dancing in full view of everyone with a stiff. Before I have time to reply, she's taken my hand and is leading me to the dance floor. I suddenly feel nervous and my forehead starts sweating.

'Urm, Geraldine, I, urm . . .'

It's no use – as Madonna belts her way through the first verse, Geraldine puts her arms around me and pulls me towards her. By now I'm sweating so much that my glasses keep slipping down my nose. I feel awfully uncomfortable and she must be able to sense it.

'What's the matter, Charlie, do you think I'm a dog?'

My shoulders tense up and my mouth goes dry.

'No, of course I don't. You're really, urm . . . you're really . . . fit.'

The next thing I know she's lunging forward and clamping her mouth onto mine. It's horrible. Her lips are soft and wet and she rams her tongue into my mouth and starts moving it around in circles. I try my best to do the same but am worried about dribbling down my chin. And I'm not sure what to do with my eyes – am I supposed to close them or keep them open? Over Geraldine's shoulder I can see Vince Hargreaves scratching his balls and looking around for someone to pick on. I stick my tongue further into Geraldine's mouth and try not to squirm as she clasps hold of my cheeks and thrusts my head aggressively from side to side. I accidentally dislodge her brace with my tongue and we have to pause for a second while she reattaches it. When we move back into position, our glasses hit each other and I have to bend my head to the left to avoid another collision. This is my first ever snog and I'm really not enjoying it. Quite frankly, I don't understand why everyone goes on about it all the time. I feel like I'm drowning.

All of a sudden, a voice in my head tells me that I'm snogging the wrong person. If I'm honest, I'd much rather be snogging Matt McGregor. But giving in to this urge would mean I'm just the kind of dirty queer everyone says I am. No, there's no way I can let that happen. I wonder what Geraldine would say if she knew what I'm thinking. I try to shake the idea out of my head and concentrate on being a good snog.

As 'Crazy For You' reaches its crescendo, Geraldine begins sucking violently on my lips and gnawing away at them with her teeth. I'm struggling to catch my breath and am not sure I can last much longer. I listen to Madonna singing and for the first time ever wish she'd get a move on and wind it up. I can feel a gurgling in my stomach and hot bile tickling the back of my throat. Before I have time to do anything about it, a thick liquid comes rushing up into my mouth. I push Geraldine to one side and dart towards the door.

Unfortunately, I don't make it out in time and am sick all over the corridor. I have to hold onto the wall while my eyes water and I hack up a puddle of white wine, Tia Maria, Cinzano and Coke. A group of indies spot me and start pointing. Before long there's a crowd of them looking on and laughing. Through my tear-filled eyes I can just about make out Matt McGregor sneering in the distance.

Shanaz comes over and gives me a handful of tissues.

'Come on,' she says, 'I think we'd better get some air before your mum arrives.'

Once I've cleaned myself up, Shanaz leads me outside and the two of us stand shivering by the school gates.

'Sorry about that,' I cough, 'I'm not sure what happened.'

'I was thinking the same myself. What on earth were you doing going with Geraldine Hoggett?'

'Why do you say that? Do you think she's a dog?'

'No, Charlie – the point is, she's a *girl*.'

I suddenly feel a stab of terror. It's as if I'm more exposed than I've ever been in my life. I look around to check no one's listening. 'What's that supposed to mean?'

Shanaz shrugs her shoulders. 'Well, I always assumed you fancied boys, that's all.'

'Shhh – keep your voice down!' By now I'm ablaze with anxiety. I can't believe she actually just said that out loud. What if someone overheard her?

'Don't panic,' she smiles, 'there's only us!'

I can feel the atmosphere between us sharpen. The problem is, now that she's brought it up, I can't deny it, not to Shanaz; she'll know without any doubt that I'm lying. 'Well, I don't care,' I rasp, 'I don't want to talk about it.'

'OK, OK,' she breathes. 'I'm sorry I mentioned it.'

I glance down at my watch, unable to look her in the eye. 'Anyway, what time is it? Mum'll be here soon.'

I look out to the road, the anxiety still coursing through me. The two of us plunge into a tense silence and sit there shuddering with cold. 'The Whole of the Moon' by The Waterboys can be heard coming out of the hall. The night's gone on forever and I wish Mum would just hurry up and get here.

'I tell you what I fancy,' Shanaz says after a while.

'What?' I ask, my eyes trained on the ground.

'I could murder a tin of pineapple chunks.'

I give a weak laugh.

'I tell you what else an' all,' she says.

I look up to meet her gaze. 'What?'

'After the night we've had I think we can eat them straight out of the tin.'

I draw in a shaky breath and manage to break into a smile. 'Now you're talking.'

She smiles back at me. 'But do you reckon your stomach's up to it?'

'Oh I think it'll cope.'

A set of headlights comes towards us and I recognize the number plate. It's Mum.

'Hey,' says Shanaz, 'it's only eleven o'clock – we'll be back in time for *Prisoner: Cell Block H.*'

As I watch Mum's car approach, I think back to how happy I was at the Madonna concert – and how strong I felt to be infused with the spirit of my idol. The problem is, as far as I know Madonna has no plans to tour again soon. So where on earth can I go to feel that way again?

I have to find out.

Vogue

Shanaz and I stand up and wait for the train to stop. We're excited about our first night out in Manchester but I can't help feeling a bit frightened too.

As the train pulls into Victoria Station, Shanaz pulls out *City Life* magazine, which she bought so we could work out the way to our destination. Somewhat tentatively she leads us out of the station, down Cross Street, past the Royal Exchange Theatre and then King Street with its glamorous shops. We come to the edge of St Peter's Square and stop for a moment to look at the town hall, lit up in all its Gothic grandeur. And then we turn left and walk on until we come to a small cobbled street, which is the end of our journey. The sign's supposed to say Canal Street but someone has vandalized it so it reads 'anal treet'. I gulp.

'Come on,' says Shanaz, 'don't back out on me now.'

Lately, Shanaz has been encouraging me to talk to her more and more about fancying boys. She always approaches the subject carefully as I'm still very reticent and certainly don't want to discuss it with anyone else. If I'm honest, I still don't want it to be true either but very slowly I'm starting to accept that it is. I can't imagine ever saying out loud that I'm queer but more and more people are using the word 'gay' to talk about people like me and I've always thought that's a much nicer word. I'm starting to think there might even come a day when I'll be able to use it about myself.

A big turning point came when Shanaz and I went to the pictures to watch *In Bed with Madonna*, the access-all-areas documentary Madonna filmed behind the scenes of her *Blond Ambition* tour. In it she revealed that six out of her seven male dancers were gay, as well as her brother Christopher, who designed the show and worked as her dresser. I sat in the cinema overwhelmed as I watched this close-knit group of men talking about their boyfriends and going to a Gay Pride march in New York. Finally, it felt like there were some openly gay people in my world. And not only that but Madonna made it clear in the film that she loved them all exactly as they were and talked at length about feeling a special bond with gay people because they're fellow outsiders. By the time it came to the scene in which two of the dancers snog in close-up during the game of Truth or Dare, I realized that I'd been smiling through the whole film; it was as if a fog was lifting before my eyes and the whole world was suddenly coming into focus. It didn't matter that people in the audience reacted to the snog by booing loudly and some even walked out in disgust. I sat in the darkness of the cinema feeling that familiar sensation of fear but this time mixed with a new emotion – something like defiance.

Around the same time, newspapers and magazines started to write about an area of Manchester called the Gay Village. They described it as a hub of gay bars, clubs and businesses that, although still small, was expanding rapidly – and apparently had an amazing atmosphere. It was only a matter of time till I plucked up the courage and gave in to Shanaz's suggestion that we go and experience it for ourselves.

We take our first steps onto Canal Street and walk past the New Union pub, seeing a group of men with handlebar moustaches and lumberjack shirts open the door and disappear inside. As they do so, we spot a drag queen on stage belting out 'New York, New York'. Everyone seems to be singing along and having a great night. I feel excited but still nervous too. I have to make a real effort to stop myself trembling.

Just next door to The New Union is where we're heading – a glass-fronted bar called Manto. We can already hear trendy dance music pumping out and see neon lights flashing behind windows soaked with condensation. I open the door and take a deep breath.

We step inside and straight away my glasses steam up. I take them off and wipe them on my shirt, cursing myself for looking like such a stiff. Once I can see properly I look around to take it all in. I can't believe what I'm seeing. Almost everyone in there is male and they all seem to be good-looking and fashionable. Everyone's flashing Calvin Klein underpants like Marky Mark in those new adverts and there's the distinct whiff of Fahrenheit and Obsession. Loads of people have goatee beards, Kangol caps and Palladium shoes and some are wearing little black waistcoats with nothing underneath. A beautiful boy dressed in a Breton shirt and a sailor hat gives us a sniffy look. A chiselled blond in a beaded necklace paws his black boyfriend proprietorially. And in the corner two muscular men with arms thicker than my neck are in the middle of a passionate snog. It's a world away from the Ritzy, Bolton's main nightclub where I once went with Shanaz but felt so self-conscious and out of place it was as if I was an alien who'd landed from another planet. And it's a world away from what I imagine The Star and Garter to be like, although I still don't think I'll ever be brave enough to go in there. But now here I am in Manto and it all feels so right, like I've finally found a place where I belong. Has this place existed all the time I've been cut off and festering in Bolton?

We go to the bar and buy ourselves a drink. We aren't sure what to order so ask for what everyone else seems to be drinking – bottles of beer with a slice of lime squeezed into the neck. Shanaz lights herself a Silk Cut – she's recently taken up smoking full-time, saying it makes her feel rebellious and liberated. I decline her offer of a cigarette but watch in admiration as she puffs away.

We make our way upstairs to the balcony and look down on the crowd below. I wonder if anyone else is in here for the first time. It certainly doesn't look like it – they all seem so relaxed and confident. I can't get over how different this is to anything I've ever seen before. Half of me is blown away and wants to be part of the action, the other half feels overwhelmed and completely shaken.

'This is a top buzz, i'nt it?' says Shanaz.

'Too right!' I bark, a little too enthusiastically.

Standing close by are a group of lesbians wearing jeans and braces and drinking pints. I'm intrigued – I've never seen a lesbian before, although Mum always says Fat Pat who works in the paper shop is 'a bit on the lesbian side', but that's only because she has short hair and likes playing darts. Right now, though, I'm looking at the genuine article.

'All right?' one of them says to me with a wink.

'Hiya,' I squeak, embarrassed to be caught gawping.

We finish our drinks and Shanaz decides it's time to move on. We've planned to go to a club and figure we'll have more chance getting in if we arrive early.

From what we've read in *City Life*, a new club called The Paradise Factory is *the* place to go. We really want to see what it's like so have picked up a couple of flyers in Manto that offer cheap entry if we get there before ten. But we're only seventeen and are worried about getting past the bouncer, a great big slab of a man with the scar from a knife wound on his left cheek and a ring through his nose that makes him look like a bull. Thankfully, the drink is kicking in and we're starting to relax. As we walk up to the entrance, we test each other on the birthdays and star signs we've invented to make us the right age. But the bouncer doesn't ask us any questions and steps to one side and opens the door. Once we're out of earshot, we both breathe a sigh of relief.

The woman who takes our entrance money has slicked-back hair with a kiss curl on her left cheek and is wearing a man's dinner suit and a monocle. I'm delighted – it's just like stepping into the Kit Kat Klub in the film *Cabaret*.

The first thing we do once we're inside is to explore the building. We know that it was some kind of factory years ago and then housed the offices of Factory Records, which produced indie music during the Madchester period. That era's long gone and the company has since folded. All that remains is the word 'factory' in the club's title and the industrial décor – the brick walls have been left bare, there are several iron girders holding up the roof, and the bars and DJ booths are made of chrome. It's all very stylish and modern.

My favourite floor is the first, where the DJ plays music by Kylie Minogue, Right Said Fred and a new boy band everyone's talking about called Take That. The bar staff wear red wigs and silver hotpants and most of the men on the dance floor have bodies like Chippendales and are wearing hardly anything at all. But not everyone in there's gay – there are several gay men who are clearly out with their straight female friends. The one thing everyone has in common is that they're all having great fun.

The top floor has a totally different feel. It's dimly lit and full of older men dressed either in army uniforms or in head-to-toe black PVC with holes of various sizes for their buttocks and nipples. People of bafflingly indeterminable gender are writhing around on the dance floor with whips and everywhere I look I see tattoos and piercings. In a dark corner, three people are tweaking each other's nipples and a man with a shaved head is bouncing up and down on top of another who's neighing like a horse. I've never seen anything like it and feel repulsed and terrified; I might be starting to get my head around being gay but I'm not into this kind of thing and am not sure I can deal with it.

'This is doing my head in,' I say to Shanaz.

'Yeah,' she agrees. 'Let's sack it off.'

We retreat downstairs and at the bottom of the staircase bump into two drag queens who are sucking on pink lollipops and fanning themselves with elaborate lace fans. They're caked in glittery make-up, are wearing matching pink feather boas and tower over us in platform heels. They introduce themselves as Coco and Angel and say they work in 'promotions'. I'm captivated – it's just like being in an episode of that new sitcom *Absolutely Fabulous*.

'So then, sweetie,' Coco says in a broad Mancunian accent, 'are you gay or are you normal?'

I'm taken aback and lower my voice awkwardly. 'Flippin' 'eck – you don't beat around the bush, do you?'

'Let's leave the bush out of it, shall we?' She smirks and gives a click of her fan. 'Come on, spill those beans.'

'Urm, I'm gay I suppose.' It's the first time I've ever said it out loud.

'Very good, that's the right answer. And I take it this is your first time on the scene?'

I'm embarrassed it's so obvious. 'Yeah, it is actually.'

'Well, welcome to our world!' she purrs.

'Welcome to Paradise!' says Angel in a surprisingly deep voice.

'Isn't it FABULOUS?' they chorus.

I give an amused nod as they each click their fans.

Angel turns to Shanaz. 'And what about you, sweetie? You look like a dyke if I've ever seen one.'

'Oh,' she stumbles. 'Urm, why do you say that?'

'Well, you're not wearing any make-up!'

'And look at those sensible shoes!'

'Oh right.' Shanaz is flummoxed. 'No, I'm not actually. I suppose *you'd* say I'm normal.'

Coco and Angel look at each other in mock disgust. 'Eurgh, how *hideous*!'

'Well, I'm sorry,' Shanaz stammers, 'but there's nothing I can do about it.'

'Oh don't worry, sweetie,' says Coco. 'As long as you keep yourself to yourself and don't ram it down our throats, we don't mind.'

There's another chorus of laughter.

'And anyway, you're not *normal*!' Angel pronounces the word as if she's referring to a horrifically disfiguring skin disease. 'You're Asian so it's OK.'

'Oh – what difference does that make?'

'Well,' she explains, 'in here we're all special together.'

'Yeah,' says Coco, 'we're all poofs and you're a Paki. Isn't it just FABULOUS?'

I try not to squirm as I think back to the names people used to call me and Shanaz at school. Now that we're in the sixth form, a lot of the rougher kids such as Vince Hargreaves have left, which means we're subjected to the 'p' words much less often. Not only that but I'm starting to get the impression that, as the kids in my year grow older, they seem less outraged by the idea of gay people – either that or the success of films like *In Bed with Madonna* and the popularity of clubs like The Paradise Factory are gradually getting people used to the idea that we exist, and maybe we aren't so frightening after all. Even so, my wounds are still raw and I sense they are for Shanaz too. Not that Coco and Angel pick up on any of our discomfort; they just cackle louder than ever and carry on fanning themselves. I wonder whether Shanaz is going to point out that she's Indian rather than Pakistani but it looks like she's decided to laugh it off. I join in the laughter, not quite able to believe that the same things that have always made people insult me and Shanaz are now being held up as cause for celebration.

'Off you go then, sweeties!' chirps Angel.

'Run along and kiss some boys!' adds Coco.

And with that they pop their lollipops back into their mouths.

We make our way through to the bar and order ourselves another beer. They're really expensive, though, and we know this will have to be our last. We hover around the dance floor, watching some amazing moves and trying to muster up the courage to join in. I really want to get up there but everyone's dancing is so slick that I just don't have the confidence. I look at Shanaz and can tell she feels the same.

And then it all changes.

The music stops and the high-pitched opening to Madonna's 'Vogue' rings out of the speakers. As we hear our idol inviting us to strike a pose, our inhibitions instantly melt away.

We rush onto the dance floor and find ourselves a space. Everyone around us is copying Madonna's dance routine and we throw ourselves into it too. At first we feel a bit self-conscious but know all the moves off by heart and nobody would be able to tell we've only ever performed them in our bedrooms. Every beat reverberates around my body and it's as if I'm experiencing the music properly for the first time. I remember that Madonna wrote the song after watching drag queens dance on the underground club scene in New York and am suddenly overwhelmed with joy. As I listen to her singing about the pain and heartache these gay men are trying to escape through dance, I realize just how deeply she must understand all the emotions I've been going through. As she encourages me to let my body go with the flow, I feel transformed by a new energy, as if dancing to the song is somehow setting me free.

When 'Vogue' comes to an end, we carry on dancing and don't stop once. Everything that has been worrying us seems to somehow evaporate – what we look like, what other people think of us, schoolwork, exams . . . We never want the night to end.

After what feels like ages, Shanaz glances at her watch and sees that it's nearly midnight. We look at each other in shock – the last train leaves in just over fifteen minutes and we have to move fast if we're going to catch it.

We dash across town and make it to the station just in time. We leap onto the train, puffing and panting, and find ourselves a seat and slump into it, the music still ringing in our ears.

Once we've caught our breath, we start talking our way through the night, keen to keep it alive. The train's full of people returning home after a night out. Voices are raised, people are singing and there's even a couple dancing in the aisle. Sitting on the seats opposite us are some drunken lads who look like Paul Gascoigne and are swigging from cans of lager. They occasionally glance over at us menacingly. We lower our voices to a whisper but this only makes us feel naughty and rebellious and adds to the fun.

By the time we get to Bolton, like everyone else on the train we've fallen fast asleep. The conductor walks down the carriage, shaking us all awake.

'Everybody off!' he yells. 'Last stop Bolton!'

We rub our eyes and stretch our legs. Half asleep, I hobble along to the exit and stumble down the platform. In my head I'm still in The Paradise Factory, surrounded by smiling faces and dancing away to 'Vogue'. If I've finally found a place where I belong, I can't wait to get back there as soon as possible. And whatever I have to do to make it happen, I know now that I'm prepared to do it.

I'm so lost in my thoughts that I almost walk into a sign that says, 'Welcome to Bolton'. I snap myself back to reality and begin heading up the stairs.

Express Yourself

Finally the day has come.

After months of waiting it's time for me to find out my future.

It's A-level results day and I'm in the sixth-form block at school sitting in the waiting area with Mum and Dad. They've both taken the morning off work and have gone to great lengths to look smart for the occasion. Mum's wearing a brand new pencil skirt and cardigan and has been to Klassy Kutz so Auntie Jan could cut her hair into a style called feathered bangs that's apparently all the rage. Dad's had a shave and dug out his one suit, which I've only ever seen him wear at family weddings and that one time he had to be a witness in court when Uncle Les got into a fight over some woman Mum said was a trollop. As I look at my parents now, I'm touched by all the effort they've gone to and can tell they're almost as nervous as I am.

'By 'eck, lad, keep your leg still!' Dad croaks.

My left leg's jittering and I have to press it down with my hand.

'It'll be all right, love,' soothes Mum, 'if you don't get the grades you can always stay at home with me and your dad.'

My leg starts jittering even more.

'Apparently they're looking for school-leavers down the town hall,' adds Dad with a pat on my knee. 'I'm sure they'd snap up a clever lad like you.'

I close my eyes and try to zone out of the conversation and compose myself. I haven't been able to eat all morning and am starting to feel nauseous. I decide to sing to myself to take my mind off things. The first song that comes into my head is 'Express Yourself', the same song that got me through the long, tough revision period.

At the start of term, Mr Beveridge told me several times that concentrating on my exams would get me wherever I wanted in life. I paid close attention and remembered my dream of becoming a writer and how it had come to me the first time I saw Madonna live. But since then, my head's become crowded by doubts; people like me don't become writers, and anyway, why would anyone want to read any kind of story I could come up with? Needless to say, I kept my thoughts to myself and my dream stayed buried at the bottom of my drawer, along with the essay I wrote about the Madonna concert.

In the meantime, I took Mr Beveridge at his word and buckled down for several months. Every evening and all day at weekends, I'd sit at the desk in my bedroom trying to block out all sound from the outside world. I was really strict with myself and revised for forty-five minutes then took a break for fifteen. During these breaks I'd put on music and dance around the room. The song I played most was 'Express Yourself'; I know it's supposed to be about standing up for yourself in a relationship but I listen to it as an all-purpose anthem to self-empowerment. Sometimes I'd nip downstairs to the VHS player and watch Madonna perform the song on the *Blond Ambition* tour, with her famous long hairpiece and Jean-Paul Gaultier-designed conical bra protruding from a costume that looked like armour, radiating a steely confidence and self-belief. It gave me the lift I needed, firing me up to do my best.

Now that I've made it to results day, my confidence has vanished. I'm so nervous I feel delirious and in my head I can hear the same line of the song playing over and over again. Geraldine Hoggett has already come out of the office, beaming and clutching her results slip and telling everyone who'll listen that she's going to Edinburgh University. Shortly afterwards, Matt McGregor emerged pale-faced and stunned, his angry mother prodding him and muttering disparaging remarks about Bangor Poly. I've no idea how I've done and have to force my leg down with both hands to keep it still.

My worry is that I've set my sights too high. At the start of the school year I applied to study English at Cambridge and last December travelled down on the train for my application interview. Mr Beveridge had spent several months preparing me, suggesting books I should read and films I should watch to give me something to talk about. But when the day finally arrived I felt overwhelmed and out of my depth. I worked myself up into such a state that just before I went in I spilt tea all down my shirt. The interviewers must have thought I was really uncouth and it was blatantly obvious when I started to speak that none of them could understand my accent; they looked at me with blank expressions and fumbled with their ties as I answered each question.

Things only got better when I started to talk about the books I was studying. *Jane Eyre*, *The Great Gatsby*, *Wuthering Heights*, *The Color Purple*, *The Picture of Dorian Gray* . . . For some reason, once I switched to talking about fictional worlds rather than the real one I found I could express myself better. I could feel the interviewers warming to me and when we finally shook hands goodbye I remember thinking it might not have been a total disaster after all. That is until I got outside and realized that my fly had been undone the whole time.

I slunk back to Bolton, convinced that I'd been rejected. Then just after Christmas a letter arrived offering me a place to start the following October. I was staggered. All that was left was for me to work as hard as I could to make the grades – and now I'm waiting to find out whether I've done it.

I look at my watch and follow the second hand as it moves around slowly. Shanaz is in the office at the moment and I wonder how she's done. She's certainly worked as hard as me but said she had bad luck with the questions on her Chemistry paper and really struggled to finish. I know how important it is that she does well – her mum and dad are stricter than mine and always put pressure on her to succeed. This morning, the three of them turned up stony-faced and silent. Apparently, Shanaz's mum caught her smoking in the bathroom last night and the incident prompted a huge row. They already think she's reckless and unruly just because she spends Friday evenings with me watching *The Word*. If she's gone and messed up her A-levels, they'll never let her forget it.

The door opens and I look up to see Shanaz's face. Fortunately, all three of them are grinning.

'I've done it!' she says. 'An A and two Bs!'

I jump up and hug her. 'Shanaz, that's brilliant!'

We dance round in a circle and her mum and dad look on with pride.

'So does this mean you're off to Manchester?' asks my mum.

'Too right it does!'

'And it means *I'm* going to be visiting all the time,' I beam.

The two of us laugh.

'Charlie tells us you're going to be a doctor,' my dad says to her.

'Yeah,' she replies, clearly still struggling to take it in. 'It seems funny when you say it like that.'

'Well, congratulations,' he says, 'it's crackin' news.'

'*Charlie Matthews!*' The sound echoes around the room. It's Mr Beveridge's voice.

'Yes, sir?'

'Would you like to come through?'

My stomach flips over and my knees almost give way. The thirty seconds it takes me to walk inside feels like the longest thirty seconds in my life. The three of us sit down opposite him and he says hello to my now white-faced parents.

'Right then,' he smiles, 'let's have a look.'

As he opens the envelope I stare at it so hard that my eyes go fuzzy. I swallow and my Adam's apple feels as heavy as a brick.

When he finally opens his mouth it's as if the words come out in slow motion. 'Well done, Charlie – two As and a B.'

I'm not sure I've heard him right. 'What was that? Sorry?'

He pats me on the shoulder. 'You've got what you need, Charlie – As in English and Spanish and a B in History.'

He hands me the slip of paper so I can see for myself. I stare at it so intensely that all I can make out is a random collection of tiny dots. I shake my head and regain my focus. There it is in print – two As and a B.

Dad actually leaps from his seat. 'You little belter!' he laughs.

Mum's chin starts to quiver. 'My little baby,' she sniffs.

I don't think I've ever seen them so emotional. And to think that for once they're proud of *me*. I've wanted this for so long but now that it's happening it doesn't feel real. Aren't I the crap one who only ever embarrasses or disappoints Mum and Dad?

'Congratulations!' says Mr Beveridge, interrupting my thoughts.

I can't hold back a rush of happiness more intense than anything I've ever experienced. I look at the results slip and shake my head in disbelief. I've actually gone and pulled this off. And it really is the big one. And on top of it all I can't help feeling a sneaky satisfaction that my grades are better than Joe's two years ago.

'You do realize what this means?' says Mr Beveridge in a more serious tone.

I raise my eyebrows expectantly.

'What this means, Charlie, is that suddenly everything's possible. From now on you can do whatever you want in life.'

Mum bursts into tears.

'Get out there and discover the world!' he continues. 'Go and make all your dreams come true!'

I'm not sure how to reply to this in front of my parents. 'I will, Sir,' I mumble, 'I promise.'

'Oh Charlie,' sobs Mum, 'I can't believe you're going off and leaving us.'

I'm not used to such a show of emotion, particularly in front of a teacher; Mum only usually says this kind of thing at Christmas when she overdoes it on the white wine. It tends to come just before she gets Dad and Uncle Les to hold out a length of tinsel so she can show off her limbo dancing. But now that she's saying it stone-cold sober I don't really know how to handle it. 'Don't be silly, Mum,' I struggle, 'I'll be back all the time.'

'Yeah, I know, love, but you'll move on. Sooner or later we'll lose you.'

'Course you won't, Mum,' I soothe, 'you'll never lose me.' But even as I say the words I'm not sure I mean them.

'Are you sure, love?' she asks, putting her hand out towards me.

'Yeah, Mum,' I lie, 'course I'm sure.'

As I look at the expression on her face, it dawns on me just how much today's results have changed things. All my life I've been chasing my parents' approval and looking for evidence that they love me – but now Mum's looking for the same from me. I put my arms around her and give her a squeeze.

'Come on, Maggie,' coaxes Dad, 'stop being so soft. He'll only be gone a few years and then he'll be back in Bolton. It's his home, i'nt it?'

As Mum knuckles away her tears, I know that at this point I'm expected to jump in and agree with Dad but I can only bring myself to nod weakly. The truth is, I'm overjoyed to finally be getting away from a town that's made me so unhappy. All the same, I feel a sadness that becoming the person I want to be, the person I've dreamed of being for so long, means putting a distance between me and my parents – and a distance that isn't just geographical.

Mr Beveridge stands up and claps his hands. 'Right, come on you lot – off you go and tell everyone your news.'

Mum dries her eyes with a hanky and I help her up.

'Thanks for everything, sir.'

I smile and shake his hand.

'My pleasure.'

'Yeah,' chips in Dad, 'thanks for everything you've done for our lad.'

'We really appreciate it,' adds Mum, her voice breaking. If she's that sad to see me leave, I can only imagine how hard this must be for her to say. 'If it weren't for you,' she goes on with a strained smile, 'he might have been stuck here with us!'

As she forces out a hysterical laugh, I feel another pang of sadness. Surely she can't tell how much I want to get away from here? I tell her not to be silly and try to swallow my guilt.

Mum and Dad say goodbye and start filing out of the office. Once they're on the other side of the door, Mr Beveridge taps my shoulder and beckons me back.

'Oh, one more thing, Charlie.'

'Yeah, what's that?'

He looks at the door to check they've gone. 'Whatever you do,' he says, 'don't let anyone hold you back, however much you love them. And don't feel bad about it. You need to break free now – it's time to start loving yourself.'

'Oh, right, OK.' I'm still feeling overwhelmed by the day's events and am not sure I can deal with such an intense conversation.

But he looks at me with an expression of deep concentration and goes on. 'There was a time when I had a bright future, you know, just like you. And OK, I might have been brave enough to listen to David Bowie when I was a teenager, but when it came down to it I was too frightened to follow that through and take my chance.'

'I'm sorry, sir. What happened?'

He lets out a despondent sigh. 'Oh, let's just say I was too weighed down by obligations and expectations to break free. But that's why I'm telling you now, never mind what you owe other people – you owe it to yourself to get out there and live the life that's waiting for you. Don't stay here and become a disappointed man like me.'

I nod seriously and there's a moment's silence while I think about what he's said.

'Thanks again, sir. I promise I won't let you down.'

'It's not about letting me down, Charlie,' he says. 'I don't want you to let yourself down.'

'OK, yes, sorry, I won't. I promise.'

'Good. I'll hold you to that.'

I smile and shake his hand one last time.

As I open the door to the outside world, my mind begins racing with fantasies of the future. I feel like the hero of a nineteenth-century novel embarking on my adult life, ready for a rousing and gripping adventure. I picture myself cycling through Cambridge with a mortarboard on my head and my heart flutters with excitement. For as long as I can remember I've felt like a glamorous person trapped in an unglamorous lifestyle. Well, as of today all that's set to change.

And the most exciting thing of all is that when I arrive in Cambridge I can become whoever I want – nobody will know I'm a shy, insignificant boy from Bolton. It won't be like moving from primary to secondary school, when most of the kids from my class came with me so my problems tagged along too. No, this is a completely fresh start with a whole new set of people who won't know anything about me. Now that I think about it, this is my chance to totally reinvent myself. Isn't that what journalists say Madonna does? Don't they always talk about her adopting different personas and then casting them off like a chameleon?

I resolve now that if Madonna can do it, so can I.

Part Two

Into the Groove

Less than two months after A-level results day, my reinvention is complete. And today's the day to reveal it to the world.

My metamorphosis began when I swapped my glasses for contact lenses and the feeling was liberating, almost like shedding my old skin. I've decided to gloss over the fact that I can't see properly and have to blink every few minutes just to refocus. I also worked in a shoe shop over the summer, spending all the money I earned on a fashionable new wardrobe that makes me feel much more confident, if slightly bewildered by how many things I have to get right in order to look cool. And I've followed Madonna's lead and taken up running, pounding the pavements of Bolton three times a week listening to my new CD Walkman. I've even practised speaking without my northern accent, hiding away in my bedroom and mouthing along to elocution tapes I borrowed from the local library. At first I felt like Eliza Doolittle in *My Fair Lady* but I'm convinced that speaking properly is the key to fitting in at Cambridge so I persevered. After weeks of practice I'm finally happy with the new me – and today I'm going to find out what everyone else thinks.

I'm on my way to Cambridge for the start of my first term at St Christopher's College. I chose St Christopher's as I read that it was named after the patron saint of travellers and this seemed fitting seeing as I was about to embark on a journey, probably the most important of my life. I figured I could use all the guidance I could get, even if it was just metaphorical.

Mum and Dad are driving me in their burgundy Rover, the boot and half of the back seat piled high with my books, bedding, clothes and stereo. The journey's tense as we're all a bit nervous so we rely on the radio to provide the atmosphere. Once we arrive in Cambridge we report to the porters' lodge then park the car, drop off my bike in the bike sheds, and carry all my stuff up to my new bedroom in a 1970s block at the back of the college. When we've finished, we stand around awkwardly until Dad suggests finding the local chippy. I sense he's feeling unmoored and looking around for a role, or at least some kind of toe-hold, in my new life. I tell him I think this is a great idea.

We walk into the town centre and find a fish and chip shop called Oh My Cod, although I can tell from the start that Dad isn't impressed. The staff have never heard of steak and kidney pudding, don't do gravy or curry sauce, and their chip butty, which sounds promisingly northern, turns out to be served not in a bread roll but a slice of pitta bread. Worst of all, they slather their chips with mayonnaise rather than ketchup, which for some reason Dad takes as a personal affront. I try to concentrate on the fact that the chips actually taste good and suggest we find somewhere to sit down and eat them.

We stroll along King's Parade, passing the university church and a rather grand-looking building called the Senate House, which I've already been told is where students graduate each June. I feel another rumble of nerves as I wonder again if the other students on my course will all be much cleverer than me. What if I can't keep up with them? What if I don't make it through to graduation? I tell myself that my appointment in the Senate House is still three years away and try focusing on how wonderful it is to finally be here in Cambridge. The town looks so beautiful it's impossible not to fall under its spell. I glance around and feel like I'm in *Brideshead Revisited* or E. M. Forster's *Maurice*.

I pop another chip in my mouth and we stroll on, along a row of pretty souvenir shops on our left and the imposing King's College on our right, the spires of its enormous chapel reaching up into the sky. I suggest we cross the road and sit down on the wall outside the entrance.

'This is nice, isn't it?' I say brightly.

Dad gives me a frown. 'Well, it would be if I had a bit of gravy on my chips,' he grumbles. 'You know I like them with plenty of wet.'

I try not to cringe. 'Yeah, well, maybe they do things differently down here, Dad.' I decide not to mention that that's what I'm hoping.

'All I'm saying is, just make sure you don't start asking for mayonnaise on your chips when you come home,' he goes on. 'I don't want anyone thinking you've turned into a stuck-up Southerner.'

As he stuffs another fistful of chips into his mouth, I look around to check that nobody's watching. I'm suddenly struck by how broad Dad's accent is; it's almost as if he's accentuating it to make some kind of point. And does he really have to speak so loudly? What if some of the people walking past are in my year at St Christopher's and think I'm really uncouth?

'Ignore your dad, love,' Mum jumps in, before I have time to reply. 'You just concentrate on settling in and being happy.'

'Thanks, Mum. I will.'

'Now, you will wear that cycle helmet, won't you?' she adds.

'I will, yeah.'

'And you will use that blonding shampoo three times a week?'

'Yeah, yeah, don't worry.'

'Stop nagging him, woman,' butts in Dad. 'I'm sure the lad knows how to wash his own hair.'

'All right, Frank!' she snaps back. 'I know he can wash his own hair – I just don't want it to lose its blondness, that's all.'

'Don't worry, Mum,' I reassure her, 'I'll use your shampoo three times a week. And whenever the sun's out I'll make sure I get in it.'

'Good lad,' she nods. 'Oh and one more thing; don't forget to call us every Sunday at seven. If you find a payphone we'll call you straight back.'

'Yeah, yeah.' I smile, remembering our arrangement. 'I promise I will.'

She gives me another nod and we stop talking to finish our chips. I look at Mum and Dad and realize how tiny and insignificant both of them seem, silhouetted against the towering majesty of King's. My heart flinches and once again I feel guilty for finding them annoying – and for being embarrassed by their presence. Part of me wishes they'd just leave and then I don't have to feel so bad. But another part of me knows I'm going to miss them when they've gone.

Once we've finished eating, the three of us set off back to St Christopher's. Along the way we pass St Catharine's and Corpus Christi colleges, both of them home to students I'll be mixing with at the English Faculty. What will they all think of me? Will any of them like me? I remind myself that there'll be much more chance if they get to know the new rather than the old me. It's all right to feel guilty about growing apart from Mum and Dad but at the same time I have to stick to my plan of reinventing myself.

When we arrive back at college, Mum and Dad say they'll leave me to unpack and we walk over to their car to say goodbye.

'See you, lad,' Dad mumbles, looking down awkwardly.

'Yeah, ta-ra, love,' says Mum, kissing me on the cheek.

She opens the boot and hands me a package of Lancashire cheese, Bury black puddings and some Chorley cakes Grandma made. The sight of it all lovingly wrapped up makes me feel hollowed out with sadness. 'Thanks, Mum,' I croak. 'And remember I'll be seeing you at Christmas. It's only a few months off.'

She gives me a weak smile. 'You know if it all goes belly-up before then you can just call us and we'll come and get you.'

'Thanks, Mum.'

'It doesn't matter when it is,' she insists, 'we'll drop everything and set off straight away.'

'Just as long as you don't come home supporting Cambridge United,' jokes Dad.

I shoot him a smile but it's in that moment that I remember why I'm leaving them. After all this time Dad's still making jokes about which football team I support; he still hasn't accepted the fact that I'm not into football at all. I remember what Mr Beveridge said about stopping worrying about other people and breaking free to start living my own life. I rearrange my features into a smile.

'Right then,' I say. 'Bye – and speak to you on Sunday.'

'Yeah, speak to you on Sunday.'

I watch the car drive away and wave at Mum through the window. Once it's left the college grounds I slope back up to my room and close the door behind me. This is it. I'm on my own.

I try to ignore my sadness and decide to start decorating; my room's shaped like a box and has whitewashed walls so is sorely lacking in character. The first thing I unpack from my suitcase is a poster of Madonna that I bought when Shanaz and I saw her last tour, *The Girlie Show*. It's an image of my idol with her newly cropped blonde hair but that familiar look of arrogance and power. Reasoning that I could do with some of that attitude at this crucial stage in my life, I dig out some Blu-tack and stick the poster up on my new wall.

As I stand back to look at it, I feel another tickle of nerves. Today's my big chance to make a good impression on the people I'll be spending the next few years with. Well, I'm not going to let my nerves get the better of me – or hold me back. Once I've finished unpacking I take several deep breaths and decide to dive into my new world.

I can hear the sound of Abba coming from the room next door and tentatively tap on the door. A girl called Sally wearing fluffy pink slippers answers and invites me to join her while she unpacks. She tells me very enthusiastically that she was brought up in Berkshire and was Deputy Head Girl of her school and captain of the lacrosse team. In my best BBC pronunciation I tell her I'm 'Charles from Manchester' and am here to study English. She seems completely taken in and, more importantly, seems to like me.

My next stop is a Victorian building where all the second years live, which is just across a courtyard on the other side of the bike sheds. Each of us first years has been assigned two second-year students who'll act as our 'parents' and look after us during Freshers' Week. Thinking about the name they've been given squeezes at my heart as I imagine how much classier and more sophisticated my Cambridge parents are going to be from the real-life ones I've just waved off. In the event I needn't have worried; my Cambridge parents are a dope-smoking Liverpudlian I soon realize everyone calls Council House Jack because he's an avid reader of the *Socialist Worker* and reminds anyone who'll listen that he grew up on a dodgy estate, and his room-mate Inappropriate Lee, a comically posh History student who was educated at boarding school yet is clueless when it comes to social etiquette. I discover how he earned his nickname when a first year called Caroline arrives at the door in a revealingly low-cut top. 'Great tits!' he barks, his eyes practically bursting out of their sockets.

Jack and I look at each other and cringe.

'Great welcome,' smirks Caroline, stepping around him and bouncing cheerfully into the room.

Next to arrive is a Philosophy student called Adrian who looks like John Lennon and writes poetry in his spare time. And the final member of our group is a chubby Chinese girl who grew up in Llandudno and has a strong Welsh accent. She bursts in and introduces herself as Lisa Toe. 'But you can all call me Rent-a-leg,' she jokes.

Everyone explodes into laughter but I miss the joke.

'Do you not get it?' asks Lisa, spotting my blank look. 'Lease-a-toe? Rent-a-leg?'

It suddenly registers. 'Oh yeah, right, sorry!' I try my best to laugh it off but can already feel my cheeks burning. I probably missed the joke because I'm so stressed about playing the role of the new, improved Charlie Matthews. All of which is fine but maybe I need to loosen up a bit.

'Would anyone like a drink?' asks Jack, brushing my blunder aside.

I breathe a sigh of relief.

Soon we're all sipping tea, nibbling biscuits and happily chatting away. Everyone seems warm and friendly and I can't get over how interesting they all are. I'm reassured to see that they like me too. When I tell them I'm from Manchester they're instantly impressed.

'Wicked!' squeaks Caroline Tits, as she's now known. 'Have you ever been to The Haçienda?'

'Oh, you know, once or twice.' I'm not used to lying and feel guilty. I can't bring myself to look her in the eye.

'Wow!' she gasps. 'You're so *cool*!'

I feel a flutter of excitement – my reinvention really is working.

Once the introductions are over, Jack and Lee talk us through Freshers' Week. As far as I can make out, all this involves is a series of lunches, dinners and 'squashes' – drinks parties run by the various university societies to encourage first years to sign up. According to Jack and Lee, whatever our interests, there's probably a society at Cambridge that caters for us.

'If you're a muso, there are loads of orchestras.'

'If you're a thesp, there are plenty of theatres.'

'And if you're a boatie, there are lots of rowing clubs.'

Everyone nods, considering all the options.

'Oh and I forgot,' adds Lee. 'There's even a tiddlywinks society.'

I scoff. 'You're not serious? What sort of stiffs play tiddlywinks?'

'We're perfectly *serious*,' beams Jack. 'And that's what's so great about Cambridge – you can do whatever you want and nobody judges you.'

I wish I hadn't opened my mouth and look down sheepishly.

'And besides,' says Lee, 'our tiddlywinkers won the world championships last year.'

'Right,' I mumble. 'Brilliant.'

I drain my mug of tea with a loud slurp.

Thankfully, someone suggests we all go for a tour of the college grounds and we troop outside with Jack and Lee as our guides. St Christopher's really is a beautiful place and it feels warmer and homelier than some of the grander Cambridge colleges. There are manicured lawns, well-maintained roof gardens and a grove of trees along one bank of the River Cam, with benches for students to sit and think. On our way round we meet porters, cooks, nurses and 'bedders' (who as far as I can make out are cleaners), and everyone smiles lots and tells us how much they're looking forward to getting to know us. We move on and discover a timbered Tudor courtyard, where the drama society stages a Shakespeare play every June, and an expanse of lawn along the opposite bank of the river, which is the summer setting for barbecues, parties and even open-air films. My favourite part of my new college, though, is the pretty wooden bridge that straddles the Cam and I've often seen on telly, in tourist guides and on the cover of the college prospectus. As we troop over it, I notice punts sailing down the river and academics cycling along Silver Street. It really is like being in a BBC period drama and utterly enchanting.

After the tour, we first years are sent back to our rooms to dress up for something called Matriculation Dinner. I'm glad of the break and need some time alone to get my head together. Speaking without an accent requires constant concentration and maintaining my cool façade is proving more difficult than I thought. Tonight, things are cranking up a gear and I'll have to wear my new suit and my academic gown for the first time. We're dining in Formal Hall and there'll no doubt be issues of cutlery and crockery to negotiate. Now that I think about it, I can't even remember whether it's the word 'napkin' or 'serviette' that's considered common. I suddenly realize that I'm exhausted from trying so hard. How on earth am I going to cope with Formal Hall?

As it happens, Formal Hall turns out to be exceptionally *in*formal and nobody pays any attention at all to which knives and forks I use. At the start of the meal someone reads grace in Latin but, apart from our suits and gowns, that seems to be the only concession to hundreds of years of history. Having said that, there *are* several traditions that the students are keen to uphold. The first is an activity called 'pennying'. Council House Jack explains that this means challenging someone to down their drink by dropping a penny into their wine glass. The first years soon get the hang of it and before we've even finished our starter a handful of dirty pennies are winding their way around our table.

The second custom is something known as a 'boat race'. After our main course, Inappropriate Lee stands up and explains the rules. The people at the far end of the table have to kick things off by downing their drinks in one and as soon as they've finished, the person next to them does the same. The winning side is the one who reaches the other end of the table first. Everyone leaps to their feet, wine glasses at the ready. The race begins and like a Mexican wave I watch arm after arm rise up in a fanning motion. When the wave eventually reaches me I have no intention of letting the side down. I knock back my wine in just a few seconds, wiping my mouth proudly.

There's a wonderfully carefree atmosphere in the room and

I'm swept along by a feeling of release. The more people drink, the more they raise their voices and the level of laughter gradually increases to near deafening. It doesn't take long for me to feel properly drunk and as the meal goes on I'm finding it harder and harder to speak without my accent.

'Flippin' 'eck!' I slur. 'I don't 'alf feel pissed!'

'Me too,' chirps Sally, dressed from head to toe in pink. 'Woo woo!'

Thankfully, everyone's so drunk they don't notice that I'm starting to sound like Jack Duckworth from *Coronation Street*.

Once the meal's over, we all stagger to our feet and the second years lead us outside and across a courtyard to an unmarked door.

'This,' announces Council House Jack, 'is where you'll probably spend most of your time at St Christopher's.'

There's a hush of anticipation and a few excited giggles.

With a ceremonious flourish, Jack flings open the door to reveal a heaving, sweaty mess of drunken undergraduates. Some are stumbling around randomly snogging whoever they can lay their hands on and others are standing on the furniture and dancing to Take That. Glancing around I spot a pool table, a darts board and a table football game, and around each of them people are cheering loudly whenever one of their friends scores or pots a ball. But the thing that strikes me most is that everyone I see looks like they're having enormous amounts of fun.

'Welcome to the student bar!' Jack proclaims.

My stomach jumps as if I've just driven over a hill.

'Come on!' says Inappropriate Lee. 'What are you all waiting for?'

We step inside, wide-eyed.

I look around and see that St Christopher's bar has obviously been designed with damage limitation in mind. The floor is tiled, the wooden furniture left bare and the drinks served in plastic glasses. It's not difficult to work out why.

'Right then,' says Jack, clapping his hands together, 'what are we all drinking?'

I really fancy a Pernod but quickly look around and can't spot anyone else drinking it. I discovered the liqueur mixed with water over the summer on our last family holiday to France, and decided it would become my drink of choice; I love the taste of aniseed and thought that, as the brand's continental, it would make me look sophisticated. But right now I don't want to look out of place so ask instead for a glass of wine, remembering something Dad said about not mixing my drinks. I see that the bar here is incredibly cheap and you can buy whole pitchers of Pimm's as well as something called the 'Queen Mum special' – a potent mix of gin and Dubonnet that, according to legend, is the favourite tipple of the college patron. There's even a pint glass full of cigarettes, which you can buy singly for 15p. Best of all, Jack explains that students can put all their bar purchases on credit by signing a form called a chit.

'Isn't it wicked?' he says, gleefully signing his first chit of the evening.

The music changes and a song by Wham! blasts out of the sound system. Everyone drunkenly roars their approval. There's a heady excitement in the air and people are flitting round and introducing themselves to each other. To my surprise, there are several who want to meet Charles from Manchester.

A dark-haired, slightly thickset girl wearing a velvet dress and a purple neck scarf comes over and introduces herself as Amelia.

'Hi,' I say, struggling to stop my accent breaking through. 'I'm Charles.'

'Charles?' she smirks. 'Doesn't anyone call you Charlie?'

'Oh right, I suppose they do, yeah.' We both laugh.

'And what are you studying, Charlie?'

'English.'

'I'm doing Languages. Or Modern and Medieval Languages as everyone calls it here. Hey, do you fancy a fag?' She holds out a packet of Marlboro Lights, a brand that has only just launched in Britain but in a few months has managed to obliterate all the competition, at least among teenagers and twentysomethings.

I ask myself if I really want to smoke then look around and see that everyone else is. 'Yeah, go on then.'

We both light up and take a deep drag.

'So where are you from then?' I ask, breathing out my smoke.

'Well, I live in North London but my parents are Italian,' she says, and I suddenly understand where her caramel skin and thick black hair come from. 'They run a restaurant in Maida Vale. How about you – where are you from?'

I clear my throat to try to remove all traces of Jack Duckworth. 'Manchester.'

'How funny – you sound like you're from Bolton.'

I feel a stab of panic and take a drag on my fag. 'Really? What makes you say that?'

'Well, my brother's girlfriend's from Bolton and she sounds just like you.'

I'm stumped. 'Oh, yeah, well, I suppose I *am* from Bolton – sort of.' I wonder whether I should stop drinking now before I blow it completely. 'I spend a lot of time in Manchester, though. You know, out clubbing and stuff.'

'Really? I'm not that into clubbing to be honest. I mean, I love the music and the dancing and all that but I've never really felt cool enough in clubs. I find it all a bit intimidating.'

I feel stupid now and hope I haven't put her off. I take a swig of my drink. 'Actually,' I stammer, 'come to think of it, I haven't been out clubbing for a while really.'

'Oh yeah, why's that? Are you attached now?'

I feel a prickle of discomfort run up my neck. I'm already anxious about broadcasting my sexuality around Cambridge – I've no idea how people will react. My plan for the moment is to be mysterious and enigmatic and to keep them all guessing as to my sexual preference, at least until I've worked out whether it's safe to come out of the closet. All right, over the last few years acceptance of gay people has continued to grow, something I've noticed from the greater number of straight people going for a night out in Manchester's Gay Village, some of them even pretending to be gay to get into The Paradise Factory. The problem is, I'm entering new territory now and have no idea what people think about gay men in Cambridge. I'm suddenly hit by a memory of the kids at school all signing that piece of paper calling me queer and realize there's no way on this earth I can risk that kind of thing happening again.

'Oh no, I'm single,' I say, attempting to fob Amelia off. 'I just didn't really get time for clubbing over the summer – you know what it's like.'

'But what about here?' she goes on. 'Are you the only gay bloke or have you spotted any others?'

I can feel myself blushing to the tips of my ears. Is it really that obvious? 'Oh, urm, I, urm, I don't know really.'

'Sorry.' She frowns. 'You *are* gay, aren't you?'

My mouth suddenly goes dry. 'Yeah,' I rasp. 'Yeah, I suppose I am.'

'Well,' she trills, 'if you do want to meet people, apparently there's a LesBiGay society that meets once a week. My second-year parents were telling us about it this afternoon.'

'Oh. Right.' I'm not sure what to say. Is it all going to be this easy? But how can things be so different here? Is it just because people are cleverer than at my old school or has the world moved on more quickly than I thought, leaving Bolton lagging behind?

Amelia stubs out her cigarette in an ashtray and I do the same. 'Anyway, see if you fancy it,' she says. 'I'll go along with you if you want.'

'Great, thanks.'

She drains her glass and leaves it on the side. 'Right – I'm off to the bar. What are you drinking?'

I think about it for a moment. 'You know what,' I say, standing tall with a new self-confidence, 'I'll have a Pernod, please.'

She smiles. 'One Pernod coming up!'

Just then, the music changes and I recognize the opening notes of Madonna's 'Into the Groove'. All over the bar people jump to their feet to dance. Some of them aren't very good but nobody seems to care. They evidently aren't bothered about listening to music that makes them look cool either. And that's when it hits me. I suddenly see how stupid I've been to waste so much effort pretending to be someone else. What's the point? Everyone here's being themselves and it doesn't look like anyone's trying to trip anyone else up. Now that I think about it, I don't know why I've been so bothered about my accent either. So far today I've heard all kinds of accents and no one has commented on any of them – Geordie, Irish, Essex and even Cornish. I'm certainly not the odd one out.

As I listen to Madonna, I think of my idol's various reinventions over the years and realize that she might have changed her image several times and explored new interests and influences in each video or tour, but that's very different to pretending to *be* someone else. Whereas I've been lying about who I am as a person, which is all wrong, even if the person I am will no doubt start evolving now the world around me is changing. But I can't force myself to be someone I'm not – and I can't force myself to speak without a Bolton accent either. In that moment I vow that I'm going to stick with my accent, even when I'm sober.

I suddenly feel overcome with excitement and look around the room to take it all in. In the corner, Council House Jack is mid-debate, railing about the injustice of the British class system to a posh-looking boy wearing brogues. Adrian's smoking roll-ups and reciting a poem he's written called 'Shitfaced on Cider' to a guy who has long straggly hair and is wearing Jesus sandals. Inappropriate Lee's leaning against the wall snogging Caroline Tits while she bats his hand away from her boobs. Rent-a-leg has joined the rugby crowd, who are playing drinking games and making the loser down a cocktail into which they've each dropped one of their pubes. And Sally's standing on a table and dancing away, utterly unconcerned about looking cool, alongside a line of girls who are all wearing different coloured dresses and together look like a rainbow. Best of all, they're all dancing to Madonna.

'Well, what are you waiting for?' asks a voice behind me. It's Amelia, returning with our drinks. 'Aren't you getting up to join them?'

'Yeah,' I say, 'I think I am.'

Material Girl

'Wicked party, Charlie!'

'Yeah – cool ball!'

It's the last day of summer term and the May Ball is in full swing. The entire grounds of St Christopher's College are filled with students in black tie and ball gowns, eating candy-floss and toffee apples and drinking champagne. Music is provided by string quartets and jazz quintets and there are bands playing everything from Britpop to glam rock. There's barn dancing, break dancing and belly dancing, and circulating among the guests are fortune-tellers, fire-breathers and sword-swallowers. Best of all, everyone's congratulating *me* on a wonderful evening.

Earlier in the year I was appointed one of the ball organizers and since then have rushed around Cambridge finding clowns, masseurs and tattooists to entertain the guests. I managed to book a top-name hypnotist and was particularly pleased when I discovered an Egyptian snake-charmer living in a nearby village called Slip End. So far, all the artists have turned up and they're dotted around the college doing their stuff. The only one missing is our star performer, a Madonna tribute act called Mad Donna. She's due on stage in just forty minutes but there's still no sign of her.

I check the dressing rooms one last time but find that she still hasn't arrived. I look at the time on the college clock tower and see that the situation really is getting urgent. I decide to go and wait at the tradesman's entrance, where Mad Donna has been instructed to arrive and park her car; that way as soon as she shows up I can whisk her through the various courtyards and make sure she gets on stage on time.

I fight my way through crowds of people all enjoying themselves – and eager to express their appreciation.

'Charlie, you're amazing!'

'Charlie, I love you!'

As I listen to their praise, I think back to my first school disco at the age of fifteen, when I snogged Geraldine Hoggett then threw up in front of everyone. Back then I was relegated to the periphery of the action, loathed by all the other teenagers and ridiculed by the popular crowd. But now here I am just a few years later at a far more exciting event and right at the centre of it all. It's utterly intoxicating and I still can't believe it's happening. Even though we're coming to the end of my first year at Cambridge, part of me is still convinced that it's too good to be true and very soon I'll be given a rude awakening. I hope to God that rude awakening isn't going to happen tonight.

I push open the creaky old gate and stand in the back street waiting, checking my watch every thirty seconds and nibbling my nails. I've already called Mad Donna's home number three times but there's no answer and I've no other way of contacting her.

I step back inside the college grounds to check that everything else is carrying on fine. After a quick scan around I satisfy myself that all the guests are still throwing themselves into the May Ball experience. The belly dancer's proving a big hit with Inappropriate Lee, who's following her around, his eyes transfixed by her navel. Caroline Tits is surrounded by the barbershop choir, swallowing oyster after oyster and licking her lips flirtatiously, her breasts almost spilling out of her low-cut gown. And the dodgems we've hired are proving popular with Rent-a-leg, who's spent most of the evening downing tequila shots with the college hockey team. I spot her ramming her dodgem a little too aggressively into the one driven by my next-door neighbour Sally, who's turned up wearing a tiara, waving a wand and dressed from head to toe in her favourite colour pink. As Rent-a-leg repeatedly slams into her dodgem, Sally's tiara gradually becomes dislodged and her wand goes flying across the court, landing in a glass of champagne being drunk by committed Socialist Council House Jack.

I check my watch again. It's now just gone eleven o'clock and Mad Donna still hasn't arrived. Considering she's supposed to be performing at half past, I wonder whether it's time to start thinking of a plan B. What will everyone say if she doesn't turn up and I've effectively failed to fill the top performance slot? Will they all realize I'm crap after all?

I decide to check the street outside one last time. As I open the gate, I see a clapped-out old Ford Cortina chugging its way towards me. It draws up alongside and a head of brassy blonde hair pokes its way through the window.

'Oi! Are you Charlie?' asks the driver in a broad Birmingham accent.

'Yeah! Are you Mad Donna?'

'That's me, poppet!'

I breathe a huge sigh of relief. 'God, am I glad to see you. I thought you weren't going to make it!'

'So did I for a minute. This journey has been one huge pain in the snatch!'

As she parks the car, she explains that she broke down on the way here and that when the repair man finally showed up, he asked her to perform a quick chorus of 'Like a Virgin', which only delayed her even more.

'Sorry about that,' she giggles, touching up her hair. 'But I do like to please my public. I guess me and Madonna have got that in common – as well as the fact we practically look like twins.'

She steps out of the car and I see that she's wearing black leather trousers, some kind of snakeskin-print blouse and an excess of fake tan. Twins? She looks more like Rod Stewart than Madonna. This is a complete disaster. What if the entire ball falls flat once she takes to the stage?

Well, there's not much I can do about it now. The main thing is making sure she gets onto the stage on time. I suggest we go straight to the changing rooms and help her with her cases. I weave through the crowds and she clatters along next to me in her stiletto heels with about as much grace as a five-year-old who's raided her mum's wardrobe. As she does so, she warbles her way through some kind of warm-up.

'Eeee. Aaaa. Eeee.'

Unfortunately, she sounds like Rod Stewart too.

'So,' I ask nervously, 'which songs are you going to perform?'

'Oh you know, all the classics – "Dress You Up", "Holiday", "Vogue".'

I try not to cringe as I imagine her performing the songs on stage. Is she about to piss all over the music that's made me the person I am, the music that's got me all the way from Bolton to Cambridge?

'Oh and I thought I'd start with "Material Girl",' she adds cheerfully. 'The toffs always love that one.'

Hearing her criticize my friends feels like I've been slapped around the face. 'Just a minute,' I say. 'What do you mean, toffs?'

'Oh you know, Sloane Rangers, Burlington Berties, Hooray Henrys – call them what you want.'

'But I don't know what you're on about,' I insist, 'the people here aren't like that.'

At that moment, Inappropriate Lee blunders past in pursuit of a now tiara-free Sally. 'I say!' he barks in his plummy voice. 'Mind if I tickle your tonsils?'

Mad Donna shoots me a withering look. 'Whatever you say, poppet, whatever you say.'

I show her into the changing rooms and tell her I'll wait outside while she gets ready. As I'm pacing around on the other side of the door, I spot a passing waiter and grab a glass of champagne, sinking most of it in one. I wonder what my dad would think if he could see me now. When he dropped me off in Cambridge at the start of the year he warned me not to become a 'stuck-up Southerner' and here I am just eight months later dressed in black tie and swigging champagne, something I'm pretty sure he's never done in his life. But the thing is, I still feel like the same person, and ever since trying to pretend I was someone else when I arrived in Cambridge, I've always been careful to stay true to myself. Granted, I'm now mixing with some people who have lots more money than me and tickets to the ball cost hundreds of pounds, but being on the committee means I didn't have to pay for mine. And besides, I've worked really hard all year; I was so terrified that everyone at Cambridge would be much cleverer than me that I went to every lecture and spent ages writing every essay to make up for it. Now that I've made it through my first year, don't I deserve a little reward?

I tip back the rest of my glass and leave it on the side.

In the distance I can just about make out Amelia having her caricature painted by a sparrow-faced street artist I found near the kebab van on Market Square. I decide to go over and say hi.

Standing next to her is her boyfriend Anthony, a History of Art student who paints and sculpts his own work in his spare time. Anthony spent his gap year travelling around India and Nepal and his room at Cambridge is full of ethnic wall-hangings and grainy photos of grubby-faced kids leaning against mud huts and battered old farm machinery. I love listening to him talk about the experience and how the whole thing 'realigned his planes of spiritual perception'. And Amelia's totally in love with him. We already have a sweepstake going on which Cambridge couple will be the first to make it to the altar and most people agree it'll be Amelia and Anthony.

'All right there, you two?'

'Oh hiya,' replies Amelia. 'What do you think of my portrait?'

I peer forward to see the work in progress. The caricaturist is accentuating her looks to draw her as a middle-aged Italian mamma wearing an apron, stirring a bowlful of pasta and fighting off an army of snivelling brats. 'Oh yeah,' I tease, 'it's very accurate!'

Anthony leans over and has a look. 'Mmm . . .' he muses, stroking his chin, 'I'd say it's . . . an interesting interpretation . . . of the interplay between your inner self . . . and the cultural identity you've inherited . . .'

'My God, Anthony,' Amelia snorts, 'it's only a caricature.'

'Excuse me,' pipes the street artist. 'I think he's spot on!'

We're all laughing when Mad Donna re-emerges, her transformation complete. She's wearing a pink dress similar to the one Madonna wears in the 'Material Girl' video, complete with diamanté jewellery, a fake fur stole and a wig of blonde curls so cheap it looks like a bale of hay. She actually looks worse than when she arrived. A chill runs down my spine.

Now that I think about it, I've no idea *what* she's going to be like on stage. Someone Uncle Les met in The Flat Iron said he'd seen her perform in the local Labour club and she'd been 'top class'. When I got in touch and spoke to her on the phone, she sent a VHS of one of her performances but I didn't have a machine to watch it on so, as time was running out, decided to take a chance. Now here I am standing next to a Madonna impersonator who looks more like a two-bit fairground stripper than my idol. Well, it serves me right for listening to Uncle Les about someone his friend saw performing in a working men's club. What's the saying, 'You can take the boy out of Bolton but you can't take Bolton out of the boy'?

'How do I look, poppet?' Mad Donna asks, tilting her leg coquettishly.

'You look wicked,' I lie, reasoning that the worst thing I can do now is to dent her confidence just before she starts her act.

'Come on then,' she says, with a wiggle of her bum, 'take me to those toffs!'

I lead her to the stage and we wait in the wings for a few minutes while the Footlights comedians finish their act. Mad Donna hands her backing track to the techies and quickly checks her hair and make-up in a compact.

'Why are *you* looking so nervous?' she asks me. 'I'm the one who's about to go on stage.'

'Yeah and I'm the one who might be about to see his amazing new life come crashing down around him,' I want to say. Instead I force a smile onto my face. 'I'm not nervous,' I insist. 'I'm really looking forward to seeing your show.'

A few minutes later, it's time for her slot and I give her a nod of encouragement as she steps into character and bursts onto the stage.

'Hello, Cambridge!' she purrs in a mock American accent. 'Are there any material girls out there?'

Most of the audience scream yes and the music starts over their cheers. I take my position to the left of the stage and can feel my body shrinking in on itself as I watch.

From the moment Mad Donna begins to sing it becomes clear she has a voice like hell yawning – and she's a lousy dancer too. But the funny thing is, nobody else seems to notice. Every time I look, the entire audience is roaring in approval.

'Charlie,' shouts Sally, spotting me hovering around the edges, 'this singer's *wicked*! Where did you find her?'

I'm just about to yell the answer back but she disappears into the crowd, flapping her arms around as if she's been plugged into the electricity supply.

Just as Mad Donna's launching into her second chorus, Amelia edges over and bumps me on the shoulder. 'You all right, Charlie?' she says into my ear.

'What do you think?' I shout back. 'God, this is so embarrassing!'

'No, it's not,' Amelia says. 'It might not be the most polished performance I've ever seen but she's really getting them going.'

'Yeah but I wanted to impress everyone, Amelia. I wanted them all to think I was brilliant.'

'You *are* brilliant, Charlie! You don't have to do anything to impress us; we love you anyway.'

Despite myself I can feel my mouth twitching into a grin. 'Really?' I ask. 'Do you really mean that?'

'Yes! Now stop worrying. And stop trying so hard. You've got us already, Charlie. We're in the bag.'

Now I can't stop my grin growing until it lights up my whole face. It stays there until Mad Donna finishes the song, ending a clumsily executed dance routine with a mischievous smack on her bum.

The crowd erupts in applause so loud I nearly stagger back from the impact. And the cheering continues as Mad Donna launches into her next song.

Maybe the night hasn't turned out so badly after all. I fringe my way around the crowd, picking out several of my friends throwing themselves into another vintage Madonna song. OK, one or two of them might be posh but what I like about the people here is that they're all so individual. At the front of the dance floor I can see Council House Jack, his bow tie hanging unfastened around his neck; he might have broken all the rules of Socialism by spending hundreds on a ticket to the ball and then pouring champagne down his throat, but earlier this year he campaigned against rising room rents in college and even staged a protest for a few days by chaining himself to the Queen Mum's tree. Dancing next to him is Sally, who now runs Cambridge RAG and flutters around college organizing a whole series of wacky events that involve parachutes, processions and pancakes. Just a few feet behind her stands Adrian, guzzling from a bottle of champagne to celebrate winning the university poetry prize with a composition he wrote about a one night stand between a student and a cleaner called 'Bedding the Bedder'. And elbowing her way through to the toilets is Rent-a-leg, both hands clasped firmly over her mouth. 'I think I'm going to chunder!' she heaves before realizing that she isn't going to make it and emptying her guts out into the river.

As I stand watching them all, I realize that I don't care if Mad Donna thinks they're toffs; I love my new friends and, more than anything else, I'm so pleased that they love me. And, however much Amelia insists that they love me whatever I do, I'll never stop trying to impress them.

And then I remember that there's another friend I need to impress, one I've hardly seen since I started at Cambridge. It's a friend who I was always sure was in the bag but recently I've started to worry might have fallen out of it. Sometimes I even think I might be on the verge of losing her. Well, next week I'm going to find out for sure. Because next week I'm going to Manchester – to visit Shanaz.

Justify My Love

What am I doing here? What have I let myself in for?

I'm in Manchester on a night out with Shanaz; it's the end of our first year at university and my term finished before hers so I've come to visit. I thought the trip would be fun and soften the blow of having to leave Cambridge and go home for the summer. I also thought it would help bring us closer together after sensing for months that we've been drifting apart. But our night out's only just started and I'm actually feeling bored.

'Isn't this amazing?' Shanaz bellows into my ear.

'Yeah, it's wicked,' I shout back, glad she can't see my eyes so she can't tell I'm lying.

We're in a club called Sankeys Soap, which is in the basement of an old soap factory in the Ancoats area, just on the edge of Manchester city centre. It took us ages to get here and we had to trudge through street after street of what looked like post-apocalyptic industrial wasteland. When we finally arrived, we had to wait in the queue for nearly an hour, before kowtowing to a squadron of bouncers who for some unfathomable reason were obsessed with confiscating everyone's chewing gum but didn't see fit to do the same with their drugs. Now that we've made it inside the club, I can see that the décor isn't too dissimilar to The Paradise Factory, with exposed brick walls and steel girders holding up the ceiling. Unfortunately, the atmosphere couldn't be more different.

I look out over the dance floor and see that it's already rammed with people dressed in baggy jeans or dungarees, T-shirts bearing the brand names Fila and Mossimo, and trainers by Converse or Travel Fox. Everyone's waving their arms in the air to catch the lasers that are shooting around, dancing to music that has no tune, melody or even vocals – just a pounding, repetitive beat. I wonder if it's house or techno. Or could it be drum and bass? Whatever it is, I can't get over how unpleasant it is to listen to. I wonder if it sounds different when you're on drugs.

'Now are you sure you don't want one?' asks Shanaz, as she shakes out a little plastic bag of pills.

'Yeah,' I say firmly, 'I'm all right, thanks.'

Before coming here, Shanaz told me everyone would be taking Ecstasy, which they all call 'E'. But I don't really want to; I've told her it's just not my thing but the truth is I'm a bit frightened of it. What if I'm the one who has a bad pill and goes into some kind of seizure in front of everyone? Didn't something similar happen to River Phoenix? No, I can't risk that and I certainly can't risk dying and my parents thinking I was a secret drug addict the whole time. I only hope not taking Ecstasy doesn't set me apart from everyone else.

I watch as Shanaz doles out the pills among her friends from uni. Altogether there are four in the group. There's a smiley fair-haired boy who looks like a cross between Keith Harris and Orville, has massive gaps in between his teeth, and sways from side to side when he's speaking. There's a red-headed girl with extreme sloping shoulders who looks like she could do with some vitamins and a good night's sleep. And there's a raw-skinned blond boy who's so skinny his cheeks are concave and he reminds me of Gabby Annie in The Flat Iron. The three of them were introduced to me by the nicknames Tricky, Hickey and Twiglet, and there were stories behind each name that everyone found hilarious – everyone apart from me. I wonder if Shanaz would feel the same way about the nicknames I have for my friends in Cambridge.

Right now the four of them are excited about the pills they've just taken and for the next half an hour we huddle at the side of the dance floor while they talk about how they can feel they're 'coming up', which as far as I can tell means the Ecstasy has started working. Apparently it's normal to feel nausea when this is happening and at one point the ginger girl says she can feel a bit of sick in the back of her throat, but everyone assures her this is a good thing as it means she's 'coming up hard'. They all drink water and from time to time remind each other to sip it slowly rather than gulping it down in one go. It all seems very complicated – and not much fun at all. But I don't want them to think I'm uncool so I stay silent and sip on my Diet Coke.

Mind you, Shanaz's friends probably think I'm uncool already. While they're all dressed in the latest street fashions, I'm looking unmistakably *high* street in my beige chinos and vertical block-stripe shirt from GAP, together with the hair I've finally managed to grow into curtains, just now that it's starting to fall out of fashion. As if to attract more attention to my lack of cool, it's quite obvious Shanaz is the trendiest one in their group; she's had a complete makeover since moving to Manchester and is wearing Triple Five Soul dungarees with one strap hanging down to show off a No Fear T-shirt, and has her long hair up in double buns that I'm sure I've seen on that

Icelandic singer Björk. Not only that but she's had her tongue pierced, which I can only imagine will make her parents rail with disapproval. It strikes me that, after just a year in Manchester, Shanaz is much more confident than she used to be, and much more assertive. In fact, from the way she interacts with her new friends it's clear she's the leader of the group.

'Come on, guys,' she commands, waving her arms to beckon them forward, 'let's do this!'

I hold back as the four of them take their first steps onto the dance floor and begin dancing in an identical way to everyone else. For a while I stand watching them but within minutes I'm bored again. I remember what my mum used to say when I complained about being bored as a child; that only boring people get bored. Well, I don't want to be boring. I absolutely don't want to be boring.

I decide to have a wander around the club and discover a chill-out area, a second room with a dance floor upstairs and a cobbled courtyard, where I go for a fag. And then I walk around again – and again. But it's no use; whatever I do I just can't snap out of my boredom. Oh God, maybe I *am* boring!

I wonder if Shanaz thinks so because I'm not doing 'E'. When I spot her leaving the dance floor to get some more water, I decide to grab her and try engaging her in a conversation.

'Hey,' I shout into her ear, 'do you remember the first time we went to The Paradise Factory?'

She grimaces at me as if trying to make out what I'm saying is painful. 'You what, Charlie?'

'I said, do you remember the first time we went to Paradise?'

'Sorry, you're going to have to speak up.'

This time I yell at the top of my voice. 'I SAID, DO YOU REMEMBER THE FIRST TIME WE WENT TO PARADISE?'

She shakes her head as if what I'm saying is an unwelcome irritation. 'Sorry, Charlie, I can't hear you.'

I try my best not to look downcast. 'Oh forget it,' I say, 'it wasn't important.'

I stand to the side as Shanaz buys four bottles of water and then skips back onto the dance floor, where she distributes them among her friends and is rewarded by warm smiles, hugs and even a few kisses. She responds with similar expressions of affection. Clearly the Ecstasy everyone's taken is bonding them together, leaving me on the outside. To them at least, I *must* be boring. It's no wonder Shanaz wants to leave me at the side of the dance floor and spend the night hanging around with her new, much cooler friends. I wonder if I should have taken some Ecstasy after all. Maybe then Shanaz would still want to hang around with me.

Never mind, it's too late for that now; they're already well away, while I'm standing here festering in my own boredom – or possibly my boringness. When no one's watching I sneak a look at my watch; it's only midnight. The club doesn't close for hours yet. And whether I'm bored, boring or both, I don't think I can bear it much longer.

Hours later, the club finally closes and we're kicked out and onto the street. As we walk through Ancoats, I'm desperate for the night to be over, then I can just go to sleep, but unfortunately nobody else feels the same. They're all hungry so we stop off at a kebab shop and then, once we get back to their halls of residence, Shanaz invites everyone back to her room, for what she calls a 'chill-out'.

Shanaz's university bedroom is one of the grottiest I've ever seen. The walls are bare, the laundry basket is overflowing, and the floor is scattered with ashtrays stuffed with cigarette ends and mugs with dark brown rims and what looks like green mould in the bottom. The curtains are hanging off the rail and, as far as I can tell, remain permanently closed. The only furniture is a single bed with a duvet that looks like it hasn't been washed since the start of term, a desk with an anglepoise lamp and a kettle peeping out from underneath a chaotic mess of textbooks and ringbinders, and a wardrobe that has its doors covered with a collage of brightly coloured flyers advertising clubs with names like Bugged Out, Carwash and Wiggly Worm. I look at the collage and realize how carefully it's been put together; it must have taken Shanaz hours. Clearly she cares more about clubbing these days than she does about anything else. I wonder how she can have changed so quickly.

We sit down and one of Shanaz's friends, who I think might be the one called Tricky, starts rolling a spliff. It seems to take him forever, although it's a ritual everyone else savours, and a long discussion ensues about the quality of the 'gear' they're about to smoke compared to what they had last week and the week before. I wonder when I can go to bed but know there's no chance of that soon; I'm supposed to be sleeping on the floor in a sleeping bag. I can feel a yawn coming on but try to direct it through my nostrils so no one will notice. I need to get up and move around or I'm in serious danger of nodding off.

'Shall I put some music on?' I suggest brightly.

'Yeah, go on,' says Shanaz, 'let's have something chilled.'

I pick my way across the room and start rifling through her CD collection. There are albums by Orbital, Portishead, Primal Scream and The Chemical Brothers, and DJ mix compilations from superclubs Cream, The Haçienda and Ministry of Sound. But where's Madonna? After much searching I finally find a few CDs buried away at the back. I pick out 'Justify My Love' and decide to put on the William Orbit mix Madonna performed on *The Girlie Show*, first of all because it has a relaxed, laid-back beat but also because I remember Shanaz loving it. I slide it into the CD deck of her stereo and hit Play.

As soon as everyone recognizes the song, they unleash a torrent of objections and look at me as if I've just suggested we engage in bestiality.

'Get it off, Charlie!' Shanaz practically shouts in my face. 'I said to put on something chilled!'

I watch in dismay as she stands up and presses Stop. In that moment it's as if she wilfully destroys everything that bound us together as children. I feel betrayed. I feel abandoned. And I feel angry at myself.

'Come on, Charlie,' she says, directing her comment towards everyone but me, 'I grew out of Madonna ages ago.'

I pull a face and whisper, 'Sorry.'

She lets out an exasperated sigh and puts on a compilation CD from a nightclub in Ibiza called Café del Mar. 'This is more like it,' she announces and her friends express their agreement. She looks happy again and sits down on the bed with the rest of the group.

I settle down in a corner, feeling outcast and hoping to blend into the background. The four others pass the spliff between them and a conversation ensues about a trip they're planning to Ministry of Sound in London to see DJs I've never heard of called Judge Jules and Jeremy Healy. I can't think of anything to contribute and knead my eyelids to try to stay awake. I can't fall asleep. I really can't fall asleep.

As I watch Shanaz holding court among her new friends, I wonder how in just a year we can have ended up having such different lives. And to think we always planned on sharing our university experiences, even though we knew we were going to different places. But I can see now that we're not just in different places but different cultures too – and that makes me worry that Shanaz and I might drift apart forever. I try not to panic, telling myself that we've been through so much together that this new distance between us can only be a temporary thing. But I look at her interacting with her new friends and can't escape the fact that she enjoys being with them much more than she does with me. What have I done wrong? Is this what all my friends will do in the end?

I realize then that I can't let this happen. I have to do everything I can to make my friends in Cambridge love me. Amelia may have said they're already in the bag but I can't risk losing them like I'm losing Shanaz. No, I have to come up with something I can do in my second year to really impress them.

Just when I'm trying to work out what it is, I'm unable to resist my tiredness and fall fast asleep.

You Must Love Me

We're standing hand in hand in a circle and my eyes are following the direction of the game. I feel like Madonna backstage before a gig, warming up with her band and dancers. I really want the show to go well and concentrate on channelling all my positive energy.

'Fuzzy duck.'

'Fuzzy duck.'

'Fuzzy duck.'

'Fuzzy duck.'

'Does he?'

My eyes swivel as we change direction.

'Ducky fuzz.'

'Ducky fuzz.'

'Ducky fuzz.'

'Does he?'

We change direction again and I try to stay focused, determined not to be the one to break the chain.

'Fuzzy duck.'

'Fuzzy duck.'

'Fucky duzz. Oh *bugger*!'

Everyone falls about laughing at my mistake.

It's the evening of our dress rehearsal and a nervous tension is in the air. I look at my watch and, now that we've done our warm-up exercise, know it's time to get going. 'Right, I'm off, everyone. Knock 'em dead!' I leave the room and bound upstairs to the auditorium, trying not to imagine how nerve-racking it'll be when the room's full of people. I really hope everyone likes the show.

The student theatre in Cambridge is a professionally run venue that over the years has trained directors like Peter Hall and Trevor Nunn and actors like Ian McKellen and Emma Thompson. By the time I come along, it's looking the worse for wear but inside creativity's still thriving. Already this term I've seen comedy revues called *Masturbation: The Musical* and *Whoops Vicar is that Your Dick?* as well as a raft of alternative, student-written plays such as *Lady Bracknell was a Lesbian* and a 'theatrical experiment' involving two actors, a word association game and a white sheet. To me, it doesn't matter what I'm watching; I'll sit in the audience, daydreaming about the theatre's glamorous past and wondering which of the performers on stage are going to be the stars of the future.

At the end of my first year, after months of hanging around the theatre, someone suggested that I direct a play myself. At first I didn't have the confidence to put myself forward but when I thought it over during the summer holidays I remembered that I've always loved reading or watching other people's stories and all directing involves is *telling* other people's stories. Part of me couldn't help thinking back to my dream of becoming a writer and coming up with a story of my own, but the problem is I'm still not convinced that I have anything to write about – at least nothing interesting. Directing solved the problem; all I had to do was choose a ready-made story that I found interesting and concentrate on telling it as best as I could. I had to give it a go. And besides, I was looking for a way to impress everyone so they wouldn't go off me; if I could get this right, it would do the job brilliantly.

Last term I submitted my formal application to mount a production of *Evita*, inspired by Madonna's role in the film version of the musical. I was thrilled when my proposal was accepted and resolved to throw myself into the role of director. Since then I've spent my whole time wearing black polo neck jumpers and smoking menthol cigarettes through a long silver holder. In doing so I don't think I'm being remotely pretentious or trying to become someone else; I'm simply altering my image to suit the way my life's evolving.

The well-organized Amelia is the perfect choice of producer and she's thrown herself into her role by buying one of the new generation of mobile phones, which has a pull-up aerial, snaps open and shut, and has to rank as the most sophisticated invention I've ever seen. By now Amelia's my closest friend in Cambridge and I can't imagine what I'd do without her. We've chosen to live in rooms opposite each other in our second year, eat most of our meals together, and often help each other through work crises. I went to visit her at home in North London during the Christmas holidays and she cooked me a delicious lasagne in the family restaurant and then took me to see Buckingham Palace and Trafalgar Square, which was totally spellbinding to a boy still adjusting to life outside Bolton. Back in Cambridge I was thrilled that, when I told her I wanted to direct a play, she was keen to get involved – and I'm over the moon that we're now doing it together.

Amelia's boyfriend Anthony is our set designer and he's spent hours agonizing over photographs of 1940s Argentina so that his creation is as authentic as possible. He spent last summer travelling around South America and returned with yet more ethnic trophies and tat. He fell in love with the continent and said that he saw designing our production of Evita as a chance for his soul to 'reconnect with the essence of Latin America'. I have to admit, whatever he's up to spiritually, his set looks great.

I settle into my seat in the stalls and take out a pad to write notes. The process of directing the play began a few months ago, when Amelia and I giggled our way through a weekend of open auditions and then I kicked off rehearsals with a series of trust-building exercises, which basically involved fumbling around blindfolded or throwing actors in the air and catching them. I organized a series of improvisational activities so that the cast could engage with their characters and spent hours immersed in earnest discussions about narrative development. I'm enchanted by the idea of bringing to life a whole other world with its own characters and dramas and it's all so much fun that I've started thinking that when I graduate I might pursue a career in the theatre. Right now, though, I have a dress rehearsal to think about. And I need to make sure my production of *Evita* is going to dazzle everyone.

'OK guys, let's get this show on the road!'

The lights dim and the music begins.

The role of Eva Perón is being played by Natasha Nuttall, an attractive blonde waif who's at Emmanuel College, studies English and has a soft spot for old-fashioned Mills and Boon romances and classic chickflicks like *Cocktail*, *Pretty Woman* and *Top Gun*. Once she was cast, Tash and I threw ourselves into protracted debates about the character of Eva Perón and what motivated her in life. But even though we've now made it to the dress rehearsal, I'm still not convinced we've got it quite right.

The curtain goes up and Tash takes to the stage as the teenage Eva. Right from the start I have the niggling feeling that something's missing. Tash is brilliant at capturing the character's energy and determination but for some reason I'm still not engaging with her performance. As I watch her sing and dance on stage, my mind begins wandering to Madonna's performance on screen. And that's when it dawns on me. Until the film, Eva was always played as a heartless megalomaniac with a passion for theatre and dressing up. But what Madonna brought to the role was a humanness and vulnerability. And this is missing from Tash's interpretation.

I'm just wondering how to broach the subject with her when I'm distracted by the first of many on-stage disasters. The actor playing Ché nearly breaks Tash's kneecap during their waltz and she's forced to hobble her way through the rest of the routine. Not much later, she belts out 'Don't Cry for Me Argentina' with such gusto that the balcony of the Casa Rosada gives way and she has to be rescued from falling by her audience of adoring peasants. And during a sombre moment halfway through Eva's funeral, one of the pallbearers stumbles and drops the coffin, initiating a wave of uncontrollable laughter that sweeps through the on-stage mourners, an activity I discover has the appropriate name of corpsing. It's obvious that there's still serious work to be done – and we desperately need to do it before opening night.

Once the rehearsal's over, the entire cast and crew adjourn to the theatre clubroom to talk things through.

'I'm really sorry about the balcony . . .' mumbles Anthony. 'But don't you think it complemented . . . the atmosphere of moral and physical decay . . . that pervades the second half of the piece . . . ?'

'Anthony,' I gasp, 'what are you on about?'

Thankfully, the no-nonsense Amelia comes to my rescue. 'Oh cut the artistic analysis, Anthony – just make sure it's fixed by tomorrow.'

In the midst of all the chatter Tash approaches me and asks if we can talk. Once I've given everyone else my notes, we sneak off to the pub down the road – I can tell from the intense look on her face that this is going to take a while. The two of us have got to know each other well while rehearsing and I've already discovered that behind her dazzling confidence lies a mass of insecurities. I remind myself now to tread carefully.

'What did you think?' she asks once we're sitting down. 'Was I totally *awful*?'

'No!' I breeze. 'You were brilliant!'

'Do you really think so?' She kneads her rings nervously. 'I'm not so sure, Charlie. I'm not convinced I'm capturing Eva's spirit.'

'Hmm.' I pretend to think it over. 'Maybe you need to ease off on the anger a bit. Try to soften that aggressive edge.'

'But my whole interpretation of Eva is that she was utterly consumed with anger and absolutely *desperate* to prove herself.' As she speaks she waves her hands around wildly and grasps fistfuls of the smoky air between us. 'That's what first engaged me about the character – her *incredible* drive to be someone.'

'But try to get to the bottom of that anger, Tash. See if you can access the feelings behind it. Try to think of that lonely little girl and how difficult it must have been for her, rejected by her dad, shunned by society for being illegitimate, and stuck in a back-of-beyond existence where she didn't really fit in and nobody understood her. That's the character *I* first engaged with. Surely that's what motivated her to become such a success?'

She nods her head thoughtfully and purses her lips.

'Try to see Eva as someone who felt hurt and unloved and just wanted people to like her,' I go on. 'I'm pretty sure *that's* the way to win over the audience.'

I stop before I go any further. I feel like I've somehow started talking about myself and feel a little disarmed.

'I'm feeling your empathy, Charlie.' Tash takes hold of my hand and gives it a squeeze. 'I'm *really* starting to feel it.'

She looks away pensively and I wonder what's going through her mind. Like the character she's playing, Tash comes from an unsettled family background; her mum died when she was twelve and her dad has shown little interest in her since, sending her off to boarding school just a few weeks after the funeral. As I watch her now, nodding to herself and biting her cheek, I hope she's drawing on her own experiences to connect with the character. After all, isn't that what Madonna said she did when working on the film?

Several cigarettes later, our discussion's cut short by the ringing of a bell.

'Last orders at the bar!'

'Come on,' I say, finishing my drink, 'I'll walk you home.'

The two of us set off towards Emmanuel, still analysing Tash's performance on the way. As we walk through the town I realize just how much it already feels like home. We pass the Round Church, outside which a few months ago Sally had our entire year group dressed up as Mr Men and Little Misses collecting money for RAG Week. We cross All Saints Passage, where I remember Rent-a-leg throwing up against a wall after getting completely hammered during a night in St John's bar. And we stop off at the kebab van on Market Square, where Amelia and I first met Anthony while we were stuffing our faces after a long night dancing in Sin nightclub.

We press on, past more and more beautiful buildings. When I first arrived in Cambridge, the older students insisted that, like everyone else, I'd soon get used to the architecture and stop noticing its beauty. But that hasn't happened to me so far and I'm sure it never will.

When Tash and I eventually arrive at Emmanuel, we're just saying goodbye outside the porters' lodge when she spots a dark-haired boy heading through the gate.

'Hey Charlie,' she says, a sudden twinkle in her eye, 'there's someone over there I want you to meet . . .'

Before I have time to argue she's shouting over to the boy. 'Nick! *Nick!*'

He turns around and gives a look of recognition. He walks towards us and I see that he has piercing blue eyes and a smile that lights up the whole of his face. His cheekbones are so prominent that they've got to be visible from outer space and his jet-black hair is so glossy I can practically see my reflection in it. I have no idea why but I feel like I've just been winded.

'Charlie,' gushes Tash, 'this is my gorgeous friend Nick.'

I hold out my hand and just about manage to curl up my trembling lips into a smile.

'Hi,' he replies, flashing us another grin.

'Nick,' Tash rattles on, 'this is my *enormously* talented friend Charlie – he's directing my *totally* wicked new play!'

'Oh right, cool.'

I feel goosepimples tingle along my arms but can't think of anything to say.

Luckily, Tash is happy to spout her way through an update on today's rehearsal. As she does, I hear all her words blur into each other and find myself staring at Nick's face. For some reason, Tash's interpretation of Eva Perón suddenly seems unimportant.

I don't know why but as I stand there mesmerized by Nick's face, something tells me that my whole life's about to change in a way that I wasn't expecting. This isn't just about finding my creative voice anymore – this new emotion is something else and right now it feels incredibly powerful.

Whatever's happening, I somehow know that from this point on there'll be no turning back.

Rain

As I walk over to Emmanuel, the sky's the colour of a particularly painful bruise. I've forgotten my umbrella so am hoping it won't start raining till I've made it across town. I don't want to look like I'm entering a wet T-shirt competition – not least because there's no chance I'd win. And tonight I need to look as good as I possibly can.

Our run of *Evita* ended a few weeks ago and the production was a big success. But life has moved on already and suddenly Valentine's Day has arrived. There are all kinds of activities going on around the university; Amelia and Anthony have gone to a jazz and cocktails event in Pembroke and there's a big Blind Date event going on in all the colleges in aid of Cambridge RAG. I'm on my way to a party being thrown by Tash – a party at which I hope to finally begin my love life.

Unfortunately for Tash, she's throwing the party to get over the latest upset in hers. While we were working on the play, she was going out with an orthodontically perfect American called Brock, who was a few years older than us and studying for a PhD in engineering. He grew up on a farm in the Midwest and had a jaw that looked like it was made out of iron, hands that were as big as shovels, and calves that resembled a pair of giant hams. For a few months, Tash was convinced he was 'The One' and told anyone who'd listen that when she graduated the two of them were going to move to New York, where she'd launch her career as a professional actress. But then out of the blue, Brock dumped her for a cupcake-pretty Christian called Melody, who Tash insisted was so boring she could cure insomnia. Since then we've all assured her that he clearly can't handle a woman with any emotional depth and must be one of those men who needs to go out with someone bland just so he can feel like the king of the castle. But she's still struggling to get over the split, which is why she's decided she needs to be around friends on Valentine's Day.

Tash has also told me that her friend Nick's on the guest list and it's him I'm most looking forward to seeing – and him I want to look my best for. Until I met Nick I didn't really think about men, other than in the abstract, theoretical sense. All right, I've kissed a few guys on nights out in Manchester's Gay Village, but that's only when I've been drunk, and I've always been too nervous to give any of them my number in case they call and my parents answer. If anyone asks me why I don't have a boyfriend here in Cambridge I tell them I'm too busy with academic work and student theatre, sometimes throwing in a joke about being so crap at attracting guys that I couldn't pull the ring off a Coke can. The truth is, though, deep down I find the idea of having a boyfriend slightly revolting. What would we do, walk down the street holding hands?

But then I met Nick and everything changed. Ever since that night Tash and I bumped into him after the dress rehearsal of *Evita*, I haven't been able to stop fantasizing about the two of us being boyfriends. I picture us lounging around the gardens of St Christopher's in the springtime, or strolling along the Backs together as the sun sets over Cambridge. Suddenly the idea of two men holding hands doesn't seem quite so revolting and going out with Nick is the one thing I want more than anything else in the world. But I'm still terrified about the idea of having sex; every time I imagine it I can't help thinking about all the things the kids at school said about gay sex being excruciatingly painful and giving you AIDS. Of course I've learnt by now that it's quite easy to avoid catching the virus that leads to AIDS by wearing a condom – but I still suspect that gay sex hurts and I can't shake off the idea that it's slightly dirty. How can I when nobody's ever really told me otherwise?

As I stroll towards Emmanuel, I tell myself that Nick might just represent my first real chance to lose my virginity, if only I can be brave enough to see it through. But the first thing I need to do is to get to Tash's room before it starts raining, or else Nick will take one look at me and run a mile. In the distance I hear the sound of thunder and break into a jog, holding on to the bottle of cheap white wine I'm taking and the bunch of roses I've bought Tash as a Valentine's present. When a bolt of lightning splits the sky, I run across the road, ducking into the shelter of the porters' lodge just as it begins tipping it down. Relieved that I've dodged a soaking, I slip under the arches and head towards Tash's room.

Tash lives on the top floor of a Georgian building in a spacious set with its own en suite bathroom and kitchen area. The main living space is piled high with Mills and Boon novels, and decorated with posters of the films *Ghost* and *Sleepless in Seattle* as well as some of the plays Tash has appeared in at the student theatre, all of them scrawled with drunken messages from fellow cast members eager to express their never-ending friendship at the last-night party. Along one wall is a tatty old sofa covered by a lavender throw and in the middle of the room is a clutch of beanbags on which Tash and I often lounge around and smoke cigarettes. For tonight's party she's hung lengths of pink silk over the lightshades, strung chains of red love-hearts around the ceiling, and piled plates of Cupid-shaped cookies on the coffee table.

'Charlie!' she gushes as she opens the door. '*Wicked* to see you!'

I glance over her shoulder and quickly ascertain that Nick hasn't arrived yet. The discovery comes as something of a relief as it means I can have a drink and take the edge off my nerves before seeing him.

Tash thanks me for the flowers and puts them in a pint glass she tells me she nicked from the student bar ages ago. 'I knew it'd come in handy one day,' she says, plonking it down on the coffee table. She gestures to the flowers and thanks me for the present. 'It's almost enough to make me forget I've been dumped.'

Once I've reassured her yet again that Brock didn't deserve her, she forces a smile onto her face and takes me into the living room to introduce me to the other guests. None of the names lodge in my mind but there are a few people I've met before; there's a blonde girl with a bony décolletage who played violin in the orchestra for *Evita*, a statuesque African girl whose father, Tash told me, is the richest man in Nigeria, and a Theology student with ginger dreadlocks who always seems to smell like an old pond. Tash's invitation instructed her guests to 'Bring a lot of bottle' and it looks like everyone has; there's a mountain of white wine stacked up in the sink and as I glance around the room people aren't so much drinking it as tossing it back.

'Oh and you must meet my lesbian friend, Bud,' Tash says, steering me towards a chubby girl who looks like Zippy from the children's TV programme *Rainbow*. '*All* my friends are lesbians,' Tash declares proudly, despite the fact that as far as I can tell there's only one in the room.

I pour myself a glass of wine and sit down next to Bud, who tells me that she's recently split up from her girlfriend, a Pakistani girl from Bradford who apparently grew up in a very anti-gay environment and still isn't comfortable enough with her sexuality to have a relationship. 'I just don't think she's ready to accept it in herself,' Bud muses. 'And if she can't love it in herself there's no way she can love it in someone else.'

I nod sympathetically but suddenly feel worried that Bud might have had a conversation with Tash and might be trying to hint that I'm in the same position as her ex-girlfriend. Well, if she is then she's wrong. Or at least she will be after tonight. I excuse myself to top up my glass and corner Tash in the kitchen.

'Tash,' I whisper, 'when's Nick getting here?'

She smiles knowingly and looks at her watch. 'In about half an hour; he had to see some friend in a comedy show first.'

'Cool,' I reply, filling my glass to the brim. 'And does he know I'm here?'

'*Totally!*' she erupts. 'He's *really* looking forward to seeing you.'

However many times she's told me this already, I still can't accept that it's true. 'Seriously?' I ask. 'But he's only met me once.'

'Yeah, but maybe that's all it takes. And don't forget he noticed you when he came to see me in *Evita*.' She explains once again that Nick came to watch our show halfway through its run and spotted me on the other side of the auditorium but had to dash off afterwards because of some other commitment.

'Oh yeah,' I nod, pretending I've forgotten. 'And what did he say about me again?'

'*Charlie*,' Tash breathes, rolling her eyes, 'how many times do I have to tell you? He's *totally* into you. Now relax. And make sure you don't get too pissed!'

As she skips off into the seating area, I make my way over to the sofa and sit on the arm next to a knot of arty types. I try to join their conversation but just want the time to pass as quickly as possible. A mouthy posh girl with terrible split ends tells a long story about travelling around Uganda during the summer and almost being raped by a baboon. 'Honestly,' she announces to the others, 'I woke up in the middle of the night and there it was, wanking over me!'

Everyone claps their hands over their mouths in horror, and then the conversation somehow moves on to a discussion of people's worst ever sexual experiences. Before long, some of the guests are sharing stories of how awful it was to lose their virginity. I try to zone out and not listen to their chatter about bleeding, fainting and, in the case of one guy, ending up in A & E after tearing his foreskin. I hope to God Nick turns up soon.

A few minutes later there's a knock at the door and, finally, there he is. He's wearing a bicep-hugging jumper, perfectly fitted jeans and a big, beautiful smile. My heart gives a little wobble. He's even more gorgeous than I remember. I make sure I avert my eyes before he spots me gawping at him and suddenly feign interest in everyone's stories. 'Oh my God,' I gasp at no one in particular, 'that sounds *horrendous*!'

Out of the corner of my eye, I watch Nick as he follows Tash into the kitchen and pours himself a glass of wine. The two of them chat for a few minutes and then I can just about make out Nick stepping forward to join the rest of the guests. Shortly afterwards there's a tap on my shoulder. I feel a jolt of electricity run down my spine but somehow manage to project an expression of something approaching nonchalance. I turn around to face him.

'Oh hi,' I say, 'it's Nick, isn't it?'

'Yeah,' he grins, 'and you're Charlie.'

'I am, yeah.' I notice that he has eyelashes so long you could brush the floor with them. I try to stay calm. 'So where've you been tonight?'

Nick tells me he's been to see a friend in a comedy revue called *Funny Ha Ha*, which he assesses as 'the right side of average'. 'But the truth is,' he explains, 'I'm much more into theatre than comedy.'

He goes on to tell me that his biggest passion is acting and that, like Tash, when he leaves Cambridge he wants to act professionally. I'm sure he'll have no problem as he's so charismatic – not that I'm going to tell him that as I've been well briefed by Tash beforehand. Instead, I share with him that my ambition is to become a director. 'At least I think it is,' I add, deciding to forget about my dream of becoming a writer. 'I think I'd like to direct for the theatre.'

At this, Nick sits next to me on the arm of the sofa. When his leg touches mine I have to concentrate all my energy on making sure my excitement doesn't register on my face. We begin talking about some of the plays we've each seen in Cambridge and I'm surprised to find that, despite my nerves, the conversation flows easily. Before I know it, half an hour has passed and our glasses are empty. I offer to go to the kitchen to fill them up, and within seconds Tash is at my side.

'Check you out,' she hisses in my ear, 'you two are practically having sex on my sofa!'

I quickly glance to see that Nick isn't looking but he's flicking through some old theatre programmes on Tash's coffee table. 'Really?' I whisper. 'So do you think he wants to pull me?'

'Charlie,' she says, 'he's all over you like a sloppy quiche! Honestly, it's totally going to happen. And on Valentine's Day too. Oh it's so *romantic*!'

I fill our glasses with wine but make a note that this drink will have to be my last; it's fine to use booze to loosen up but the last thing I want is to get shitfaced if anything *is* going to happen between me and Nick.

Tash must be reading my thoughts. 'So are you going to shag him?' she asks. 'Because you *totally* should.'

In a flash, all the things people were saying about their first time and all the things people used to say to me about gay sex begin pinballing around my mind. Assuming Nick *does* want to have sex with me, and that's one hell of an assumption, am I really sure I can go through with it?

'I've no idea, Tash,' I say, trying my best to sound coy rather than terrified. 'But when I do you'll be the first to know.'

I walk back over to the sofa and Nick and I begin talking again. I don't know how I get through the conversation as I can barely take in a word he's saying and it's almost as if my comments are saying themselves. All I can think about is the possibility that tonight might be the night I finally lose my virginity. And not just that, but with someone I really like.

When Nick has emptied his glass he puts it down on the table and stands up purposefully. 'Well,' he says, 'I'm kind of tired. I reckon I might make a move.'

In an instant I feel myself deflate. All this time I've been thinking he wants to have sex with me and now he's telling me he wants to go to sleep. 'Oh, right,' I manage, 'yeah, me too.'

'Come on then,' he says, 'let's go.'

As I stand to leave, I feel a weird mixture of disappointment and frustration but also a dash of relief; at least I won't have to confront my fears about sex just yet. And maybe Nick and I will have a little snog as we say goodnight. That's probably the right thing to do anyway; it's probably better to ease myself into things rather than having sex as soon as I've got to know him.

Nick puts his hand on my elbow and begins to guide me out of the room. I wave at Bud and a few other people I've spoken to and we stop by Tash to say our goodbyes. Once Nick's back's turned, she looks at me and mouths, 'Good luck!'

I try shaking my head to let her know that nothing's happening but it's too late. Nick sweeps me into the corridor and down the stairs.

When we get to the bottom he opens the door into the courtyard. It's one of my favourites in Cambridge as the surrounding walls are made out of stone the colour of butterscotch. The only thing is, it's still pissing down with rain.

We stand cowering under the arches. 'Shit,' I say, 'I haven't brought an umbrella.'

Nick frowns at me. 'Well, we can't have you getting wet, can we? Maybe you should come back to mine.'

I feel a spike of terror. Is this it? *Does* he want to have sex with me?

He looks deep into my eyes and doesn't blink. 'You know, I'm sure it'll have stopped raining by the morning.'

OK, so now there's no doubt what he's asking. This is it. This is my chance. But can I really go through with it?

At that moment Madonna's 'Rain' begins playing in my head. I don't care that it's corny; right now I need to hear it. I need to feel inspired by my idol. I need her to give me the courage to do this. And as I listen to her singing about falling in love as the rain comes down, I can feel my courage rising.

'So what do you say?' Nick asks.

He touches my cheek with his finger and I'm so ablaze with desire, excitement and fear I can almost feel my skin blistering. He leans forward and kisses me softly on the lips. It's a kiss I can feel right down to my toes.

'Yes,' I whisper. 'Yes, I'll come to your room.'

He grins at me and I find myself grinning back at him.

But then Nick's grin quickly switches to a grimace. 'There's only one problem,' he says.

'Oh no, what's that?'

'My room's in the next court along so we might get a bit wet on the way.'

'Oh right,' I say, by now almost panting. 'I don't think that'll be a problem.'

Nick holds out his hand and I lace my fingers through his.

We set out into the rain.

Cherish

The sun's shining and it's spring in Cambridge. The smell of freshly mown grass is in the air, the ducks on the river are trailed by ducklings, and the weeping willows along its banks are coming into leaf. It's all very beautiful and the perfect setting for romance.

Nick and I are out punting – we've already glided along the Backs and are now making our way to the nearby village of Grantchester. I'm not very good at punting, though, so Nick's having to do all the work. I had a go in my first term but wobbled around so badly that I fell in the river and swallowed so much dirty water that I spent the next few days puking up in the sick bay. Luckily, Nick's taken charge this time and I lie back in the punt, thankful that I'm wearing sunglasses so he won't realize just how much I'm staring at him. He looks manly and masterful and when he smiles at me I feel so happy that it actually hurts. I can't resist serenading him with a song I've been unable to get out of my head for weeks now. It's 'Cherish', possibly the most upbeat, cheery love song Madonna's ever made.

Since that first night I went back to Nick's room, my life has changed more than I ever thought it could. Yes, we had sex but it wasn't painful or dirty, it was beautiful – and in the days and weeks that followed we haven't been able to stop doing it over and over again. I'm suddenly aware of my body and what it can do in ways that didn't cross my mind beforehand and I can hardly take my hands off Nick's. Discovering sex has transformed me and I'm sure everyone can read it on my face. It's like part of me wasn't really awake until now but has suddenly come roaring to life. I'm so happy that when the crocuses and daffodils begin sprouting along the banks of the Cam I'm convinced they're all smiling at me. For the first time in my life, I understand what Madonna's going on about when she sings about true love. The lyrics to songs like 'Cherish' make so much more sense.

All these feelings have taken over my life and I haven't been able to concentrate on work for weeks. In lectures and supervisions I find myself gazing out of the window and I can't stay focused for long enough to write an essay. I'm supposed to be working on one this afternoon but for the first time since arriving in Cambridge I'm going to have to ask for an extension on my deadline.

Now that Nick's in my life I want to be with him every second of every day. It doesn't matter what I'm doing as long as we're together. I love watching him shave, contorting his face into all kinds of funny positions. When he's working at his desk I'll lie next to him and play with his feet. And at night I'll cuddle up to him and rest my head on his chest, the lyrics to 'Cherish' tinkling away in my mind.

Nick rests the pole in the water and suggests we take a break. He's been at it for hours now and is starting to look tired. He manoeuvres the punt under a weeping willow as the sun's getting strong and balances his way along to lie down next to me.

'Isn't this wicked?' he says.

'Yeah, it's like being in a fairytale.'

He takes off my sunglasses and looks deep into my eyes.

'Charlie,' he says, 'has anyone ever told you you're gorgeous?'

I can feel myself getting out of breath. 'No,' I stammer, 'no, they haven't.'

'Well, you are. You're the most gorgeous boy I've ever met.'

I feel like I want to cry and struggle to stop my chin from wobbling. No one's ever said anything remotely like that to me before and it never occurred to me that anyone would. But hearing Nick say it to me is so powerful that it's almost like he's blasting away all my imperfections. If he thinks I'm gorgeous, maybe I am.

'Hey,' I struggle, anxious to stop my voice from cracking, 'you do realize what day it is today?'

'No – what day is it?'

'It's our four-week anniversary.'

He looks at me and smiles. I can now spot his smiles a split second before they spread across his face.

'I can't believe I've had a boyfriend for *four whole weeks*,' I go on. 'Isn't it amazing?'

His face drops. 'Urm, Charlie, urm . . . Haven't we talked about that?'

'What?'

'The whole boyfriend thing?'

'Oh yeah, sorry – I keep forgetting.'

Unfortunately, Nick's keen that I don't use the word 'boyfriend'. He prefers us to say that we're 'seeing each other' as apparently it's less formal. I don't see what the problem is and when he isn't there I love referring to him as my boyfriend.

The only snag is, I have to remember not to use the word when I'm actually with him.

'OK,' I correct myself, 'so we've been *seeing each other* for four weeks. Is that better?'

'Much better,' he says, cuffing me playfully on the shoulder.

It's at times like this that I feel really inexperienced when it comes to relationships. As I've never had anything approaching one before, I'm often unsure of the right thing to say or do and have spent much of the past month pestering Tash and Amelia for advice. In my head I relive our conversations.

'The first time you fall in love,' Amelia explains, 'it's completely intoxicating and really easy to get carried away.'

'But what do you mean "the first time"?' I protest. 'I only want to fall in love once.'

'Yeah well, I thought that with my first love and that's probably why I ended up getting so hurt.'

Just before Amelia arrived at Cambridge she was dumped by the man she now refers to as her first love. She spent her gap year working as an au pair with a family in Italy but ended up falling for the father of the family. The two of them embarked on a passionate affair until his wife found out, at which point Amelia was unceremoniously sent packing – and left utterly devastated.

'You know what,' she says, her voice softening, 'at the time I was so knocked for six I didn't see how I'd ever get over it. But now I see that it wasn't that special an experience at all – it was just something I had to go through, something everyone goes through as part of growing up.'

I nod respectfully but can't help thinking that just because Amelia has been devastated by her first experience of love, that doesn't mean that we *all* have to be. I can't bear to see the feelings I have for Nick reduced to some kind of rite-of-passage I'll one day look back on as 'not that special'.

I wait for Amelia's sadness to fade then argue, 'But what if me and Nick aren't like other couples? What if what we've got really *is* unique?'

'I hope you're right, Charlie, I really hope you're right. But you've got to realize that everyone feels that the first time they fall in love. I mean, think about this rationally – you've only known Nick for four weeks!'

I pout at her. 'Actually I've known him for six weeks; we've been *seeing each other* for four. And anyway, it doesn't always take long. Haven't you heard of love at first sight? Madonna sings about it all the time.'

She sighs in mock exasperation. 'Yeah, but I haven't heard of it lasting very long – not in real life anyway. Look, one thing I've learnt from past experience is no matter how strongly you can feel about someone in the beginning, you never know how a relationship's going to turn out in the end. So all I'm saying is, take it easy at first and don't make any big declarations about being in love just yet.'

It's frustrating to hear Amelia talk about something that's so intensely, indescribably special in such a level-headed, logical way. If I follow her advice and hold back my feelings, how will I ever experience true love?

Thankfully, Tash is being far more optimistic about the whole thing. She's currently having an affair with one of her lecturers and will tell anyone who'll listen that she's convinced he's 'The One', squealing with delight as she imagines the day he'll leave his wife and fully commit to her. Together, Tash and I have also fantasized about my future with Nick, deciding that after Cambridge, the two of us will move to London and live together in our first flat, a stylish loft conversion in a bohemian part of town. I'll become a top theatre director and be showered with Olivier Awards while Nick will become a major star and act in all my plays. When things really take off, we'll move to New York to launch ourselves on Broadway. I'm convinced it's a perfect plan and feel encouraged by Tash's agreement.

'Just imagine,' I gush to Nick now, 'in a few years' time we could be doing this in Central Park!'

He sighs and runs his finger down my cheek. 'You really are sweet, Charlie.'

'I can just see us now,' I go on, 'lying in the park sipping champagne with the Empire State building rising up behind us.'

He smiles and trails his hand in the water. I feel my heart pull and reach out to run my fingers through his hair.

'Ah-ah!' He flinches, jumping up immediately. 'Don't touch the hair!'

'Oh yeah, sorry, I forgot.' I curse myself for spoiling the moment. Oh maybe I'm not very good at this after all . . .

'How many times have I told you?' he goes on. 'You *know* it takes me ages to style my hair!'

Nick has explained on several occasions now that he has to take care of his appearance if he's ever going to make it as a successful actor. He goes to the gym four times a week, uses more hair and skincare products than I knew existed, and once a month plucks his eyebrows, which I didn't for a minute consider that anyone did. All of which is fine as it makes him even more good-looking than he is naturally. I just have to remember that he doesn't like me touching his hair.

'Sorry,' I mumble again. 'I'll try to remember next time.'

'Oh don't worry about it,' he smiles. '*I'm* sorry for snapping. Come here.'

He stretches out his arms and I lie back in them. As I snuggle up, breathing in his scent, I wonder what the two of us would look like on the poster for a romantic Hollywood film. Nick's heartbreakingly handsome, much more so than any actor I've seen at the pictures – Brad Pitt, Johnny Depp, Patrick Swayze . . . I'd rather have my Nick any day. For the last few weeks I've been bursting to tell him that I love him but have stopped myself. And I'm not sure I can any longer.

'Nick,' I say, 'there's something I've wanted to tell you for a while now.'

'Oh yeah? What's that?'

'I, urm, I – I've never said it before but . . .'

'Go on.'

'I'm a bit nervous . . .'

'Oh come on, Charlie, spit it out.'

'I, I, I love you, Nick.'

He looks away from my eyes and into the water. There's a pause and he nods. 'I know, Charlie. I know.'

A tense silence descends between us and in my head I hear my nerves screeching like fingernails being dragged down a blackboard. 'I know,' he just said, 'I know.' Surely what he should have said was, 'I love you too'? Or does that mean he *doesn't* love me? I suddenly feel vulnerable and exposed and my heart begins beating so fiercely that I'm worried Nick will actually hear it. Maybe Amelia's right and I *am* moving too fast. Oh I hope I haven't just blown things.

'Listen, Charlie,' Nick begins ominously, 'I really like you. I really *really* like you . . .'

I can sense there's a 'but' coming and feel my shoulders growing tense. 'But you don't love me? Is that what you're trying to say?'

'No! It's not that I *don't* love you. It's just that I think it's a bit too early to be talking about love at all.'

I grimace. 'Sorry. I guess I just couldn't help myself.'

'I know and it's all very sweet. But you're just moving a little fast for me, that's all.'

As I listen to him gently pushing me away, I'm terrified I've messed it all up. Oh what's the matter with me? Why can't I just relax into the relationship rather than being so desperate for him to love me?

'OK, right,' I manage, forcing myself to smile. 'Well, from now on I'll just have to put the brakes on, won't I?'

He screws up his face. 'Do you mind?'

'Course not,' I lie. 'I've waited this long – a bit longer's not going to hurt, is it?'

'Thanks, Charlie.'

'Don't worry about it.' I pick up my sunglasses and clamp them over my eyes; I don't want him to see how disappointed I am. 'Now come on, hadn't we better get back to town?'

Nick regains his position at the head of the boat and begins punting us back along the river. I can't bear to dwell on what's just happened and decide that singing a Madonna song is exactly what I need to take my mind off it. I'm just about to burst into an encore of 'Cherish' when I check myself and decide it would probably be better if I sing it in my head rather than out loud.

Oh I might be inexperienced at relationships but I know one thing for sure – I *am* in love. And the feeling's incredible. Nick will fall in love with me one day . . . What I feel for him's so strong and so *real* that I can't possibly see how it could be wrong. I'll just have to make a big effort not to bring up the subject again until he does.

And besides, before I can properly celebrate being in love, there's something else that I have to get out of the way first. It's something I've been meaning to do for a while now but have been putting off out of sheer fear. Before I fall any further in love, there's an important conversation I need to have with Mum and Dad.

Secret

During the Easter holidays I finally feel ready to have that conversation. I've decided to tell Mum and Dad about me and Nick. I've decided to come out to them as gay.

I take a deep breath and mentally prepare myself – I'm about to experience what by all accounts will be one of the most momentous events of my life. But after finally making my parents proud of me for going to Cambridge, I'm dreading going back to the days of disappointing them. I can remember only too clearly how I felt as a child, trying to be good at football to please my dad but failing miserably and only ending up embarrassing him and feeling like I wasn't good enough. What's he going to say when he finds out I'm gay?

I'm back in Bolton and sitting in The Flat Iron with Mum, Dad and Joe. The interior's recently been refurbished in the style of an English country pub. There's a pretend log fire and fake wooden beams running across the ceiling and they now serve food like traditional roast beef, chicken tikka masala and scampi in a basket. I'm not sure I like it but at least they've expanded the range of drinks they serve and, to my great relief, they've even started stocking Pernod. I take a swig of mine and try to calm my nerves. I'm so terrified of what I'm about to do I've been biting my nails all day and when I nibble at my thumb I rip off a strip of skin and the blood starts flowing. I take out a tissue and press it to the wound. I'll just stop this bleeding then I'll make my announcement.

Despite all the changes to the pub, I look around and see that it's still frequented by the same crowd of regulars. Gabby Annie's in her usual seat, still toothless and sipping away at her favourite Mackeson Stout. Keeping one eye on the door and one hand on his holster is John Wayne, who by now has a cowboy shirt and waistcoat to go with his hat and boots. And standing behind the bar is a slightly older-looking Babs Flitcroft, although I notice something about her today that isn't quite right. I peer closer and manage to work it out. For the first time ever, Babs has a smile on her face.

''Ere,' says Mum, leaning towards me, 'you do know Babs and your Uncle Les are courting?'

'No! Really?'

She nods authoritatively. 'Apparently they're quite serious.'

'So do you think they'll get married?' asks Joe, who by now has lost his ponytail and pierced eyebrow and is a big fan of Britpop. He's also finished his degree in Economics and has stayed on to live in Newcastle and train as an accountant. I can't help feeling a sneaky satisfaction that, if my academic career has trumped Joe's, my professional career is bound to as well, especially if I succeed in my ambition of becoming a theatre director. But then I remind myself that I have to get over the idea that the two of us are always in competition. It might have been unavoidable when we were young but surely I should have grown out of it by now? I decide to re-focus on the subject of Uncle Les and Babs Flitcroft. It's a welcome distraction while I build up the courage to make my announcement.

'Yeah, what do you think, Mum?' I ask. 'Are they going to get married or what?'

Mum swills her white wine around the glass as she thinks it over. 'It wouldn't surprise me if they did, yeah.'

'Well, God knows what he sees in her,' pipes up Dad. 'She's a right misery.'

Mum hisses at him. 'Keep your voice down, Frank! You can be so negative sometimes.'

He laughs out loud. 'Excuse me, you're the one who said she has a face like a cow licking piss off a nettle.'

'Frank!' she says, elbowing him. 'Mind your language in front of the kids.'

'Maggie, they're hardly kids anymore.'

'Anyway,' Mum goes on, ignoring him, 'in case you haven't noticed, Babs hasn't been half as miserable since your Les started taking her out. I reckon it's really romantic.'

As she witters on about their new relationship, I find myself wondering what she'll think when I tell her about me and Nick. Will she think that's romantic too? I feel another pang of panic as I remember what I've got to do. My thumb's stopped bleeding but I pretend not to notice and press the tissue onto it anyway.

To try to calm myself down I wonder what Nick's doing now. He's spending Easter skiing in Switzerland with some friends and I picture them eating fondue in a restaurant or resting in the chalet after a hard day on the slopes. I imagine it's me out there with Nick and see the two of us rolling around in a passionate embrace in front of a real log fire. I suddenly feel his absence like a sharp pain in my chest. Now that has to be true love.

Burp! Dad lets out a gush of wind. 'I tell you what – the beer hasn't half gone downhill since they did this place up.'

'Bloomin' 'eck, Frank!' snaps Mum. 'I wish you wouldn't burp out loud!'

'Oh stop nagging, woman! Better out than in I always say, eh lads?'

Joe and I smile but inside I find myself feeling embarrassed. Ever since I started at Cambridge, whenever I come home I can't help noticing how unrefined Mum and Dad can be. I wonder what my other friends from Cambridge are doing for Easter. They all seem to have much more interesting and sophisticated home lives than me. Amelia's probably sitting down to a meal with her Italian family at their restaurant in London – I picture them all laughing heartily like something out of an advert for olive oil or Dolmio. I know that Tash is spending Easter with her stockbroker dad and the latest in his series of apparently gold-digging girlfriends at his holiday home in the South of Spain. She said she was dreading it because she always feels in the way when her dad has a new girlfriend but to me the whole thing sounds like a plotline from a Jackie Collins novel. And here I am sitting in The Flat Iron talking about Dad's wind – what a difference. Gabby Annie shuffles past us to the bar and we all look over to see if she's left a damp patch behind her. Unsurprisingly she has.

During the pause in conversation I warn myself to stop being distracted from the announcement I've got to make. The longer I leave it, the more difficult it'll be. In fact, now's the perfect time to broach the subject. I stretch my legs under the table and prepare to dive in.

'Oooh, don't look now,' interrupts Mum, 'but your Auntie Jan's new fella's just walked in!'

Thankful for another diversion, I swivel around in my seat. 'Where? Who?'

'Ssshhh!' Mum hisses before I can get a proper look. 'Pretend you haven't seen him!'

The man in question walks past us with his head down and disappears into the beer garden.

'Oh thank God for that,' breathes Mum.

'What's going on?' Joe asks. 'Why are you trying to avoid him?'

She sighs and rolls her eyes. 'Well, in case you boys haven't noticed, when it comes to picking men your Auntie Jan has a knack for backing losers. She's fallen head over heels for this guy and won't accept he's bad news.'

'But what's up with him?' I ask, keenly. 'Why are you so sure he's bad news?'

'Well, for a start your Grandma's seen him out with some girl who works in that new nail salon in town.'

'What, the one with the rude name?' I ask.

She smiles tightly. 'Yeah, that one.'

'What's it called again?' teases Joe, desperate to make Mum say the name out loud.

'I don't know, love,' she barks. 'I can't remember.'

'*I* know!' says Dad, a naughty twinkle in his eye. 'It's called Hand Job.'

Mum pulls a face like she's sucking on an out-of-date lemon. 'Yes, all right, Frank, thank you for that.'

'My pleasure, Maggie.'

'Anyway, the point I'm trying to make is not only is this bloke seeing the girl from the nail salon but I was talking to Fat Pat in the paper shop the other day and she reckons he's knocking about with Shirley Stubbins too. You know Shirley – the one with five kids by five different men? She was on the Vanessa Feltz show last month!'

'Poor Auntie Jan,' I say. I close my eyes and wish she could find herself a boyfriend as special as my Nick. My morale plunges as I remember my mission.

'Talk about love is blind,' Mum tuts. 'She keeps going on about him looking like that Liam Gallagher from Oasis. I'm not kidding – he's a window-cleaner who lives on Corporation Row!'

'I actually quite like the bloke,' mutters Dad. 'I bumped into him at the football the other day and we had a pint together after the game.'

Mum elbows him in the ribs. '*Frank!*'

Joe perks up at the mention of football. 'Hey, wasn't it a good match, Dad?'

'I know, lad, it were beltin'!'

The two of them launch into an in-depth discussion about the current form of Bolton Wanderers and I breathe another sigh of relief. I'm off the hook for the time being.

Joe might have given up playing football in his late teens, something I can't help thinking was down to the realization that he wasn't quite good enough to make it professionally, but he's still an avid fan, going with Dad to watch our local team play every time he's home. Ordinarily I'd feel a stab of jealousy and a sense of frustration that this is a conversation I can't possibly join in. But all I can think about now is the conversation I've promised myself I'll bring up tonight. And however sick the idea makes me feel, I can't put it off any longer.

'Mum and Dad,' I begin falteringly, 'there's something—'

'You know, I wish you hadn't given it all up, Joe,' Dad breaks in nostalgically. 'Just think – if you'd stuck at it, you could be playing for the Wanderers yourself by now.'

Joe looks uncomfortable and I can't help feeling a rush of

satisfaction. This is quickly followed by a wave of guilt – I hope it doesn't make me a bad person. Never mind, at least it's given me another few minutes before I make my announcement.

'But it's not as simple as that, Dad,' Joe says. 'And anyway, it's not as if I've sat on my backside for the last few years.' He explains how hard he's worked on his degree and how much he's putting into his accountancy exams at the moment. Just then I spot my chance to steer the conversation in vaguely the right direction. I have to be brave. I have to do this.

'Oh don't talk about exams,' I say. 'I've got to start revising myself soon but I've so much other stuff going on next term.' Now's my opportunity to hit them with the news that I've got a boyfriend.

'Oh yeah?' says Joe. 'Like what?'

'Well, urm . . .'

I lose my nerve.

'. . . I'm directing an open-air Shakespeare play in the Tudor court in college.'

'Bloomin' 'eck, yeah,' remembers Mum. 'That'll be smashin', love.'

'Beltin',' agrees Dad.

'Well, you must try and come down,' I say. 'It'll be during May Week, in the second week of June.'

Mum looks confused. 'Oh. I thought you said it was May?'

'No, May Week's in June – everybody knows that!' I sound annoyed and feel another wave of guilt. 'Sorry, I suppose it is a bit confusing.'

'Well, whenever it is,' says Dad, 'we'll be there, lad.'

'Wicked! And, urm, there's another reason I'm looking forward to next term.' Now really is my chance – I *have* to see it through this time . . .

'Oh yeah, son, what's that?'

My heart's thumping so hard I can feel it throbbing in my temples.

Come on, Charlie, you can do this . . .

'I, I, I, I-want-to-get-back-and-see-my-new-boyfriend.' I blurt it out all in one and listen to the words echo in the silence around me.

There's such a long pause I'm not sure Mum and Dad have understood what I've said.

'You what, love?' asks Mum eventually.

I take a deep breath and clear my throat. I force myself to mouth the words again, this time slowly and clearly. 'I want to get back and see my boyfriend.'

There it is. I've done it.

There's another silence and Mum and Dad look like they've been hit in the face. After a while, Mum puts her head in her hands and Dad looks up to the ceiling. Joe shuffles in his seat awkwardly.

Shit, what have I done?

Well, there's no turning back now; my secret's out of the closet and I can't put it back in.

'Howdy, cowboy!' The silence is interrupted by the sound of John Wayne greeting one of his friends. 'Get off your horse and drink your milk!' he drawls in a bad American accent.

I try not to notice the sharp pitch of anxiety thrumming in my ears and do my best to gain control of the situation. 'So yeah, urm, that's it,' I stammer. 'Haven't you got anything to say?'

'Well, I don't quite get it, son,' says Dad, his face getting whiter by the second. 'Are you telling us you're *gay*?'

I squirm to hear him say the word out loud. 'I suppose I am, yeah,' I manage.

'Well, that's nice, love,' struggles Mum, fiddling with her rings as her neck begins to flush bright red.

Joe stares into his pint glass and takes a swig. It's as if a gloomy shadow has suddenly been cast over our table. I feel sick as I watch Mum and Dad's recent pride in me instantly evaporate, giving way to a much more familiar look of disappointment. My eyes begin stinging as if I'm about to cry. I concentrate all my effort on trying to keep my chin from quivering.

'So that's it?' I just about manage to croak. 'Is that all you're going to say?'

'Well, there's not much we *can* say is there, lad?' The look on Dad's face says everything I need to know – he's devastated.

Mum gazes into the air thoughtfully. 'I suppose we always knew you were a bit different to other boys . . .'

'Hmpf,' grunts Dad. 'But we didn't think it'd come to *this*.' He purses his lips and starts tapping on the table with a beer mat. The rest of us fall silent and stare at his hands. In the background I can hear the sound of a clock ticking. I feel gouged out by the intensity of my anxiety.

Mum does her best to force a smile. 'So who is he then, this fella?'

I spot a chance to lighten the tone and leap at it almost hysterically. 'His name's Nick, he studies English, he's at Emmanuel with Tash, he's going to be an actor, everybody loves him and he's absolutely *gorgeous*! I can't wait for you to meet him!'

The two of them look terrified. I hope I haven't gone and made things worse.

'Oh I'm not so sure about that, son,' says Dad. 'Whatever you get up to in your own time is your business but me and your mam don't actually want it ramming down our throats.'

I have to stop myself from gasping out loud. Did he really just say that or did I imagine it?

I do my best to calm myself down. I look at my hands and see the bloody tissue I've been clutching the whole time. When I open my fist now it's stuck there in a damp, sweaty lump. I drop it into the ashtray and wipe my hands on my jeans.

'If you want to go off and be gay,' Dad clarifies, 'then that's your choice. But you can't expect me and your mam to be pleased about it.'

'But Dad,' I bleat, 'I haven't chosen to be anything – this is just the way I am.'

He holds up his hand as if he isn't listening. 'Ah-ah. You've already said your piece, lad. Now that's the last word I want to hear on the subject.'

'Oh right, urm, OK . . .'

He stands up and claps his hands together. 'Right, now who's having another drink?'

I sit still, watching him stride over to the bar and not sure how I should be feeling. It's all so confusing – I'm relieved to have finally revealed my secret but feel guilty, sad, shaken up and sorry for causing my parents so much distress. And if I'm not mistaken there's a tiny bit of defiance mixed up in there as well. But more than anything else I feel scared about the future. Have I just made the biggest mistake of my life?

Mum leans over and gives my knee a little squeeze. 'Don't worry, love,' she soothes, 'your dad'll be all right soon. He just isn't very good at talking about this kind of thing, that's all.'

I'm on the verge of replying when I'm interrupted by the sound of Joe clearing his throat. I realize then that he still hasn't said a word on the subject – since I told them my news he's sat there in silence, gazing into his pint glass. I suppose now that it'll give him another reason to think he's better than me and I'm sure Mum and Dad will think so too. As soon as he opens his mouth I know I'm right.

'Why did you have to go and do that, Charlie?' he asks.

I can feel the anger unravelling in me. 'You what?'

'Upsetting Mum and Dad? Didn't it occur to you before you made your little announcement that they weren't going to like it?'

'But it's not *my* fault, Joe!'

'Oh yeah, well, whose fault is it then?'

I sit there, speechless and seething.

'Come on, boys,' Mum breaks in falteringly, 'let's not fall out about this . . .'

'But Charlie,' Joe steams on, 'I don't understand why you can't just be normal. I mean, what's wrong with liking girls like the rest of us?'

'Joe,' I stammer, 'don't you think I've asked myself that a few times?'

'Yeah, well, why don't you do something about it then?'

'Like what? What do you suggest, Joe?'

Just then Dad comes back with a tray full of drinks and a couple of bags of crisps. 'Here we are,' he says, tossing the crisps onto the table, 'a nice pub salad.'

Joe and I fall silent and look down awkwardly. While Mum opens up the crisps, the two of us wait for Dad to speak.

''Ere Joe,' he bellows as he sits down between us, 'did you see that crackin' goal by McGinlay the other day?'

Of course Dad would talk about football. How else would he cope with the situation?

I tell everyone I need to go to the loo and sneak out of the back door of the pub to get some air. I feel like the damp tissue

I was clutching onto, all battered and bloody and pounded to a pulp. I emerge into an alleyway and lean against a redbrick wall while I gulp in a series of deep breaths.

After a few minutes, I take out a cigarette and light up. As I pull on the nicotine and exhale the smoke, I can feel my tension slowly unwinding.

Well, I've gone through with it. And it was the scariest, bravest thing I've ever done – or am ever likely to do – in my whole life.

Despite Mum and Dad's reactions, now that I stop to reflect on it, I'm proud of myself for opening up to them, for laying myself on the line and being so honest. And they might not be happy about it but at least I've been true to myself.

That doesn't mean I'm not worried about how much I've damaged our relationship, but the truth is, if it is damaged then that's only because of their reactions to something that was there all along. What am I supposed to do, lie to them about it for the rest of our lives? Pretend to like girls just to please them, even if that means I can never be happy? And it's not my fault the news I'm gay has come as such a shock. The signs were always there – everyone at school spotted them way before I'd got my head around it. So why didn't my parents? Why didn't they take the trouble to understand me and find out what it's like to be gay so they could make it easier for me? Isn't it a parent's duty to love and nurture their child, without putting any conditions on that love?

As the thoughts ricochet around my mind, I can feel my anger building. And that's something I really wasn't expecting. The few accounts of coming out I've read in that new gay magazine *Attitude* have often involved the son feeling desperately grateful for the slightest crumbs of acceptance his parents throw his way. Anything short of full rejection or disownment is usually accepted with a kind of wretched relief. Well, I don't see why I should feel that way.

There's a big stone lying on the cobbles and I kick it into a patch of weeds at the bottom of the wall. If I *am* going to hold together my relationship with my parents, I need to somehow put a lid on my anger before I go back inside.

I stub out my fag and pop a piece of chewing gum in my mouth. Mum and Dad hate me smoking and they're bound to be able to tell I've been out for a fag. Never mind, I've just told them I'm gay, I reckon this is the one day I can get away with it.

I take a moment to compose myself then push open the door and walk back into the pub. I look around and am surprised to see that for everyone else life is carrying on as if nothing's happened. Gabby Annie's back in her seat sipping her Mackeson Stout and Babs Flitcroft's polishing glasses behind the bar with a faraway look in her eyes. Don't any of them realize what I've just done?

On the other side of the room I can see Mum, Dad and Joe desperately trying to carry on as normal. Dad's in the middle of telling some story and Mum and Joe are laughing at a slightly manic pitch. How dare they ignore my feelings and try to carry on as if nothing's happened? Don't they have any idea how tough this has been for me?

I suddenly realize just how much easier it would be to leave my family behind and cut them out of my life completely, to go back to Cambridge where I'm surrounded by people who love and accept me as I am. But something tells me I won't do that. No, I won't take the easy way out. I won't give up on them yet.

I walk over and sit back down.

True Blue

'Wow, you look amazing!' I tell Inappropriate Lee, who's wearing a black PVC gimp suit and a blindfold with ripped eyeholes, and is carrying a rather scary whip that he insists on cracking at every opportunity. 'That's such a wicked costume!'

All my friends have turned up in fancy dress at a party I'm throwing to celebrate my twenty-first birthday. The venue is the Old Hall of St Christopher's, a wood-panelled room with a brightly coloured, ornamental ceiling that reminds me of the gingerbread house in Hansel and Gretel. Watching over us on the far wall are portraits of the king and queen who founded the college and built into the stained-glass window are several reproductions of their coat of arms. Despite the fact that the room's nearly 550 years old, it's available for hire to students for the sum of just £25 per night. So far this year it's hosted all kinds of fancy dress parties with themes such as Pimps and Prostitutes, Slinky or Kinky and Slag or Drag. The theme I've chosen is very simple but hasn't been done before. The theme I've chosen is Madonna.

Obviously, this means dressing up is more difficult for the boys than it is for the girls, although Inappropriate Lee has managed brilliantly with his tribute to 'Erotica'. I've opted not to go in drag after my disastrous experience performing 'Dress You

Up' at school years ago. Instead I'm wearing the top hat and tails that Madonna wore as the ringmaster during her *Girlie Show* tour. I'm delighted to see that the costume comes with a cane and I get really into twirling it around in front of me as I stride through the party checking that everything's going well.

A vintage Madonna song is playing on the rather primitive sound system and everywhere I look people are dancing and drinking. I'm already quite drunk myself and it's obvious that several other people are too. Rent-a-leg is running the bar, wearing a tight basque her body's spilling out of along with fishnet tights and a black feather boa. She's creating a punch by pouring the bottles of alcohol everyone's brought into a huge plastic bin I've decorated with Madonna posters. Unfortunately, she isn't mixing it according to any kind of recipe and the resulting concoction tastes like a cross between Listerine mouthwash and a severe case of bad breath. Thankfully, most of the guests are sipping away regardless.

I'm feeling on top form and buzzing with satisfaction at the sight of the party in full swing. I had a difficult Easter at home with Mum and Dad; after coming out to them they refused to talk about the subject again, making me feel like I'd never be able to be my true self around them. I just about got through it but by the time I got back to Cambridge I felt like the emotional equivalent of an open wound. So this party is coming at just the right time; it's bound to take my mind off the situation at home and remind me of everything I love about the life I've made for myself.

I scan the room and it's great to see that so many friends have turned up to help me celebrate. Tash is skipping and simpering around in a full 'Like a Virgin' style wedding dress complete with veil and bouquet. She's recently been dumped by her lecturer boyfriend and, after a week of moping around in her pyjamas watching *Dirty Dancing* three times a day, has decided to face the world again. A few feet away from her is Caroline Tits, who's turned up in the long hairpiece and conical bra Madonna wore for the *Blond Ambition* tour. The two girls are currently vying for the attention of the rather handsome captain of the university boat club, who's come to the party in full drag, wearing a flamenco dress similar to the one Madonna wore for 'La Isla Bonita' but with what has to be three-day stubble and make-up that looks like he's put it on in the dark. After seeing how heartbroken Tash was earlier this term, I can't help hoping that she wins, even if her target isn't currently looking his best.

Shanaz has come down from Manchester especially for the party and has ditched her cool street wear to dress up in a baseball outfit like the one Madonna wore in the film *A League of Their Own*. I'm so pleased she's been able to make it as I'm still feeling sad about how much we've grown apart since we went to separate universities. We still see each other at home in the holidays but now that she's living in a student house in Manchester she only comes home for a few days at a time. Over Easter I was desperate to talk to her about coming out to my mum and dad but she didn't want to discuss it for long, preferring to go on and on about a visit she'd just made to the Liverpool superclub Cream. She talked for ages about the drugs she'd taken and exactly how they made her feel, peppering her account with stories about her amazingly cool uni friends. Once again, I found myself resenting them and hating the fact that Shanaz clearly enjoyed spending time with them more than she did with me. Couldn't she remember how close we were? Didn't it matter to her anymore? Whatever the answers, I'm pleased that I've managed to get her down to

Cambridge for the first time, although I'm a bit worried that she won't fit in with my friends and will feel the same way as I did in Manchester.

'How's it going?' I ask hopefully. 'Are you having a good time?'

'Charlie,' she beams, 'this is absolutely hilarious! I've just been talking to some total letch who keeps telling me how much he wants to pull a "hot Asian babe".'

'Oh yeah,' I say, 'that'll be Inappropriate Lee.' I look to my left and see him slinking around in his gimp suit and cracking his whip.

'And there's some weird Scouse bloke in full drag who keeps banging on about Socialism,' she giggles.

'Council House Jack,' I say as I spot him on my right dressed as an early Madonna, complete with bangles, pixie boots, lacy gloves and a black bra wrapped around his head like some kind of helmet. I wonder whether maybe this isn't the best way for her to meet him for the first time.

'What a *weirdo*!' Shanaz scoffs.

I can feel my smile waning. 'But you are enjoying yourself, aren't you?'

'*Yeah!* I've never seen anything as funny in my life!'

I find Shanaz's laughter a bit offensive but try not to show it. I really want her to like all my friends and it's hurtful now to hear her openly making fun of them. I decide that maybe I should introduce her to Nick instead – he'll be sure to make a much better impression. But I look around and can't see him anywhere. Why's he so late?

Standing on the door checking people's invitations is Anthony, who's dressed as the Pope, and Amelia, who's come in Madonna's outfit from 'Papa Don't Preach', complete with a

T-shirt bearing the slogan 'Italians Do It Better'. At the beginning of term, Amelia told me she doesn't think Nick's right for me and her comment hit a raw nerve as I was already starting to worry that he might think *I'm* not right for *him*. When I came back from Bolton I really needed him after the emotional upheaval of coming out to my parents. But if anything he backed away and made excuses about having work to do when I wanted to see him. As a result, I've become increasingly tense around him and haven't been able to sleep properly, thrashing around in bed all night trying to work out what on earth I'm doing wrong. I'm beginning to give up hope of him ever telling me he loves me.

At that point the door opens and Nick finally makes his entrance. He's dressed as the Spanish bullfighter from the 'Take a Bow' video and he even has a red cloth that he whirls over his head with a flourish. As soon as I see him, I feel a familiar fluttering sensation in my stomach. Thank God he's made it at last. I excuse myself from Shanaz and go over to greet him.

'Hiya,' I say, kissing him on the cheek. 'Where've you been?' I realize I sound a bit tetchy.

'Sorry,' he says, looking down sheepishly. 'I had some things to do.'

There's an awkward pause while I wonder what he could possibly have been doing until nearly ten o'clock on a Saturday.

'To be honest,' he goes on, 'it took me ages to get into this costume.' He twirls around so I can take it all in. 'What do you reckon? How do I look?'

There's no doubt about it – with his dark skin, jet-black hair and brooding good looks, he makes a very attractive matador. 'You look gorgeous!' I gush.

He flashes me one of his magical smiles and I feel my heart

tighten with longing. Oh *why* can't he just fall in love with me? Can't he see how amazing it would be if he did?

'Come on,' I swallow, holding out my hand, 'let me introduce you to my best friend from home.'

I pick out Shanaz in the crowd and head over to her with Nick in tow.

'Shanaz,' I begin, tapping her on the shoulder, 'this is Nick.'

'*Nick!*' she trills. 'I've heard so much about you!'

'Oh really?' he asks, turning to give me a smirk. 'What's he said about me then?'

'Oh nothing,' she breathes, 'just that you're the most gorgeous man he's ever met and he's madly in love with you and wants to spend the rest of his life with you. How's that for starters?'

I can feel the heat prickling my face and my palms beginning to sweat. Nick's fiddling with his red cloth awkwardly.

'Oh well,' he stutters, 'it's a bit early to be talking about that kind of thing . . .'

'That's not what Charlie says,' she rattles on. 'According to him the two of you are going to move to London after Cambridge and get a flat together and everything.'

My buttocks are clenched with embarrassment and I try staring fixedly at Shanaz to get her to stop.

'You know what,' she steams on, 'he told me the other day that going out with you is like something out of a Madonna—'

'Yeah, thanks Shanaz,' I interrupt hastily. 'We were just on our way to the bar actually – do you mind if we come back later?'

'Oh, urm, no, urm, don't worry about it.'

I take Nick by the arm and sweep him away. 'Sorry about that,' I breeze, 'I think she must be a bit tipsy.'

'Charlie,' he replies, 'do you think me and you could have a talk at some point?'

I feel a stab of panic. 'Yeah, course we can!' I chirp. 'Can I urm . . . Can I just introduce you to my brother first?'

I desperately check around for Joe and spot him dressed as Dick Tracy in a huge yellow overcoat and matching fedora, flirting with three early Madonnas wearing rosary beads, BOY TOY belt buckles and nothing at all around their midriffs. Joe's travelled all the way down to Cambridge from Newcastle, although I'm sure he doesn't want to be here and has only made the effort to impress Mum and Dad; once I invited him he must have known that it would look unbrotherly if he refused. Mind you, I don't particularly want him here either and only invited him because I thought it would look unbrotherly if I didn't. Anyway, now that he *is* here I'm going to make a point of introducing him to Nick; there's a slight chance that if Joe meets him he'll understand why I've fallen in love and me being gay will suddenly make a lot more sense. At least that's what I'm hoping.

I march over and burst in, giving the early Madonnas the eye so they'll leave us alone. 'Joe,' I announce cheerfully, 'I'd like you to meet Nick.'

Nick steps forward and the two of them stand facing each other, stock still like two cowboys in a spaghetti western. I half expect the theme tune to *The Good, the Bad and the Ugly* to come bursting through the sound system. I can feel my bones sharpen.

'So you're the brother,' sneers Nick.

'And you're the boyfriend,' spits Joe.

'Urm, actually,' I say, 'Nick and I are kind of *seeing each other . . .*'

There's a taut silence.

'Anyway, urm, Joe's . . . Joe's an accountant,' I yelp, desperate to change the subject.

'Well, not yet,' says Joe, 'but I will be once I've passed my exams.'

Nick stifles a yawn. 'But don't you find it boring? All those numbers and figures?'

'Urm, no, not really.'

'Well, *I* couldn't do it,' Nick says. 'What a waste of a life.'

I can sense Joe tensing up further. 'Yeah, but presumably you'll need an accountant one day,' he hisses. 'You know, on the off-chance that you ever get any acting work.'

'Oh and you'd know about that kind of thing, would you?' Nick hits back. 'Have you ever actually been to the theatre?'

This is far worse than I imagined. I'm not sure how to handle things but know that I have to move quickly to avert a crisis.

'Hey Joe,' I say brightly, 'have I introduced you to Tash yet?' I take hold of his arm and deftly steer him away.

'What a *tosser*!' he mouths, looking over his shoulder.

'Well,' I say, 'you weren't particularly nice to him either. You didn't give him a chance.'

'Charlie, what are you on about? He completely laid into me for no reason!'

'Yeah, well, he was probably sticking up for me. He knows you don't approve of him and me being together. How else do you expect him to react?'

'Charlie, that's out of order. Have you ever thought that it might have been difficult for me to come here? Do you think I actually enjoy watching my own brother flouncing around holding hands with blokes?'

He winces as he says it and I think back to how I felt about the idea of two men holding hands before I met Nick. I too found it distasteful until I discovered how wonderful it feels to be in love. Well, I don't care what Joe thinks – and he isn't going to make me go back to being ashamed of myself.

'Oh bollocks, Joe,' I throw back at him. 'You've just got the hump because you're not the golden boy for once. You can't face it that it's *my* party and it's *me* getting all the attention. And you deliberately set out to sabotage it!'

'Charlie, that's complete bullshit!'

'Is it? Is it really?'

The two of us stand still for a moment, spluttering with rage.

Oh why do I always let him get to me so much? I take a deep breath and tell myself to calm down. It's stupid to have a big argument here in the middle of my own party. And I'm certainly not going to spoil my big night for Joe.

'Look, I'm sorry, Joe,' I manage in a much softer tone, 'but me and Nick are going through a bit of a rough patch at the moment. Maybe it was the wrong time for you to meet him after all.'

He looks at the floor and shifts from one foot to another. 'Yeah, well, I'm sorry too. I have to admit, I was a bit arsey with him. I suppose I'm still trying to get my head around the gay thing.'

I'm not sure how much either of us believes what we're saying but not only am I determined not to let Joe spoil my party, I also don't want him going home and telling Mum and Dad I fell out with him. I expect he's thinking the same thing and that's why he's eager to keep the peace.

'I tell you what,' I offer, 'why don't we just forget that the last half-hour ever happened?'

'All right,' he concedes, 'maybe we should.'

I hold out my hand and he shakes it.

Relieved to have averted a crisis, I realize that I need to keep Joe occupied. I look around to see if I can spot Tash and just about make her out in the distance. She's dancing with a rather bedraggled Rent-a-leg, who by now has deserted her post behind the bar and is flailing herself around to the music, completely out of time and looking more like something out of *The Rocky Horror Picture Show* than Madonna. I politely pull Tash away and introduce her to Joe. Thankfully, they seem to hit it off straight away and before long Tash is wearing Joe's fedora and he has her wedding veil plonked on top of his head. I decide to make my excuses and head for the bar – I need a drink before I can face Nick again. I down three glasses of punch one after the other and then shudder as the aftertaste hits me.

I look around for Nick and catch sight of him leaning on the grand piano talking to a boy dressed in full military garb as Juan Perón. To my astonishment, they're gazing into each other's eyes and leaning closer and closer together.

Oh no. Please don't let this be happening.

'Hey, Charlie,' comes a voice from behind me, 'is everything all right with you and Nick?' It's Adrian the poet, who, despite wearing a blonde wig and a pink dress similar to Madonna's in the 'Material Girl' video, still manages to look uncannily like John Lennon.

'I don't know,' I croak, blinking as I struggle to take it in. 'It doesn't look like it, does it?'

He starts to stammer a reply but before he can finish I leave the room, grabbing Amelia on the way. As we dash across the Tudor courtyard I quickly explain the situation and then lead her to the hidden toilets better known to students as 'the secret pisser'. I'm in dire need of an emergency conference.

'Oh Amelia,' I moan once we're safely locked in a cubicle, 'this whole night's turning into an absolute nightmare!'

'Don't say that,' she says. 'It's a wicked party and you shouldn't let anyone spoil it.'

'Yeah, well, I think it's a bit late for that. Shanaz completely showed me up in front of Nick, me and Joe have just had a blazing row, and now Nick's flirting with some guy dressed as Colonel Perón.'

'Hmm,' she muses, biting her lip, 'he isn't Chinese, is he?'

'Yeah. Why do you say that?'

'Charlie, this probably isn't the right time to tell you but I think that's the guy he went skiing with at Easter.'

'You what? I thought he went with a group of friends?'

'Well, that's not what I heard.'

Of course he didn't go with a group of friends. Of course he went with somebody he fancies more than me.

I let out a mournful sigh. 'But why didn't you tell me this before?'

'I did try,' she frowns, 'I tried broaching the subject several times. But you didn't seem to want to listen.'

I look up at the ceiling. 'Oh God – how totally humiliating! I feel like such a dick!'

She puts her hand on my shoulder and gives it a squeeze. 'Don't feel like that, Charlie – *you've* done nothing wrong.'

'Hmpf! Apart from falling for a guy who's totally out of my league. And then coming on so strong that I completely scare him off. God, I can't believe how stupid I've been to ever think someone like Nick would fall in love with *me*.'

'Now you really are being silly.'

'Am I? Am I really? Look in there, Amelia – the evidence suggests otherwise. You know, however hard I try, I guess I'll just always be some unpopular freak from Bolton.'

Amelia puts her hand on my shoulder. 'Charlie, you're all worked up and you're obviously not thinking straight; that's not true at all. Just think about all those people in there tonight – the party's full to bursting and they're all your friends. *They* all love you, Charlie.'

I scoff. 'Yeah and Nick's about to get off with someone else in front of the whole lot of them.'

The very thought of it makes my body freeze. I love being at the centre of such an amazing group of friends and I'm thrilled that they've all come together to celebrate my birthday. But my boyfriend (or whatever he wants to call himself) is about to blow it all by rubbing my nose in my inadequacies in front of them all. Well, I'm not going to let him get away with it. I stand up sharply.

'Listen, I'm really sorry, Amelia.'

She looks confused. 'What for?'

'For not listening to you in the first place. If I'd followed your advice months ago, I wouldn't be in this mess now.' Or at least I wouldn't be about to be humiliated in public. I open the door and walk out.

'Oh don't worry about that!' she calls after me. 'Charlie, that's not important at all!' Her words echo behind me as I stride across the courtyard.

I storm into Old Hall and go straight over to the bar. I'm already feeling drunk but want to get totally obliterated now. Willing Nick to fall in love with me has been completely exhausting and I've just about had enough. But as well as being furious with him I'm much more furious with myself and just want to drink through it. I down some more punch with an angry edge and survey the room with a new determination.

Everywhere I look, people's disguises have disintegrated into a drunken mess. I can just about make out Caroline Tits, whose conical bra is by now so skew-whiff that one boob's much higher than the other. Rent-a-leg can't stand up straight after breaking one of her stiletto heels and I watch her crash into Council House Jack, who's feeling his way forward, his black bra now wrapped around his eyes like a blindfold. Just behind them stands Tash, looking rather less like a virgin than when she first arrived, her lips clamped onto Joe's and her hand rummaging around in his trousers. He's obviously calmed down since our little altercation. But where on earth's Nick?

I finally spot him, leaning against the stone fireplace, twiddling flirtatiously with his matador's red cloth and pawing at Perón's military medals – in full view of everyone. I watch him with my bleary eyes and can feel an intense rage rise up within me. It might be my fault he's cheating on me but that doesn't mean I have to stand for it.

By the time I've fought my way across the room, Nick looks like he's on the verge of making the initial lunge forward into a full-on snog. I tell myself that if I wait any longer then things are going to get *really* humiliating. I take a deep breath and step unceremoniously between them.

'Oh hi, Charlie,' Nick says calmly. 'This is one cool party!'

'I know,' I say, 'and it feels absolutely wicked to be so *fantastically popular!*' I look at him expectantly but there's no reply. All around us I'm aware that people are stopping what they're doing to come over and listen.

'Anyway,' I continue, 'what's going on with Colonel Perón

here? The two of you look like you're about to get off with each other!'

Nick glances around anxiously. 'Charlie, urm, this is my friend Jon – we met a couple of months ago.'

Jon nervously holds out his hand but I decline to shake it.

'So you're the guy he's been two-timing me with!' I wail.

By now the entire room has fallen silent and I'm aware of countless pairs of eyes looking at us. I don't know what to say next but know that I have to see this through. And now everyone's watching I have to somehow save face too.

Nick seems slightly shaken by the turn the conversation's taking. 'Listen, Charlie,' he says, 'I did explain several times that I didn't want to get too serious . . .'

'And what's that supposed to mean? I thought we were "seeing each other"!'

'Yeah, exactly. Which means we're free to see *other* people too.'

'But I don't *want* to see any other people!'

'Yeah, well, I'm sorry, Charlie, but I do.'

I stand silent for a moment, struggling to take it all in. Although at the same time it makes complete sense. Nick always told me this was how he felt but for some reason I chose not to hear it, for some reason I chose to carry on. And part of me always knew it would end like this. Part of me was always expecting it. Well, it's one thing for him to tell me I'm not good enough for him in private but another thing for him to do it by cheating on me in public.

'You absolute bastard!' I gasp. 'You completely led me on!'

'Charlie, that's not fair. I didn't ask you to fall in love with me!'

With every word it feels as if he's humiliating me even more – and twisting in the knife of my self-loathing. I can't listen to any more.

Unsure of what else to do, I step forward and slap him across the face.

All around me there's a sharp intake of breath and I feel like I'm living through a particularly melodramatic episode of *Dallas*. Nick's mouth gapes wide open as he rubs his stinging cheek with his hand. The only sound that can be heard is that of Madonna singing about true love in 'True Blue'.

As I listen to the song, I can feel my chin starting to tremble. For a brief moment I'm able to view the scene as an outsider and see myself standing there yelling at Nick, surrounded by all my friends. I wonder how on earth I've ended up in this position when just a few weeks ago I was convinced I was in the midst of true love.

Thankfully, someone goes over to the sound system and switches off the music. We're plunged into a tension-filled silence and I tell myself that I have to round things up soon before I lose my nerve and burst into tears in front of everyone. I brace myself to deliver my parting shot.

'From now on, Nick, you and me are *over*!'

There's another gasp from the crowd and I can hear my words reverberate around the room.

'Did you hear that? You're *dumped*!'

I nod my head triumphantly and there's a sudden eruption of gossipy chatter all around me.

Nick stares at me in disbelief. 'But Charlie, we weren't—'

'Charlie nothing,' I yap, cutting him dead. 'You're a slimy, self-obsessed sleazeball and you can pick up your red rag and leave right now. You too, Perón – come on, off you go!'

I watch as Nick straightens himself up, struggling to maintain his pride. For a second I almost cave in and take it all back. Out of the corner of my eye I spot Joe and try not to look at him. I know he's apologized but, after what happened earlier, I'm sure he'll be loving every second of this.

I realize that my arms are shaking and I do my best to keep still. Amelia catches my eye and gives me an encouraging wink. I step to one side as Nick turns and flounces out, Perón scurrying along behind him.

Everyone around me cheers.

'Well done, Charlie!'

'That was so *cool*!'

I smile and thank them but can't take my eyes off Nick as the door closes behind him. Oh being in love with him was so exhilarating and uplifting and made me feel like maybe I just might be a slightly better person than the one everyone hated for all those years. When I was seeing Nick I didn't remember all the things people used to say about me – and they certainly didn't seem to matter. But it turns out the kids at school were telling the truth all along and now I just feel rotten inside. Rotten but also in a weird way *right*. Because I can't help thinking I've got what I deserve.

I decide to plaster on my brave face and swallow my emotions. My Adam's apple feels like it's swollen to the size of a football. I clear my throat and struggle on.

'Right then,' I trill, clapping my hands together loudly, 'let's get on with this party. Now who's going to switch that music back on?'

Ray of Light

I can't believe that after just three years in Cambridge, it's already time for me to leave. It's a bright summer's day and the town is looking particularly beautiful. All along the Backs the college gardens are in full bloom and tour guides punt wide-eyed tourists up and down the river as smiling students cycle past, enjoying the attention. I lap it up for what I know will be the last time.

My academic career ended this morning with a graduation ceremony in the Senate House with Mum, Dad and Grandma watching from the audience. I was really nervous about them coming down to Cambridge as things are still awkward between us. Dad's so unhappy about me being gay that he's forbidden me from telling Grandma, insisting that she'll find it way too upsetting. More upsetting for me is his resolute refusal to discuss anything to do with my personal life in case the gay thing somehow crops up. Obviously, this rules out having any kind of meaningful conversation whatsoever but we somehow manage to muddle on. On the surface we probably seem like a perfectly functioning family but I feel uncomfortable with the understanding we've gradually settled into and I object to the fact that I'm supposed to sympathize with how difficult Mum and Dad are finding the fact that I'm gay; doesn't it occur to them that I might have found it difficult too?

Thankfully, I manage to control my anger at my graduation, possibly because there are so many other emotions swirling around. After the ceremony, we all spill out onto the lawn of the Senate House, where my fellow students and I congratulate each other while armies of tourists look on from behind the railings. We each pose for photos in our caps and gowns, our families eager to document what everyone keeps telling us is a key moment in our lives. My mum snaps off several shots I'm sure will be made up of two thirds sky with me, Dad and Grandma in the bottom corner of the frame, while Dad takes so long pressing the shutter button that by the time he takes each photo we've all started frowning and looking away. But however the pictures turn out, it's clear my family are enjoying my graduation experience.

'Well done, lad,' says Dad, putting his arm around me and giving me a squeeze. 'You've made me proper proud.'

'Yeah,' adds Mum, 'and don't think we don't know how hard you've worked. You've come a long way to get here, much further than a lot of your friends. I hope you remember that.'

I nod and smile but, although it's lovely to receive their praise, I realize for the first time that I don't feel pathetically grateful.

After we're ushered out of the grounds of the Senate House, we have a meal scheduled in the same room where my life in Cambridge began – St Christopher's Formal Hall. Mum and Dad initially seem intimidated by the whole thing and I recognize on their faces a feeling of awkwardness I remember from my own first time in Formal Hall. I whisper to them which knives and forks they should be using and they look at me with a gratitude that I can't help finding affecting.

Luckily, Mum and Dad get on well with the other parents at

lunch so I don't have to worry about them not fitting in. We sit next to Amelia's family and Mum chats away to her mum about cooking and contraception while Dad becomes engrossed in a discussion about the Italian football league with her Juventus-supporting dad. Unfortunately, one person who doesn't fit in quite so well is Grandma, who's like a fish out of water from the very start. She smothers her food in salt, asks for brown sauce with the main course and then heaps five teaspoons of sugar into her cup of tea. At the end of the meal she casually lights up a Benson and Hedges and the catering staff have to rush over and usher her outside. I spot Dad cringe with embarrassment and realize right then that he reacts to his mum in exactly the same way in which I react to him and my mum. I suddenly feel guilty and creep outside to join Grandma.

'Hey Gran, have you got a spare fag?'

Her face brightens up. 'Course I have, cocker!' She fumbles in her handbag and lights me a cigarette. 'I didn't know you smoked.'

'Yeah, well . . . You won't tell Mum and Dad, will you?'

'Will I 'eckers like!'

We giggle conspiratorially as we each chuff away on our cigarette.

'*I* don't know,' she sighs after a while. 'Who'd have thought one of my lot would end up down here? Graduating from Cambridge University!'

I smile. 'What do you think of it, Gran? Did you enjoy the ceremony?'

'Well, it was very posh but I didn't have the foggiest what it all meant. All that kneeling down and pulling on the old bloke's fingers. *And* it was all in Latin. How was I supposed to follow that?'

'Yeah, well, don't tell anyone but I couldn't tell what was going on either. To be honest I don't think anyone could.'

We both chuckle and breathe out a cloud of smoke.

'How about the meal, though?' I ask. 'Did you enjoy that?'

'Oh I'm not sure really – it was a bit different to what I'm used to. You have to remember I was brought up on fish-head soup and sugar butties. The only treat I got was when it was my birthday and my dad would let me have the top off his boiled egg. To be honest, cocker, I don't really know *what* to think about this kind of do.'

I smile and take a drag on my cigarette. 'Well, whatever you think, please don't feel out of place.'

'I'll try not to, cocker.'

At that point we're called back in for the speeches.

'Come on,' I say, stubbing out my cigarette. 'We'd better make a move.'

She touches my arm and pulls me back. 'You know what, Charlie? I might feel a bit daft in there but you've still made me a very proud grandma. And this is one of the happiest days of my life.'

'Aw, thanks, Gran.'

'No, thank *you*, Charlie. It's all down to you; you did this on your own. And it's all right for us to feel proud of you but you must make sure you feel proud of yourself too.'

I can feel my chin start to wobble as the tears well up in my eyes. 'Thanks, Grandma. That means a lot.'

She drops her cigarette onto the floor and stamps it out. I hold out my arm so she can link it but she starts rummaging around in her bag. ''Ere,' she says with a naughty wink, 'do you want a mint?'

We shuffle back into the hall and make it to our seats just in time to hear the speech by the College President. Professor Potts is a short, portly man with eyebrows as thick as moustaches and the ruddy cheeks and penis-veined nose of a heavy drinker. He looks like he's had a few too many today – he staggers over to the microphone and slurs his way through his final address to those of us who are leaving.

'This is your time,' he booms directly into the microphone, causing the speakers to screech with feedback. 'And you owe it to us all to make the most of the chances you've been given.'

As he speaks, I tingle with excitement at the thought of the dazzling future that lies ahead. I can see that Dad has a lump in his throat and Mum has a tear in the corner of her eye. After everything that's happened between us recently, I can't help smiling inside.

'Now get out there and make it happen!' Professor Potts slurs before stumbling to his chair and dropping into it with a thud.

A few hours later, our President is safely in bed and the graduation formalities have come to an end. Caps and gowns have been discarded and the students have changed into much more comfortable clothes to enjoy the summer weather. Amelia and I lead our families out of college and across the river to our favourite pub, The Mill. We spread a pair of rugs out on the lawn by the river and settle down to an evening lolling around and drinking Pimm's.

From where I'm sitting, I overhear the names Cher and Barbra Streisand and realize that Mum's chatting to Amelia's mum about how it's actually becoming quite fashionable to have a gay child. As I listen to her speak I wonder who she's trying to convince – Amelia's mum or herself. Thankfully,

Dad's sitting out of earshot, absorbed in a debate with Amelia's dad about the comparative merits of Italian pasta and the British chip. And Anthony comes to join us and begins an impassioned explanation of his artistic motivations to my distinctly bewildered-looking Grandma.

'What fascinates me about sculpture . . .' he says, 'isn't the piece itself . . . but the cracks it leaves behind in the mould that shapes it . . .'

I watch as Grandma gazes at him blankly.

'For me as an artist . . .' Anthony goes on, 'the relationship between sculpture and mould . . . is an organic metaphor for . . . the dynamic interplay between the individual and the society that forms us . . .'

There's a pause and Grandma grasps nervously for another cigarette. 'Well, by gum,' she mouths, 'it sounds smashin', cocker.'

Before long we're joined by Tash, whose dad and new stepmother disappeared as soon as the graduation ceremony ended, making some excuse about having a cocktail party to attend in Chelsea. She brushes this off as she floats in, saying a sunny hello to everyone and then lying down in the sun next to Amelia and me. She promptly spreads out a stack of bridal magazines on the grass for us to inspect.

'Now, do you think I should go for a ring like this one that Prince Rainier bought Grace Kelly?' she breezes. 'Or would you prefer something like this that Richard Burton gave Liz Taylor?'

Perhaps unsurprisingly, things ended between Tash and Joe when he went back to Newcastle after my party. He rather abruptly put a stop to anything developing, saying he wasn't ready for a long-distance relationship and knew that it wouldn't work out anyway. Obviously Tash and I had spent ages joking about how funny it would be if we were in-laws, but I'd found it difficult to have one of my best mates gushing about how great my brother was and was secretly relieved when it ended. Fortunately, Tash soon got over the disappointment and within months had fallen madly in love with an eerily humourless, white-blond law graduate called Mauritz, who speaks like Arnold Schwarzenegger and looks like a Swedish hitman from a Bond film.

'Now Tash,' says Amelia, 'don't you think you're jumping the gun a bit? I mean, you've only known Mauritz a short while.'

Tash holds up her hand and brushes aside Amelia's objections. 'Yeah, but you know how it is,' she breathes. 'When you realize someone's The One, it *totally* feels right straight away.'

I can tell that Amelia's losing her patience and decide to move the conversation on. I ask the girls how they're feeling about leaving Cambridge after all this time. Amelia says that she's calm and confident about the future; her plan is to train as a teacher so she can support Anthony while he launches his career as an artist. For the second half of her degree she changed subjects from Languages to Sociology because she couldn't bear to leave Anthony for the third year abroad and then to graduate a year after him. She's made no secret of her dream of getting married and starting a family as soon as possible, a dream she reiterates for us now.

'Oh I know it might not sound particularly ambitious,' she says, 'but I sometimes think that all I want out of life is to be just like my mum and dad. I mean, if Anthony and I get to grow old together surrounded by a load of kids, then that'll do me to be quite honest.'

'And where do you think you'll settle?' I ask.

'Oh back in North London, eventually. I don't want to be

too far from my mum and dad, especially once we start having a family.'

I think back to what Mum said about me coming further in life than some of my friends. From what Amelia's saying, her ultimate goal is to end up right back where she started. So maybe Mum's right. Then again, Amelia isn't desperate to escape a hometown that didn't accept her, a thought I'm now able to experience without any guilt.

Tash has very different plans to Amelia and she's itching to put them into action. Her dream's still to become a professional actress and she's already managed to find herself a hotshot agent.

'My only problem now,' she sighs, 'is convincing a casting director to take a chance on me. I mean, how am I going to stand out from all those desperate wannabes, manically flashing their eyes and teeth and pouting away with their blow-job lips?'

I laugh but can't help worrying how she'll cope. There's no question that she's very talented but I've already learnt enough about the theatre to know that doesn't necessarily guarantee success. And Tash's fragility might be what makes her a great actress but that same quality might also make her unable to deal with rejection or criticism.

'What do you think, guys?' she asks hopefully. 'Do you think I'll make it?'

'Of course you will,' we both chorus. 'There's no question at all!'

'Just think,' she squeaks excitedly, 'in a few months' time I could be standing on the West End stage, taking my first bow to *rapturous* applause! I bet my dad would stick around then . . .'

I give her a supportive smile, knowing how much his earlier departure must have hurt her. But I admire the way she isn't letting it stand in the way of achieving the future she wants.

I too am brimming with determination to make my mark on the working world. When I split up with Nick I decided to forget about true love for a while and instead to concentrate on my career. Over the last year my open-air production of *Twelfth Night* was a big success and I also directed a popular take on *A Streetcar Named Desire* by Tennessee Williams. It all served to further distance me from my original dream of becoming a writer and to reinforce my ambition of becoming a professional theatre director. Ever since finishing my finals, my mind has whirled with images of West End openings, five-star reviews and thunderously loud standing ovations. There's no doubt about it – right now I'm ready for a high-powered life in the premier league of glamour. And I'm bursting with so much positive energy sometimes I feel like I can fly.

The idea makes me think of Madonna's latest album, *Ray of Light*. During our final term at Cambridge, it's been a big favourite with the girls and me and the title track has become something of an anthem for us. With its infectious energy and frantic drive it's the perfect complement to our outlook right now and just before graduating we gave each other a silver bracelet engraved with a variation on the main lyric – 'Quicker than a ray of light we're flying'.

The bracelets were intended as good luck charms for the future and as I look at mine glinting in the sunlight I feel a rush of excitement thinking of everything I'm going to achieve. It's been great to see Mum and Dad proud of me again today but that's nothing compared to how I'm going to make them feel soon.

Professor Potts was right – this is my time. And nothing in the world is going to hold me back.

Part Three

Causing a Commotion

It isn't until months and months after graduation that I'm finally on my way to my first day's work. As I stride along to my new office, I try to will myself into feeling confident. I really want to make a good impression, not least because it took me so long to find this job.

After leaving Cambridge I slunk off home to Bolton and straight away began looking for employment. I wrote to every theatre in Britain but didn't secure a single meeting. Trying not to be too disheartened, I wrote to them all again offering my services for free but still no one was interested. The steady trickle of rejection chipped away at my self-confidence and there were days when I thought it had damaged my soul.

I took to spending hours on end lying on my bed listening to Madonna, trying to convince myself that I *was* good enough to be employed and I *would* find a job. It didn't help that Shanaz had gone straight into her training to be a doctor so didn't really understand what I was going through and nor did anyone in my family, who've always seemed suspicious of a career I think they imagine will take me further away from them. I began to think my time in Cambridge might have been a brief bright spot in what was otherwise going to be a dull, unexciting life.

Just when my morale was at its lowest I spotted an advert for a job as a trainee researcher on a cable TV channel specializing in 'adult entertainment'. By this point my finances were becoming a serious problem and I had to consider any option that would allow me to start paying off my debts. So I sent off my application, went for an interview and somehow got the job.

At the moment, anarchy's in fashion on TV and series like *The Big Breakfast* and *Eurotrash* are hugely popular. The show I'll be working on is a magazine series called *The Third Nipple* and is billed as a 'wacky weekly round-up of the wild and the weird'. Professor Potts certainly didn't mention anything like that in his speech after our graduation ceremony. I look at my bracelet engraved with the lyrics to 'Ray of Light' and wonder whether a more appropriate choice might have been 'Causing a Commotion'.

I decide to put on a brave face and remind myself that Madonna was forced to slave her way through a series of dead-end jobs before eventually achieving her ambitions. Didn't she work as a cloakroom attendant in a nightclub and even a waitress in Dunkin' Donuts at one point? Well, in the long run it obviously didn't do her any harm. In fact, I'm sure she's spoken in interviews about some of these experiences making her stronger. I feel reassured and decide to face the challenge before me head-on.

The good news is that my new job's based in London so I didn't waste any time in moving into a flat with Amelia, who's already well into her teacher-training course, and Tash, who's newly single again after Mauritz dumped her for a frizzy-haired hippie called Sheila who apparently doesn't wear a bra or deodorant. Tash was so upset that she broke her own record of watching *Dirty Dancing* seventeen times in one week and only snapped out of it when Amelia and I forced her to come out flat-hunting with us. We skipped around London together, chatting away about whether we should opt for a flat like Gwyneth Paltrow's in *Sliding Doors* or Hugh Grant's in *Notting Hill*. Unfortunately, we soon discovered that all the three of us could afford were a few damp rooms in Hackney above The Booze Brothers, a shabby off-licence run by two unfeasibly tattooed Scotsmen.

On the day we moved in, there was a tramp sitting outside our door drinking Special Brew, a rusty old shopping trolley parked against the wall and a rat the size of a small dog scurrying across the pavement, nibbling on an abandoned Barbie doll with only one leg. I looked down the street and could see three big yellow police signs asking for witnesses to come forward in cases of armed robbery, serious assault and gang violence that had recently taken place in the neighbourhood. It wasn't exactly what I'd expected but I was determined not to feel too down about it. I quickly adjusted the cinematic London playing in my head from the idyllic, wholesome setting of *Four Weddings and a Funeral* to the much edgier urban grit of *Lock Stock and Two Smoking Barrels*.

Now that I've settled into the flat I'm ready to start work. Granted, my new job's far from perfect but I'm just going to have to make the most of it. I swallow my pride as I head towards *The Third Nipple*'s production offices in the basement of an industrial estate in Mile End. I'm wearing the smart new suit my parents bought me as a graduation present, carrying everything I need in a briefcase with my brand new Motorola mobile phone clipped to my belt. I obviously can't afford one but scrimped and saved for months, telling myself that the only way to earn the respect of my future colleagues was to adopt the look of a top TV executive. I desperately hope it works and try to think positively so that I'll give off an aura of gravitas and authority.

When I arrive at the offices I'm met at reception by a young mixed-race girl who introduces herself as Charlotte, the series runner. She's dressed in the ultra-trendy combination of cargo pants and tight-fitting vest top that reminds me of something I've seen in an All Saints video. I tell her I'm Charlie and that I'm nervous about my first day's work. She looks me up and down disapprovingly and I wonder if maybe she doesn't like the suit. 'Innit' is all she says, although I have no idea what she actually means.

I make another attempt at conversation as we trot down the stairs to the basement. 'Our names are quite similar,' I observe brightly. 'Does anyone call you Charlie?' She seems entirely uninterested and continues chewing her gum in silence. I hope they aren't all going to be like this.

As we enter the basement, I'm confronted by the sight of the entire team looking up from their desks to check me out. The first thing I notice is that every single one of them is casually dressed – and several of them are wearing the latest fashions. I suddenly become aware of just how formal and out of place I look, and smile awkwardly. My stomach plummets as it dawns on me that I'm in the process of making a complete fool of myself.

With an obvious lack of enthusiasm, Charlotte leads me around the office and introduces me to the team. Thankfully, everyone else is much friendlier than she is. There's a Production Manager called Cathy, a thin-lipped Northern Irish woman who I can't help thinking looks like Marge Simpson dressed in double denim. She speaks so fast it's hard to keep up with her and as she does so subjects those around her to a relentless spray of saliva. 'Great to meet you,' she says, a drop of spit landing right in the corner of my eye.

Next up is a posh-looking reporter called Elizabeth who's wearing a Hackett sports top and a gold signet ring and speaks in a voice so plummy that it's difficult to tell what she's saying. Charlotte introduces her as 'Fuck-It Liz' and I soon learn that she's earned this nickname because of her staggeringly frequent use of the F-word. 'Fucking nice to meet you,' she offers, obviously not wanting to disappoint.

Shortly afterwards, another reporter comes over and introduces himself. 'Hi Charlie,' he says in the campest voice I've ever heard, 'I'm Mike Brewer.' About five years older than me, Mike's gym-honed and immaculately groomed with short dark hair, a nicely maintained tan and a smile that reveals a perfect set of dazzlingly white teeth. He's dressed in Acupuncture trainers, baggy combat trousers and a black hoodie I'm sure I saw J from 5ive wearing on *CD:UK*. I'm just about to breathe a sigh of relief that no one's commented on my own fashion faux pas when Mike bursts in as if reading my thoughts. 'First things first,' he chirps, 'what on *earth* are you wearing?'

I squirm. 'Er, it's, it's – it's a new suit.'

'Well, I can see that. It's just that the last time *I* wore a suit, I was at a pinstripe party in a bar full of benders in King's Cross. Didn't anyone tell you? *Nobody* wears a suit on telly!'

I blush bright red and don't know what to say.

'Oh don't worry about it, Cambridge boy – give us a couple of weeks and we'll soon break you in.'

He cackles naughtily and I manage to force out a nervous laugh.

Mercifully, at this point Charlotte moves me on to show me to my desk. Straight away I notice there's a computer on it. I hand-wrote all my essays at Cambridge and haven't really used computers, let alone email or the internet that everyone seems to be talking about these days. It all seems very modern and hi-tech and I suddenly wish I were back in the old library at St Christopher's.

Before I have time to worry, Charlotte whisks me onwards and deposits me in the office of the Series Producer, Fran Tucker. Fran stands up to meet me and I see that she's about thirty-five, has short, spiky hair, and is wearing a Stussy track-suit and big plastic glasses. There's something about her that reminds me of a pit bull terrier. 'Hi,' she booms in a surprisingly masculine voice, 'you must be my new bitch.'

'Urm, yeah,' I stammer, not sure of the appropriate response, 'I'm Charlie Matthews.'

She pumps my hand and I do my best to give her a smile.

'Fran Tucker,' she bellows, 'but you can call me Mother-tucker.'

I wonder if she's what people call a ball-breaker. I suspect she probably is.

We sit down opposite each other and Mothertucker talks me through how things work on the show and what my responsibilities are. She explains that I'll be working alongside the two reporters, helping them develop story ideas, carry out the research and then assisting on shoots. She warns me that I'll be 'thrown in at the deep end' and it'll be a 'baptism of fire' and is keen to impress upon me that 'the most important thing in this game is to be proactive'. 'But there's nothing to worry about,' she says. 'Spend a few days getting up to speed and we'll touch base towards the end of the week.'

Before I have time to stop and think, a meeting's called and everyone clusters around Mothertucker in an area of the office that consists of two enormous sofas and a coffee table. I sink into one of the sofas until my bum's practically touching the floor and lay my briefcase flat on my knees. Mike and Liz plonk themselves on either side, sandwiching me in tightly. I must look like a total stiff and curse myself for doing such a bad job of projecting the image of a top TV executive.

Mothertucker begins proceedings by formally introducing me and welcoming me onto the team. 'Now as you can see,' she booms, 'Charlie's joining us from Cambridge so he might need some Londonizing.'

Everyone laughs and my heart begins pounding so violently I can hear it in my ears. I unbutton my collar and loosen my tie. So much for 'getting out there and making it happen'. I wonder what Professor Potts would say if he could see me now.

There's a pause and I wonder if I'm supposed to say something. I'm just about to open my mouth when Mothertucker rattles on and initiates a discussion about last week's programme.

My new colleagues spend the next half an hour earnestly dissecting every finest detail of a piece of television that included a report on a new stage show called *Naked Men Talk Cock*, an interview with an S&M dominatrix who used to be a novice nun, and a profile of a dance academy in Tooting that is cashing in on the new craze for lap dancing by offering lessons in stripping, flirting and pole dancing. I look at my bracelet and think it really should read 'Causing a Commotion'. I remember how invincible I felt on graduation day and shudder in humiliation. I certainly won't be winning my first Olivier any time soon.

'And now for something completely different,' bellows Mothertucker. 'Who wants to get the ball rolling with ideas for this week's show?'

Mike jumps in first with a suggestion to film behind the scenes of a new one-man show starring a man who paints portraits with his penis. 'God knows how he does it,' he says, 'but clearly his dick's very talented. I was thinking I could go backstage and see if he needs a fluffer.' I'm about to jump in and ask what a fluffer is when I realize from the expressions on everyone's faces that I'm the only one who doesn't know. I decide to keep quiet.

'That idea gets the green light,' announces a businesslike Mothertucker, jotting down notes in her pad. 'Now who's next?'

Cathy pipes up and suggests an interview with Desperate Dawn, a porn star who's attempting to break the world record for having sex with the highest number of men in one film. 'The film's called *The Crack of Dawn*,' Cathy elaborates, sprinkling a cloud of saliva onto the whole team, 'and we're being offered access-all-areas on set. I think it sounds like a great craic!'

Fran doesn't seem too impressed. 'Same old, same old,' she dismisses with a wave of her hand, 'and it's a bit vanilla for *The Third Nipple* – let's put it on the backburner for now.' I wonder how many more clichés she'll use during the course of the meeting. 'What I really want is for you all to think laterally,' she continues, 'to think outside the box.'

At this point, Liz suggests a report on a group of S & M enthusiasts she's discovered whose activities apparently deviate from the usual master/slave routine. 'This bunch of freaks fuck off into the forest and dress up as fucking ponycarters,' she explains. 'Basically, half of them put on upper-class Victorian costumes and the other half are harnessed up like fucking horses and then they pull them along in full-on fucking ponycarts. I think it'd be funny as fuck if I went along with them on one of their outings and joined in with the whole fucking thing. Except for the fucking, that is!'

I gulp and realize that during her entire speech I've been fiddling nervously with my bracelet. What on earth have I let myself in for?

Mothertucker's a little more enthusiastic. She nods decisively and announces that she's a 'happy bunny'. 'That certainly hits my spot,' she approves.

I notice that everyone's looking at me expectantly.

'Charlie,' Mothertucker barks, 'you're in the hot seat. Fire away!'

I can feel my mouth going dry. Now's the moment for me to come forward with an idea of my own. All of a sudden it's as if the last three years haven't happened – I feel like that clueless boy from Bolton again, desperate to make a good impression and terrified of what people will think of me. I suddenly wonder how on earth I've ended up in this ridiculous position, pitching for programme ideas on some tacky soft porn channel I haven't even watched. I have to stop myself from screwing up my face but then remind myself that I've no choice but to make the most of it. I decide to do my best to loosen up and not be so repressed or inhibited.

'The only thing we're missing,' Mothertucker goes on, 'is something really topical, something that makes us look like we've got our finger on the pulse.'

'Oh!' I blurt out. 'I've got it! I read in the paper this morning that it's National Disability Week . . .'

As I speak, I become acutely aware of the sound of my own voice and realize that I'm looking out onto a mass of blank expressions. I suddenly wonder why I ever thought National Disability Week would interest the viewers of a cable porn channel. Never mind – it's too late to turn back now. 'Urm, c-c-could we maybe do something to tie in with that . . . ?'

There's a stony silence and I notice Charlotte trying to stifle a giggle. Mothertucker looks at me with her mouth wide open. After what seems like ages the silence is finally broken by Mike.

'Actually,' he says, 'Charlie might have a point.'

'Go on,' says a dubious-looking Mothertucker, 'I'm all ears.'

'Well,' he says, 'couldn't we do something about sex for the disabled?'

I sense several eyebrows being raised with interest.

'I mean, just because you're in a wheelchair doesn't mean you stop wanting to have sex, does it?'

'Hmm,' muses Mothertucker, 'now we're cooking on gas.'

'Apparently,' Liz joins in, 'there are hookers in Amsterdam who cater especially for the fucking disabled.'

This wasn't quite what I had in mind but Mothertucker inches forward onto the edge of her seat.

'Hey, we could always interview that topless model,' chirps Mike. 'You know – the one with the peg leg.'

Mothertucker looks ecstatic. 'Now we're all singing from the same hymn sheet!'

'And what about all those dwarves who work in porn?' spits Cathy. 'Couldn't we interview some of those too?'

'Bullseye!' spouts Mothertucker.

'Just a minute,' I venture, 'I don't think you can count dwarves as being disabled . . .'

'Oh don't worry about that,' she says, 'it's all swings and roundabouts – six of one and half a dozen of the other.'

'The thing is, though,' I point out, 'I really don't think we should sensationalize the subject.'

Mothertucker pretends she hasn't heard me and ploughs on. 'Right, that idea gets the go-ahead. Now let's strike while the iron's hot and get onto it PDQ!'

I'm not quite sure what I've done but decide to put aside my objections and look on the positive side; I've just got my first story on TV.

'Charlie Matthews,' gushes Mothertucker, 'you're a broadcasting genius!'

I start to feel better and can almost sense my confidence rushing back. If my new boss thinks I'm a genius then maybe this whole set-up isn't going to be such a disaster after all. I reason that I might not be on the verge of becoming an internationally celebrated theatre director but reassure myself that maybe I'm more suited to the much more down-to-earth medium of TV. Now that I think about it, theatre can be terribly stuffy, po-faced and worthy – maybe telly will be a better fit for me. And working on *The Third Nipple* might just turn out to be a masterstroke in career planning.

The outlook suddenly seems much brighter and I give my new colleagues a big smile. 'Causing a Commotion' indeed! I've only been here a few hours and it looks like I'm settling in nicely.

Now if only I wasn't wearing this stupid suit.

Music

Over a year later, my work on *The Third Nipple* pays me an unexpected dividend. It gives me something I've waited my whole life for – the chance to meet Madonna.

This comes at a time when the world's gone Madonna-mad once more. Her song 'Music' is at number one in the charts and she's brought the cowboy look back into fashion. Following her lead, I've ditched running and taken up yoga, as has everyone else from Tash and Amelia to Geri Halliwell and Ricky Martin. And best of all for those of us who live here, Madonna has made London the coolest city in the world.

Ever since she fell in love with Guy Ritchie and moved to the UK, I've been able to feel Madonna getting closer. I've seen paparazzi photos of her out and about in places I know and have even been to and have become convinced that it's only a matter of time till I get to meet her. Every morning while I sit on the Tube, I plan what I'll say during our first conversation; I've decided that I won't gush all over her as it's really important not to seem like too much of an adoring fan. Instead, I'll be the epitome of cool, earning her respect by coming across as confident and self-assured. Tonight it looks like I'll finally be getting the chance to put my plan into action.

It's a Thursday night and I'm queuing to get into my first

showbiz party with Mike Brewer. Although we've always had a laugh working together, so far I've been careful to decline Mike's invitations to go out at night; I don't want to be a prude but I just can't get used to the way he talks about sex so openly – and so explicitly. But when he asked me to be his guest at the opening of a new nightclub in Soho, I knew it was an invitation I couldn't refuse. I'm beside myself with excitement to be part of this glamorous new world and tell myself that tonight, the all-important boundary between celebrity and civilian is about to be broken down. The only problem is, the party's bound to be so glitzy that I'm worried I'll look out of place and someone will denounce me as a fraud.

'What name is it, please?' The woman on the door is dressed in a sharp, all-black trouser suit and glares at me with an expression approaching contempt.

'Urm, Charlie Matthews,' I offer, expecting her to say that there's been some mistake and I'm not invited after all. At this point an actor from *Heartbeat* waltzes straight past with a leggy blonde on his arm. The photographers begin clicking away and I'm almost blinded by the flashbulbs. My heart thumps furiously in my chest. Maybe Madonna's in there already . . .

'Hmmm.' The woman looks me up and down with a frown. My hair's now short and spiky and I'm wearing flared beige cords with an obligatory cowboy shirt, desperately trying to give off the message that I'm laid-back about my innate sense of cool. There's a lengthy pause before the woman finally says with a scowl, 'Go right in.'

I practically skip down the stairs and bounce into the main club. When I arrive there I stop to survey the room. The entire space has the feel of a nineteenth-century French whorehouse;

the walls are lined with plush red velvet, people are lounging around on chaises longues and everywhere you look there are huge mirrors with ornate gold frames and chandeliers that dazzle from above.

I'm captivated by the glamour and keep telling myself in disbelief that I've just arrived at my first celebrity party. So far I've spotted a daytime TV presenter, two Page 3 girls, a handful of mildly talented footballers and some of the evictees from that new reality TV show, *Big Brother*. Mingling among them are an army of people who Mike calls 'liggers' – managers, agents, publicists, stylists, hairdressers, make-up artists, personal assistants and even the odd TV researcher like me. But none of these people make any impact on my line of vision – I'm somehow able to block them out so that I only notice the famous people.

Just then a redhead who slept with a married footballer and now presents her own late-night TV show walks past me dressed in a bikini top and a camouflage belt she's wearing as a skirt. I feel like I've stepped into the pages of that new magazine *Heat*, my favourite since it launched a few months ago. Sadly, I can't see Madonna anywhere but suppose it's still early – she probably doesn't want to be the first to arrive and is planning on making a big entrance.

Evidently, Mike's mind is on something other than spotting celebrities. 'My God, it's wall-to-wall dick in here,' he says. 'It's practically a cock carpet!'

My eyes bulge – I'm still finding it difficult to get used to Mike's cheery lack of self-censorship.

We venture further inside and a swarm of incredibly skinny waitresses begin circulating around us, handing out unfeasibly lightweight canapés. I reach out and grab one and as I begin chomping away Mike glowers at me. 'Eating is cheating,' he scowls, before dragging me off in the direction of the bar.

When we get there I'm amazed to discover that whatever drinks we want are free all night. Now that's *seriously* glamorous. I decide to push the boat out and go for a Cosmopolitan as this is what the girls drink on *Sex and the City*. The TV series is a house favourite and Tash, Amelia and I snuggle up on the sofa every Wednesday night to howl with laughter at the adventures of Carrie, Charlotte, Miranda and Samantha. Unfortunately, I now discover that their cocktail of choice tastes so sickly that it makes me wince. I continue sipping away regardless, safe in the knowledge that I'm radiating vibes of extreme taste and sophistication.

'So, have you got a boyfriend at the moment?' asks Mike.

'Nah, I'm afraid not. How about you?'

He mimes outrage. 'Are you taking the piss? I don't do relationships – fuck 'em and fuck 'em off, that's my motto!'

I try not to squirm.

'In fact,' he goes on with a sparkle in his eye, 'there's a few benders from my back catalogue here tonight . . .'

'Really? Who?'

He looks around the room and points out a barrel-chested fortysomething in a suit with blond hair and a ginger beard. 'Now I wouldn't recommend *him*,' he sniffs. 'His dick's so small it's like a swollen clit. Honestly, it didn't even touch the sides.'

I gulp.

Next, he points out a rather slight-looking young boy with a baby face who can't be more than eighteen. 'Now that one over there's a completely different ballgame – they call him the pocket rocket because of his whopper cock. I swear to God, it's like a tube of Pringles – a real liver-lifter!'

He flashes me a mischievous grin and I look down awkwardly.

'You want to get in there,' he rattles on. 'He's a sensational shag and he can suck the handle off a door.'

I wriggle on the spot uncomfortably. 'To be honest Mike, please don't take this the wrong way but I'm not really into casual sex.'

'Sorry, did you just say something?' he teases. 'My eyes have glazed over.'

'I know it's a bit uncool but I think sex is something special and intimate between two people who care about each other.'

He feigns an expression of deepest boredom. 'Listen, Cambridge boy, take it from me – there's no point looking for love because it doesn't exist. All men turn out to be bastards sooner or later, it's just that some of them are better at hiding it.'

'But they can't *all* be bastards,' I argue. 'There are millions of men out there and I'm only looking for one!'

'Oh we've all been through that phase – you'll soon snap out of it.'

I'm just about to fight my corner when Mike grabs me by the arm with a gasp. 'Rat-a-tat-tat!'

'You what?' I ask. 'What are you on about?'

'Hot tattoo alert! Check out that fit guy over there. I *love* a man with tats!'

Mike looks the man up and down like a searchlight. I notice that on his left arm he has a tattoo of the Virgin Mary but one that looks like she's got Bell's palsy. 'Yeah,' I manage, 'he's very handsome.'

'Handsome?' Mike practically spits back at me. 'He's fit as fuck! Here, hold this – I'm going to go and ask him for a light.'

And with that he's off. I watch him approach the man and run his hands up and down his chest while he's lighting his cigarette. I've never seen anyone make it so obvious they're up for sex. Within minutes, the two of them are snogging passionately at the side of the dance floor.

I'm not quite sure what to do with myself now that Mike's pulled. I'm already feeling more than a bit tipsy and have to grasp hold of a railing to steady myself. I scan the room for Madonna but there's still no sign of her and I'm suddenly hit by a terrifying thought. What if she comes in now and spots me on my own looking like I've got no friends?

I decide to quickly make conversation with some of the other guests. After all, that's what people do in the party photos in *Hello!* and *OK!* magazines. I scan the room and the first person I see is a middle-aged woman wearing thick silver eye shadow, a sequinned boob tube and a diamanté tiara. I go over to say hello and she introduces herself as 'Helena, darling'. She explains that she runs her own PR firm and my eyes light up as I realize that she must be the London equivalent of Samantha Jones. I listen mesmerized as she tells me of her trips to Harley Street to be 'kissed by the Botox fairy' and her racy past working as a hostess on *Play Your Cards Right* and then a cheerleader on *Gladiators*. She's so sophisticated and savvy that I can't believe she's talking to me – she even insists on calling me 'darling' about three times per sentence! She obviously wouldn't do that to just anyone and must really like me. I glug my Cosmopolitan with a new confidence.

After about half an hour Helena Darling has to leave for the toilet to do something she calls 'shaking the lettuce'. I assume she means taking the latest kind of designer drug and wink at her knowingly. She smothers me with air kisses and tells me to

'Stay showbiz!' before clicking off into the distance in her strappy silver stilettos. As I watch her leave, I feel a glow of satisfaction at how easily I'm fitting into London's glamorous party scene. I'm obviously in my rightful place on the cutting edge.

The only slight cloud on the horizon is that I've lost count of how many drinks I've downed and am starting to feel pissed. As I carry on drinking, making friends with the other guests proves to be more and more difficult. The next person I speak to is a Venezuelan beauty queen called Celestina, who I manage to offend by asking if anyone ever calls her Semolina. Then I strike up conversation with a transgender magician called Anna Cadabra, who gets the hump when I mess up her trick by forgetting the card I was supposed to memorize. And finally I introduce myself to a statuesque model called Verina who storms off in a sulk after I mistakenly call her Verruca. By now I'm starting to feel in serious danger of falling over the cutting edge.

My stomach begins aching and I decide that it would probably be a good idea to take a quick toilet break and try to pull myself together. By this stage, getting from one side of the club to the other takes several minutes and involves numerous collisions with drunken dancers. When I eventually get there, I lock myself in a cubicle and straight away begin throwing up. I can't understand it – the girls on *Sex and the City* are constantly downing Cosmopolitans and *they're* never sick. As I puke myself inside out, I wonder if I might have caught food poisoning from that canapé I ate earlier. Just then I vomit so violently that one of my contact lenses jumps out and disappears down the toilet bowl. I'm mortified – just a few minutes ago I thought I was coping so well.

At that moment I hear the introduction to 'Music' and a cheer of approval coming from the dance floor. I suddenly remember that Madonna could be arriving at any minute and hurriedly start to clean myself up. I dry my eyes, pop a chewing gum in my mouth and rush outside and onto the dance floor.

I soon realize that with only one contact lens I can't see properly and have to close one eye and peer around with the other to see what's happening. I can just about make out that the dancing's getting more and more outrageous – all around me people are latching onto anything that remotely resembles a pole and writhing up and down as if in a state of intense sexual ecstasy.

I join in and dance away to the electro-punk beat, trying my best not to bang into anyone. Even with my severely impaired eyesight, as I look around it strikes me how different the party has become from the sophisticated soirée I expected. The venue's now uncomfortably hot and most of the guests are dripping with sweat. Once-immaculate hairstyles have unravelled into unkempt messes, shirts have been ruined by spilt drinks and dresses have been ripped open to reveal way too much thigh. Inches away from me, I spot a children's TV presenter running his hands all over the boobs of a well-known lingerie model. There are smashed glasses and fag butts all over the tables and half-drunk cocktails piled up at either side of the dance floor. In fact, my first celebrity party has turned out to be not too dissimilar from a night in St Christopher's bar or even the school disco I went to when I was fifteen. I become aware of a rancid stench and look down to see that I'm standing in a puddle of almost luminous pink sick.

Madonna still hasn't turned up so I resign myself to the fact that I probably won't be meeting her tonight after all. I decide not to be too disappointed – the state I'm in now, maybe it's no bad thing. I wipe my foot clean and decide to look around for Mike.

After several laps of the club I eventually catch sight of him looking the worse for wear, coming towards me down a narrow corridor, ricocheting from one wall to the other. He struggles to steady himself with an empty cocktail glass in one hand and a half-eaten canapé in the other. He's chewing gum furiously and there's a discarded fag butt stuck to the side of his cheek.

'How's it going?' I ask, shouting into his ear. His eyes are all over the place and he's having trouble focusing on my face. 'Sensational! I'm just on my way to the shithouse *if you know what I mean.*'

'Oh right,' I nod, desperate to use the correct jargon, 'are you going to shake the lettuce?'

He blinks at me in confusion. 'What are you on about, Cambridge boy? Shaking the lettuce is what birds do when they have a piss.'

I blush bright red. 'Oh right, yeah, sorry.'

'*I'm* going to meet that guy with the tats to size him up.'

'Course you are, yeah, sorry.' I shudder with embarrassment – Mike can obviously see right through me. 'To be honest,' I go on, 'I think I'm going to head home now.'

'But it's only one o'clock!'

'I know but I'm feeling rough – I've already vommed and I've lost a contact lens and can't see properly.'

He pauses as if he's thinking it over. 'Oh don't worry about it – if that guy's up to scratch I'll be taking him back to mine anyway. Give me half an hour and I'll be pushing back like a goat on a cliff edge.'

I cough to try to hide my shock. 'Oh, OK, right . . . Well, I'd better be off . . . Bye then.'

'See you!'

I turn and fight my way up the crowded stairs, picking my way between couples of varying combinations of gender and sexual persuasion. Everywhere I look, people are snogging fervently, their hands straying up shirts and down skirts. I push my way out into the open air and with my blurred vision stumble towards a waiting taxi, the sound of 'Music' still ringing in my ears. I try not to notice how unglamorous everything suddenly looks and keep telling myself that I've just been initiated into London's glittering party scene.

Yes, I've arrived.

And I might not have met Madonna but now that I've had my first glimpse of life on the A-List, I know that day can't be far off.

Don't Tell Me

I'm transfixed. Two of the most gorgeous men I've ever seen are standing right in front of me. One of them's white with floppy hair, the other one's black with a shaved head, and they both have fantastic bodies. They're wearing shorts and V-neck T-shirts and as they throw a Frisbee to each other, the muscles on their arms stand out like pistons on an engine. I can't stop staring – and neither can Amelia.

'If only Anthony could look like that,' she drools.

I sigh. 'I can't believe how fit they are.'

'Just a minute,' she says, 'I thought we were saying "hot" now?'

We've recently decided to call men 'hot' rather than 'fit' as it sounds more *Sex and the City* but in the near delirium of desire I've forgotten all about it. 'Oh yeah,' I concede, 'they're so *hot*!'

We're in St James's Park, where we're having a picnic lunch. We've just been to our regular yoga lesson in Victoria and often come here afterwards if the weather's good, spreading our foam mats out on the grass to enjoy the sunshine. Even though it's not really in keeping with the ethos of yoga, we spark up two Marlboro Lights, collecting our ash in an empty lager can someone left lying on the grass, and Amelia opens our bottle of screw-top white wine, which she pours into the plastic glasses we nicked from next to the watercooler in the gym.

'Amelia,' I announce, 'we are living the dream!'

Sitting next to us are an affluent-looking couple in their thirties who are sipping champagne and nibbling at smoked salmon and continental cheeses they've brought in an expensive-looking hamper. We wish we could afford that kind of luxury picnic but neither of us is earning much money and we're still struggling to pay off student loans so it's a Boots meal-deal sandwich and packet of crisps for us with a bottle of the cheapest wine we could find. But neither of us is complaining. And we're certainly not complaining about the view.

Just then we remember that Tash is about to start her audition and tear our eyes away from the Frisbee players to text her good luck. She wasn't able to come with us today as she's in a tiny theatre above a pub in Deptford to audition at a casting for 'an intense lesbian psychodrama' called Arse Over Tit. I really hope she gets the part and text her that if there's any justice, she will.

I put my phone down and stub out my cigarette in the lager can. I ask Amelia how her work's going and, as we eat our sandwiches, she talks me through the latest news from her job teaching at a school full of infant reprobates in Peckham. Although it's hard work and some of the kids are much more unruly than she expected, she seems to be coping well and is glad to have started work after a long year of teacher training. It's Anthony's career she's worried about; he's spending the day at his studio in Stepney Green, pondering a change in artistic direction. Since graduating from Cambridge he's been trying to find a gallery to represent him but hasn't had any joy and has recently announced that his 'practice needs to evolve to produce work that challenges our preconceptions about artistic worth'. From what Amelia can gather, all this involves is lying in bed until late morning then sitting around the studio all afternoon drinking coffee and smoking dope.

We're interrupted when the Frisbee lands at our feet and I stand up to throw it back to the hot men. They nod and wave their thanks then continue to toss it between them. I wonder how two grown men can be so amused by the simple act of throwing a plastic plate from one to the other. But they look so happy – and when they smile, they're both so cute.

'What do you reckon?' I ask Amelia. 'Do you think they're straight or gay?'

'I don't know,' she answers. 'They *seem* straight but they're very well groomed and well maintained.'

'You can say that again.' I watch as the black one wipes the sweat off his forehead, the curl of his bicep silhouetted against the sun. 'God, I hope they're gay. I really hope they're gay.'

'Yeah and if they are, let's hope they're not together,' chips in Amelia.

'Shit, yeah,' I say, 'I didn't think of that.'

I peer closer, examining the men's interaction for signs they might be a couple. From where we're sitting we have the perfect vantage point; we're on top of the little hill next to the pond, just across from the bridge where all the tourists take photos against the backdrop of Buckingham Palace looking one way or the newly erected London Eye looking the other. It's a Saturday in late September but unseasonably warm, which is why so many people have come out to make the most of what might be the last sunny weekend of the year. Dotted around us are a group of Indian women dressed in multi-coloured saris and eating what looks like a full Indian banquet, a clutch of teenage Caribbean boys playing non-stop cricket with a tennis ball, and a gaggle of noisy Spaniards celebrating someone's birthday with a cake they demolish in minutes. Strolling along the path are a couple of Muslim women in headscarves pushing their toddlers in buggies, and two nuns who at first I'm convinced are in fancy dress until they come closer and I realize they're genuine. I tell myself that what I'm seeing is just a glimpse of life in London, on display in all its glorious diversity.

But I can't stop my eyes being drawn back to the two men playing Frisbee. For a moment they stop to swig from cans of beer they've left in the shade, propped up against the trunk of a massive oak tree. And then, completely unprompted, they start peeling off their shirts. Their bodies are just as amazing as we imagined.

'Oh my God,' I say to Amelia, 'I think I'm going to pass out.'

'Look at the abs on the white one,' she says, her usually calm voice descending into a guttural groan.

'Never mind that,' I gasp, 'get a load of the V on the other.'

For a few minutes we sit in silence, our eyes following the men's every move. It's a good job we're wearing sunglasses so they can't tell how much we're gawping at them. Despite the fact we've no money, we recently splashed out on fake designer eyewear we bought for a fiver on Camden Market; while Amelia's wearing a pair of Aviators with orange-coloured lenses she's convinced she's seen on Britney Spears, I'm wearing a pair of black frameless plastic ones that look just like those worn by Dane Bowers in that new video he's made with Posh Spice. As we use them to shield our gaze, we tell each other that buying them was the best fiver we ever spent.

We continue to stare as the boys interrupt their game to greet two blonde girls who are walking towards them with a portable CD player and big plastic bags from Pret A Manger. The girls are both stunning and impeccably fashionable, wearing the latest trend of low-rise jeans, halter-neck tops and beaded chokers, with stripes of chunky highlights running through their hair. Much more importantly, they greet the two Frisbee players with long, intimate kisses.

'Uh-oh!' says Amelia. 'I think that answers your question.'

'Oh no!' I pant. 'So they're straight *and* attached. That's so unfair!'

I watch in disbelief as the two girls tear themselves away from their men to start taking out all manner of delicious-looking food from their bags and spreading it out on a picnic rug. I look at the nibbled crusts left over from my bog-standard cheese and pickle sandwich sitting on the edge of my yoga mat, hardening in the sun. I toss them into our rubbish bag and light another cigarette.

'You know what,' says Amelia, 'I've been thinking about this and I think you need to go more gay.'

'More gay?' I ask, breathing out my smoke. 'What are you on about?'

'Well, what I mean is, it's great that you spend so much time with me and Tash, but I wonder whether you should start making gay friends and going to gay places.'

I raise my eyebrows. I haven't really considered that my life isn't very gay but, now that Amelia mentions it, I can see that she's right. She and Tash might accompany me to the odd gay bar, just as Shanaz used to in Manchester, but the truth is I always feel slightly self-conscious flirting with men or snogging one in front of a straight friend, so I tend to hold back. 'All right,' I reply, 'but the problem is, I don't really know any gay people. Who would I make friends with?'

'Well, what about Mike from work?'

I swallow. I do like Mike and I did enjoy going to that club opening with him but all he talks about is pulling and having sex. Other than being gay, I can't see that we have that much in common.

'Why are you pulling a face?' Amelia asks. 'What's wrong with Mike?'

'I'm not pulling a face!' I protest, quickly softening my features. 'There's nothing wrong with Mike.'

'Well, why don't you go out on the town with him then? You've said yourself he's always asking you.'

'Yeah, I know, it's just . . .'

'Just what?' she says. 'You're frightened of him?'

I take a deep drag on my cigarette. 'Amelia, I'm not frightened of Mike.'

'You know, you never went to that LesBiGay group at Cambridge . . .'

'And? What's that got to do with anything?'

'Well, it's just, I wonder if you're a bit frightened of the whole gay thing, that's all.'

I'm just about to argue with her when I decide to stop and think about what she's saying. I never did fancy going to LesBiGay meetings and I never have fancied going on a night out with Mike. I stub out my fag. Maybe Amelia has a point.

'You know we've just done this anti-bullying training at school,' she continues, 'and one of the things they taught us about is the long-term damage bullying can do to the way people see themselves. So if a kid's given a hard time for being ginger, for example, he's not going to love his red hair. Or if he's called speccy four eyes for wearing glasses he's hardly going to grow up loving his glasses. I wonder if something similar's happened to you with being gay.'

I fall silent and begin pulling tufts of grass out of the lawn. I've only given Amelia a brief summary of what happened to me at school as I don't like talking about it now it's in the past. I certainly don't like to think it's had any lasting effect on me; I wouldn't like to give those kids at school the satisfaction. But at the same time, I think I *am* a bit frightened of going out with Mike. So maybe the two things *are* linked, even if I don't want them to be.

'The thing is,' I point out, 'I know what Mike's like and if I go on a night out with him, all he's going to want to do is get off with someone and go and have sex.'

Amelia shakes her head. 'Oh come on, Charlie, nobody can be that two-dimensional – there must be more to him than that. Why don't you try and get to know him a bit better?'

Just then, I recognize the opening to Madonna's latest album and look over to see the two blonde girls have put it on their CD player. Things are looking up; they might have called an abrupt end to our floorshow but at least they're providing some decent background music.

'You know, if you don't make friends with Mike and start going to gay bars,' Amelia goes on, 'how are you ever going to find a boyfriend?'

I pick up the pile of grass I've made and scatter it onto the lawn. I hadn't really thought I was looking for a boyfriend but, now that Amelia mentions it, I think I probably am. OK, it took me a while to get over Nick and after that I was distracted by my final year at Cambridge and then finding a job and settling into London. But I've done all that now. Isn't it about time I reignited my quest to find love?

'Yeah, OK,' I admit, 'I suppose you're right. Maybe I do need to get over myself.'

'I mean, don't get me wrong, sitting in the park with you is lovely for me but eyeing up straight boys isn't much use to you, is it?'

I look over at the two straight men and their girlfriends and see they're now lying on their picnic rug, cuddling and nuzzling each other. When the song comes to an end, one of the girls gets up and skips the CD onto 'Don't Tell Me', my favourite song on the album. As I listen to the lyrics, I realize that Madonna's much older than me but she never gave up on love and now she's found it – and has recorded songs like this about how happy it's made her. Well, maybe it's time I took a leaf out of her book, just like I used to.

'All right,' I announce, 'I'll speak to Mike this week and see if he's still up for taking me out.'

'Great,' Amelia says, smiling. 'But don't look so worried. You never know, you might actually enjoy it.'

I look over at the straight boys as they put their arms around their girlfriends and start snogging in the sunshine. Both couples seem so into each other it's almost as if they've stopped noticing everyone around them. I can't help thinking how nice that must feel.

'Who knows?' I say to Amelia, a twinkle appearing in my eye. 'Maybe I will.'

Beautiful Stranger

'Right then,' beams Mike, 'what are we going to call ourselves?'

'Oh, I don't know,' I say, 'what's everyone else called?'

We look at the screen and read the names *latinlovegod*, *hunglikeadonkey* and *cumhungryhomo*. My eyes bulge. I might have accepted that I've been a bit frightened of Mike but he isn't making any allowances for my uneasiness.

'Urm, how about, urm . . . How about *slapandtickle*?' I suddenly picture me and Joe chasing Uncle Les's ferrets around Grandma's garden when we were little.

Mike looks at me and frowns. 'I think you'd better leave it to me, Cambridge boy.' I watch his fingers hit the keyboard and type in the codename *bangupforitbenders*. I take a deep breath.

It's Saturday night and the two of us are sitting in Mike's flat in Soho, where he's invited me for dinner. The meal consisted of overcooked soggy pasta smothered in a jar of Chicken Tonight (without any chicken), and then half a tub of out-of-date, frozen-solid Haagen Dazs for pudding. As soon as we finished, Mike insisted that we sit down and watch a DVD on the new player he's just bought. At the moment everyone's raving about DVDs and I've been looking forward to checking out the picture quality for myself. I asked Mike if he has

Moulin Rouge, my current favourite film, but he smiled mischievously and produced a film I hadn't heard of called *Chitty Chitty Gang Bang*. It only took one glance at the case for me to work out it was a hardcore porno about some kind of orgy that takes place on the bonnet of a vintage car.

After I told him I wasn't really in the mood for a DVD, he suggested instead that we log onto his favourite internet site for a quick 'crotch watch'. I've read about Gaydar in a Sunday supplement recently and thought it sounded like a fun way to find potential boyfriends. Looking at the site now, it's blatantly obvious that the object of the exercise isn't to forge relationships but instead to find partners for casual sex.

Mike types in his postcode and straight away a list flashes up on-screen of men who are online in the same area ready and willing to meet up for sex. There are hundreds of them and each has a detailed profile that includes information on the size of their penis, the amount of body hair they have and what they like sexually, as well as an all-important gallery of photos. With just a few clicks of the mouse, Mike launches straight into a conversation with *hotandhorny69*. I try not to grimace as I watch the words race across the screen, amazed that the chat can be so frank and upfront. Within ten minutes Mike announces that he's preparing to 'clinch the deal' and starts entering his home address and phone number.

'Just a minute,' I jump in, 'you're not seriously going to invite this guy round, are you?' Until now I honestly thought that the whole thing was a game and didn't for a moment consider that we'd actually follow it through, least of all for some kind of threesome.

'Course I am, Cambridge boy. What else do you think I'm going to do?'

'I don't know, I . . .'

'Don't worry,' he reassures me, 'we don't have to do him at the same time; we can always go one after the other.'

'Oh, right,' I stammer, desperate to come up with some other way to get out of it. 'But what if he turns out to be a serial killer?' Now that I think about it, I suddenly find the idea of a stranger coming round to the flat utterly terrifying.

Mike laughs. 'What are the chances of that, you daft bender?'

'But don't you think it could be dangerous?'

'No, not really. Most of the blokes on here are ordinary guys who just want to empty their sack every now and again. What's so scary about that?'

I try not to cringe. 'Look, Mike – no offence but this whole internet thing isn't really my bag. I'm not being funny or anything but I think I'd rather pull the old-fashioned way and just meet someone in a bar or something.'

He looks at me with what seems to be a mixture of understanding and pity. 'Oh don't worry about it – it's no big deal.' He turns to the screen and tells *hotandhorny69* that he doesn't want to meet up after all. 'Sorry mate,' he types, 'I've just had a wank.'

'Is that it?' I ask.

'Yeah,' he nods, 'he'll get the message.' He stands up and puts on his coat. 'Come on,' he says, 'we're off into town.'

'Oh. Are you sure you don't mind?'

'Nah. It's Saturday night – just think of all those fit benders in Soho.' He licks his lips and shoots me a naughty grin. 'My dick's dripping with pre-cum at the thought.'

Half an hour later we're standing at the back of a gay bar called Rupert Street, shouting over a soundtrack of alternating Britney,

Kylie and Destiny's Child. The place is packed full of perfectly plucked pretty boys dressed in an almost identical uniform of clothes bought from H&M, Topman and that new Spanish store everyone's obsessed with, Zara. Everywhere I look, people are eyeing each other up and pointing out men they fancy to their friends and pulling partners. Mike's no exception.

'If you had to shag one person in this bar now, who would it be?' he asks. '*I'd* do that Latino guy with the tats.' He points at a dark-skinned man standing by the door. 'Rat-a-tat-tat! And look at the size of his arms. I love a man with big arms. Arms are the new cock.'

I look around to make my selection but nobody strikes me as being particularly attractive. 'To be honest, Mike, I know this is really uncool but I can't be arsed pulling some random bloke if it doesn't mean anything.'

'Oh God, not again! Well, in that case, stop moaning and go and find yourself a boyfriend – you'll be bored shitless after a few months, believe me!'

'But don't you see? I don't just want *any* old boyfriend. I want to fall in love.'

'Yeah, well, we've all been there, you know. You don't think *I* started off like this, do you? I'll have you know it's not that long since I was looking for the same thing as you.'

'But Mike,' I splutter, 'I had no idea. What happened?'

He lets out a long sigh. 'Oh you know . . . Life.' He takes his straw and begins stabbing at the ice cubes at the bottom of his glass.

I sense that he doesn't want to open up any more but I can tell from the look on his face that Amelia was right and there is more to him than all the banter about casual sex. 'So were you ever in love with anyone?' I press.

'If you must know, I was, yeah.' He pauses for a moment and I notice a faraway look in his eye. 'His name was Stevie and he was from Brixton. He was built like a brick shithouse and drop dead gorgeous. And yeah, before you ask, he was covered in tattoos.'

'I wasn't going to say anything.'

'Yeah, well, anyway, I was only eighteen and I'd just moved to London and started going out on the scene. One night I came to a bar like this and there he was. To be honest I didn't notice him at first but he must have spotted me because he came over and introduced himself. And he was nice. I liked him.'

'So what happened?'

'Well, believe it or not, I didn't shag him straight away. I was actually quite classy back then. But once I did it didn't take me long to fall madly in love with him. And I know it seems a bit daft now but we moved in together after a few weeks.'

'Mike,' I gasp, 'I'd never have thought.'

'Yeah, well, that's only the half of it. I actually took him home to meet my mum and dad. You can imagine how that went down in our little village in Norfolk. They'd only just got used to the fact that I was gay and then I turned up with a six-foot-three Muscle Mary with shitloads of tattoos. I didn't care, though. All I cared about was Stevie. He made me so happy.'

'Oh Mike,' I gush, 'that's so romantic.'

'Hardly,' he sniffs, giving his ice cubes another stab. 'It only lasted six months.'

'Why? What happened?'

'Let's just say I realized I couldn't stay with him if I wanted to survive.'

'What do you mean? I don't get it.'

'Well, to cut a long story short, Stevie told me he wanted an open relationship, I told him I didn't and then he just went and had one anyway. I was so devastated it almost killed me.'

'But Mike,' I say, 'that's terrible. I'm so sorry you had to go through it.'

He sucks up the rest of his drink with a loud slurp. 'Yeah, well, I'm over it now. And it's a long time ago. I was a different person back then.'

'Yeah, but you don't have to be, you can still be that person. I've been hurt before but I want to fall in love again. Just because it didn't work the first time doesn't mean it won't the next time.'

He shakes his head firmly. 'No, no, there won't be a next time, not for me anyway. Falling in love's too painful, why would I want to do that again? Ever since I split up with Stevie, the forcefield's been up, the armour's on and I don't do emotion. I told you, fuck 'em and fuck 'em off, that's my motto.'

Listening to Mike explain how he got to this point makes me like him much more – but I can't bear to think of the younger him convincing himself the only way to get through the pain is to force iron into his soul. 'But don't you think deep down part of you wants to fall in love again?' I insist. 'Could that be why you keep going for guys who remind you of Stevie?'

I see a flicker of vulnerability in his eyes but then he shakes his head. 'Nice try but no. It's just about sex now, nothing more, nothing less. And I happen to find tattoos sensationally attractive.'

I'm not sure I believe him. 'But don't you think if you tried to see beyond that, you might find an individual who can make you feel happy again? Just like you were with Stevie?'

He sets down his drink and dusts his hands. 'Oh give it up, Cambridge boy. I learnt my lesson the hard way and it's about time you learnt it too. Because, like it or not, we're living in the same world.'

'Yeah, but Mike—'

'But nothing,' he interrupts. 'That's the end of the conversation.' He pulls his wallet out of his pocket. 'Now, you can stand there like a loser looking for love but *I'm* off to the bar.'

He joins the crush of people waiting to be served and I look on, tapping my foot to the music. I can't help wondering what Mike was like at my age and wish I'd met him earlier so I could have stopped him becoming so cynical. And I totally understand why it happened but at the same time I'm determined not to let the same thing happen to me.

At that moment, the song changes and the introduction to Madonna's 'Beautiful Stranger' comes pounding out of the speakers. As I listen to the lyrics about falling in love at first sight, I start to smile. Surely finding someone to fall in love with can't be *that* difficult. Now that I think about it, there are loads of good-looking men in the bar. How do I know that one of them isn't right for me?

I survey the room and spot a tall, olive-skinned man with dark hair and bright green eyes. He's talking to a friend by the jukebox and I inch closer and see that he's handsome and seems mature and less affected than most of the men in here. I feel butterflies flutter in my stomach as I gaze at him. He's perfect and just what I'm looking for. After a while, he glances over and returns my stare. He smiles and I feel my knees go weak.

'Oh I'm dying of thirst,' chirps a voice behind me. 'My mouth's as dry as a nun's cunt.'

Mike's back from the bar and holding out a glass of Pernod for me. I manage to grab hold of it without losing sight of the gorgeous guy.

'My God, do you want to make it any more obvious?' Mike says.

'What do you mean?'

'That dark-haired bender over there. You can't stop staring at him and your tongue's practically hanging out of your mouth!'

'Oh, right, sorry.' I snap myself out of the trance and turn to face Mike.

He launches into a story about some ex-pull he's just bumped into but I can't concentrate and my eyes keep wandering to find the face of my beautiful stranger.

'Look, Charlie, why don't you just go and talk to him?'

'Oh I don't know, I suddenly feel all shy. What can I say to him?'

'How about, "Are you top, bottom or versatile?" It usually works for me.'

A crease of confusion scratches across my face. 'Sorry, Mike, but I don't get it.'

He rolls his eyes. 'Oh Charlie, come *on*! It's about what they do in bed. You know, are they the postman or the letterbox or both?'

I'm aware of flushing a deep shade of crimson and look around to check no one's listening. Is that seriously what he's suggesting as a chat-up line? 'But Mike, I can't say that!'

'Why not? It's important to establish these things right at the beginning.'

'Well, maybe that's true but I don't think I'd be able to pull it off. And I can't mess this up – I *really* like this guy.'

'My God, you haven't even spoken to him yet! Go on, you've got thirty seconds or else *I'm* going up to him and doing the my-mate-fancies-you routine. Now get a move on!'

I look ahead and am relieved to see that my beautiful stranger's friend has gone to the bar. Now's my chance to make a move. He catches my eye and I sidle over to him bashfully. 'Hi,' is all I can manage. My voice comes out in a high pitch and I cough to clear my throat.

'Hi,' he replies and smiles. 'Is that Pernod you're drinking?'

'It is, yeah. How do you know that?'

'I'm French,' he laughs, 'I'm from Provence, where everyone drinks Pernod.'

I try to contain my excitement. 'And what's your name?' I ask.

'Christian.' This is too good to be true – he even has the same name as Ewan McGregor's character in *Moulin Rouge*! 'And you?' he asks in a strong French accent. '*Comment tu t'appelles*?'

'*Je m'appelle Charlie*.' I hold out my hand and he shakes it.

'*Enchanté*.'

He explains that he moved to London a few years ago to start work as a fashion designer for a high-end store. I immediately imagine him pinning chic outfits onto impossibly glamorous models backstage at a fashion show and then taking to the catwalk himself to lap up the applause. As the conversation continues, it becomes clear that Christian's everything I've wished for. He's intelligent and articulate, has a good sense of humour and looks genuinely interested when I talk about what I do for a living. Best of all, he seems keen on me – the two of us keep exchanging looks that last a bit too long and then smiling at each other and looking down shyly. This is it, I tell myself, this man could make your life complete!

At that point Christian's friend returns and introduces himself as Daniel, a visiting cousin from Bordeaux. I call Mike over and soon the four of us are chatting away. But only half an hour later, Christian tells us that he has to go home; Daniel's flying back to France early tomorrow morning and they have to get an early night. I try not to look too disappointed but my heart sinks as we say our goodbyes. We exchange phone numbers and Christian holds my gaze for what seems like an eternity. 'I'd really like to see you again,' he says.

'Oh you will,' I reply confidently.

As I watch them go, I let out a wistful sigh.

Once they're out of the door, I turn to Mike. 'My God, I think I'm falling in love!'

'Steady on, cowboy, you haven't even shagged him yet!'

'Yeah, I know, but he's amazing, Mike. I've never met anyone like him. Don't you think he's *perfect*?'

'Oh everyone's perfect,' he shrugs. 'Until you get to know them.'

I tut and shake my head. 'You're such an old cynic!'

'You will be too one day, you mark my words.'

'Well, after tonight I wouldn't bank on it . . .'

'Hey, I've got a joke for you,' he says, obviously keen to change the subject. 'What did the lemon say to the orange?'

'Urm, sorry, I don't know.'

He holds up his empty glass. 'Your round. Come on, get them in – mine's a gin and slim.'

As I move to the bar and add myself to the throng, all I can think of is Christian and wherever I look I see his green eyes gazing back at me. I stand waiting to be served and lose myself in fantasies of the two of us strolling through the streets of Paris and sipping champagne in the real-life Moulin Rouge.

Yes, he has to be right for me. And falling in love with him is going to be so easy.

Like a Prayer

A few months later my fantasy's coming true – my romantic hero and I are on our way to Paris for Valentine's weekend.

For the first time ever, I'm travelling on the Eurostar and I find it amazing that you can catch a train in Waterloo Station, travel through a tunnel under the English Channel and then re-emerge in Northern France little more than an hour later. Christian's sitting next to me and when I look at him I feel like I'm going to explode with bliss. He's turned out to be a wonderful person and a thoughtful and attentive boyfriend. He surprises me with romantic text messages several times a day and often brings me flowers and presents just so that he can see me smile. It's certainly a big contrast to my first relationship with Nick, which began on another Valentine's Day several years ago. I know for sure that Christian wouldn't ever cheat on me and this gives me a sense of security that I haven't experienced before.

'This is so *fantastique*,' Christian says in his seductive French accent. 'Two whole days in Paris with my boyfriend all to myself.'

I smile and rest my head on his shoulder.

The best thing about being in a relationship with Christian is that he doesn't object to the word 'boyfriend'. In fact, I remember him calling me his boyfriend on our very first date. Right now he stretches his arm around me and I snuggle up to him and cuddle his chest. I feel good. I feel special. I feel like I'm the best person in the world.

Half an hour later, our train arrives at the Gare du Nord. We catch a cab and drive south towards the Latin Quarter, where we've booked a room in the Hotel Spartacus. The cab pulls up outside the main entrance, next to a statue of the gladiator himself. As we step inside, we see that the hotel has been decorated according to a Roman Empire theme; everywhere we look there are sculptures of emperors and gladiators and the walls are crammed full of paintings of the Colosseum and the Forum. It's all a bit tacky but most of the other hotels were booked up, and of the ones that were available, this is all we could afford.

'Charlie,' Christian says, 'if I'm staying here with you then this is my favourite hotel in Paris.'

I gaze into his striking green eyes and am convinced I feel a crackle of electricity pass between us.

Over the next two days, we devour every inch of a city Christian knows well from childhood visits and more recent trips to Paris Fashion Week. As he shows me around, I feel totally carried away by its stirring beauty and inspiring atmosphere. All weekend the sky's bright blue and the air crisp and fresh. We spend our time ambling along the Left Bank and gazing at the river from the Pont Neuf, my mind racing with images from avant-garde black and white films like *À bout de souffle* or *Bande à part*. We sit on a bench in the Jardin du Luxembourg and Christian reads dramatic love poems to me by Baudelaire and Verlaine. We weave our way through the narrow lanes and antique street lamps of Montmartre and I imagine the two of us in a painting by Renoir. And we saunter arm in arm through the corridors of the Louvre, stopping occasionally to look more closely at paintings of famous lovers.

'Charlie,' says Christian, 'you're more special to me than all these works of art put together.'

He squeezes my hand and looks into my eyes. I feel my heart flutter as if he's seeing right through to my soul.

The only low point of the weekend happens when we make a short pilgrimage to see the real Moulin Rouge on Valentine's Day itself. I discover that the club, for me the very epicentre of love and romance, is in reality tatty and run-down. It's surrounded by kebab shops and unshaven, shabbily dressed men hassling tourists to buy tacky souvenirs. We originally planned to go inside for a drink but decide against it when we read that the entertainment for the evening is some kind of topless dance show featuring a troupe of cancan girls wearing garishly coloured feathers and very little else. I feel a crushing sense of disillusionment and suggest to Christian that we must have somehow made a mistake. He looks in our guidebook and reads out loud that my favourite film was apparently shot entirely in a studio in Australia and had nothing to do with the original building in Paris. I feel cheated and decide that it's time to move on. But from that moment I can't shake off the idea that something's not quite right.

'Don't worry, favourite boy,' soothes Christian, as he puts his arm around me, 'what we have together is far more important than any film.'

Later that evening, he takes me for a romantic meal at a stylish restaurant in the Marais. We sip expensive champagne we can't really afford and hold hands in the candlelight as a distant pianist plays love songs by Maurice Chevalier and

Charles Trenet. It should all be like a dream come true but I can't help thinking back to our trip to the Moulin Rouge and feeling a bit deflated.

'Charlie,' Christian says, stroking my hand gently, 'before I met you my life was a cappella. Now you're my boyfriend it's like I'm accompanied by a whole orchestra.'

It's the most romantic thing anyone's ever said to me but for some reason it doesn't make me feel better. I smile at him weakly.

As the meal goes on, I find myself wondering if I really am in love with Christian. Once the thought's lodged in my mind there isn't anything I can do to get rid of it and by the time we reach dessert I'm becoming increasingly plagued by the worry that I don't feel quite as strongly about him as I did about Nick. Back then I was stunned by the force of my feelings and felt so in love that I sometimes wondered if I was going insane. But this time around, if I'm honest with myself, I don't get quite the same feeling in my gut every time I see Christian. I'm thrilled to have a boyfriend and feel loved but is that the same thing as being in love with him? Or am I so in love with the idea of being in love that it's blinding me to reality?

I brush aside my doubts, telling myself that the reason I feel differently about Christian is because I've grown up a lot since my mad schoolboy crush on Nick and am in a much more mature relationship now. This time I'm going for long-term success rather than the flash-in-the-pan, the Liberty X rather than the Hear'Say. Surely it's bound to feel different?

I decide to stop worrying and instead to fantasize about the two of us in a love scene from a film like *Les parapluies de Cherbourg* or *Les amants du Pont-Neuf*. I instantly feel better and by the time the meal has ended am overwhelmed by a renewed rush of happiness. I simply *have* to be in love with Christian – he's everything I've ever wished for.

Outside, it's a beautiful moonlit night and we decide to stroll back to our hotel past the Hôtel de Ville, over the river and across the Île de la Cité. As we pass Notre-Dame Cathedral I notice that inside it's lit up and we can't resist sneaking in to see what's going on. It's the end of some kind of service and the congregation are getting up from their seats and starting to file out. We creep in behind them and begin wandering up and down the side aisles, stunned by the splendour of the architecture. Beneath a statue of Jesus on the cross I notice two French women so absorbed in prayer that they don't even see us passing right in front of them. They have tears in the corner of their eyes and expressions of such fixed concentration that they might as well be in another world.

I've never been particularly religious and have always viewed God in the same way as I see Father Christmas, the Easter bunny and the tooth fairy – as a comforting white lie Mum and Dad told me so that the world would seem like a nicer place. But standing here now in this breathtaking monument to his glory, I can see how over the centuries so many millions of people have been overwhelmed and seduced by religious passion.

Christian leans into my ear and begins singing a song I immediately recognize as Madonna's 'Like a Prayer'. I look at him affectionately and join in. As the two of us begin singing together, in my mind I see Madonna's video for the song, which is set in a church and mixes images of religious devotion with scenes of a more earthly passion. I think about the song's lyrics and tell myself that what Christian and I have between us is similar to what other people feel for their God.

'Charlie,' Christian says once we've finished singing, 'I'm going to tell you something very important.'

'Yeah? What is it?'

He pauses to make sure he has my full attention.

'I love you.'

I'm completely taken aback and listen to the words echo in the cathedral around me. I suddenly realize that my whole life I've been waiting for this moment and now that it's finally arrived it feels somehow unreal or otherworldly. No one's ever told me they love me before, not even Mum after she's had a few drinks. And now Christian's saying it to me and looking at me intently to make sure I understand. And it feels amazing. It's like his love washes away the stains caused by all the bad things that have ever happened to me.

I can feel a tear springing up in the corner of my eye. Christian raises his hand to touch my cheek and I become aware that my chin's trembling with emotion.

'I love you, special boy,' he repeats, 'and I want to be with you forever and ever.'

All at once I become aware of how lonely I've been for the last few years and want to cry with joy and relief now that it's come to an end. My doubts about Christian instantly disappear and in my dazed state I repeat to myself that he's exactly the kind of man that I've wanted all along. What on earth have I been worrying about?

'I love you too,' I say, convinced that in that moment I'm happier than I've ever been in my whole life.

I have no idea that I'm wrong.

Borderline

'Chomp chomp chomp.'

I shiver with irritation and can feel my body grow tense.

'Chomp chomp chomp.'

The sound's unbearable. Can't he try to make less noise?

'Chomp chomp chomp.'

If he doesn't stop soon I'm going to have to say something.

'Chomp chomp—'

Right, that's it.

'Christian!' I snap. 'Can't you close your mouth when you're eating? Honestly, it's making me feel sick.'

He looks surprised. 'Sorry, special boy,' he replies rather meekly. After a couple of seconds he turns back to his paper and carries on chomping. I busy myself in the kitchen, banging pots and pans together to try to block out the noise.

It's less than a year since our trip to Paris but already the romantic dream's turning sour. There it is, after months of pretending I'm finally facing up to it. Christian may be everything I've wanted in a man but for some reason I can't fall in love with him. I know I've told him I love him several times and I've been so carried away when he's told me he loves me that I convince myself I'm feeling it – but the truth is I don't. I've tried everything I can think of and have willed it to happen with so much energy that right now I feel emotionally drained. I'm racked with guilt about the whole thing and hope that it doesn't mean that deep down I'm a bad person. What's wrong with me that I can fall hopelessly in love with someone who treats me like crap but now I have a boyfriend who adores me and treats me well, I just can't love him back?

It's eight o'clock in the morning and Christian and I are getting ready for work in the flat in Clapham that I share with Amelia and Tash. A big improvement on our first flat in Hackney, our latest place has three double bedrooms and a spacious living room where we love throwing dinner parties for our old friends from Cambridge and the new friends we've made through our jobs in London. On the downside, it's situated on a busy main road so the windows are always black with dirt, and along one side runs a railway line that makes the entire building rattle whenever a train passes. But still, it's an upgrade and if the sun's out we can climb out of the hall window and onto the flat roof of the property below, stretching out to sunbathe and telling each other how lucky we are to have our own glamorous roof garden.

Last night, Christian stayed over as both of the girls were out – Amelia was sleeping at Anthony's and Tash was spending the night with a Glaswegian theatre director and former heroin addict who she met on the set of an experimental opera about Dolly the sheep. Christian wanted to watch *Moulin Rouge* as it was on telly for the first time but I couldn't be bothered and went to bed early, making an excuse about having an important day at work. I've moved on from *The Third Nipple* and am now working on a series of comedy interviews with celebrities called *Idol Banter*, and I do have an important day coming up; we're filming an interview with Sierra Harley, an actress who became famous for playing a serial-killing superbitch in a TV soap and is now publishing her first diet and detox manual. Deep down, though, I know that isn't the reason I don't want to spend time with Christian – and realize I've been making excuses more and more often lately.

I look over at him as he slurps away on his breakfast, splattering milk all over the table and dropping flakes of cereal onto the floor. For some reason it's taken me until now to notice that he's a disgusting eater. But now that I have I just can't stand it. I go to the stereo and put some music on at full blast to drown out the noise. The song I decide to play is Madonna's 'Borderline'.

Now I'm being honest with myself, I can admit that I've been feeling irritable around Christian for months – and that only makes me feel guilty and ashamed of myself. As a result, when we do see each other, whatever spark of electricity that existed between us just isn't there anymore. Tash told me the other day that she thinks we're entering the final act. When I consider it now, I have to agree with her.

As Madonna sings about her boyfriend pushing her love for him over the limit, I look at Christian and once again feel repulsed by the sound of him chomping away on his cereal. I suddenly become aware that he has a thousand annoying habits I absolutely can't bear. I hate his constant pawing at me in public and when we share a bed at night I detest the way he gives off so much heat, cuddling up to me tightly so it feels like I'm sleeping next to a radiator. I've always loved his French accent but now it's started to aggravate me and I find myself tensing up when he makes mistakes with his English. His romantic lines that once melted my heart now turn my stomach, especially when I hear them trundled out in clichéd romantic films. And worst of all, I want to scream out loud when he refers to having sex as 'making love'. Mike's always jokingly maintained that this is 'strictly a dumpable offence' and I'm starting to see his point.

But however negatively I feel towards Christian, the worst thing about the whole situation is the way it makes me feel about myself. Whenever I stop to think about it I prickle with frustration at myself for not being able to fall in love with him. Just what's *wrong* with me?

The girls and I have spent several nights tucked up on the sofa under a duvet, drinking herbal teas and endlessly discussing my dilemma. In my head I replay our last conversation about the subject.

'You can't force yourself to fall in love,' Tash offers sympathetically. 'Emotions aren't something you can turn on and off like a tap.'

'But it's so unfair,' I sulk. 'He's so right for me.'

'Yeah, well, you can't fall for someone because they sound good on paper, you know. He's obviously just not The One.'

Amelia isn't convinced; she has a very different take on why my relationship isn't working out. 'Usually, if a person can't fall in love with someone who treats them well,' she explains, 'it's because they don't think they deserve to be happy. It's the same reason they fall in love with someone who treats them badly, because that's what they think they deserve.'

'Oh I don't know,' says Tash, pulling the duvet around her defensively. 'I've dated plenty of bastards in my time but I don't think I ever *wanted* them to hurt me. I just fell in love with them and that's what happened.'

'But *why* did you fall in love with them?' counters Amelia.

'Have you ever asked yourself that? Because sometimes if things happened to us when we're young and for whatever reason we grow up thinking we're not good enough, that can be what makes us fall in love with people who'll only confirm that belief.'

Now it's my turn to be defensive. If what Amelia's saying is right, does that mean I'm destined to fall for bastards for the rest of my life? 'Yeah, yeah, it's fine for you to sit there psycho-analyzing us,' I begin, 'but the truth is that falling in love with someone is something magical and amazing that just can't be explained. That's why every time two people find each other and fall in love it's like a little miracle happens.'

'*Totally!*' jumps in Tash. 'You can't decide to fall in love with someone just because you know they'd make a good boyfriend. It's not something you can *manufacture*, Amelia. And whatever people say, there's only one reason why relationships don't work out.'

Amelia rolls her eyes fondly, accepting she isn't going to win us round. 'Oh yeah and what's that?'

'Because one person just isn't as in love as the other one is,' Tash answers definitively. 'It's as simple as that. The magic just doesn't materialize. So don't be so hard on yourself, Charlie. There's plenty of people who've been in this position before you.'

I smile as I remember her advice – and how eager I've been to believe it. But it still doesn't make things any easier. I simply can't get my head around why the sheer joy I felt in Christian's company when I first met him can have gradually given way to the physical repulsion I feel now. But that's effectively what's happened and it's left me feeling empty and angry at my own miserable failure.

As 'Borderline' begins to fade away, Christian finishes his breakfast with one last slurp and bounds over to kiss me goodbye. 'Have a good day, favourite boy!'

I force myself to smile but as I look into his bright green eyes I know for sure that we can't go on like this. Whether our relationship has run its course, I've only deluded myself into thinking I was in love with him in the first place, or I just can't love him because he's nice to me, I have absolutely no idea anymore.

I move over to the window so I can look down onto the street and watch him leave. As he comes out of the door, he turns around and waves. I wave back, bristling in irritation. There's no doubt about it, I have to end our relationship – and I know just how much this is going to hurt him. And it's so unfair on him because he's done everything right. I'm the one who's done everything wrong.

I continue watching as he walks down the street and then rounds the corner and disappears from view. I wonder if my last chance of happiness is disappearing with him.

Live to Tell

A few weeks later I've done it; I've broken up with Christian. But, even though I was the one who instigated the split, I'm still feeling miserable. I'm hoping that a trip to Bolton for Christmas might be just the thing to restore my spirits.

I'm driving home in the first car I've ever owned; it's a knackered old Seat Ibiza that I bought from the stubbly Greek Cypriot who works in the shop across the road, who confidently informed me that it goes like 'shit off a shovel'. I put my foot down and see that he wasn't wrong. In fact, the only problem with the car is its dodgy sound system; the button that controls the power and the volume has broken off and the first CD I put in there has somehow got stuck. I realize very soon that the same song is jammed on repeat and whatever I try I can't switch it off. Right now the last thing I need is to hear 'Live to Tell', Madonna's saddest ever break-up song, all the way back to Bolton.

I try my best to be positive about things but the soundtrack to the journey makes it impossible. As I drive up the motorway my mind wanders and I imagine myself forty years from now, sitting in an empty flat alone and listening to the same sad Madonna song over and over again. When I think about it, I can't imagine ever being in a relationship again and am seriously worried that I'm incapable of falling in love with someone who loves me. I suddenly have a premonition of dying a lonely old man like Benny Hill and people only realizing I'm dead when the neighbours notice the stench of rotting flesh coming from next door.

By the time I arrive in Bolton four hours later, I've heard 'Live to Tell' nearly fifty times and feel on the verge of a deep depression.

I drive down the quiet cul-de-sac where Mum and Dad live and straight away spot their house glowing in the distance. Every December they cover it with flashing neon lights and this year's design includes snowmen, reindeer and a huge Father Christmas on a sleigh that travels from one side of the house to the other. I cringe – I'm really not in the mood for festive fun. I park the car on the street outside and with a sigh of relief cut Madonna off mid-line. I never thought I'd be so pleased to hear her stop singing.

From the outside, Mum and Dad's 1960s pebble-dashed semi looks the same as it always has, with the same corrugated-iron carport on the side to shelter Dad's work van. Inside, it hasn't changed that much either, at least not since I moved out to go to Cambridge. Each room's decorated with brightly coloured, busily patterned wallpaper that's bordered with chains of flowers or arrangements of sea shells, and finished off with soft furnishings and lampshades that together form clashing combinations of ruffles, tassels and ribbons. Hanging on almost every wall are photos of me and Joe at different stages of our lives and faded prints of Monet's water lilies that Mum bought from Athena in the early '90s. Everywhere you look there's still evidence of Mum's love of plants – by the door there's a huge rubber plant that looks like it belongs in the

Amazon jungle and the front room's still dominated by the sprawling ivy that now trails along the floor and up the walls in every direction imaginable. A few days ago I saw a remarkably similar house on TV's *Changing Rooms* and cowered in embarrassment as the experts savaged its owners' bad taste.

It's here in Mum and Dad's house that I've spent every Christmas so far, and this year I'm sure that the festivities will follow the same pattern as they always have. I'm not far wrong. On Christmas Eve, a sheepish-looking Dad sneaks into my bedroom covered in Sellotape and wrapping paper and begs me to wrap up his presents for Mum. And on Christmas morning, Mum gives her usual moans about Dad's uselessness in the kitchen and then asks me to give her a hand lifting the turkey in and out of the oven.

This year, however, there's one major change. Mum's decided to follow one of Nigella Lawson's recipes and cook goose for Christmas dinner rather than turkey. The only problem is that she's bought a bird so big that it won't fit in the oven.

'Flamin' 'ell!' she fumes, almost dropping it onto the floor.

The goose's neck is too long and no matter which way round we try it, we can't force it in. We spend the next ten minutes hacking it off with a carving knife before finally managing to cram the bird into the oven.

'Well, that's the last time I try to be classy,' Mum huffs, leaning against the wall. 'I wish I'd got one of those cheap turkeys from down the market now.'

'Come on, Mum, it'll all be worth it in the end. I'm sure everyone'll be impressed.'

'Hmpf! Your dad probably won't even notice!'

We sit down to catch our breath and she pours each of us the first sherry of the day. I stretch my legs out to relax and Mum immediately spots the opportunity for an intimate chat.

Over the last few years Mum's gradually come round to the idea of me being gay and I'm beginning to think she actually quite likes it. Of course Dad still won't have it mentioned in his presence but I sometimes wonder if this adds to the appeal for Mum. She loves sneaking into a corner to secretly chat to me about my love life, and after years of not being able to talk about it at home I have to admit that I enjoy it too. It certainly makes a change from the anger I felt towards my parents shortly after coming out. But that started to fade long ago and I don't even feel much anger towards Dad anymore as I realize I don't want to talk to him about my love life anyway; it's not as if it would play to his conversational strengths.

Mum, on the other hand, is another matter. I remember now that I made the unfortunate mistake of telling her that I was in love with Christian; I suppose part of me hoped that when the rest of my family saw how happy we were as a couple, they'd have no choice but to accept me the way I am. It's only now that I understand just how much that strategy's backfired.

'So what went wrong?' asks Mum. 'Did he pack you in or did you pack him in?'

As she bombards me with questions I not only feel humiliated but ashamed of myself too. Oh *why* couldn't I have fallen in love with Christian?

'Ooh I've just thought,' Mum says. 'You know Pam Barker's son's gay? *He* lives down South, somewhere called Pinner. Is that near you?'

'Not really, Mum – Clapham's on the other side of London.'

She ignores me and breezes on. 'Well, apparently he's got

really into internet dating – according to Pam it's a big thing for gays. You should try it, Charlie.'

'Mum, I know all about internet dating and let's just say it's not really my thing.'

'Well, in that case why don't I ask Pam for her son's number? He sells ice cream in a theatre *and* runs *The Sound of Music* fan club – I'm sure you'd get on really well.'

'Look, no offence, Mum, but can we just talk about something else? I really don't want to discuss my love life right now.'

'What's the matter, love? Have I hit a raw nerve?'

'You could say that, yeah.'

'Well, it helps to talk about it, you know. Bottling it up's the worst thing you can do.'

'Honestly, Mum, I promise I'm not bottling it up. All I've done for the last few weeks is talk about it.'

'Not to me you've not.'

I can see the hurt register on her face and am felled by a wave of guilt. For years I've resented the fact that I can't talk about anything to do with being gay at home and now here's Mum trying to help and I'm shutting her out.

At that moment, Dad walks through the door, clearing his throat loudly. 'How's that turkey doing then?'

I don't know whether he heard us or not but I stiffen up all the same.

'Actually, Frank,' says Mum, fixing her features into something approaching a smile, 'this year I'm doing goose – it's a Nigella Lawson recipe.'

'Oh, is she that posh bird off the telly?'

'Dad!' I groan. 'She's the *Domestic Goddess*!'

'Yeah, well, whoever she is, she's not bad-looking for a Southerner.'

Mum rolls her eyes at me and stands up to baste the goose.

A few hours later, the fully cooked goose sits in the centre of the table and we're all gathered around it ready to tuck in. We've been joined by Grandma, who's getting frailer in her old age and has recently moved into an old people's home, and Joe, who's travelled down to Bolton from Newcastle with his long-term girlfriend Sarah. Sarah has a strong Geordie accent, is even more into football than my dad, and is fond of telling everyone that as a teenager she once appeared as an extra in *Byker Grove*.

At the start of dinner, Sarah and Joe announce that they've just got engaged and are planning to buy their first house together in the New Year. Everyone's ecstatic and there are gasps of amazement from each side of the table. I try my best to look happy for them but can't help feeling a resurgence of the jealousy that has so often soured my relationship with Joe. It isn't just that I want what he has but also that it reminds me of what I've failed to get for myself. But I tick myself off for being self-absorbed, telling myself that it isn't always about me and I should be happy for my brother.

'Oh that's brilliant, Joe,' I jump in quickly.

'Yeah, that's beltin' news,' says Grandma.

'Congratulations, son!' beams Dad.

In the midst of all the excitement, Mum leans over to me and whispers, 'Cheer up, love – I'm sure there are plenty more lightbulbs in the chandelier.'

All of a sudden I'm eight years old again, with Joe reflecting my failings right back at me in front of the whole family. I can't believe that so many years have passed yet so little has changed. I force a weak smile but Dad spots it across the table and can tell that there's something wrong.

'Come on, lad,' he says, 'get some food down you. I bet you don't get turkey like that down London!'

Mum smiles through gritted teeth. 'Actually, Frank, I think I've already told you – it's goose.'

'Right, yeah, sorry . . .' he mumbles. 'Urm, how's work, Charlie? Is it still going well?'

'Great, thanks,' I say, brightening up. 'Have I told you I've just been promoted to producer?'

'That's brilliant news!' everyone cheers.

'Yeah,' I reply, 'so I won't have to worry about money anymore.'

'Fantastic,' says Joe. 'I'm so pleased.'

I wonder if he's genuinely pleased for me or if, like me, he's just pretending because we're in front of Mum and Dad.

'What are you going to be working on next then?' he asks.

'Well, it's an extreme makeover show called *Revamp the Tramp*. It's kind of like Trinny and Susannah but with homeless people as guests. They reckon it's going to be big.'

As everyone oohs and aahs Mum leans over again to whisper in my ear. 'Well, you never know,' she says, 'you might meet some nice gays working on the team. It's true what they say – it always happens when you least expect it!'

I roll my eyes in exasperation.

'Haway,' says Sarah, perking up. 'Talking about telly, did I ever tell you about the time I was on *Byker Grove*, like?'

'Yes,' hisses Joe, 'we've heard that story *several* times.'

She folds her arms in a sulk.

'I tell you what, Charlie,' Dad joins in, 'I was reading in the paper the other day that the media down London is apparently staffed entirely by cocaine addicts.'

Mum looks outraged. 'Well, I hope *you're* not doing cocaine, Charlie!'

'Course not.'

'According to what I read,' Dad goes on, stroking his chin, 'some people in London even snort it off their desks.'

Everyone around the table gasps and Mum begins to flush at the neck.

I sit up in my seat with a scowl. 'Well, I can promise you now that I've never seen anyone snort cocaine in any office I've worked in.'

'Eeh, it's a dangerous place, London,' offers Grandma. 'Bombings, stabbings, gang-rapes . . .'

'Don't you think you'd be better off living up here, lad?' asks Dad.

'But my job's down there, Dad.'

'Well, couldn't you get one up here?'

I decide not to answer and reach for the stuffing, piling a load more onto my plate. Doesn't it occur to them that I don't *want* to live up here? Can't they see that I've only been happy since I left?

''Ey,' says Grandma, leaning forward so she has everyone's attention, 'I was talking to Fat Pat the other day and *she* once met a TV producer. Apparently he was into prostitutes.'

'Bloomin' eck, Charlie,' fumes Dad, 'I think you better had move up here!'

'Look, will everyone stop fussing,' I say, trying my best not to sound exasperated. 'Thanks for your concern but I'm quite happy living in London.'

‘But we worry about you, lad,’ says Dad. ‘It’s not safe down there.’

‘Yeah, well, don’t – I can look after myself.’

‘You know what, love,’ says Mum, leaning in again so that no one can hear, ‘if you are moving back to Bolton, maybe I should introduce you to my new hairdresser, Carl. He wears ever so colourful waistcoats and knows the words to all Barbra Streisand’s show tunes. I’m sure he dances at your end of the ballroom.’

I look at my plate and stab into a chipolata. This is like torture.

‘’Ere Maggie,’ Dad goes on, holding out his empty plate, ‘is there any more of that duck?’

Mum looks as if she’s about to explode. ‘Bloomin’ ’eck, Frank! How many times do I have to say it – it’s flippin’ GOOSE!’

‘All right, keep your hair on. Turkey, duck, goose. I wasn’t *that* far off!’

She buries her head in her hands. ‘Oh, I bet Nigella Lawson doesn’t have to put up with this!’

I sneak a look at my watch, wondering how long this will go on for – and wishing I could escape.

A few hours later, everyone’s busy preparing the house for the traditional Matthews family drinks party. Dad’s putting his favourite Tina Turner album on the stereo while Mum’s making sure she has all the guests’ Christmas cards on prominent display.

‘I cannae wait to meet the rest of the family like,’ says Sarah.

‘And just think,’ says Mum cheerily, ‘the next time we’re all together will be at your wedding.’ She looks at me and mouths, ‘Sorry, love!’

First to arrive at the party is Auntie Jan, who's turned her back on flings with bad boys and settled down with a retired sunbed salesman called Stan in his villa (with a swimming pool!) in Tenerife. Uncle Stan has dyed-black hair, leathery brown skin and an addiction to green Smints, which he pops into his mouth two or three at a time. He's about twenty years older than Auntie Jan and clearly devoted to her; he calls her his princess and constantly showers her with gifts of lacy lingerie and flashy jewellery. Right now, the two of them burst through the door in a blaze of colour, looking as if they've just stepped off the beach.

'Ooh,' says Uncle Stan, shivering, 'this country's so *cold*!'

Jan takes off her sunhat and shades and gives us all a big smile. '*Buenos días*, everyone!' She goes round the room giving out kisses and then sidles over to me, hiding away in a corner. 'Hiya sunshine, how's your French fella?'

I grimace. 'Oh yeah, we, urm, we split up actually.'

Her face falls and then rises again as if she's just had a brilliant idea. 'Never mind – I met a lovely air steward on the plane over here . . .'

Next to arrive are Uncle Les and his wife Auntie Babs, who as soon as she got married seemed to go back to looking just as miserable as she always did beforehand. Nine months after the wedding, Les resigned himself to selling his pet ferrets Slap and Tickle when Auntie Babs gave birth to twin daughters. My cousins are nearly six now and already big fans of Britney Spears and Christina Aguilera. Today they bounce through the door dressed in shiny hotpants and matching crop tops emblazoned with the word 'Juicy', bursting with excitement to tell everyone about the glitter make-up and karaoke machine Father Christmas brought them.

'Merry Christmas everyone,' sighs Les wearily. 'Now, I

couldn't half do with a pint.' I can't get over how much Les has aged over the last few years. His muscles have withered away, his hair's thinning and whenever he yawns, which is more and more often these days, I can see a handful of gold fillings buried at the back of his mouth. Worst of all, the hair on his chest is starting to go grey. I hope somebody gives him a pint soon so he can regain some of his sparkle.

As is par for the course at Mum and Dad's Christmas party, the adults instinctively divide themselves into two groups according to sex. The men make for the kitchen area, where they stand around the huge barrel supping bitter out of pint glasses and discussing football and cars. And the women settle down in the living room, where they chat for hours about pregnancy and childbirth. As usual, I don't really know what to do with myself. Joe always gravitates towards the pack of males while Sarah slots perfectly into the group of women. But I don't fit easily into either group and start to feel like an awkward teenager again, skulking around nervously like the odd one out.

I decide instead to go and sit with Auntie Jan; after all, when I was growing up, she was always the single one, the slightly wild one who didn't fit in with all the much more conventional couples. I'm intrigued to know how she managed to stop fancying bad boys and fall in love with a man who loves her. I wait till she goes to the loo then corner her on her way back downstairs. We sit next to each other on the bottom step and, after a few minutes' preamble in which she tells me all about her favourite air steward performing the entire dance routine to Kylie Minogue's 'Can't Get You Out of My Head' in the aisle of the aeroplane, I manage to bring the conversation around to the subject I want to discuss.

'So what would you say you fell in love with about Uncle Stan?'

Jan begins tracing the rim of her glass of Cava with her finger. 'I don't know,' she breathes. 'I suppose he made me feel safe. Yeah, I think that's what got me.'

'But he's very different from the kind of man you used to go for.'

She scoffs and takes a swig of her drink. 'You're telling me. The *last* thing the others made me feel was safe.'

'So what changed? Why did you suddenly find that attractive?'

She stops and thinks it over. 'You know what, Charlie, everyone used to tell me not to go for bastards – your mam used to say it all the time. But I couldn't help it, that's just what I fancied.'

'But *why* do you think you fancied them?'

'Funnily enough, a friend of mine once did a course in psychology and she told me it was all to do with low self-esteem. She came up with some theory about me thinking I was in your mam's shadow because she was always our dad's favourite, she was the pretty one who everyone fancied, she was the natural blonde while mine was out of a bottle . . .'

'And do you think there was anything in that?'

'I think there probably was, yeah. At least I accepted it at the time. But the frustrating thing was, knowing *why* I fancied men who treated me badly didn't *stop* me fancying them. And I started to think it never would. Until I met Stan.'

'So what do you think happened? Did the message just gradually sink in?'

'I guess it did, yeah, very slowly. I tell you what, though, I wish I could take hold of the girl I was then and give her a good shake. I mean, can you remember some of the blokes I used to go out with?'

'Well, yeah, some of them weren't the best.'

'And that's putting it mildly. God, I was such a silly cow. You know, when I see young people now making the same mistakes I did, I just want to scream in their face. I mean, some of them are so stupid they can't see the blindingly obvious.'

At this point I start to feel uncomfortable and shift around on the step. 'Well, yeah,' I attempt, 'but finding the right person can be hard sometimes.'

'I know it can, sunshine. And that's why I really want to introduce you to this air steward . . .'

After a few minutes of listening to her insist she's found my ideal match, I drain my glass dry and excuse myself to go to the loo.

On the way back, I notice that the door to Mum and Dad's bedroom is open and I go in and find Grandma having a quiet moment to herself. She's sitting on the edge of the bed and wringing her hands, desperate to smoke a cigarette but knowing that she'll incur the wrath of the entire family if she does so. On her first night in the old folks' home she smuggled in a packet of cigarettes and sneakily lit one once she'd been put to bed. The smoke set off the fire alarm and the nursing staff were forced to haul all the residents out of bed, into their wheelchairs and Zimmer frames, and out onto the street. The next day, Dad and Uncle Les received an angry phone call from the Matron telling them that Grandma would only be allowed to stay at the home if she gave up smoking. From the look of her now, she's still in the throes of major withdrawal symptoms.

'Ooh, I'm gaspin' for a tab,' she moans.

I decide that it would be best to distract her and ask if

there's any local gossip. She immediately perks up and starts telling me about Shirley Stubbins, who now has six kids by six different men and has apparently left the father of the latest for a binman who once auditioned on *Pop Idol*.

'It's pathetic!' yaps Grandma. 'People these days have no staying power. When I was a girl you found yourself a fella and then you made do with him.'

I realize that I'm wincing and try not to feel judged. Images of a dead Benny Hill come flooding back into my mind.

'But what if you knew you'd made a mistake?' I ask.

'Tough luck! You made your choice and you stayed put, whatever happened. All this moaning and whingeing about falling in love, it's a load of old claptrap. We were far happier back then because we were more realistic. If we wanted to dream then we went to the pictures.'

I'm not sure I can listen to any more and start to think of how I can change the subject.

'Anyway, cocker,' she bulldozes on, 'are *you* courting yet?'

'Actually, Grandma,' I break in, suddenly struck by inspiration, 'I've just remembered – I've got a secret stash of fags on top of my wardrobe.'

Her face instantly lights up and she forgets all about what she was saying. 'Ooh have you, cocker?'

'Yeah. Do you fancy one?'

By the time we rejoin the party it's obvious that people have already had too much to drink. The men are joking loudly about the excuses their wives use for not having sex, while the women are cackling their way through anecdotes about their husbands' sexual inadequacies. I look around the room and recognize the drunken mess I know only too well from most Christmases since me and Joe were teenagers. Dad's standing in the centre of the kitchen performing his usual impression of George Formby, using the frying pan he bought Mum for Christmas as a ukulele. Mum's climbed up onto the table, rolled up her blouse to expose her midriff and is showing off the belly dancing moves she picked up on a recent package holiday to Turkey. My little cousins are performing an inappropriately risqué dance routine as they sing along to Christina Aguilera's 'Dirrty' on their karaoke machine. And Jan's showing Les and Babs a plastic surgery catalogue and trying to pick the new pair of boobs that Stan's promised to buy her for Christmas. Stan himself looks on adoringly, popping a constant stream of green Smints into his mouth and sipping beer from a pint glass that he doesn't realize has half a mince pie at the bottom.

Watching from the sidelines is my future sister-in-law Sarah, wearing an unmistakable expression of 'What have I let myself in for?' Her face reminds me of when I was a kid and how much I used to wish that my family were like the ones I watched on telly in *Diff'rent Strokes* and *The Cosby Show*.

All of a sudden I feel like a caged beast and need to get outside. For some reason I'm desperate to jump up and down and shout and scream out loud. I have to make a real effort to control myself.

'What's up, Charlie?' Dad booms. 'Do you want a beer?'

'Oh go on then, I think I could probably do with one.'

He goes into the kitchen and comes back with a freshly pulled pint of bitter. 'There you go, lad,' he says, looking around to check that everyone's listening, 'I bet you don't get beer like that down London!'

The whole house shakes with laughter.

I wonder if anyone will notice if I slip out to the car and listen to 'Live to Tell' for the hundredth time . . .

You'll See

I look up at the bride and groom, their bodies glowing with a happiness that's so vivid it seems somehow otherworldly. I look away and glance around me at the rest of the guests basking in the joy that almost bounces off the blissful couple. It's no use; the more I try to get into the spirit of the occasion, the more I feel overcome by a choking sense of isolation.

It's Shanaz's wedding day and she's marrying an osteopath called Ravi who she met at the hospital in Manchester where she recently qualified as a registrar. On their first date she found out that his parents go to the same temple as her mum and dad and told me that soon after that she realized she was in love. I can't get over how quickly she's changed yet again. Needless to say, her tongue piercing has long since disappeared and it seems like ages ago that she was a hardcore clubber. It feels like a whole other lifetime since the two of us used to sit around her room listening to Madonna, two rejected children clinging onto each other for survival.

Shanaz has chosen to celebrate her wedding in India on the outskirts of Delhi, where her family is originally from. A few days ago, I flew over for the start of the celebrations. Coming to India made me feel genuinely excited; I looked forward to visiting the Maharajah's palace Shanaz had told me her grandma escaped from to marry a stable boy. And I imagined myself in a scene from a Bollywood film wearing a turban and dressed all in white, perched on top of an elaborately decorated elephant as a troupe of dancing children scattered rose petals before me.

I'm here with Joe, who I can only assume has been invited as my guest because I'm single. I'm nervous about spending time with him, partly because our relationship has always been fractious but also because I've avoided seeing all my family or going home at all since Christmas. I've tried telling myself that this trip might be just what I need to stop resenting Joe as the brother who represents everything I'm not and to start seeing him as an individual I might just like if I only give him the chance. After all, it's always been on holidays that we've got on best, when we've been at one remove from some of the issues that come between us at home.

Things start well enough on the plane. We get tipsy on free booze, play endless increasingly absurd games of I Spy and reminisce about some of the great times we've had on family holidays.

'And it's not over yet,' I say with a smile. 'I might as well tell you now that when we get to India I fully intend to ride an elephant to the hotel.'

'Oh you do, do you?' Joe laughs fondly.

'Yeah!' I insist. 'So I hope you've brought your camera with you. Because I'm ready to take the lead role in my own Bollywood film!'

We laugh and chink our drinks together before looking out of the window and getting excited about our arrival.

Unfortunately, when we land in Delhi there are no signs of any elephants so I have to give up on my fantasy and instead we board a taxi that seems to be powered by pedals, smells like an open sewer and is driven by a hunchback with only one tooth. We set off for our hotel under a pounding rainstorm and our driver weaves his way through the busy streets, dodging stray chickens and monkeys, horse-drawn carts, herds of free-roaming cows, and motorbikes carrying whole families, all the time tooting his horn and wobbling his head at us with a smile. I hold onto the car door and grit my teeth. This is hardly the stuff of a Bollywood film.

Four days later it's still raining and Joe and I are standing sheltering under a vast tent-like canopy, the sound of a constant drum roll in our ears and the smell of incense heavy in the air. Kneeling on a raised platform before us is Shanaz, wearing a cerise and peach sari, gold rings through her nose, ears and all the way up her arms, and an elaborate bejewelled headdress that is nearly two feet tall and makes her tower over all the guests. She looks beautiful.

I watch as Shanaz and Ravi exchange matching garlands and then step on and off some kind of sacred stone. All the time a bare-chested priest stands beside them chanting verses in a foreign language and then he winds a thread of cotton around them twenty-four times. I'm not sure what it all means and pretty soon my mind starts to wander. Although I'm pleased that Shanaz is so obviously happy on her wedding day, I can't help also feeling a sense of sadness. Whichever way I look at it, Shanaz's marriage effectively rules out any chance of our friendship going back to what it was, when as children we lost ourselves in our joint imagination, picturing ourselves rebelling against the lives that were destined for us, a life Shanaz has now decided to embrace – in a way I don't see how I ever can.

Before coming to India, I tried looking on the bright side and imagined Shanaz and I would bond during all the activities in the week leading up to the big day. I pictured us in a scene from *Monsoon Wedding*, laughing and joking as we painted her hands with elaborate henna designs. But I soon discovered that most of the events scheduled in the lead-up to the wedding divided the guests into two groups strictly according to gender. Most importantly, men were forbidden from attending the *mehndi* evening, which sounded to me a bit like a western hen night and by far the most fun. I did try accompanying Joe to the equivalent male activity but felt really out of place and slipped away as soon as I could, making excuses about a bad case of jetlag.

Right now I'm distracted from my thoughts by the priest stepping forward to tie Shanaz and Ravi's costumes together in some kind of symbolical knot. As he does so I catch sight of Shanaz's henna tattoos and remember her explaining to me that, according to tradition, the groom's initials are always hidden somewhere in the design and it's up to him to find them once the couple are alone on their wedding night. I look again at the designs and am surprised to find myself feeling a pique of jealousy.

Yesterday afternoon, I managed to get Shanaz all to myself for a couple of hours in her family home. Joe was staying in the hotel bar to watch some kind of football game on satellite TV and Shanaz's family had driven to the airport to welcome another wave of guests. According to Hindu custom, Shanaz wasn't allowed to leave the family home after her *mehndi* so she invited me round to keep her company.

I jump into another rickety cab, curious to see the Maharajah's palace I've heard so much about when I was young. I try not to get my hopes up too much and resign myself to the fact that it will probably be a bit dilapidated by now. But when I eventually arrive, after another hair-raising journey across the city during which I'm thrilled to spot a real elephant but then mortified when we nearly run it over, I'm surprised to find that the family's Indian home is a modestly sized, fairly average-looking modern building not too dissimilar inside from the kind you might find in Bolton. I'm puzzled.

'So tell me,' I ask, once we're sitting down in the living room each with a glass of pineapple lassi, 'whatever happened to the Maharajah's palace?'

'You what?' she replies in a Bolton accent unchanged by her journey halfway across the world. 'What are you on about?'

'Don't you remember? The story about your grandma running off with that stable boy . . .'

'Oh *that*!' she smiles. 'You don't still believe that, do you?'

'Well, why shouldn't I? You've never told me not to.'

'Well, I'm telling you now, Charlie. Of course that's not true. My God, I thought you'd have sussed that one out ages ago!'

I feel a bit daft and suck noisily on my straw. Am I really stupid not to have worked it out for myself?

Shanaz chuckles with a look of nostalgia. 'You know, I used to love making up stories like that to impress people.'

'But you didn't need to impress *me*, Shanaz.'

'I know, I know. But I probably needed to impress myself . . .' She twiddles the straw in her drink as she thinks it over. 'Oh I used to hate being Indian, Charlie. Surely you must have guessed that much.'

'But you always seemed so proud of it . . .'

She waves her hand dismissively. 'Oh yeah, I put up a good front, I'll give you that. But I hated everything about it. I used to dread unpacking my lunchbox at school and taking out my chapattis and bhajis. I used to get so upset when everyone started taking the piss. All I ever wanted was to eat jam butties and Penguin biscuits like the rest of you.'

'But I always thought you couldn't care less what anyone said. I always thought you were so feisty and independent.'

She smiles fondly. 'I *wish*! I used to feel so ashamed when my mum turned up at the school gates in a green and yellow sari with a bright red bindi in the middle of her forehead. Don't you remember the time Vince Hargreaves and his mates pinned me down in front of everybody and drew a whopping big bindi on my head in permanent marker?'

'Well, yeah, of course I do. But for some reason I always thought you rose above it. I honestly thought it didn't bother you.'

'Yeah, well, it did. And it did for longer than I'd admit to most people. You know what, I used to lie in bed at night wishing I wasn't Indian, tensing every muscle in my body so hard that I was convinced it had to make me wake up "normal".'

I'm suddenly hit by the memory of doing exactly the same thing – only in my case wishing I wasn't gay. But I tell myself that none of that matters anymore, not now that I'm out and proud. 'Thank God it never worked!' I smile at Shanaz brightly.

'Yeah, now I can agree with you,' she replies. 'But back then I wouldn't have thought in a million years I'd ever end up sitting here in India covered in henna tattoos and getting ready for a full-on Hindu wedding.'

I give her an understanding nod. It's years since Shanaz and I have sat down for a proper heart-to-heart and I want to make the most of it. I have to stop being selfish and thinking about where her marriage leaves me. 'So what happened?' I ask. 'What made you come round?'

'Oh I don't know. I suppose somewhere along the line I realized that all that not-wanting-to-be-Indian stuff was completely exhausting and utterly pointless. I mean, what's the point trying to deny your family or where you've come from? It's not as if it's ever going to make any difference, is it?'

I shrug. 'I suppose not, no.'

'And if I'm totally honest,' she goes on breezily, 'then falling in love with an Indian had a lot to do with it too.' She holds up her hennaed hands and giggles with delight as she strokes them. 'You know what – I can't wait to get married tomorrow and then I can wear my bindi for everyone to see!'

I feel a smile spreading across my face. 'In that case, I can't wait to see it either.'

'And how are things going with *your* love life?' she asks, shuffling forward in her seat. 'Has there been anyone since Christian?'

I shrink back. 'Oh no. I've had a few dates and things but not with anyone important. I'm not sure it's ever going to happen for me, to be honest.'

'But Charlie,' she gasps, 'that's not like you. You're the last person I expected to get jaded!'

I'm just about to explain that it's not so much that I'm jaded, more that I'm worried I'll only ever be attracted to people who treat me badly. I'm just about to explain that I've recently found myself dating men I suspect aren't that interested in me, or having the occasional one night stand with a man who's made it quite clear he isn't looking for a relationship. I'm just about to explain that I'm frightened I might be my own worst enemy and will never allow myself to be happy.

I'm just about to explain that she might be able to make peace with her background and marry someone who brings her back into the fold but that option simply isn't open to me. But then I stop. How could I possibly make Shanaz understand all this? Even though we grew up together and I always thought our situations were so similar, they suddenly seem so different.

'Oh don't worry about it,' I say. 'You're getting married tomorrow! Now come on, tell me everything that's going to happen . . .'

The next day I find out how a Hindu wedding works for myself. I stand mesmerized by the sight of Shanaz decked out in all her finery and radiating pleasure as she gazes into the eyes of her husband-to-be. The priest lights a small fire and the two of them take seven steps around it, all the time reciting their vows. Once this is complete, Ravi presents Shanaz with some kind of symbolic necklace. Judging from the looks on the faces of the more experienced Indian guests around me, I guess this means that from now on they're married.

I join in with everyone's cheering and applause but inside can't help feeling lonely. This is a familiar sensation by now as back home several of my friends have started to get married too. Amelia and Anthony have finally set a date and are busy planning every last detail and Joe will be marrying Sarah at her parish church in Newcastle shortly after we get home. At times it feels like everyone around me has started to couple up, even those I least expected. One of the first to go was Inappropriate Lee, who retired from his years of lechery and tied the knot with an overweight, dowdy librarian who's already pregnant with their second child. And Caroline Tits gave up her years of flirting and stunned us all by suddenly producing a childhood sweetheart who works as a long-distance lorry driver and then promptly marrying him. 'Oh he might not be perfect,' she explained to her bemused friends, 'but at least he's there.'

It's as if all of a sudden, having someone to marry is the most important thing in everyone's life and I'm starting to understand Bridget Jones's feelings about 'smug marrieds'. But unlike Bridget, I know that there's no happy ending in store for me – even if I do find someone to share my life with, it's not legally possible for two men to get married so there's no chance of me ever enjoying a day like today. It's slowly dawning on me that whatever I do in life, I'll always be shut out of the golden circle that seems so important to everyone else.

Once I've made sure no one's looking I pull out a hipflask of neat gin I've hidden in my pocket and take a deep swig. A few people warned me that booze is strictly forbidden at Hindu weddings so I planned ahead and brought along a little something to help me through the day. I don't often drink gin and discover now that I quite like the taste. I already downed three stiff doubles mixed with tonic before leaving the hotel this morning and with a little top-up now and again I can easily feel the effects. For some reason, though, the more I drink the more depressed it seems to make me. I can't understand it – it certainly never has that effect on Mike and he drinks it all the time. Weddings obviously just aren't my thing. Maybe I need to drink more.

Shanaz moves forward and bows her head so that her new husband can sprinkle some kind of red powder over her hair and then apply the bindi that's the sign of a married woman. She told me beforehand that this would mean the ceremony has come to an end and I can't help but feel a slight relief that it's finally over. All the guests move forward to throw petals and rice over the newlyweds and there's something about the intensity of happiness concentrated in such a small area that makes me feel squalid inside.

I'm just about to sneak another quick swig of gin when I discover that the flask's almost empty. Not to worry, I remember that I've stashed another full bottle in the bushes outside. As soon as I can, I slip away from the crowds and creep outside to fill up my flask.

Just as I'm crouching over on the ground trying my best not to spill any gin, Joe appears next to me with a furious look on his face. 'What do you think you're up to?'

I look around shiftily to check that no one else is watching. 'Oh nothing. I'm just having a nice leveller, that's all.'

'But you're not supposed to drink at a Hindu wedding.'

'I know but it doesn't really matter; nobody'll know if you don't let on. And anyway, I'm not a Hindu so it doesn't count.'

'Well, neither am I but I'm not drinking.'

The note of condescension in his voice riles me so much that it's as if it lights a touchpaper. I draw myself up to my full height and look him in the eye. 'Yeah, well, maybe it's easier for you, Joe – maybe you fit in more. After all, you're getting hitched yourself in a few weeks. And let's be honest, we might be on the other side of the world but the drill isn't that different, is it?'

'Charlie, what are you on about?'

'Oh nothing you'd understand. You're part of the golden circle, remember?'

'The golden circle? What golden circle?'

'Don't worry about it, you wouldn't get it.' I shoot him a defiant look and slot the flask back into my pocket.

'Come on, mate,' he coaxes, 'you don't need to do this.'

I hesitate, telling myself that Joe and I have been getting on better than we have for years. Do I really want to jeopardize that now?

'It's been a great holiday and a great day,' he persists. 'Please don't do anything to spoil it.'

But as he says the words I know I won't be able to stop myself. 'Actually, Joe,' I erupt, 'for some of us it hasn't been a great day. Because, in case you haven't noticed, when it comes to this kind of thing some of us are outsiders.'

From the look on his face this is something that's never even crossed his mind. 'I – I'm sorry—'

I don't give him time to reply. 'But the thing about being an outsider is I don't have to play by the rules.'

'Charlie, what do you mean?'

'Watch.'

I take a deep breath and stride back to the tent with a new sense of purpose.

A few hours later I'm so drunk I can hardly stand up. I've spent ages dancing to traditional Indian sitar music and must have shovelled about five different types of curry into my now severely bloated stomach. Thankfully, I spot a sofa and slump into it, surrounded by a group of British medics I remember meeting when I went to visit Shanaz at university, although they've changed so much since then they're barely recognizable.

'We've spotted a place we really like in Didsbury,' says the one I think people used to call Tricky, 'but it's just one street away from the catchment area for the best primary school.'

'Well, if I were you I'd think again,' says another who I'm convinced was called Hickey. 'I checked out fees at a few private schools the other day and they were astronomical.'

The entire group seems gripped by the conversation but I know I'm not going to be able to join in. How can everyone here, even the people who used to be so much wilder than me, have grown up so quickly? And how can they have all left me behind? I feel racked by a crippling sense of depression and stagger off to sneak another nip of gin.

On the way I spot the microphone Ravi and his family used for the speeches and the temptation's too great. I go over to grab it and the first song that comes into my head is Madonna's 'You'll See', her boldly rousing celebration of singledom. I've already been humming it to myself for most of the day and launch into it now, belting out how proud I am not to need anyone else in my life. Despite my drunkenness I can remember every line and boom out the song with defiance, accompanied by the occasional blast of feedback. It's quite uncanny how much the lyrics sum up the way I'm feeling right now. Maybe I'm not on my own after all, I think to myself. No, I'm not – when everyone else has deserted me Madonna's still there as always, understanding exactly how I feel.

Some of the guests start to gather around me and an old woman who looks like Grandma Kumar claps her hands excitedly. 'Oh I didn't know there was karaoke! What fun!'

I'm just catching my breath to give the next line everything I've got when the microphone's rudely snatched from my hands. I look down and see Joe. 'Come on, mate,' he says, 'I think it's time we made a move.'

Before I have chance to protest he's marched me through the tent in full view of everyone and bundled me outside and into a waiting taxi. A crowd of guests follow us to the exit, open-mouthed. It's obvious from their horrified expressions that everyone except me is stone cold sober. I gaze at them through the car window but by now my vision's completely blurred and all I can take in is a cacophony of colour and what seem like a billion bindis all merging into one.

I'm still singing away in a crumpled corner of the back seat by the time we reach our hotel. I step onto the pavement and my legs give way, bringing me crashing to the floor a second time. Joe has to lift me up, lug me across the lobby in front of the shocked reception staff and then slowly heave me upstairs and into the bedroom.

As soon as he shuts the door behind us, I collapse onto the bed fully clothed. There are a couple of stray sequins from somebody's sari stuck to my left cheek and I can't be bothered to take out my contact lenses or brush my teeth.

'Oh Joe,' I moan, lying face-down on the pillow, 'I feel so rubbish!'

He looks at me and sighs. 'Well, I know you're not going through the easiest time at the moment but this is your best mate's wedding day – you should be happy for her.'

'I am, I am,' I cry, 'I honestly am. So I don't understand why I feel so *low*.'

'Well, it's obvious, isn't it? That'll be the gin – hasn't anyone ever told you it's a depressant?'

He pads into the bathroom and I turn over and groan. All I want is for this black mood to end but it doesn't seem to be lifting at all. And Joe might be right about the gin making me feel depressed but deep down I know this is about more than that.

I lay my pillow sideways and snuggle up to it as if it's another person lying next to me. I remember Grandma telling me that when Grandad died, the only way she could get to sleep at night was by cuddling up to a pillow and pretending it was him. I snuggle up to mine now but am not sure who to imagine it is. I realize that there isn't anybody I'd like to have lying asleep next to me and feel stupid for trying. I remember the lyrics to 'You'll See' and remind myself that I don't need anyone else. I'm fine on my own.

God, I hope I feel better in the morning.

Hollywood

Six months later, I still don't feel better. And I still haven't worked out why. But I have been given a glimmer of hope that leads me somewhere completely unexpected – all the way to Hollywood . . .

It's a hot summer's day and I'm in Los Angeles, driving down Sunset Boulevard with the wind in my hair and the sun on my face. I'm excited to be in a city I've always wanted to visit and on the stereo a track from Madonna's latest album is playing, a track in which she celebrates the magic of Hollywood – a town that encourages everyone to shine as brightly as possible.

I'm here to shoot the first episode of an alternative travel show called *Dyke on a Bike*, which is a cross between the kind of satirical travelogue made popular by Louis Theroux and the tongue-in-cheek investigative reporting of Ruby Wax. Our presenter is Bernie Baxter, a former Olympic cyclist who won three gold medals in Sydney and was recently made a dame. Bernie isn't what you'd expect from a typical dame; she wears her hair in a Mohawk, has a dirty laugh that sounds uncannily like Sid James, and has worked her way through a string of celebrity girlfriends that have made her a tabloid star and earned her the catchphrase, 'When Bernie strikes, they all turn dyke'. The TV executives at a hip, youth-oriented digital channel have decided she's the perfect choice to front her own travelogue, billed as an irreverent exploration of the myths of international travel.

I turn down a street lined with palm trees and look up at the Hollywood sign glimmering at me from the hillside. Inside I can feel my excitement swelling. I tell myself that this trip could represent a real turning point in a career that, if I'm honest, hasn't inspired me in ages. My professional ambitions may have moved on from my goal of becoming a theatre director and it may have been years since I remembered my dream of becoming a writer, but I'm gradually coming to the realization that making lightweight TV programmes isn't making me happy. Maybe film will be the art form in which I can really shine. Maybe this new TV show will be my first step into an industry that'll make me feel truly fulfilled.

Before long, my mind's whirling with images of glitzy red carpet premieres and triumphant Oscar acceptance speeches in front of hordes of Hollywood stars. Film's obviously a much more exciting, dynamic medium than television – and so much more glamorous. Why's it taken me such a long time to see it's the right one for me?

I tell myself not to get too carried away dreaming about the future but to focus on the task in hand; I'm here with a TV show called *Dyke on a Bike* and the whole point of my visit is to take the mickey out of the place.

The first few days of the trip have been set aside for me to check out the various locations and meet our guests. Just driving around the city now, I realize I won't have a problem finding stereotypical images of America to set the scene. On every street corner there are old-fashioned American diners and branches of 7-Eleven and Starbucks, and everything from the fire hydrants to the signs saying 'WALK' and 'DON'T WALK' look like props from a Hollywood film. There are cops on motorbikes who remind me of the characters in *CHiPs*, and everyone who passes by has teeth so white that they reflect the sunlight and make me squint, even with my sunglasses on.

'Bring it on!' beams the youthful researcher sitting in the passenger seat next to me. Sam Campbell, or Scramble as everyone calls him, only graduated from university less than a year ago and is bright-eyed and keen. He has messy surfer hair and wears a baseball cap, an American football top and jeans that are so loose-fitting that his tight white underpants and half of his backside are permanently on show to the world behind him. Scramble's a fan of all things American and despite coming from Skegness even speaks in an affected transatlantic accent. As a self-confessed film buff, he's been straining at the leash to come to Hollywood and right now is overwhelmed by what he sees. 'This is unreal, dude,' he drawls. 'I can't believe I'm actually here!'

The following morning, we're woken up early by jetlag and take advantage of it to start our shoot. First on our filming schedule is the obligatory opening sequence of our dyke arriving at this week's destination on the back of her bike. After that we meet up with our first guests – a pair of generic, personality-free Hollywood princesses called Sweetness and Serenity. We film the two of them on a shopping trip to Rodeo Drive, when they're driven around by their own personal chauffeurs and spend enough money to bankroll a small country on their seemingly limitless credit cards. Bernie follows them through a succession of designer stores, all the time asking for their opinions on the latest news such as the role of

Saddam Hussein in the Iraq war. 'Excuse me?' they say with a vacant look in their eyes. 'But when does that movie open?'

Next on our agenda is filming a long sequence at a plastic surgery clinic to uncover the real story behind the latest hit TV show, *Nip/Tuck*. Back in London we managed to secure access to the operating theatre and take advantage of this to shoot a couple of particularly gruesome operations. Then we interview Lavish Delgado, a former Playboy bunny girl who became world famous when her ninth nose job went wrong and left her with a black hole in the centre of her face. She chats to Bernie about LA's obsession with physical perfection and how her career has tanked since her plastic surgery disaster. 'The only job I've been offered recently,' she moans, 'is the serial-killing monster in *Shit-scared 6*.'

The centrepiece of our programme is a behind-the-scenes report from a glitzy film premiere. In keeping with the theme of our programme, Bernie intends to use this to chip away at LA's glossy façade. On the last night of our trip we arrive at the cinema, push our way through the crowd of fans and show our passes to the security guards who escort us under the crash barriers and behind the velvet rope.

'Man, I can't believe I'm actually at a full-on film premiere,' drools Scramble. 'This is a total trip!'

His relentless enthusiasm is starting to annoy me but I manage to keep it to myself.

After a seemingly interminable wait there's an explosion of camera flashes and we see the lead actress step out of her stretch limo and onto the red carpet. Tiffany Turner is a big-busted blonde who grew up in a trailer park before going on to become a major international celebrity when a video of her having sex with the heir to a fast-food empire somehow surfaced on the internet. A hush of excitement descends over the crowd as they watch her turn this way and that, pouting for the cameras as they flash back at her. It's as if she's glowing with a palpable sense of charisma and I can't take my eyes off her. As she looks around, she fleetingly catches my gaze and for that brief moment I feel like the most special person in the world.

A minor panic erupts as an officious-looking PR girl in a white trouser suit notices that Tiffany's stepped in some chewing gum and has a piece of toilet roll trailing from her dagger heel. 'Well, hurry up then!' the actress snaps at her, holding out her heel. 'Hurry up and get it off me!'

As the PR girl kneels down to pick off the chewing gum, Bernie hisses at our cameraman, 'Quick! Make sure you get a shot of that!'

Next to arrive is Carlos Martel – the male star of the film and a Hispanic former WWF wrestler with a frighteningly muscular body and an even more frightening reputation for being a hard man with a penchant for punching photographers. The film's publicists are keen to start the rumour that the lead couple have fallen in love off-screen as well as on but Bernie's more interested in exploring the rumour that the hard man's gay and only landed the part in the film because he's sleeping with the head of the studio. I direct our crew to follow the two stars as they move towards each other and pose for more photos while the crowd of fans chant their names. They make an awkward, clunky couple and it's difficult to imagine them in a real-life relationship.

'Oh I love your new lips!' I hear the wrestler squeak to his co-star in a surprisingly camp off-screen voice. 'Where did you get them done, honey?' I listen to him ooh and aah as she babbles on about her latest collagen treatment, his limp wrist all the time hanging safely behind his back. His fans might be taken in but I can't help thinking that he's a textbook case of looks-like-Tarzan-talks-like-Jane.

Scramble's enthusiasm goes into overdrive. 'Dude, this is off the hook! Carlos Martel a closet case – now that's *unreal*!'

I try not to show that by now I'm finding him seriously irritating; everything we've filmed is soulless and fake and it turns out that this premiere is no different. I decide not to think about what this means for my plan of moving out of TV and into film.

Our camera carries on rolling as the golden couple make their way down the assembled line of TV, radio and print journalists, stopping to engage in a strictly timed four-minute chat with each, during which they manage to pretend they're close friends with the interviewer while also giving exactly the same carefully rehearsed answers to an identical list of pre-approved questions. Our camera follows them along the line, filming the entire series of supposedly informal chats – our intention is to edit their repeated answers together to expose just how inauthentic the whole set-up is.

'This is stonking,' beams Bernie. 'It's more of a con than I expected!'

Once they've reached the end of the line, the stars make their way through to the auditorium where they join the film's director in front of the screen and smile sweetly as he makes a short speech to introduce the movie. As I listen to him, I try to stay positive, telling myself that one day I could be doing his job, commanding a whole team of creatives on the set of a major Hollywood blockbuster – with all the panache of a star conductor leading an internationally acclaimed orchestra.

After a couple of minutes, the actors and director say they hope everyone enjoys the film and then sneak out of a side entrance, where a limo's waiting to speed them away. 'Let's get out of here,' I hear the wrestler pout to his co-star. 'This premiere is so *over*!'

We manage to capture their exit on camera and then Bernie jumps into the shot to ask why cinema audiences should be expected to watch the film if the lead actors can't even be bothered to sit through it themselves. I have to admit, now that I've seen what happens at a premiere, the whole thing does seem like a sham. I think again of the lyrics to Madonna's latest album and suddenly remember that, far from being a celebration of the American dream, the album's actually intended as a satire on it. I guess I'm experiencing the very thing she sings about.

I feel stupid now for getting overexcited and resolving to pursue a career in film. How childish of me to think that jumping ship from TV to film could ever solve all my problems. The truth is the world I've just witnessed is not only dishonest but even feels a little sordid. I look down at the bracelet Tash and Amelia gave me when we graduated and read the inscription with the lyrics to 'Ray of Light'. I suddenly feel self-conscious and tuck it under my shirt sleeve.

The following morning we drive the car out of the city and up into the hills to film Bernie's closing piece-to-camera in front of the Hollywood sign. Unfortunately, on our way we have to stop to put the roof up as it starts pouring with rain. Los Angeles is the last place on earth I'd expect it to rain and as I look out of the windscreen I see that the bad weather is giving the city an entirely different look. Affluent areas like Beverly Hills suddenly seem tacky and ostentatious and the poverty around run-down neighbourhoods like Korea Town is much more noticeable. I'm really starting to dislike the place.

We jump out of the car to quickly knock off the final shot of the programme. Bernie straddles her bike in front of the Hollywood sign and gestures to the city below. 'If this is the American dream,' she says, her Mohawk drooping in the rain, 'then it's my worst nightmare.' She cycles out of shot and on to her next destination.

By the time we've finished, we're all wet through and looking forward to flying back to London. Only Scramble is still enjoying the experience, pressing his head against the car window to take it all in. 'Dude,' he drawls, as we slide down the hill and back into the city, 'this place is far out!'

I lean forward and turn on the stereo. I need to hear another blast of Madonna's 'Hollywood'.

'Well,' I announce, 'I won't be coming back to Hollywood any time soon.'

'Gee,' whistles Scramble, 'whatever happened to make you so cynical?'

Cynical? Nobody's ever called me cynical before. Is that really what I'm becoming?

I'm not sure how to answer his question. In the end I sigh and say, 'Life, just life.'

I turn the music up louder and, as I do, feel a sudden wave of homesickness. I've no idea where it comes from but in an instant I'm overwhelmed by an urge not just to go back to London but to travel all the way back to Bolton and see Mum and Dad.

The feeling takes me by surprise but it's very real. I realize I want to tell my parents about the shoot I've just done, how fake everything is here and how Tiffany Turner and Carlos

Martel showed themselves up to be total frauds. I want to have a laugh with Joe about all the celebrity parties I've been to in London, which I can now admit are just as soulless and tacky. And I want to open up to everyone and let them know how unhappy and unfulfilled I'm starting to feel – even if I am very different to them all.

The more I think about it, the more I realize how desperate I am to go home and reconnect with the shy, frightened boy I was so many years ago, the boy who didn't fit in and felt rejected by the world but somewhere deep inside always knew that he was loved by his family. I want Mum to look after me like she used to do when I was ill, making scrambled eggs and mugs of hot OXO and fussing around me as I lie on the sofa surrounded by cushions. I want Joe to annoy me by playing football in the back garden, constantly kicking his ball against the wall with the same repetitive thud. And I want Dad to come home after work, smelling of chips and mushy peas and whistling a tune by George Formby or Gracie Fields.

Yes, I've just about had a gutful of Hollywood. What I really fancy right now is a trip home to Bolton.

Part Four

Oh Father

The sky above me is slate grey, a colour that always reminds me of drizzly afternoons like this one in Bolton. A sharp wind blows through the trees and I pull my coat around me to keep warm.

Ahead of me walks Mum linking Grandma's arm by her side. Next to me is Joe, the two of us standing bolt upright and staring straight ahead. Although we're at the front of a procession of nearly a hundred people, the only sound to be heard is the shuffling of feet, the wind in the air and the occasional awkwardly stifled cough. I continue staring ahead and slowly follow the coffin inside and down the aisle to the front of the crematorium. It's Dad's funeral and I remind myself that I have to be strong and hold myself together.

Although Joe and I spent much of the past week organizing the ceremony, now that it's here I can't remember anything we planned. I sit in my pew and pick up an order of service, trying to concentrate as the vicar introduces himself to the mourners.

Over the years I've seen so many funeral scenes on TV and at the cinema that I always thought when I ended up at one myself, it would all be completely familiar. And in some ways it is. But in others it's totally different. For a start, all the funerals I've ever witnessed, from *EastEnders* to *Evita*, have been highly dramatic affairs with horse-led processions through the streets and grandly decorated coffins being slowly lowered into the ground as grief-stricken mourners wail and convulse in abject misery. But this funeral seems peculiarly undramatic and almost haunting in its ordinariness. When we first arrived at the crematorium, we had to wait at the gates while the service before us finished and everyone left. Now that we've made it inside I'm surprised to see that the chapel's carpeted in a sickly green and its walls are panelled in some kind of cheap-looking fake wood. Blocking the side aisles are a couple of knackered old storage heaters barely giving off enough warmth to heat a room a fraction of the size. Everyone pulls their coats around them and blows on their hands to keep warm. The whole scene is so sharply in focus and so eerily *real* that it makes me feel light-headed and dizzy.

As the vicar leads the congregation through a tentatively mumbled hymn to which nobody seems to know the tune, my mind drifts back over the events of the past week.

A few days after returning to London from my trip to LA, Mum wakes me up in the middle of the night with the news that Dad has suffered a heart attack and been taken into hospital.

'But don't worry, love,' she coos, 'the doctors reckon he'll be as right as rain in no time.'

I jump straight into the car anyway and race up the motorway ahead of the rush-hour traffic. As I arrive at the hospital and dart through the corridors looking for the right room, Mum's words whirl round and round in my head like a washing machine stuck on spin.

'He'll be as right as rain, he'll be as right as rain, he'll be as right as rain . . .'

I go over them so much that soon they stop making sense and I start to wonder if I'm actually going a bit delirious. More to the point, when I eventually make it to Dad's bedside, it's immediately clear that he's anything other than as right as rain.

Needles are sticking out all over him, he's buried under a web of tubes and the entire room is filled with machines and monitors that tick and beep at various ominous-sounding intervals. Mum, Grandma and Uncle Les turn to face me and explain that Dad suffered a second heart attack while I was driving up the motorway and hasn't regained consciousness since. Things aren't looking good.

'I've already lost one son,' Grandma mumbles, 'I'm not sure I can handle losing another.'

'Oh he can't give up on us now,' sniffs Les. 'He can't go and conk out at fifty-six.'

'Let's all try to stay positive,' chirps Mum in a voice that's at odds with her ashen, panicked-looking face. 'He's tough as old boots is our Frank. He'll be as right as rain by the end of the week.'

I really wish she'd stop saying that but decide it's probably best if I agree with her. I've never seen Mum looking so on edge and want to do everything I can to keep her calm. As we all stand around Dad willing him to get better, I can't help thinking that the image we form must look like one of those dramatic deathbed scenes you often see in Renaissance paintings. I suddenly feel very frightened and out of my depth and wish Joe would hurry up and get here. I can't even think of anything to say – everything I try sounds either terribly banal or like a clichéd line from an episode of *Casualty*.

For the next few hours, doctors and nurses fuss around Dad and there's an awkward moment when a consultant bombards

Mum with questions about his eating and drinking habits and I listen in disbelief as she breezes her way through a pack of lies about his almost total aversion to alcohol and his practically pathological hatred of fatty food. 'Chips?' she gasps, her hand over her mouth. 'He never touches them.'

I've always known Dad doesn't lead a particularly healthy lifestyle but somehow never imagined he'd end up in the state he's in now. To me he's always been such a big, powerful presence that he dominates whatever space he's in. I can't conceive of anything ever defeating him physically but here he is now lying powerless and pathetic, trapped inside a body that isn't so strong after all but is slowly failing him as everyone he used to tower over stands around watching. It's as if we're looking at a completely different man to the one who's known around Bolton as Frank the Tank.

'Come on, lad,' coaxes Les, 'you have to get better, then you can see the Wanderers win the League.'

'Yeah,' says Mum, 'and I'll cook a big pan of corned beef hash when they do and have everyone round to ours to celebrate.'

Maybe Mum's tactic is working – by lunchtime Dad starts to rally a little and even drifts back into consciousness occasionally. 'What's everybody making a fuss about?' he manages to splutter at one point. 'You're not getting rid of me that easily.'

It's around this time that Joe arrives from Newcastle and things really start to look up. Dad stays awake for long enough to have a conversation with him about the route he took down the motorway and then he spends a long time telling us that he's convinced he's 'turned the corner' and we should all trundle off home and get some sleep. There's no chance of that but Mum and Grandma do relax enough to go and get a cup of tea from the canteen and Les nips outside to make a few phone calls.

Once they've all gone, I notice Dad's expression change. 'I'm glad I've got you lads on your own,' he wheezes. 'There's something I need to talk to you about.'

'Go on – what is it?'

He tries to sit up a little and winces with the pain. 'If anything happens to me now . . .' He stops for a second to catch his breath. 'If anything happens to me now, you will look after your mam, won't you?'

'Course we will,' I offer.

'No, but I want you to really look after her, Charlie. You know, move back to Bolton – both of you.'

I feel a sudden stab of panic. However terrible I feel about what's happening now and however unsatisfied I've started to feel with my life and career in London, I know there's no way I can promise to move back home. Even if I have been feeling homesick lately, how can I live here when as a child I was so desperate to escape? As I look at Dad waiting for a reply, I feel that familiar knot of frustration, resentment and guilt. Am I really that selfish that I can't even agree to please my dying dad?

'Of course we will,' soothes Joe. 'In fact, me and Sarah have already been talking about moving down to Bolton for a while now.'

Dad lies back and smiles.

'*Anyway*,' I burst in nervously before he has time to question me any more, 'don't go worrying about things like that – you've got to concentrate on getting better.'

My diversionary tactic seems to be working. 'Oh you are good lads,' he breathes, 'and you've always meant the world to me.'

As he speaks, I can feel the panic gripping me tauten its hold even further. Dad never talks like this and I'm not sure how to handle it. The truth is I've wanted him to say I mean the world to him for so many years but now that he has, I feel strangely shaken and am not sure how to reply.

'I love you both very much,' he goes on. 'And you know you've always made me a very proud dad.'

'I love you too, Dad,' replies Joe.

'I – I—'

Before I have time to reply, the doors swing open and a nurse bursts in to check on the monitors. I bolt away from the bed a little too quickly and begin to pace the room. I know I've got to tell Dad I love him too, however difficult it is. I can't manage it just now, though. Not to worry, I tell myself, there'll be plenty of time later.

But there isn't any time later.

A few minutes after I fail to reply, Dad has another, much bigger, heart attack. And this one kills him.

Now here I am sitting at his funeral, feeling sick with guilt and grappling with yet another way in which I've failed him as a son.

'If you'd all like to stand,' says the vicar, 'and join me in saying the Lord's Prayer . . .'

There are relieved expressions all around as the congregation realize they can join in with this one and decide to belt it out at the tops of their voices. 'Our Father, who art in Heaven . . .'

As they speak, I close my eyes and try to shut myself off from what's happening, blocking out the words until they become a mess of random noise. Once I feel like I'm safely on my own, in my head I begin reciting the lyrics to 'Oh Father',

Madonna's song about her own difficult relationship with her dad. When I was a teenager I'd spend hours shut away from the world in my bedroom, listening to my idol singing about how much her dad used to hurt her and her refusal to let him hurt her anymore. I'd play the song every time I was trying to calm down after some kind of confrontation with my own dad. Sometimes I'd get so worked up I felt like I was going to explode with frustration at my inability to be the son he wanted. I don't understand why all these years later I find myself standing at his funeral feeling exactly the same way. In 'Oh Father' Madonna sings about being able to move on – so why can't I?

As a child I'd get so angry at Dad that sometimes I even thought that things would be easier if he were dead. Just remembering this now, I feel the full weight of guilt pressing down at the back of my throat. Oh it's all so confusing. My whole body throbs with a chaos of emotions – from grief to self-loathing, from love to regret.

I open my eyes just as the congregation's coming to the end of its 'Our Father'. The vicar invites everyone to sit down and there's a general shuffling around as Joe moves out from his pew and up to the altar. We decided earlier this week that, as the eldest son, he'd be the best person to deliver the eulogy. I watch him now slowly tapping on the microphone and then clearing his throat before he begins.

'When I was little,' he starts falteringly, 'I used to think I had the best dad in the world . . .'

I sit back and listen to Joe's fond memories and his anecdotes about all the happy times he spent with Dad. He reminisces about Dad teaching him how to ride a bike, taking him to boxing lessons at the Lads' Club, and standing in the cold and rain every weekend to cheer him on as he played football. All around me people smile in recognition of the man they knew but I can't help thinking that this isn't quite the dad I remember.

Just as Joe's telling the story of the two of them travelling down to London to watch Bolton Wanderers win some cup match at Wembley, I feel the corners of my eyes stinging and my mouth start to melt into a frown. All of a sudden I'm powerless to stop the tears falling and once they've started my whole body begins shaking. Very soon I've drenched the only tissue I brought with me and am having to make a real effort to stop myself from sobbing out loud. I hope that nobody's noticed the state I'm in but Mum reaches across and gives my knee a little squeeze. The tears carry on falling. Oh why couldn't I tell him I loved him? Why couldn't I tell him when he's the one person I loved more than anyone else?

' . . . And now that I'm much older,' I hear Joe saying in conclusion, 'I can honestly say that I was right all those years ago – I *did* have the best dad in the world.'

He turns to walk back to his seat and the congregation burst into applause. I know now that I really have to pull myself together and stop crying. With a supreme effort I sniff up and dry my face on my sleeve.

Thankfully there isn't much more of the ceremony to get through. There's another nervously sung hymn, a few more prayers that don't seem to make any sense, and then a strange moment when the coffin chugs away on a conveyor belt, disappearing behind some velvet curtains where I can only assume there's a furnace waiting. Tash warned me about this beforehand so fortunately I'm prepared for what could have been a shockingly functional sight. I've spoken to her on the phone a lot over the past week and remember her saying that she still feels traumatized now by the vision of her mother's coffin chugging away from her when she was twelve. Apparently her own grief was complicated by the fact that her mother abandoned the family home a few months earlier to make a new life for herself with another man. I was shocked when Tash told me that she still feels angry with her mum now and isn't sure if she'll ever get over her death. I hope losing Dad doesn't have the same effect on me.

Once the funeral's over, everyone troops back to The Flat Iron, where the landlord has reserved a seating area for us and Auntie Babs has laid on a buffet tea. There's a lot of talk about how Dad wouldn't have wanted people to be too upset that he's gone and Uncle Les proposes several toasts to his memory. All the regulars come over to tell us how sorry they are and Joe reads out a card from the manager of Bolton Wanderers expressing his sadness that one of their most loyal supporters won't be coming to watch the team play anymore.

None of this seems to be any comfort to Grandma. She sits slumped in a corner with a defeated expression on her face, tugging away unapologetically on a cigarette. 'I can't believe I'm going through this all over again,' she says machine-like, staring straight ahead. 'Anyone would have thought once was enough.'

'Oh give it time,' says Auntie Babs, 'give it time.'

'But it doesn't get any better,' Grandma breathes, 'I already know that from the last time.'

I shiver and look away. People often use the word 'numb' to describe how they feel when this kind of thing happens. But I don't just feel numb, I feel a curious combination of numbness and a heightened sensitivity, as if all my emotions are sharper and more intense than they have ever been before.

I spot Mum sitting on her own at a table, sipping a white wine and lost in her thoughts. I move over to sit next to her.

'Are you all right, Mum?'

'Yeah, course I am, love. How about you?'

'Oh, you know . . .'

There's a long pause and she twiddles her glass. Without her saying a word, I know exactly what she means. I don't think I've ever felt as close to her as I do in this moment.

'When do you have to go back to work, love?' she asks after a while.

I feel another snag of guilt but decide not to let it get the better of me. 'Not for another week or so yet. They've been very good about it. And I'll still come up at weekends.'

Thankfully Joe hasn't mentioned Dad's dying wish for me to move back to Bolton since our conversation in hospital. I briefly gave him the usual explanation about having to be in London for work and so far he's been unusually sensitive about it.

Mum looks out of the window and her eyes mist over. 'You know what, Charlie, I can't believe I'll never see him again. It just doesn't make any sense.'

'No. I'm not sure I can get my head round it either.'

'The worst thing is, I keep waking up in the morning and feeling cheerful. And then I get that horrible sinking feeling and remember he's dead. It's like having to live through the whole thing all over again, every single morning.'

'Oh you'll get used to it, Mum. At least that's what everybody keeps saying.'

'But what if I don't want to get used to it? I mean, if getting used to it means waking up in the morning and knowing he's dead straight away I don't think I *do* want to. At least this way I can kid myself he's still alive for a few seconds every day.'

I nod my head as if it's a dead weight. Mum takes a sip of her drink.

'You know what, Charlie,' she goes on, 'I can still picture him now, sitting right there in that chair.'

I smile. 'This was his favourite table, wasn't it?'

'Yeah. He said he could sit here and keep an eye on the whole pub.' She leans forward on her arms. 'You know, we were sitting here when you told us you were gay. Do you remember?'

'Course I do. It's not the kind of thing you forget.'

'Although I sometimes think your dad would have liked to.' She gives a big sigh and falls quiet. I try to stop the lyrics to 'Oh Father' rushing back into my mind. No, I won't let him hurt me anymore.

'You know what, Charlie,' she goes on, 'you mustn't be too hard on your dad about the way he was with all that. You have to remember he was from a different generation.'

'Yeah yeah, and he hadn't met any gay people before . . .' I'm surprised at how obvious the anger sounds in my voice.

'Not exactly – it was a bit more complicated than that. Oh I know when he refused to talk about it, it can't have been easy. But one thing I know for sure is that he only ever wanted you to be happy. And one day you'll understand that.'

'But Mum,' I gasp, 'what you're saying doesn't make any sense. Didn't Dad understand that *he* was the one making me unhappy?'

'Now that's unfair, love. Your father was a good man and I

think you know that deep down. Joe says he told you he loved you just before he died . . .'

'Yeah,' I mumble sheepishly, 'he did.' I don't mention the fact that I wasn't able to tell him I loved him in return.

'Well, there you are,' Mum goes on softly. 'He thought the world of you lads and don't you forget it.'

I know that it isn't her intention but with every word it feels like she's rubbing salt into my wound. I feel utterly wretched.

She stands up and straightens her skirt. 'Now come on, love, we can't sit around here moping all night.'

'No, I suppose not.'

'As everyone keeps saying – it's not what Frank would have wanted.'

I manage to muster up a weak smile. 'No. And I know it's the kind of thing people always say at funerals but in this case they're probably right.'

'Well, come on then.' She finishes her drink and dusts herself down. 'Let's see that brave face of yours. It's time we gave your dad a beltin' send-off.'

As I force out another smile, I can feel the bitterness and frustration simmering away behind it. I'm an ungrateful, selfish, terrible human being. And there's no chance of me ever being anything else now Dad's dead.

Erotica

Where am I?

I'm so drunk I can barely remember who I am, never mind where I am.

And then it comes back to me; I'm on a night out with Mike and we're in Vauxhall in South London, leaning against the bar in a dodgy nightclub called Sabre. It's dark and dingy, smells of stale beer and vomit, and the drinks are served in cracked plastic glasses. Along each wall stand lone men, skulking in the shadows as they clutch their drinks and leer at anyone who walks past.

Mike's a big fan of the club because of its well-known theme nights. Thursday's uniform night, Friday's underwear night and tonight – Saturday – is football kit night. Mike's come dressed in a rather worn Arsenal kit while I'm wearing a spanking new Bolton Wanderers strip. I wonder what Dad would say if he could see me now.

The thought of Dad makes me want another drink. I call the barman and order another round. As soon as my drink arrives, I tip half of it down my throat. We've already been drinking for hours now and I've got through so many cigarettes that my chest feels tight every time I breathe in. I try dancing sexily when the DJ plays 'Erotica' but give up when I realize I've lost all sense of co-ordination. I focus my energy on trying to resist an attack of hiccups, telling myself that it would be completely *un*sexy if I let them take hold.

'So come on, Mike,' I slur, 'if you had to shag one person here now, who would it be?'

'Hmm.' He scours the room for talent, bleary-eyed. 'Let's see.'

'*I'd* do him over there,' I jump in, 'the one with the huge chest and the Man United kit.'

'Nah.' Mike turns up his nose. 'He's a typical prawn – tasty body but ugly face.'

'So what?' I shrug, my mouth curling into a wicked grin. 'I could always turn the lights off first.'

'Atta boy!' Mike cheers. 'Or then again, you could always D.I.D.'

I'm disappointed at myself for missing out on an in-joke. 'D.I.D.?'

'Do It Doggie.'

As Mike bursts out laughing, I can't help following suit. I've been seeing more and more of him lately and, now that I've got over myself and loosened up about his sexually explicit banter, I have to admit he's a brilliant laugh – especially on a night out.

'Oooh, just a minute,' he breaks in after a while, 'now *he's* not bad over there.' He rather unsubtly points out a black guy in a West Ham strip with Celtic bands tattooed on his arms.

'Rat-a-tat-tat!' I say. 'I thought you'd like him. I can read you like a pamphlet.'

'Yeah, he's gorgeous,' he purrs. 'He'd look even better with my jizz on his face.'

We laugh and Mike holds up his plastic glass for a toast. 'To cock!' he trills.

'To cock!' I echo.

I stand back and watch as Mike approaches his chosen target and promptly makes his intentions known. While he's gone, I use the opportunity to do a bit of groundwork with the guy in the Man United top. I narrow my eyes to try to look sexy and lick my lips flirtatiously. He flashes me a cocky grin in return and I reckon it's a done deal.

Suddenly I hear a voice behind me that I vaguely recognize. 'Charlie, is that you?'

I turn around and come face to face with my ex-boyfriend Nick.

I instantly forget all about looking sexy and wriggle in my shoes awkwardly. I might be shitfaced but I have to try and at least come across as sober.

'Oh hi, Nick!' I just about manage to enunciate. I haven't seen him since I threw him out of my birthday party in Cambridge years ago. Unfortunately, the sight of him now gives me the attack of hiccups I've been fighting. 'Hic!'

'It *is* you, Charlie.'

Nick's wearing a Tottenham Hotspurs kit and I can see that he still works out at the gym. He flashes me one of his smiles and it lights up his whole face, just like it used to. Straight away I remember how I felt the first time I saw him smile. I'm surprised to feel my heart give a little flutter.

'Oh urm, hi Nick, urm, how are you? Hic!'

'I'm cool, thanks,' he drawls, smooth as ever.

I notice that he's starting to get crow's feet around his eyes and his precious hair is thinning on top. But it doesn't matter; he's still amazingly attractive.

'How about you?' he asks. 'How are things?'

I decide not to tell him about Dad dying. The last thing I

want is to talk about that here. 'Oh, you know me,' I sing-song, 'couldn't be better. Hic!'

I suddenly wonder what I'm doing dressed in a Bolton Wanderers kit, hiccupping drunkenly in a nightclub called Sabre. How on earth have I ended up in this state? A fantasy flashes through my mind in which Nick apologizes for his infidelity all those years ago, tells me he's always been in love with me, and wants us to get back together. Almost out of nowhere I feel a twinkle of hope.

'Hic! It's really nice to see you, Nick.'

'You too, Charlie.'

'So what are you up to now? Hic! How's the acting working out?'

'Oh, you know,' he mumbles, 'I did an episode of *The Bill* a few months back and I'm going to be a baddie in *Midsomer Murders* soon.'

'That's great, Nick, that's really brilliant.' I can't help thinking back to our last conversation, when we had a huge melodramatic row in front of all my friends, and it suddenly dawns on me just how young we were. I tell myself that now I've matured and have more realistic views on love and relationships, maybe I could put up with Nick sleeping around. Maybe it *is* time for us to give it another go. 'Hic!'

'How about you?' he asks. 'Are you a theatre director yet?'

I remember my ambition of becoming the toast of the West End, an ambition I can now see may have been born of a genuine interest in theatre but only developed to impress Nick. I blush. 'Oh no, urm, actually I'm a TV producer now. Hic!'

'Oh yeah? What do you produce?'

I do my best to sound enthusiastic. 'Well, I'm just about to start work on a new reality show called *Section the Celebrity*

– we're going to take a group of slightly unstable has-beens and put them in a psych ward and see what happens. Hic!'

'Wicked,' Nick mutters rather half-heartedly. 'Sounds fun.'

There's an awkward pause and he smiles at me again. At that moment I realize just how much I want to kiss him and my mind races with images of the two of us passionately making up and resolving that this time we're not going to split up over something as childish as a little affair. I'm aware that if I don't say something now then my chance will be gone forever.

'Nick,' I begin, 'do you ever think—'

'Hi there.'

I'm interrupted by a bleached blond in an Aston Villa strip who sidles up to Nick and takes hold of his hand. I look at him in disbelief. 'Hic!'

'Oh, right, sorry Paul, this is Charlie,' Nick explains to the newcomer. 'He's an ex-shag from Cambridge.'

I can't help flinching at the description but manage to smile feebly. 'Nice to meet you, Paul. Hic!'

'Charlie,' Nick goes on, 'Paul's my *current* shag.'

Paul giggles playfully and leans over to kiss Nick on the cheek. I feel humiliated and ashamed of myself. How could I have been so stupid as to think Nick would want to get back with me?

'So how about you, Charlie?' Nick asks. 'Are you seeing anyone at the moment?'

'No, no!' I warble as if it's a stupid question. 'I don't do relationships these days. Fuck 'em and fuck 'em off, that's my motto! Hic!'

'Oh yeah? And who've you got your eye on tonight?'

'Well, the way things stand at the moment,' I chirp, 'I'm going to be scoring with Mr Man United over there.'

I point at the bloke in question and Nick and Paul nod their heads in approval.

'Well, good luck,' says Nick, 'we're just about to shoot off for a home match if you know what I mean. We'll leave you to it.'

We say our goodbyes and Nick gives me one last smile. As I watch him leave, I realize just how attractive I still find him. If only he could fancy me.

I reach for my drink and down the rest of it in one. 'Hic!'

'Who was that?' Mike asks, reappearing next to me.

'Oh nobody important – just someone from my back catalogue. Hic!' I badly need to change the subject. 'How are you getting on anyway? Aren't you pulling that bloke?'

He sticks out his tongue in disgust. 'Nah. When I got close up he had terrible spiky teeth, it put me right off. Honestly, it'd be like dropping my cock into a box of nails.'

'Hic!' I curse myself – these hiccups are *so* unsexy! 'Well, I tell you what, I could do with another drink to take the edge off.'

'Take the edge off what?' he slurs. 'Consciousness?'

'Oh come on, you boring bender! Hic! What do you want – another gin and slim?'

'No, forget about the drinks. Your fairy godmother here's got a better idea.' He dips into his pocket and flashes me the edge of a transparent plastic bag. 'I think it's about time me and you took a ride on the white powder highway . . .'

The two of us grin at each other naughtily. My mind flashes back to how anti-drugs I used to be and how I refused to take anything when I went to visit Shanaz in Manchester, feeling alienated when everyone else bonded by taking Ecstasy. Right now I feel embarrassed by my naivety – I must have come across as a total killjoy. When I think about it now, I can't see any objection to taking drugs. In fact, the idea suddenly seems quite appealing.

On our way into the toilets I can feel my heart beating faster with excitement. As soon as we open the door, we're hit by an overpowering stench of stale urine. We wait a few minutes for a cubicle to come free and then slide inside.

Mike empties a heap of what he tells me is ketamine on top of the cistern and starts chopping it up into lines with his credit card. The process is curiously familiar from American gangster films and I feel goosepimples run up and down my arms. He takes a twenty-pound note from his wallet and rolls it into a tube, then puts it to his nose and sniffs up quickly. He hands it to me and I lean down and hoover up the rest. I immediately feel a surge of euphoria race through my body.

'Ah, that's better,' Mike quips. 'I feel sensational!'

I have to admit, it *is* an amazing feeling. It instantly makes me forget I ever bumped into Nick and wipes out all the pain I've been feeling since Dad died. It even makes my hiccups disappear.

I snort a second line and lean on the side of the cubicle to savour the effect. This really is incredible. It makes me feel invincible. It makes me feel better than I know I am. And it makes me feel *seriously* sexy.

Mike and I stride back into the club as if we're floating through the air. I feel so happy and alive and I tell myself that there's no way I'm leaving this place alone.

On the other side of the room I catch Mr Man United's eye and he winks at me roguishly. I swagger over to him and run my finger along his cheek. 'So,' I ask, 'are you top, bottom or versatile?'

Like a Virgin

God I'm tired. I'm absolutely exhausted. And I know that pretty soon the comedown's going to start kicking in. I don't think I can bear it. I have to do everything I can to hold it off.

It's getting close to four o'clock on Sunday morning and the birds are just starting to sing. As usual, Mike and I hit the town straight after work on Friday and haven't been home since. Once the clubs shut in the early hours of Saturday morning, we found a post-club event to keep us occupied for the few hours until the next round of pre-club activities cranked into gear. We've taken all kinds of powders and pills to keep us going but now that Saturday night's clubs are closing I'm starting to panic about our mammoth session coming to an end. Fortunately, Mike says he knows just the answer and I happily jump into a taxi after him.

The taxi drops us off outside Spartacus Roman Spa, in front of a huge statue of the gladiator himself. According to Mike, this place is open twenty-four hours a day, seven days a week, and is constantly full of men all looking to indulge in no-nonsense sex. I feel nervous and have butterflies in my stomach but at the same time am strangely drawn to find out what's going on inside.

'Now are you sure you want to do this?' Mike asks seriously.

'Yeah,' I insist, 'course I am.'

We go through to the foyer and I see that the interior of the venue has been decorated with sculptures of emperors, ornate Roman colonnades and paintings of the Colosseum and the Pantheon. It reminds me of the hotel where Christian and I stayed in Paris a few years ago. I try not to think about it and hand over my entrance fee.

A door swings open and Mike leads me down a long corridor to the changing rooms. Several men are standing around in various states of undress beneath bright fluorescent lighting. I suddenly feel awkward and self-conscious and Mike spots the look of apprehension on my face. 'What's up, Cambridge boy? You're not having second thoughts, are you?'

The truth is, I *am* having second thoughts; I don't want to do this at all. Despite this, I feel weirdly compelled to.

'No!' I burst out. 'Not at all!'

The two of us quickly undress, bundle our belongings into lockers and tie white towels around our waists. Mike leads me forward and through a doorway into a bar, where men in towels are lounging around on sofas and armchairs, nursing drinks and chatting. Mike strides through purposefully and bounds up the stairs to a corridor where several more men are padding around, giving each other the once-over and fondling their crotches provocatively. I stick out my chest and hold in my stomach.

The music playing is Madonna's 'Like a Virgin' and I begin mouthing along to the words. But, as Madonna sings about emerging from the wilderness and finding a man who makes her feel innocent and pure again, I start to feel uncomfortable. Evidently, I'm still very much in my wilderness with no sign of making it through.

Mike guides me along the corridor and on to a tour of the venue, which takes in a total of four floors. There's a small cinema playing hardcore porn, a full-sized swimming pool, a long row of showers, two jacuzzis, two saunas and something called a dark room, which as far as I can make out is just an empty room with the lights turned off. The rest of the venue consists of a labyrinth of winding corridors bordered on either side by cubicles of various sizes, all of them with cushioned padding on the floor. We wind our way through and I see men standing in the doorways hungrily eyeing up the passers-by. Pairs of them occasionally disappear inside the cubicles, locking the door firmly behind them. Along the walls of each corridor there are special dispensers crammed full of a brand of condoms and lubricant named Eros. Mike grabs a fistful for us both.

'Come on, sauna virgin,' he says, 'I've saved the best till last.'

He leads me to the door of a large steam room and I read an official-looking sign that says 'Strictly no poppers'. He opens the door and straight away I recognize the strong smell of amyl nitrate. Mike looks at me and grins.

We sit down on a bench along one of the walls and I look around to see what's happening. Through the thick cloud of steam I can just about make out groups of men engaging in full sex as spectators ogle from the sidelines, some of them masturbating. I can't believe it – I'm actually witnessing a full-on orgy.

My memory rewinds to my first visit to The Paradise Factory, when Shanaz and I walked into the fetish room and stumbled upon some kind of sexual free-for-all. Back then I was repulsed by what I saw and that same feeling washes over me now – only this time I can't help noticing that I also feel aroused. Just when I'm wondering how it's possible to feel aroused and repulsed by the same thing, it dawns on me that I'm not; I'm aroused by what I'm seeing but repulsed by the person watching it.

At that moment the smell of poppers hits me at the back of the throat and I can feel my veins thumping in my temples. Black spots appear before my eyes and I start to feel faint, as if I'm going to pass out. It's so hot in here I have to struggle to catch my breath and my head feels like someone's trying to split it open with an axe. The comedown I've been dreading is starting to take hold and I know that if I don't do something to fight it now then very soon I'll be past the point of no return.

'Mike,' I gasp, 'I'm just nipping outside to get some air.'

I throw myself into the corridor and lean forward onto a wall as I breathe in desperately, filling my lungs. After a few minutes I manage to compose myself and can feel my heart rate gradually slowing down.

'Are you all right, Cambridge boy?' Mike asks nervously.

'Yeah!' I breeze, forcing a smile. 'Sorry, I must have had a bad pill or something.'

We decide against going back into the steam room but spot that one of the jacuzzis is empty. The two of us lower ourselves into the water and I stretch my arms out along the side.

'So come on then,' Mike asks, 'what do you think of the place?'

'It's totally insane,' I say, 'I can't get over it – it's like a sex supermarket.'

'I know, isn't it sensational? And the best thing is, it's open all hours!'

I raise my eyebrows in disbelief. 'What gets me most is just how many men are here. And some of them are fit too.'

'Course they are. There are loads of benders out there who can't be arsed going through the rigmarole of pulling someone in a bar, having to chat them up for ages and then get rid of them in the morning. Coming to a sauna is far easier and far more honest.'

'Well, I think it's brilliant,' I chirp, 'and something tells me I'll be coming here a lot from now on . . .'

Halfway through my sentence I can tell Mike's stopped paying attention. I follow his gaze and see that he's caught the eye of a man who reminds me of an African warlord I saw on the news recently.

'Listen, Charlie,' he whispers, 'I might just leave you to have a look around on your own. I suddenly feel like stretching my legs.'

'No problem, partner. Go get him!'

I lie still for a moment and listen to the music, enjoying the warm bubbles as they swirl around me. The smell of chlorine hangs heavy in the air and reminds me of the swimming pools Joe and I spent hours playing in during our childhood holidays in France as Mum lay sunbathing by the tent and Dad played boules and drank lager with the other British dads. Just then, grief breaks through and hits me like a sharp punch to the stomach. I close my eyes and breathe in steadily to stop it taking hold. That's when I realize that it isn't just chlorine I can smell – it's semen too. All of a sudden I find myself wondering when the jacuzzi was last cleaned if Spartacus is open twenty-four hours a day. I have to get out of here; it's disgusting.

I haul myself out of the water and dry myself down with my towel. Now that Mike's disappeared, I can easily slip off home and tell him that I pulled some hot guy and went into one of the cubicles. He'll be none the wiser and I can spend the rest of the day sleeping off my comedown. The problem is, I just can't bring myself to leave.

I decide to go for a wander around and re-assume my strutting posture. I've no idea what time it is but the place is still packed. Before long a mixed-race guy with a crooked smile and closely cropped hair gives me an interested look. I don't find him particularly attractive but before I can talk myself out of it I'm following him down the corridor. My head's spinning with adrenalin as I contemplate what I'm about to do.

I half expect my conscience to kick into gear and pull me back but for some reason it doesn't. I watch the man step inside a cubicle and he turns to give me another crooked smile. As he does so I notice that he has a small birthmark to the side of his left eyebrow. For some reason this makes me smile back at him. The next thing I know, I'm following him inside. I close the door and lock it behind me.

Frozen

'Are you an alcoholic?' asks the poster glaring out from the wall. There are ten questions and apparently if you answer yes to three or more then you're officially classed as alcohol-dependent. I nervously read down the list . . .

'Once you've had one drink do you find it difficult to stop?'

'Do you enjoy the sensation of being out of control?'

'Do you drink because you can't see any reason not to?'

I answer yes to three out of three – this isn't a very good start . . .

I stop reading and look around the room. I'm sitting in the waiting area of my local genito-urinary clinic and there's a large group of people due to be seen before me. Everyone's glancing around shiftily or staring at the floor to avoid catching the gaze of others. I hide behind my sunglasses and feel dirty and degraded.

This morning, after nearly two days of constantly itching my pubic hair, I was forced to face up to the fact that I may have picked up some sort of lice. A careful examination of the region confirmed my suspicions and I immediately called Mike to ask for his advice. He diagnosed crabs, suggested I caught them from Spartacus and told me to visit the 'clap clinic' to get myself checked out. He reassured me that it wouldn't hurt a bit but, sitting here in the waiting room, I can see that he's wrong. It does hurt. It hurts a lot.

I try closing my eyes but all I can see is the face of the man I met in Spartacus, with his crooked smile and the birthmark next to his left eyebrow. OK so it's my fault I was there in the first place but what sort of a sleazeball goes out looking for sex knowing he has an STD?

I reach down to fidget with my 'Ray of Light' bracelet but it isn't there and I realize with a jolt that I haven't seen it since I took it off in Spartacus. The bastard. So as well as giving me some kind of STD, he's nicked my bracelet too. And the worst thing is, I was too stupid or too out of my head to notice.

I try to smile bravely. I reach over to the magazine rack and look for something to read. All I can find are leaflets on the re-emergence of syphilis and the danger of genital warts. 'People who lead promiscuous lifestyles,' one of them reads, 'run a far greater risk of picking up sexually transmitted infections . . .' I quickly close it and put it back in the rack. I pull my cap down over my face.

I sit there biting my nails for what seems like ages, convinced that everyone's staring at me. Just when I think I can't bear it any more, a mumsy nurse with a northern accent comes to the doorway and shouts my name. 'Charlie Matthews!'

'That's me,' I mumble, my cheeks flushing bright red. I hope nobody else heard my name.

I follow the nurse down a long corridor and into the doctor's surgery. I sit down timidly and am greeted by a smile from the opposite side of the desk. The doctor is a rotund, middle-aged man with a kindly face. He introduces himself and then without warning launches straight into a series of probing questions about my sex life.

'Do you have a regular partner or do you prefer to have casual sex?'

'Have you ever had sex under the influence of alcohol or drugs?'

'Have you ever visited a sex club or sauna?'

His tone's soft and sympathetic but mine's low and mournful. I feel conscious of the sound of my own voice and repulsed by the person sitting there detailing his sexual encounters. How on earth have I ended up in this position when all I ever wanted was to fall in love and live happily ever after? I always thought people who come to places like this were reckless and irresponsible but now I'm one of them. It's just like everyone said at school; I'm a disgusting, horrible pervert and now I'm getting what I deserve.

Once the interrogation's over, the doctor writes something in his pad and then looks up at me with a smile. 'Right, Mr Matthews, I think we should send you for a full MOT.'

'I'm sorry?'

'Oh it's nothing to worry about. We just need to get you checked out for everything – chlamydia, gonorrhoea, HIV . . .'

'HIV?' I sit up with a start. 'What do you mean, HIV?'

As I say the word, I'm hit by the image of a falling tombstone from the government's AIDS awareness campaign in the 1980s. Of course, that's what happens to people like me; we catch AIDS and die. I was stupid to ever think otherwise.

'Human Immunodeficiency Virus,' the doctor answers. 'Are you aware that it's on the increase, Mr Matthews?'

'But just a minute,' I splutter, 'there must have been some mistake – I mean, I only went to a sauna that once and I was safe.'

'Well, that's good news but it would be too early to see if

you were infected this weekend anyway. I'm talking about previous sexual activity. Are you *always* safe, Mr Matthews?'

Suddenly I'm not so sure. 'Urm, I think so . . .'

'Hmm, you only think so. Well, do you always remain completely in control of yourself? You know we can all do stupid things when we're drunk or on drugs . . .'

As I think back over my recent sexual history, I realize I've had sex with so many men, often when I was so off my face I can't even remember all of the details. 'Urm, I'm not sure . . .'

'Well, I think we should get you checked out,' says the doctor. 'Just to be on the safe side.'

I writhe around in my seat. I wasn't expecting this and am still struggling to take it all in. 'But . . . I . . .'

'Oh I'm sure you'll be fine,' he reassures me.

'But what if I'm not?'

'Then it's better to find out now so that we can get you the treatment you need.'

I picture myself lying in a hospital bed like Dad, covered in wires and tubes and listening to the beep of a distant monitor. The image leaves me shot through with a terror that's almost blinding. I can't believe that Dad's only been dead a few months and here I am being told I'm putting my own life in danger. I suddenly think about how difficult it would be to tell Mum I have a condition that could lead to death. She'd be devastated if anything happened to me. I couldn't do that to her, the very thought of it's too upsetting to contemplate.

'You do know,' the doctor coaxes, 'that with the treatments currently available, in very few cases now does HIV lead to AIDS. In other words it's far better to find out if you're HIV positive at an early stage and then we can do everything possible to keep you well.'

Right now, this feels like little consolation. But I can hardly refuse. 'Urm, OK. Yeah, I suppose I'd better have a test.'

Before I have time to change my mind, I'm led through to a whitewashed room where the same mumsy nurse is waiting for me. She covers a bed in a roll of blue tissue paper and asks me to lie down. For the next fifteen minutes I listen to her make small talk about the weather while she pokes around my genitals, takes blood samples from my veins and inserts medical swabs into various orifices. The worst is a penile swab, which Mike didn't mention but I'll certainly never forget. I shut my eyes tight as the nurse fumbles around with my private parts, asking in a sweet voice if I've been anywhere nice on holiday this year. And with that she inserts the swab up into my penis, twists it around and then yanks it back out again. I yelp with pain and jolt upright from the shock.

'Right,' smiles the nurse, snapping off her rubber gloves, 'we'll see you in a few hours for your results.'

As soon as I can, I slink away and out of the hospital into the street. I'm supposed to be going shopping with Amelia this afternoon as she's on half-term but I know there's no way I can face that now. I wonder if I should make up some excuse about a last-minute shoot coming up at work or tell her the real reason I have to cancel. What if she's as disgusted in me as I am in myself? But then I remember that Amelia's never judged me or disapproved of my behaviour and has recently made it clear that she's here to help if I need her. I decide to give her a call.

I quickly summarize what's happened and before I can ask her to come and meet me she says she's on her way. We arrange to meet on the other side of the river in St James's Park so I begin dragging myself across Westminster Bridge and Parliament Square. I'm still dumbfounded by everything that's happened so hardly notice the crowds of workers and tourists swarming around me. At one point I catch sight of a rather drawn, sad-looking man reflected in a window. I do a double take and realize it's me.

When I get to the park I sit down on a bench overlooking the pond. I remember when the girls and I first moved to London we spent lots of our weekends in the royal parks, eating sandwiches, drinking wine and chatting about our plans for the future.

I hope I haven't just shattered that future.

As I wait for Amelia to arrive, I take out my new iPod and hit play. The introduction to Madonna's 'Frozen' sounds and the lyrics burst out with piercing clarity. I listen as Madonna encourages me to let the hurt inside of me die, warning me not to let my heart stay frozen. I switch off the iPod and put it back in my pocket.

Before long, I spot Amelia walking towards me and the first thing I notice is she's smiling. I don't think I've ever been so happy to see a smile on someone's face. When she reaches me she holds out her arms and wraps me in a hug.

'Oh Charlie,' she says as I cling onto her.

'Oh Amelia,' I reply, my voice cracking. 'I'm so sorry.'

'Sorry?' she asks, stepping back. 'What do you mean, sorry?'

'Sorry for being such a fuck-up, sorry for making such a mess of everything.'

She gives me a stern look and gestures for us to sit down on a bench. 'OK, so first of all, you've nothing to be sorry for. Secondly, you haven't made a mess of everything.'

'Well, you could have fooled me.'

'Charlie,' she says, 'your dad's just died. It doesn't surprise me you've been struggling.'

I give a little laugh. 'Yeah, well, that's one way of putting it. But I can't blame it all on Dad dying. Joe hasn't fallen apart, has he?'

In the distance I can hear the ducks quacking. A pair of foreign students walk past, chatting excitedly in German.

'Charlie,' Amelia retorts, 'I think we both know Joe hasn't had as much to deal with as you.'

'What do you mean?'

'Well, he didn't grow up gay for a start. You know, I think we've got to be honest about what's going on here. It doesn't surprise me that if you always thought your dad disapproved of you being gay then now he's gone you're going to try and punish yourself for it.'

'Punish myself? For being gay? Do you really think that's what I've been doing?'

'Well, don't you? I mean, I don't know all the details but it strikes me that a lot of it has been like an exercise in self-harm – and it's all been played out in gay bars and clubs. Or from what you're telling me now, through gay sex.'

There's a long silence while I think about what she's saying. 'Shit, yeah, you're right. I never thought about it like that.'

'Yeah, well, it seems perfectly obvious to me – and perfectly logical too.'

I notice that my hands are twitching and I sit on them to keep still. 'But Amelia,' I argue, 'I'm happy with my sexuality. I'm proud of being gay.'

'I know you are, Charlie. But this stuff is buried deep. Even though you know it's totally fine to be gay, deep down you can't help believing some of the things people used to say about you.'

Her words knock the breath out of my throat; I remember

thinking exactly that when I was in the clinic, I remember believing what people said and thinking I was getting what I deserved.

'Oh Amelia,' I moan, 'I hate to admit it but what you're saying's spot on. What if it's too late, though? What if I've already fucked up and caught HIV?'

She gives me a rub on the shoulder. 'Well, if you have we'll work through it.'

As she says the word 'we', I realize that one little syllable is possibly the loveliest thing I've ever heard. 'Really?' I ask. 'Do you really mean that?'

'Of course I do.'

'So you won't be disappointed in me?'

'Absolutely not. Charlie, I told you a long time ago, I'm in the bag. Remember?'

I can't help smiling at the memory of the conversation we had at our first St Christopher's Ball. 'Yeah, I remember. How could I forget?'

'Good,' she says. 'And nothing's changed since then so you still don't have to try and impress me. But it's about time you stopped trying to impress yourself. You know, it's OK to fuck up, Charlie. It really is OK.'

I nod and force out a smile. 'Well, we'll soon find out if I have, won't we?'

She rubs her hands together. 'Come on, what time do we get your results?'

I consult my watch and see that we need to start heading back to the hospital. Amelia links my arm and we stand up and walk out of the park, over Parliament Square and back across the river. When I spot the hospital looming ahead of us, I feel gripped by panic and can hear what sounds like radio interference in my ears. My body suddenly feels so heavy I can barely move my legs.

'Come on,' says Amelia, squeezing my arm, 'you can do this.'

I fill my lungs with air and we head inside.

When we arrive at the GU clinic I take the same seat in the reception area and Amelia sits next to me. The room's still full of people but this time I don't notice them and don't care who sees me.

Eventually my name's called and I suddenly feel breathless. With Amelia by my side, I haul myself up and over to the doctor's surgery. But the receptionist stops Amelia and tells her she isn't allowed in with me. She's just about to make a fuss when I tell her not to.

'Don't worry,' I insist, 'I can do this bit on my own.'

'Are you sure?'

'Yeah, I'm sure.'

I knock on the door and let myself in.

As I walk over to the seat, the doctor glances up at me from his desk. When I ran through this scene in my head beforehand, I thought I'd be able to guess the result of my test as soon as I saw his face. But now that I'm here, my mind caves inwards and I can't order my thoughts.

'Ah, Mr Matthews,' the doctor says in a matter-of-fact tone, 'I have good news and bad news.'

All I hear are the words 'bad news'. I can feel all the blood drain from my head and my legs almost give way. I worry that I'm going to faint so grab onto the chair and lower myself down slowly.

'The good news,' he says, 'is you're HIV negative.'

My whole body relaxes. 'Oh God,' I almost cry, 'thank God. Oh thank God.'

'The bad news,' he goes on, 'is you have an infestation of lice.' He hands me a bottle of shampoo. 'Now, it's nothing serious – one application of this will soon shift it.'

I look at the bottle and blink. I'm so relieved not to have HIV that I can't take in anything else he's saying; he might as well be speaking to me in another language. 'Th-th-thank you, doctor. Thank you very much.'

'Yes, well,' he replies, 'just think yourself lucky that's all you've got this time.'

I swallow and nod.

'And let this be a wake-up call to you. I *don't* want to see you here again.'

'Oh you won't,' I mouth. 'Honestly, you won't.'

As I say goodbye and stand up to leave, I want to scream out loud and jump up and down as high as I can. I'm healthy and well and the feeling's incredible.

I head towards the door, repeating in my head that under no circumstances am I ever stepping foot in this place again. I'm giving up casual sex and if that means I also have to give up drugs and cut down on booze, then that's fine; I'm prepared to do whatever it takes. This has been one of the worst days of my life, but oddly enough it strikes me now that it could also turn out to be the best day of my life. Because today I've been given another chance. And right now I'm going to seize it.

Nothing Really Matters

I cuddle the baby in my arms and sway from side to side to try to get him to sleep. He's stopped crying now but his eyes are still wide open and he's looking straight at me. His eyelashes are long and feathery and there's a thin coating of downy hair on his head. His little fingers with their tiny nails wrap themselves around my thumb and squeeze onto it tightly. A rush of warmth washes over me and I can feel my heart melting in my chest.

'Shhh,' I whisper, 'it's time to go to sleep.'

My new nephew yawns at me and wriggles drowsily. The two of us waltz slowly around the room I slept in as a child, which Mum recently redecorated as a guest bedroom both for me and her new grandson. It's here that Dad sang 'Two Little Boys' to me and Joe as we sat up in bed refusing to go to sleep. I decide to sing a lullaby now and the first song that comes into my head is Madonna's 'Nothing Really Matters', which she wrote for her own daughter when she was a baby. Her lyrics about abandoning the self-absorption of youth to focus on loving and caring for a new life make so much sense to me now I'm an uncle.

Through the open window I can hear a gentle wind rustle

through the cherry blossom trees, which once again are blooming to mark the onset of spring. I've been travelling home from London quite regularly lately, but this time when I arrived in the street, I was greeted by great big clouds of pink and remembered picking handfuls of the blossom when I was a child and mixing it with water to make perfume for Mum. Standing in the same spot all these years later, I picked some blossom from one of the trees and breathed in its sweet scent. It was a comforting smell and I knew I was home.

My choice of lullaby's working – I look down and see that the baby's eyes are slowly closing. Today has been a big day for him. Just a few hours ago he was taken to church to be christened Frank Charles Matthews. All day long he's been on his best behaviour and only cried once when my twin cousins argued over which of them was going to hold him next and almost tore his arms off in the process. He sat quietly through the entire service, bouncing on his dad's knee in the same christening gown Joe and I wore as babies nearly thirty years earlier. And he listened carefully to the vows I made as godfather to care for him and guide him through life by my own example.

I have to admit I'm slightly surprised when Joe asks me to be godfather – and tells me he and Sarah have chosen Charles as the baby's middle name. We're sitting in Mum's living room going through some old family photos and he just comes out with it. Although we've been getting on much better lately, at first I'm not sure if he's joking.

'But Joe,' I say, 'what's brought this on?'

'Oh you know . . . Let's just say that being a dad has made me realize how important family is.'

'Well, I've been thinking the same thing since Dad died. Even so, I thought I'd be the last person you'd ask to be godfather.'

'Why do you say that?'

'Oh I don't know . . . I just wasn't particularly sure you liked me.'

'Hmm. I suppose I have been a bit hard on you sometimes.'

'Well . . . I . . . I don't know – possibly, yeah.'

'Look, I'm sorry if at times I haven't been the most supportive big brother. But the truth is, Charlie, I've always . . .' He stops and wrings his hands. 'I've always . . .' He looks up as if searching for the right words. 'I've always been a bit jealous of you.'

'*You*? Jealous of *me*?'

'Yeah. Is that so hard to believe?'

I give him a shrug, speechless.

'Oh sure,' he goes on, 'I was good at football and all those kind of things but you were so much cleverer than me and much more fun to be around, always laughing and joking. I remember when you went to live in Cambridge and Mum said the soul had gone out of the house. I really hated you when she said that!'

'But that's so weird,' I say. 'I always thought Mum and Dad were disappointed that I wasn't more like you.'

Joe shakes his head and smiles. 'What, boring predictable Joe? Nah – you were the special one and didn't I know it? Dad always used to tell me to keep an eye on you at school and look after you if anyone gave you a hard time.'

'But they did – everyone gave me a hard time!'

'I know and I feel guilty about that now. But I was so jealous of you back then that I couldn't bring myself to look out for you at all.'

I hold up a photo of the two of us on holiday in France for the first time. We're standing at the side of the swimming pool with our fingers on our noses, getting ready to see who can jump the highest and make the biggest splash. It's weird to think that we've both lived through the same experiences but saw things so differently. I give a little chuckle. It's a huge relief to know that, all through our childhood, Joe was feeling the same emotions as me, that he envied and even hated me just as much as I hated him.

'Yeah, well, it's OK,' I offer, 'because I was really jealous of you too. And I'm sorry for all those times I put you down or scoffed at you if you got something wrong. You know, I feel terrible admitting this now but when you stopped playing football part of me was pleased your dream was falling apart.'

He gives a knowing smile and rolls his eyes. 'That's OK,' he says, 'it's nothing I didn't feel when something similar happened to you.'

'No, but it's important that we get it all out in the air now,' I insist. 'And it's important that we've both said sorry.'

He holds out his arms and I let him envelop me in a big hug. As I clutch onto him, it occurs to me that although we're very different, we still fit together just right. And hugging my brother feels good. It feels really good. Evidently, Joe thinks the same, as after a while it becomes clear that neither of us wants to break the hug. Rather than pulling back, I squeeze onto him tighter and as I do so tears begin to squeeze out of my eyes.

Perhaps sensing that I'm a little overwhelmed, Joe finally breaks away. He clears his throat and says, 'Anyway, none of that childhood stuff matters anymore. The fact is we'll always be brothers and that's far more important than anything else.'

I knuckle the tears out of my eyes. 'Yeah, I suppose you're right,' I manage.

'I mean, when you think about it,' he continues, 'it doesn't actually matter whether we get on or not – we'll always be brothers, whatever happens.'

'Yeah, I hadn't thought of it like that.' I look at the photo again and put it back in the drawer.

'But for the record, I'm glad we *are* brothers.'

'Yeah, me too.'

'So what do you say? Will you be Frank's godfather or what?'

I can feel my face breaking into a huge grin.

I'm still grinning at the memory now.

By this time my baby godson's sleeping soundly. I stop singing for a moment to listen to his rhythmic breathing.

Coming from the living room downstairs I can hear the occasional raised voice and hope that it doesn't wake him up. After the ceremony all the guests came back to Mum's house to wet the baby's head with a barrel of beer and a buffet. Grandma sat in her new wheelchair telling anyone who'd listen about giving birth to all three of her babies without any pain relief on the kitchen table at home. A by-now prune-skinned Auntie Jan teased my sister-in-law Sarah about baby Frank being born only eight months after the wedding and Uncle Stan ribbed Auntie Jan about becoming an elderly-sounding Great Aunt. Standing on either side of the barrel, Joe and Uncle Les supped their pints and led an impassioned debate with Sarah's Geordie parents about whether baby Frank would grow up to be a Bolton Wanderers or a Newcastle United supporter. I made a point of asking what will happen if he doesn't support either team or – even more unthinkably – grows up to have no interest in football whatsoever. Joe smiled and said he'll love him just as much.

Baby Frank gives another wriggle in my arms and I shift his weight to make him more comfortable. Looking down at him now, I realize just how much my perspective on life has changed since he was born. I feel a much stronger sense of responsibility than I did before and am filled with a new excitement about the future.

I move over to the baby's cot and lean over to lay him down gently. It feels weird to think that just a few weeks ago he was just a blurry image on a scan yet here he is now, a brand new person with his whole life stretching ahead of him.

There's a quiet tapping on the door and Mum pokes her head around the side. 'All right, love?' she coos.

'Yeah,' I whisper, 'he's fast asleep.'

'Oh that's smashin' – you must have the knack.'

She creeps over to have a look at her grandson sleeping soundly in his cot. 'Aw, isn't he beautiful?'

I nod and smile. 'He is, yeah.'

'And I tell you what, he doesn't half look like you did when you were his age.'

'Really?'

'Yeah, he's a dead ringer. Let's hope he hits the jackpot and gets your hair colour too.'

I can't stop myself from laughing out loud; after all this time, Mum's still obsessed with the blondness of our hair. 'Yeah, fingers crossed.'

We both gaze down at baby Frank as he wriggles around in his sleep and gives us a little gurgle. A thin trail of whitish, milky fluid trickles out of the corner of his mouth and I bend down to wipe it up.

'You know what,' Mum breathes, 'when you were little your dad used to spend ages watching you asleep in bed.'

'Did he? You never told me that before.'

'Oh yeah. He felt so protective – he was terrified about anything happening to you.'

'But I don't remember him being like that. Why was he so worried that something would happen to me?'

'Oh well . . . He always used to say you reminded him of his brother.'

'What, Jim? The one who died?'

'Yeah, poor Jim.' Her eyes mist over and I wonder what she's thinking. She waits for a moment before going on. 'You know he was gay, your Uncle Jim?'

I'm stunned. 'No. Nobody's ever told me before.'

'Well, he was. Although nobody used the word "gay" in those days. Nobody really talked about it at all if they could avoid it. Poor Jim . . .'

I'm not sure how to react. So many thoughts are running away with themselves in my head. I try to pull myself together and express one of them. 'So what did Dad think about that? Having a gay brother?'

'Oh believe it or not, he was actually very understanding. But it was all so different then – I know you had a hard time growing up but when your Uncle Jim was young it wasn't even legal, let alone accepted. He must have found it hard because he moved down to London as soon as he could and more or less cut himself off from everybody up here. We knew he worked in a gay nightclub and there was some talk of him being on drugs but that was about it. The next thing we heard was when he died.'

'Wasn't he killed in a car crash?'

'Well, yeah, in a fashion – he threw himself off a bridge and onto a road. You were about eight at the time.'

The news is all coming as a complete shock. Although I have vague memories of an uncle I never knew dying and everyone being really sad about it and going to his funeral, the details were kept from me and Joe so we didn't really understand what was happening.

'But Mum, I had no idea.'

'No, well, nobody liked talking about it much, particularly your grandma. It was all very upsetting.'

As I look at the pained expression on her face, I feel another stab of guilt for some of my behaviour over the last few years. How could I have treated myself with such little self-respect? Am I really that different from my Uncle Jim?

I wait for my insides to settle then ask, 'But why did he do it? Does anybody know?'

'He did leave a suicide note, talking about how lonely and unhappy he was. I haven't seen it for years but I remember it saying something about wishing he was normal . . . Yeah, that was it – he said he wished there was a pill he could take that would make him wake up normal. Isn't that awful?'

I feel my heart contract as I remember feeling the same way when I was little. Clearly, Jim and I aren't that different after all.

I let out a ragged breath. 'God, Mum, this is heartbreaking.'

'I know, love. But now you understand why your dad worried about you so much. He used to say you were just like Jim. Apparently, when he was little he used to skip around the house singing pop songs too. And you always seemed such a happy child – your dad couldn't bear the idea of you ending up as unhappy as Jim did.'

'But why didn't you tell me any of this before?'

'Oh your dad didn't want me to. He always said he'd tell you himself when your grandma died. Who would have thought he'd beat her to it?'

I sit down on the side of the chest of drawers and try to take it all in. I can't help thinking that what Mum's just told me changes so much, that I don't have to go on feeling like I let Dad down for the rest of my life. All that time I thought he wanted to change me but he actually wanted to protect me from what happened to Jim. And his methods might have been muddled but at least he had good reason.

'You know what, love?' Mum asks. 'I think sometimes people underestimate just how difficult it is being a parent – watching your children grow up into their own people and then seeing them grow away from you. When you told us you were gay, your dad thought he was going to lose you forever. He thought you were going to disappear into some gay ghetto, just like your Uncle Jim. So he preferred not to think about it and just shut it out. Now, that might not have been the right way to deal with it but that's the way your dad was I'm afraid.'

I lean back and take in a deep breath. I had absolutely no idea Dad felt like this. Despite everything I thought, he loved me for who I was, not for the person he wanted me to be.

Just then the baby gives out a little cry and Mum leans forward to stroke his hair and soothe him back to sleep. I see the love and affection on her face and realize that all those years ago Dad probably looked at me with exactly the same expression. I can't help wondering how a father and son who loved each other so much could ever have caused each other so much pain. If only I'd explained to him that being happy didn't mean I'd have to grow away from him, not anymore, not now the world's changing. If only I'd opened up to him, I could have understood how he felt and tried to take him along on my journey with me. I feel stupid now for spending most of my life running away from him. I don't even know what I was running away from any more. Well, it's too late for me to do anything about my relationship with Dad but it isn't too late for me to bridge the distance that has opened up between me and the rest of my family.

'Mum,' I attempt, 'you know I love you, don't you?' It's weird hearing the words coming out of my mouth but surprisingly easy to say them.

She takes hold of my hand and gives it a squeeze. 'Yeah, of course I do, love.'

'No, but seriously,' I persist, 'I know you know but I still think it's important to say it sometimes. And it might not be something we do in our family but I'd really like us to start.'

She nods as if taking it in. 'OK, well, let's do that.'

'You know, maybe if someone had said it to Uncle Jim he might not have been so unhappy. Maybe if someone had said it to him he might still be alive now.'

'Well, now you put it like that I wish we had.'

I spot a flicker of guilt pass across Mum's face and don't want her to think I'm criticizing her. 'Mum, there's no point regretting that now. But we can learn from what's happened. And I don't want to do anything else we might regret.'

'No, you're right there, love.'

'So anyway . . . I love you, Mum.'

'I love you too, Charlie.'

I'm surprised by just how good hearing Mum say the words makes me feel. I suddenly feel calm and relaxed and happy. It's almost like magic. In fact, it works so well that the two of us stand there for a moment, awash with joy at the knowledge that we love each other. Other than this, nothing really matters.

After a while, baby Frank gives another gurgle. I look over at him asleep in his cot and feel a rush of goosepimples tingle up my arm. There might not have been much happiness in my life lately but I can suddenly glimpse a whole lot of it spreading itself out before me. And I can see now that so much of it's going to come from spending time with my family – my family who love me.

'Come on, Charlie,' says Mum, 'let's leave him before he wakes up.'

We creep out of the room grinning at each other and then turn to have one last look at the baby. Mum closes the door and I begin following her downstairs.

After just a few steps I stop and tell her I need to go to the bathroom. It suddenly occurs to me that there's something else I need to do and I need to be on my own to do it. I climb back up the last few stairs and step inside the blue-tiled room, locking the door behind me.

I lean my hands on the sink and take a long, probing look at myself in the mirror. Hearing about my Uncle Jim and how similar his feelings were to mine has made me understand not just how awful his life was but how difficult some of mine has been too – and I feel a huge swell of sympathy for the boy I was that had to go through it. Not just that but, even though I've made plenty of mistakes in life, I can see now that I'm a brilliant, special person for surviving.

I stare deep into my own eyes and let this understanding sink in. I can feel a new love for myself growing and soothing my entire being from within. I remember years ago Mr Beveridge telling me it was time to start loving myself and

I realize it's taken me this long to do it. But now that I have, all I want to do is care for myself and look after myself and treat myself with the respect I deserve.

'I love you, Charlie Matthews,' I find myself saying out loud, 'I really really love you.'

As I do, I know these are the most important words I'll ever say.

I'll Remember

I stretch out on the golden sand and feel the sunshine kiss my skin. The only sound I can hear is the rhythmic lapping of the waves and the occasional turning of a page as Tash and Amelia flick through their beach reading on either side of me. I look around, keen to savour the beauty of the scene. There's a light salty smell in the air and I breathe it in deeply.

As the midday heat kicks in, I dig my bottle of water out of my bag and take a swig. 'Does anyone want a drink?' I ask the girls.

'No, thanks,' they reply.

'Amelia,' I press, 'is there anything else I can get you?'

Amelia looks up at me and smiles. 'Charlie, I'm not an invalid. It's sweet of you to ask but you really don't need to.'

'OK, OK,' I say. 'But if there's anything I can do, just let me know.'

'I will,' she breathes, 'I will.'

The girls and I are on holiday, ostensibly to celebrate our thirtieth birthdays but in reality to lift Amelia out of the slump she's been in for months. It all started when her parents split up after it emerged they'd both been having affairs for years. And then Anthony suddenly left her the week before they were due to get married, saying that he felt trapped in the relationship and had never really wanted marriage or kids but only went along with the idea to please her. Both events left her reeling and she went from being the rock the rest of us relied on to an insecure wreck who came home from work every day, put on her pyjamas and refused to leave the house. So I came up with the idea of this holiday, eager to do whatever I could to pay her back for all the times she's helped me out of a crisis. Thankfully, she agreed – and so far it seems to be having the desired effect.

All of a sudden, Amelia puts her book down and looks at the two of us with purpose. 'You know what,' she announces, 'I think I'm glad Anthony dumped me.'

Tash and I sit up with a start. 'What?' we splutter. 'Where did that come from?'

She gives us a mischievous smirk. 'Well, you know, he *was* a bit pretentious.'

I can't stop myself from bursting out laughing; after months of nursing Amelia through her heartache, I'm overjoyed to see her smiling again. 'Atta girl! It looks like somebody's ready to start fighting back.'

'And, you know,' she goes on, 'he was a bit of a waster too. All that money I spent on supporting him and all those grand plans he was constantly spouting on about – but most of the time he just sat on his arse smoking dope.'

Tash claps her hands with delight. 'Amelia, you are *totally* over him!'

Amelia's smile brightens further. 'I think I am, yeah – finally. And you know, I really am glad he dumped me. Because if he didn't want the same things as me then sooner or later he was going to bail on the relationship anyway. And it's better that he did it *before* we got married and had kids than afterwards.'

I nod. 'Well, yeah, that's a good way of looking at it.'

'And let's be honest,' pipes Tash, 'if he didn't want the same things as you then he can hardly be The One, can he?'

A crease appears on Amelia's forehead. 'Well, I'm not so sure about that. First of all, you know I don't believe in The One – at least not in the same way as you do. And, more to the point, if Anthony wasn't right for me then I have to take some of the blame for falling in love with him.'

'What do you mean?' I say. 'How were you supposed to know he wasn't right for you if he wasn't honest about what he was looking for?'

'Yeah, well, we were together for ages so it's not as if I wouldn't have had a chance to pick up on it. I'm pretty sure now that he gave me hints; I just chose to ignore them. And now I've got to work out why.'

'Well,' I say, gesturing to the beach around us, 'it's a good job we're on holiday then, isn't it? Because you've got plenty of time to work it out here.'

We're staying in the South of Spain at Tash's dad's holiday home, in a small village not far from the Mediterranean coast. The last time we came here was just after we graduated, when we were all excited about getting out into the real world and achieving our dreams. We had no money so spent most of the holiday sunbathing on the beach and walking into the local village at night to get drunk on cheap wine in a bar on the main square. I remember us annoying the locals by relentlessly putting 'La Isla Bonita' on the jukebox and singing along at the tops of our voices until the early hours. This time around, we're far happier spending our evenings cooking healthy meals in the house, enjoying the occasional bottle of fine wine or practising our yoga as we watch the sun set.

I reapply my suncream as Tash plunges back into *The Lady and the Highwayman*, the latest in a pile of slushy novels she's brought to Spain for the holiday. Despite being single again and having her heart broken by every man she's fallen in love with, Tash is still a die-hard romantic and holds onto the hope that one day she'll meet The One. This is presumably what's on her mind now as she turns the pages of her latest novel. I imagine that her choice of reading material has the added appeal of distracting her from the fact that her career isn't going much better than her love life. After a run of badly written roles in underfunded fringe productions, she hasn't acted for a year and has taken a job in a railway station pasty shop so she won't have to ask her dad to keep paying her rent. It isn't an easy time for her and I admire the fact that she's somehow finding the inner strength to keep going.

I turn onto my other side but can't make out the title of the book Amelia's reading – although it's safe to say it'll be some kind of self-help manual; she's brought a pile of them with her.

'Listen to this, guys,' she says then reads aloud, '*According to leading psychologists, those of us who cling onto dreams to get us through a challenging period in life often struggle to cope with the realization that those dreams aren't going to come true – and maybe weren't even real in the first place.*'

'Mmm,' says Tash, 'that makes sense. At least it does for me. I mean, every time I start a new relationship I get all overexcited thinking it's going to be like a passionate romance from a Mills and Boon but then it always goes wrong and I end up feeling cheated and utterly devastated. Maybe if I didn't have such high hopes to start off with then I wouldn't end up so disappointed.'

'And you know what,' says Amelia, 'all this time I wanted to live up to the idyllic family set-up I thought my parents had but it turns out that was a flawed idea all along. I'm starting to think part of me always knew that their marriage wasn't happy but couldn't handle it. And that's why I've spent my life chasing the fantasy of having it myself.'

I begin sifting sand through my fingers. 'Yeah, but what about me?' I ask. 'Which fantasy have I been chasing?'

The two of them look at me, open-mouthed.

'Oh come on, Charlie, it's obvious!' Amelia replies.

I frown. 'Is it?'

'Totally!' agrees Tash.

'You've spent your whole time idolizing Madonna,' Amelia explains, 'and wanting everything in your life to be as perfect as you think she is.'

I shrug self-consciously. 'Do you really think so?'

'Yes I do. And don't you deny it! Now it's about time you accepted that she isn't perfect – she's only human like the rest of us.'

There's a pause and in my head I hear the lyrics to Madonna's 'I'll Remember'. My childhood idol is saying goodbye to someone she's loved, someone she's drawn on for the strength she needed to get through life. But now she feels strong enough to fly off on her own. Maybe I need to do the same.

I look down at the newspaper I've been reading, with its front-page report on Madonna's fall from her horse the day before. For some reason, the article really shook me up – I never expected this kind of thing to happen to someone I've always thought was so strong and found it difficult to picture her lying in hospital with several broken bones. But when I think about it now, I don't understand what I ever imagined would happen to her if she did fall off a horse. Did I honestly think she'd bounce back, completely unharmed?

'Oh all right,' I say, 'so maybe I am guilty of building Madonna up into something she's not. I suppose it sounds a bit daft when I think about it now. I mean, she can't be perfect, can she?'

'Course she can't,' Amelia goes on, 'I'm sure even she'd admit she's made the odd mistake – just like the rest of us.'

'*Totally*,' agrees Tash, 'look at some of her dodgy ex-boyfriends.'

'Or that awful cover of "American Pie".'

'Or more than a few duff films.'

'OK, OK,' I laugh, raising my hands in defeat. 'So she's not perfect, you win. But maybe I've always *wanted* to keep Madonna on a pedestal, maybe I've always needed that dream to hold onto. God, now I'm starting to sound like your self-help book.'

'Well, another thing the book says,' offers Amelia, 'is that if you're made to feel there's something wrong with you when you're growing up then you can often invest your dreams with more hope and cling onto them more intensely – because you think they can make you all right, they can make you good enough.'

'I can certainly empathize with that,' agrees Tash.

'Me too,' I say thoughtfully. 'And when you put it like that it's quite obvious; I always thought if I could be more like Madonna then everyone would love me and I'd be happy.'

'And I always thought if my life was like a romantic book or film then I'd be happy too. Although I've no idea why when every bloke I've ever been in love with has only gone and messed me around. You know, if I stop and think about it I can't *seriously* have believed any of that stuff but I think I was always too frightened to face up to the alternative.'

'Well, I'd love to say I didn't seriously believe Madonna could solve all my problems,' I joke, 'but to be honest I think I did. Or at least I forced myself to when things weren't going well in my life. It was like I *had* to believe there was some way of changing things, there was some way of escaping my reality or turning it into something else.'

Once again I think of the lyrics to 'I'll Remember'. I try to shake them out of my head.

'So where does that leave *The Lady and The Highwayman*?' asks Tash, holding up her book. 'I suppose after what we've all said I should probably throw it away?'

'No!' laughs Amelia. 'You can still enjoy it for what it is. Just don't try applying it to your life, that's all.'

'And can I still listen to Madonna's music and watch her videos and see her on tour?'

'Course you can! But you've got to let go of the idea that you're not good enough and she's some kind of goddess that can make you better. You've got to start believing in yourself and not in some distant pop star – however brilliant you might think she is.'

After a few moments of reflection, the girls lean back in the sun. I stand up and bat the sand off my hands. I stride out towards the sea, wincing as the hot sand burns the soles of my feet. I reach the water's edge and bend down to dip my fingers in and then step forward so that the waves can lap around me.

An unexpected rush of happiness comes out of nowhere and almost overwhelms me. At that moment it suddenly dawns on me just how wonderful my life is. Sure, it can be a bitch sometimes. I might not have become a film or theatre director, I might be disillusioned with my career in TV and I might have given up on the idea of finding my true love. As of today, I might even have accepted that Madonna isn't perfect. But despite all that, I'm standing on the beach in Spain, I'm perfectly healthy and the sun's shining. So yes, my life *is* wonderful.

Standing a little further down the shoreline I notice a young mum with her toddler son who's weeing into the sea and giggling. I splash my feet around in the water. If this is as good as it gets, then I'm pretty sure it's good enough for me.

Sorry

A few months later, I'm doing the weekly shop at my local supermarket when I have an unexpected encounter – and one that I have no idea will be so important.

As I push my trolley through the entrance, Madonna's latest album is playing on the sound system. Critics are saying *Confessions on a Dance Floor* is her best offering yet and its success has dragged disco back to the top of the charts around the world. My favourite singer has abandoned the message-heavy social commentary of *American Life*, pulled on her pink leotard and given us music that's simple, fun and celebratory. Just listening to it now brightens up the mundane reality of today's shopping.

I've just finished work and it's been a really enjoyable day. My latest job is producing a late-night religious discussion series called *The Actress and the Bishop*, which is presented by a classical stage actress notorious for her love of gin and Havana cigars and her frequent use of the words 'bugger' and 'cunt', alongside a leather-wearing, Harley-Davidson-riding clergyman who's heavily into body piercing and insists we all call him Trevor. The show's great fun to work on but what I particularly like about it is that as well as discussing the latest spiritual issues, it also explores related lifestyle topics such as parenthood, relationships and what everyone these days seems to call 'work/life balance'. It feels like it has more substance than some of the programmes I've produced in the past and probably because of this I'm now enjoying my working life more than ever before.

As I recognize the introduction to 'Sorry', I toss my shopping into the trolley in time to the music. Pernod, bubble bath, pineapple chunks – all the essentials for a good night in. I look down my list and see that I still need to pick up some toilet roll. I head over to the relevant aisle and begin staring at the innumerable brands, deliberating over whether to buy luxuriously soft 'Sheer Velvet' tissue or whether to do the right thing and buy the recycled stuff that sometimes scratches my bum a bit. It's then that I feel a tap on my shoulder and turn around to see a face I vaguely recognize.

'Hey,' its owner says brightly. 'How are you?'

I smile as I struggle to work out who it is.

Standing before me is a mixed-race man in his early thirties with a crooked smile and closely cropped hair. I have no idea how I know him but think that if I play along with the conversation, maybe I'll be able to work it out at some point along the way.

'I'm really well, thanks,' I sing-song. 'How about you?'

'Oh you know, I'm fine. It sure is neat to see you again.' I notice that he has an American accent but that doesn't help me place him. There's an awkward pause while I scramble around for something to say.

The man eventually breaks the awkwardness by laughing out loud. 'This is so funny,' he says. 'You don't remember me, do you?'

'Course I do,' I lie, not wanting to offend him. 'What makes you say that?'

'The look on your face, man.' He's clearly teasing me and I start to wonder if he's actually flirting.

I glance away coyly.

'OK then,' he goes on, 'where did we meet?'

'Urm, urm . . . Was it . . . ? Urm . . .'

I peer at him and trawl my memory. I notice that he has a small birthmark next to his left eyebrow. Now that I *do* recognize! 'Wait a minute . . .'

'Yeah?'

'Spartacus Roman Spa!'

'Got it in one.'

I instantly forget about my embarrassment and feel an urge to smack him across the face. 'You . . . You . . .'

Somehow I manage to hold myself back but am so thrown by the situation that I don't know how to respond. Once or twice over the last year I've sat on the Tube on my way to work, planning what I'd say to this guy if I ever saw him again. But now that I have I just stand there speechless, opening and closing my mouth like my nephew Frank doing his impression of a goldfish. As I do so, I hear the sound of an angry Madonna telling her man not to apologize for his bad behaviour because it's an apology she won't accept.

'So you're the one who gave me crabs!' I blurt out, unable to contain myself any longer. An old woman who looks like Mrs Doubtfire glances up at us from the washing powder section, pursing her lips in disapproval. I realize what I've said and blush bright red.

'Shhh!' the man whispers. 'Keep your voice down!'

I stand up straight and puff out my chest. 'Well, I think you owe me an apology, don't you?'

'Sure,' he nods, 'I'm sorry, man. All I can say is, from what I remember I was having a bit of a crazy time back then.'

'Yeah, well, join the club. Although some of us didn't use it as an excuse to go around giving everybody STDs.'

'Straight up, when I went to Spartacus that night I swear to you I had no idea I had crabs. Just going to that place was completely out of character for me.'

'Hmpf! I bet that's what they all say.' I pick up a packet of Andrex and begin examining the print on the side.

'Listen, man,' he says, 'it really is a blast to see you again . . .'

I don't respond and continue staring at the loo roll.

'And for what it's worth,' he goes on, 'I'm truly sorry about what happened. I don't suppose there's anything I can do to make it up to you, is there?'

'No, there isn't. And it's a bit late for that anyway.'

'Yeah, I know, but gimme a break, man.' He throws up his hands as if in defeat. 'I *am* trying, you know.'

I put down the loo roll and look him in the face. Maybe I am being a bit hard on him – and he does seem genuinely remorseful. What if the whole episode *was* some kind of mistake? Come to think of it, if he gave me crabs then it was only because someone else gave them to him – and who knows what was going on in that person's life? And in a roundabout way, if this guy hadn't given me crabs and sent me to the STD clinic then I wouldn't have received the wake-up call that made me turn my life around. I decide to try to loosen up a bit and change the subject.

'I, urm, I didn't know you were American,' I manage, realizing I mustn't have heard him speak when we first met. Now that I think about it, it's actually quite funny.

He wriggles around bashfully. 'Yeah, well, please don't hold it against me. My grandmother was British if that makes any difference. And before you ask – no, I didn't vote for George Bush.'

Without realizing it, the corners of my mouth have curled up into a smile. He notices and the two of us chuckle at each other nervously.

'Anyhow, I'm Justin Taylor,' he says, holding out his hand.

I take hold of it and give it a shake. 'Charlie Matthews. Pleased to meet you. Well, pleased to meet you *properly* anyway.'

However much I can see the funny side, it still feels a bit strange going through this formal introduction when we've already been so intimate with each other. It's all a bit awkward and I decide to make my excuses and head off.

'Well, urm, I hope you don't mind, Justin, but I've, urm, I've got some shopping to do.'

'Oh, yeah, sure thing.'

'See you around.' I turn back to the loo roll.

I look at the recycled tissue and decide to go for the luxuriously soft option. I toss it into my trolley and press on.

'Hey, hold on a second,' Justin calls after me. 'Aren't you forgetting something?'

I turn to face him. 'Am I?'

'Yeah, something that belongs to you . . .' He holds up his wrist and straight away I recognize my 'Ray of Light' bracelet glinting in the bright supermarket lighting. 'I take it this is yours?'

I almost jump up in the air with glee. 'Oh God, it is – yes it is!'

I take it off him and hold it up to have a good look. I'm

relieved to find that the inscription is still intact – I can't wait to tell the girls.

'You disappeared in such a hurry that night,' Justin explains, 'you must have left it behind on the floor. Anyhow, I've held on to it all this time hoping I'll run into you.'

'Oh thanks,' I gush, 'thanks so much.' I instinctively want to hug him but knowing that I've already slept with him rises like a barrier between us.

As 'Sorry' continues in the background, I realize that it's probably my turn to apologize. 'Listen, Justin, I'm really sorry I was so hard on you just now.'

'Oh don't worry about it, man.'

'No, I was out of order. I'm sorry, I really am.'

He gives me another crooked smile and I notice for the first time that he's actually quite attractive. 'Well, how about we buy each other a drink sometime and then we're quits?'

'Oh no,' I say, 'we can't do that.'

'Why not?'

'Well, just, you know . . . The way we met . . . It's all a bit sleazy, isn't it?'

He winks at me and lowers his voice. 'Look, I'll do you a deal – if you don't tell anyone about it, neither will I.'

There's a pause while I think it over. The whole scenario is hardly the ideal way to meet a bloke. In fact, it's just about as far removed as possible from the love-at-first-sight experience I used to dream about when I was young; I've already managed to break the rule about sleeping with him straight away and am pretty sure we've just had our first argument before we've even been out on a date. But despite this I feel strangely drawn to him. He seems like a nice guy and for some reason I find myself wanting to see him again. I've no idea where it'll lead, but now that I think about it, I can't see any reason not to accept his offer.

'Yeah, all right then,' I say. 'It looks like you've got yourself a date.'

'Awesome!' he grins.

'But if anyone asks, we got talking in the supermarket and that's how we met.'

'You got it. Standing by the bathroom tissue.'

'That's right – standing by the bog roll.'

We look at each other and laugh.

In a funny kind of way, it's all quite romantic.

Hung Up

It's seven thirty on a Friday evening and I'm cooking dinner at home. The meal I've chosen is one of Justin's favourites and I smile as I imagine his face when he eats it.

I've recently bought my own place, a small flat in Archway in North London, which is conveniently near the motorway that takes me back to visit family in Bolton. It's very small, with just a bedroom, lounge, kitchen and bathroom and is hardly the kind of place you'd find featured in *Elle Decoration* magazine. For a start there's a dark stain on the lounge floor where I spilt a glass of red wine, a huge crack down the middle of the bathroom sink where I dropped a bottle of aftershave, and the walls throughout the flat are peppered with holes where I've tried putting up paintings but kept missing my target. For some reason, though, none of this seems to matter – the most important thing to me is that the flat's mine. And I love it.

I've decorated my new home in bright, cheery colours, hung some Keith Haring prints on the walls and put up several photos of me looking happy with family and friends, including a big one of me and Dad on my graduation day. Almost without thinking about it I dotted several pot plants around the place, just like Mum has always done at the family home in

Bolton. I even took cuttings from some of her well-established plants and love watching them grow, feeding and watering them each week and making sure they always have enough sunlight.

But the thing I love most about my new place is the small terrace that runs over the flat roof of Turkish Delights, the kebab takeaway below. I've decorated it with plants, wind chimes and a rainbow flag, and it's just about big enough for me to put up a deckchair, where I often sit and read as the sun goes down. Unfortunately, there's an air vent in the middle that comes from the kitchens below and spews out the smell of kebab meat. When Mum visited she made a joke about it smelling like Dad used to at the end of a day's work. But in a funny kind of way I quite like it.

The food's ready and I take it off the heat. All I need now is for Justin to arrive.

It's been nine months since we bumped into each other in the supermarket and since then I've grown to like him more and more. He isn't really the kind of man I usually go for – he listens to music by rock bands like Coldplay and The Red Hot Chilli Peppers, has no interest in going to the theatre or the occasional art gallery, and as far as I know has never read a novel in his life. But he's calm and unflappable and he might not be wild or spontaneous enough for some people but I love the way he makes me feel safe and secure. I know I can always rely on him to be there if I need him.

Justin was brought up in the Midwest of America and studied at university in Chicago, where he qualified as a vet. He originally came to London in his mid-twenties on some kind of exchange programme and told me that he fell in love with the city and the way it welcomes all kinds of people from all over the world. Once he'd made the decision to settle here permanently he found himself a job at London Zoo; animals are his passion and he often talks to me about his working day, telling me stories about his current role looking after the penguins and how each of the couples are getting on bringing up their young. I love hearing him talk about their progress and seeing the proud look on his face as he shows me their photos.

When I think about it, I have to admit that on the surface it might not look like Justin and I have anything in common. He likes going for long walks or bike rides at weekends, he doesn't drink alcohol and hasn't ever smoked, and – worst of all – he absolutely hates dancing. He isn't in the least bit romantic either and often says he doesn't even know whether he believes in the idea of love. In fact, he's nothing like the kind of bloke I used to imagine myself with when I'd sit fantasizing to Madonna songs. But for some reason none of this seems important anymore. The two of us get on really well and I enjoy spending time with him. That's all I need for the time being.

Now that the food's ready I'm not sure what to do with myself. I feel strangely calm and relaxed and just fancy a cigarette. But I gave up smoking when I turned thirty, shortly after I gave up drugs and cut down on booze. I had to use the full arsenal of anti-smoking ammunition – chewing gum, patches and even those really uncool plastic cigarettes that are supposed to be just like the real thing – and even then I often ended up with all three on the go *and* a fag in my mouth. After months of trying I finally cracked it – and I'm not going to give in now simply because I'm bored.

I'm just going into the kitchen to pour myself a Pernod when

I hear the new ringtone of my mobile phone; it's the tune to Madonna's 'Hung Up'.

'Hello,' I answer.

'Hey man. I'm just walking to your place from the subway.'

'Well, the food's ready and waiting.'

'Cool. What are you cooking?'

'Corned beef hash. It's my Mum's recipe – the one you like.'

'Excellent! Are you doing some of those mushy peas too?'

'Yep. I've even got a jar of red cabbage.'

'Awesome! Catch you in a minute, man.'

And with that he hangs up.

I go into the living room to put some music on. I flick through my iPod and come to the letter M. Madonna's entire back catalogue glares out at me but I can't help going for the obvious choice and putting on the latest album. As the introduction to 'Hung Up' kicks in, I automatically begin singing along. Just as I'm really getting into it the doorbell rings and I move over to the stereo to lower the volume.

I skip downstairs to let Justin in, aware that a smile's spreading its way across my face. I only saw him last night but already I'm looking forward to seeing him again. In fact, I enjoy being with Justin so much that today I'm thinking of asking him to move in with me. I've been mulling it over a lot lately, and the way I see it, we've been spending so much time together that it seems like the logical thing to do, if only for practical reasons. The romantic I once was would never have imagined that one day I'd see the rising cost of rent and council tax as legitimate reasons to move in with someone. But I've come to accept that they are and I'm pretty sure Justin will too. Having said that, I'm a bit nervous about bringing up such a serious discussion about our future together, probably because of my past experience with men. Maybe I'll see what kind of a mood he's in before deciding whether or not to broach the subject.

The doorbell rings again and I bounce through the hall and fling open the door. There's Justin standing in front of me, holding out a bunch of sunflowers in his hands.

'Hey man,' he says, flashing me that crooked smile I've come to adore.

'Aw, are those for me?'

'Nah,' he jokes, 'I thought I'd give them to that Turkish guy in the kebab joint.'

I give him a fake scowl and snatch them out of his hand. 'Oh Justin, they're really beautiful – thanks a lot.'

'All right, all right, don't go getting all overexcited. I only got them because they were on special offer at the store on the corner.'

I pay no attention and hold them up to smell them. I'm thrilled he's bought me flowers but can't help feeling a tiny bit suspicious. Justin's never done anything like this before and part of me thinks he might only be making such a romantic gesture because he feels guilty about something. I try not to dwell on it. I examine the flowers and notice that there's a big green caterpillar crawling across one of their faces.

'Oh look,' I say, 'what should we do about him?'

He reaches forward with his index finger and expertly scoops up the insect. 'Come here, little man,' he whispers.

I watch as he jogs over to a nearby tree and gently lays it on a low-hanging leaf. He trots back to the door and gives me another smile. 'All right, the show's over. Now did you say something about red cabbage?'

I grin. 'Oh yeah, come on in.'

I skip up the stairs and lead Justin into my flat. As we walk into the living room we're immediately greeted by the sound of 'Hung Up'.

Justin looks at me with a frown. 'Man, do you mind if we turn the music off?'

'Oh but I *love* this song!'

'Yeah, well, I'm sorry but there's something I've been meaning to tell you for a long time now. And you might want a little quiet before you hear it.'

Oh no, this sounds serious. I can't stop my smile wilting. Just when I think I've found myself a nice, steady, dependable man and am thinking of asking him to move in with me, here he is getting all heavy and saying he has something to tell me. So *that's* why he bought me flowers for the first time – he obviously wanted to soften the blow. Oh I can just hear all the clichés before he opens his mouth . . .

'It's not you it's me.'

'I'm not ready for a relationship right now.'

'You're more like a brother to me than a boyfriend.'

I'm not sure I can bear the suspense. 'Oh go on then, you might as well get it over with. What is it?'

He squirms and begins fidgeting. 'It's a bit difficult for me to say. And you're not gonna like it.'

By now my heart's pounding and I feel short of breath. 'Oh come on, Justin, tell me. This is like torture!'

'Well, the thing is . . . I . . . I . . .'

I feel sick with panic.

'I . . . I . . .'

I start to feel light-headed and have to hold onto a chair.

'I . . . I . . . I-really-don't-like-Madonna.'

I stop and look at him in shock. In the background Madonna carries on singing 'Hung Up'.

'You what?' I gasp, trying not to whoop up and down with relief. 'What did you just say?'

'I'm so sorry, Charlie, but I really don't like Madonna. I've wanted to tell you all this time but I've been too frightened of upsetting you.'

I can't contain myself anymore and burst out laughing.

'So it doesn't bother you?' He blinks in bewilderment.

'Bother me? I think it's hilarious!'

'No kidding? I thought you'd be cut up about it.'

'Honestly, Justin, I couldn't care less. Now what would *you* like to listen to?'

'I dunno. Have you got anything by The Killers? Or Snow Patrol?'

'I don't think so. You have a look on the shelves while I put these sunflowers in water. There must be something you like there . . .'

I skip into the kitchen and give a gleeful squeak when I get there. So he *wasn't* trying to shake me off after all. I really have to try to stop being so cynical and always expecting the worst. I run the cold water tap and put the sunflowers in a vase. From the other room I can hear the start of the new Scissor Sisters album.

'Man, am I glad I got that off my chest!' Justin says as I reappear in the lounge.

I turn and look at him, standing there scratching his head, wearing his scuffed white trainers and a pair of faded jeans that are covered in mud, grass stains and a smattering of what I can only assume is penguin poo. I feel a swell of emotion in my chest and am sure that it's love. Oh Justin might not believe in love and I might have decided to give up on it a long time ago but as I look at him now I'm more certain than ever that what I feel for him really *is* love.

'Justin,' I smile, 'I think it's my turn now.'

'Excuse me? What are you talking about?'

'There's something I want to say to you too . . .'

The Power of Goodbye

A few months after he's moved into my flat, Justin accompanies me up north on his first trip to Bolton. It's going to be a day of goodbyes – although neither of us realizes this at first. And it starts with a hello.

It's Justin who says the word to my mum. 'Hello, Mrs Matthews, it's good to meet you.'

'You too, Justin,' Mum replies, letting out a little giggle. 'But please, call me Maggie.'

Justin flashes her his crooked smile and she gives off another giggle. I can't believe it; is Mum actually flirting with my boyfriend?

'And you must be Joe,' Justin says to my brother.

'Dead right, mate,' Joe replies, pumping his hand. 'Welcome to the family.'

'Thank you—'

Before Justin can say anything else, Mum interrupts him. 'As you can see, Charlie gets his blond hair from me. You know we're both 100 per cent natural.'

Justin nods his appreciation. 'So I understand. And you sure do have beautiful hair.'

'Oh Justin,' she howls, letting loose a whole torrent of giggles. 'You're such a charmer!'

As Joe manages to break in to tell Justin about taking my nephew Frank on his first visit to Chester Zoo, I step back and leave them to it. Everyone's getting on so well it's like they don't need me. Is it really going to be this easy?

Then I remember that I also have to introduce Justin to Grandma. And she's the one Dad always wanted me not to tell I was gay. She's the one he was most worried about upsetting. I told Mum not to say anything to her in advance and have arranged to take Justin to meet her in the old people's home.

Once I manage to prise him away from Mum and Joe, we set off – and on the way I realize I'm nervous. I've asked Grandma to wait for us in her bedroom, rather than in one of the communal areas, which always smell of boiled cabbage and are uncomfortably stuffy and full of cantankerous men and sour-faced women. I want Grandma to be on her own when I introduce her to my boyfriend, in case she gets upset and emotional.

As it happens, I needn't be nervous at all. I can tell as soon as we walk into her bedroom that she's thrilled.

'Grandma,' I announce, 'this is Justin. Justin's my boyfriend.'

She almost jumps out of her wheelchair with glee. 'Well, you took your time, didn't you?'

'What do you mean?' I splutter.

She turns to Justin and takes hold of both of his hands. 'Justin, I am chuffed to bits to meet you.'

'Likewise, Mrs Matthews, likewise.'

'You know I always knew our Charlie was gay,' she tells Justin once we've sat down. And then she turns to me and raises her eyebrows. 'I've been waiting for you to tell me for years!'

I shake my head. 'But Grandma, I thought you'd be upset.'

'Why do you say that? Because of your Uncle Jim?'

'Well, yeah, I wasn't sure if it'd bring back unhappy memories . . .'

'Does it 'eckers like.' She sits back and sighs. 'You know I *am* still devastated about your Uncle Jim – that's not the kind of thing a mother ever gets over. But the reason I don't like talking about it isn't because I didn't like him being gay, it's because it reminds me how badly I failed him as a mother. And that's something I have to live with forever.'

'Don't say that, Grandma,' I protest. 'Don't be so hard on yourself.'

'Why not? It's true – I did fail him. And I've regretted it ever since.'

'But Grandma, that's an awful thing to carry around with you.'

'I know it is, cocker. But I also know that if I had my time again I'd fight for our Jim like the fiercest lioness in Africa. So the last thing I'm going to do is get upset when my grandson turns up with a gorgeous hunk on his arm.'

As she turns to Justin and starts showering him with questions, I sit on her bed and smile. I'm surprised at Grandma's reaction to my news but relieved and happy too. I hope being able to enjoy her gay grandson helps her let go of some of her sadness about her gay son.

I look at a photo of Jim standing on her bedside cabinet. He's reclining in a deckchair in Grandma's old back garden, shielding his eyes from the sun as he smiles at the camera. He looks pretty much like Dad and Uncle Les, although there's something about his smile that hints not just at a sensitivity but some kind of sadness too. I wonder what he was like as a person and how he felt about growing up in Bolton. Now that I've spoken to Grandma about him I guess I'll have plenty of opportunity to find out.

I notice the time on her alarm clock and see it's later than I thought.

'Come on, guys,' I interrupt, 'we'd better get going. We're due at the stadium in half an hour.'

I gather together Grandma's things and hold open the door so that Justin can push her into the hall and out to the car. As I make sure she's comfortable, I steel myself for what lies ahead. I might have started the day with a round of hellos but it's time for me to say my first goodbye.

I'm standing right in the centre of the pitch in the Reebok Stadium, the home of Bolton Wanderers. Fanning out around me are thousands of blue and red seats, with the sponsor's logo sprinting across them in white. Along the top of the roof run the curved iron bars that give the stadium its distinctive appearance, and rising up from each corner are the lights that illuminate the action on the pitch. I can only imagine how it feels to be here on match days, when up to 29,000 people pile in to watch the action, most of them cheering on the home team. I've never experienced it before as, on the rare occasions Dad took me to watch the Wanderers as a child, they were playing in their old ground of Burnden Park. I've no idea where exactly in this new stadium Dad used to sit and make a mental note to ask Joe afterwards.

The club's chaplain has just conducted a formal service of remembrance, which was well intentioned and sensitively handled but didn't feel particularly personal. Now we're given the chance to conduct our own private ceremony; the chaplain backs away to leave us on our own, to scatter Dad's ashes and say goodbye.

I look around at my family; me, Mum, Joe, Grandma and Justin have been joined by Uncle Les, Auntie Babs and my twin cousins, who've been bribed into behaving themselves with tickets to see Girls Aloud in Manchester. Standing next to them is my sister-in-law Sarah, trying her best not to look harassed as she struggles to control my nephew Frank, now an adorably chubby, permanently dribbling and undeniably hyperactive toddler. And Auntie Jan and Uncle Stan have flown over from Tenerife, their deep caramel tans standing out against the dull, overcast Lancashire sky. None of us are wearing black as we agreed to come dressed in bright colours; it's more than four years since Dad died and we've decided that today shouldn't be about grief or mourning but a celebration of our relationships with him.

Mum pulls the silver urn out of her bag and gives it a little shake. 'Right then,' she says, briskly, 'there's plenty to go round. Why don't we all sprinkle a bit on the grass and say a few words?'

Even though we've decided to try to keep today cheerful, now that the moment has come the mood is sombre.

'Oh cheer up, you lot!' Mum breaks in. 'Look at the state of you!'

Her words loosen everyone up and we force out smiles and the odd chuckle.

'Pass it 'ere, love,' says Grandma, taking hold of the urn. She unscrews the top and shakes some of the ashes out onto the grass. 'You were a beltin' son, Frank,' she says, 'and your mam don't half miss you. Not long now and I'll be up there with you.'

As Les takes the urn off her to say his piece, I step back to work out what I'm going to say. I didn't know I'd have to speak as I scattered the ashes and feel a slight panic that I haven't prepared for such a significant moment. I think back to how I felt at the funeral and remember that I was happy to let Joe do the eulogy because I was so angry at Dad. I was worried at the time that I'd never be able to let go of that anger but I realize now that I have. And then I remember what I forgot to say to Dad just before he died. I know there's only one thing I can say to him now.

When Joe passes me the urn I give it a little shake and step away from everyone to make the most of the moment. I want to be alone with my dad. And, after everything that happened between us, after all the misunderstandings, I don't want there to be any misunderstandings anymore.

I look up to the sky and picture his face. The image makes me smile. I sprinkle his ashes over the ground.

'Goodbye, Dad,' I say. 'I love you.'

That evening, it's time for me to say another goodbye. It's time for me to let go of more negative feelings – this time to my hometown.

And there's only one place where I can do it.

After we've eaten a meal with my family, I tell Justin I'd like to go out for a drink and we excuse ourselves. I've decided to take him to my local gay bar – although it's a bar I still haven't been to myself. It's The Star and Garter.

As I drive us into the town centre, I tell Justin all about the Bolton I grew up in. I take him down the same route I used when I walked into town on a Saturday to buy my Madonna records. We pass what used to be Tonge Moor Library, the

Matalan store I still think of as new even though it must have been there for fifteen years, and Dave's Aquarium, which is still going strong after more than three decades in business. As we come into the town centre, there's no denying that much of it has seen better days; Bank Street is now full of kebab shops and lap-dancing bars and many of the buildings I remember from my youth are empty and boarded up or have been demolished and not replaced. I imagine seeing everything through Justin's eyes and have to admit that my hometown is what many people coming from outside would call a dump. But I don't care because it's *my* dump.

We park up on one of the top floors of a multi-storey car park and, as we leave the car, stop to take in the view across the town centre. In the distance we can see the clock tower of the town hall peeping out over the buildings around it. I tell Justin about the stone lions standing proudly on the steps and promise to take him to Victoria Square and show him one day. But right now The Star and Garter is calling.

As we walk along Bow Street and approach the pub, I notice that it looks different from the outside; it's recently been painted blue and grey and there isn't the graffiti that often defaced the walls when I was young. There are still iron bars over the windows and there still isn't a rainbow flag flying outside but the pub has survived and is very much open for business. I take a deep breath and go inside.

The first thing I notice is that the interior isn't anything like as dirty or dingy as I thought it would be. In fact, it looks pretty much like any other traditional northern pub; it has low ceilings held up by wooden beams that look to me to be genuine, and is made up of several cosy corners offering Formica-topped tables covered with cardboard beer mats and surrounded by wooden stools. The smell is familiar too; it's the same whiff of beer, wet coats and prawn cocktail flavoured crisps I recognize from The Flat Iron. And dotted around the place are a group of men and women who wouldn't look out of place in any other pub in Bolton. Nestled in the snug is a man with big hairy forearms and hands like bunches of bananas, who stifles a belch before taking another pull on his pint. Sitting on a bar stool is a middle-aged woman with striking knee chub and arms like sides of ham, scoffing a bag of peanuts and spilling half of them down her front. And in the snug is a craft-beer bore droning on to his friends about some micro-brewery he's just discovered that he insists is the best in the North-West. I turn to the bar and see there's even a barmaid with the stereotypical blonde hair and big boobs. 'I bet you wouldn't get many of those in a quarter,' I imagine my dad saying and smile at the memory.

'All right, love?' the barmaid greets me. 'What can I get you?'

I order myself a Pernod and an apple juice for Justin. It's a bit warm inside so I start to take off my jumper. As I do, Justin reaches in and pulls down the T-shirt I'm wearing underneath so that it won't ride up and expose my belly. He does this without being asked and I realize in that moment that that's why I love him.

I thank the barmaid for our drinks and we sit down at a table facing the door.

'You know, I used to be terrified of this place,' I tell Justin as I pour water into my glass.

'Terrified? Why?'

'Oh I don't know, it's just everyone used to say such awful things about it. I imagined it would be horrible inside – and that horrible things would happen.'

He nods thoughtfully. 'And what do you think now you're finally seeing it for yourself?'

I smile and give him a shrug. 'I'm surprised at how nice it is, actually. Funnily enough, it feels quite homely.'

It suddenly strikes me that 'gay' and 'home' are two concepts I always thought were mutually exclusive. But I understand now that they *can* go together after all. And, for those brave people who carried on coming into this pub when it was difficult to be gay and live in Bolton, they always *did* go together. I think about the man I once saw walking out into the street and being abused by strangers and wonder what he's doing now.

Just then a man walks in and it's someone I recognize.

No, it isn't. It can't be.

It *is*, it is him!

Without thinking about it, I shoot up to my feet.

'Mr Beveridge!'

My former English teacher turns towards me and I see that his hair's gone grey, he's filled out around the middle, and his face is much more lined than I remember. But he's dressed on-trend, wearing a shirt with a cardigan over the top, the bottom button left undone. And he looks so well he's practically glowing. 'Charlie Matthews?' he says. 'Is that you?'

He comes over and shakes my hand and I introduce him to Justin.

'It really is good to see you again,' I babble excitedly. 'I've got so much to tell you.'

'You too, Charlie,' he says. 'How about I get myself a drink and come and join you?'

'No, let me get you one,' I insist. 'Honestly, it's the least I can do.'

I go back to the bar and order Mr Beveridge a pint of bitter, anxious to get back to the table and start hearing all his news. As the barmaid pulls his pint, I turn around and see Justin leaning towards him with that overly earnest politeness he has when he speaks to people he doesn't know. I'm struck again by my boyfriend's laid-back, calm nature and remember something Amelia said to me once about some people being fireworks and others being candles. Well, Justin's my candle and that's just how I like him.

The barmaid hands me Mr Beveridge's pint and I give her the money and head back to the table. I set it on the beermat in front of him. 'There you are, sir,' I say, reverting to the way I always used to address him.

'Thanks, Charlie, but you really don't need to call me sir anymore.'

'Oh yeah, sorry. But I don't think I actually know your first name.'

'It's John,' he says, 'but you can call me Beverley – all my friends do.'

I widen my eyes but he quickly explains that all his life people used to call him Beverley to make fun of him and a few years ago he decided to reclaim the name and turn it into a term of affection. Not only that but, now Clause 28 has been repealed, he's come out as gay and all the staff and kids at school have accepted him. In fact, he's started running the school's anti-bullying initiative as well as a gay youth group for teenagers all over Bolton. He explains that he's single at the moment but has just joined a dating website to see if he can fix that – and, after seeing how many gay men now live in the area, he's feeling hopeful. I can't get over the fact I've just bumped into him and it's brilliant to see him so happy and thriving. When I tell him this, he asks what I've been up to and I fill him in on my life in London.

'And have you ever got around to doing any more writing?' he asks.

I suddenly remember my dream of becoming a writer, which I first discovered when I went to see Madonna perform live in Leeds. But after writing my essay about the concert for Mr Beveridge, I quickly lost sight of that dream. Come to think of it, I haven't even told Justin about it. 'Oh no,' I shrug, suddenly feeling self-conscious, 'that was just something I did as a kid. I gave up on that long ago.'

'Really?' he says. 'You know there's still plenty of time; most people don't start writing until later in life.'

I try to bat away his suggestion. 'Yeah, but I've got too much other stuff going on for that.' I tell him about my latest job in TV, producing the second series of *The Actress and the Bishop*. 'You know, I didn't let you down,' I suddenly feel the need to point out, 'I went out and grabbed my future.'

He takes a pull on his pint then wipes his mouth. 'Actually,' he corrects me, 'I think I told you not to let *yourself* down.'

'Oh yeah, you did.'

'So how are you doing on that front?'

'Well, I don't *think* I've let myself down.' I consider it some more. 'But I don't think I'm finished quite yet.'

Later that night, Justin and I are lying on the bed in my mum's spare room, talking over the events of the day. It's my old childhood bedroom, although now that it's been redecorated it looks nothing like it used to. All we're wearing is our underwear, our brand new matching aussieBums, and we're trying to keep our voices down so we don't wake Mum up next door.

'You know, I really appreciate everything you've done for me today,' I tell Justin as I stretch out across the bed.

'That's cool, man,' he shrugs, 'that's what I'm here for.'

'Yeah, I know, but I'm sure when we started dating you didn't think I'd be dragging you to a totally unglamorous northern pub I've avoided going to all my life.'

He steeples his fingers under his chin. 'You know, I actually found that place interesting. And I think it's helped me understand you better.'

'Oh yeah? Well, how about spending the afternoon with my family on the football pitch?'

'I think you'll find the word's "soccer",' he teases.

'Yeah, yeah, whatever.'

'No, but seriously,' he goes on, 'that was a great thing to do. I was real pleased to be there.'

I nod. 'Good. Although I still want to say thanks. Because I think today's been important for me.'

'Oh yeah? Why's that?'

'God, where do I start?' I let out a long sigh. 'Let's just say that when I used to live here, I used to lie in this room wishing I could be the same as everyone else, wishing I wasn't gay. But now I can finally see just how wrong I was.'

He flashes me his crooked smile. 'Is that so? And what's brought you to that conclusion?'

'Well, I can see now that it was a privilege being born gay. It's opened up my life for me – it's allowed me to experience not just all the good stuff but all the bad stuff too. And surely any life that's complete has to have all the different kinds of emotions in it? You know, sadness as well as happiness, pain as well as pleasure.'

'I've never thought about it like that but I guess you're right.'

There's a pause and he looks at me intently.

After a while he pulls himself towards me. 'Hey,' he says in a voice I recognize as the one he uses when he's building up to sex. As he starts kissing me and slips in his tongue, I can feel his breath quicken. I know where this is leading.

'Ah-ah, Justin, not here.'

'Not here? Why not?'

I gesture to the space around us. 'I don't know . . . It's just . . . My mum's in the other room.'

'Yeah, well, we can be quiet.'

'I know but it doesn't feel right.'

'Why not, Charlie? You're not still ashamed, are you?'

'No, it's just . . . I don't know . . .'

I stop to look at him and, as my eyes follow the curve of his thick shoulder muscles, I realize just how much he turns me on. His whole body's so perfect and smooth and the sheer bulk of him arouses me. He starts kissing me again and I can feel my own breath start to quicken. But, however much I want to have sex with him, can I really do it here?

I pull back and look deep into his eyes while I consider it. As I do, I understand that having sex with my boyfriend in my parents' house could very well be the final frontier I have to cross if I want to finally overcome any vestiges of shame about my sexuality.

I flash him a rakish smile. 'All right, come on then.'

As I pull him towards me, I realize that I might just be saying my most important goodbye of the day.

Give it 2 Me

I look up at Madonna just a few feet in front of me, jumping and skipping around the stage dressed in a variation on her signature black basque, this time matched with spangly sports gear. As she French kisses one of her female dancers, the cheers from the audience are deafening. After the flack she took for her adoption of an African child, she looks almost relieved to see that the public still love her. I touch my VIP wristband and take a moment to savour the experience. It's now more than twenty years since I first saw Madonna live in Leeds and here I am in the VIP section of her latest gig, knowing that as soon as the show's over, I'll finally get to meet her.

I'm in Paris at the legendary Olympia concert hall, where Madonna's launching her new album *Hard Candy* with a live showcase for an audience of just a thousand journalists, radio pluggers and TV producers. My old colleague Fuck-It Liz has started work in the publicity department of Madonna's record company and, amazingly, has been put in charge of the British guest list. Thankfully, as well as inviting all the genuinely important media players, she invited friends like me too. And best of all, my invitation was a plus one. After much deliberation, I decided to ask Shanaz.

Fortunately, Shanaz forgave me a long time ago for making

such a spectacle of myself at her wedding. There's still no denying that we've been growing apart for years but recently I've come to appreciate how important her friendship is to me and have started making a big effort to rectify the situation. Last year, soon after Justin moved into my flat, we invited Shanaz and her husband Ravi down to London to spend the weekend with us. The four of us saw the new production of *The Sound of Music* in the West End, took a trip on the London Eye and had a brilliant curry on Brick Lane. When Shanaz and Ravi left to go back up north I was thrilled but also slightly relieved that the four of us had got on so well.

And now, as if to round everything off nicely, Shanaz and I are revisiting our shared youth at a Madonna gig and bonding all over again. I remember how betrayed I felt when I went to visit her in Manchester and she refused to listen to Madonna as everyone sat around smoking dope in her room. But I understand now that not only was she trying to impress her new friends by showing them how cool she was, she was also trying to impress herself and silence the sound of the childhood bullies in her head, just as I was doing when I threw my twenty-first birthday party in Cambridge. Now that I think about it, it's no wonder she reacted against everyone I introduced her to and tried to embarrass me in front of Nick. In any case, none of that bothers me anymore. And Shanaz can't really have stopped loving Madonna because she accepted my invitation like a shot.

As Madonna begins performing 'Give it 2 Me', an upbeat dance-pop song and my favourite track on the album, Shanaz and I put our arms around each other and bounce along in time to the music. In that moment it's as if nothing has changed between us and we still feel just as strongly about each other as we did as children. Yet at the same time we aren't pretending and there's an acceptance that so much between us *has* changed. Our lives are so different now that we can't possibly have the same kind of friendship as we did all those years ago. But the important thing is that our friendship has survived and we're back together again watching Madonna.

The whole show's amazing and it's incredible to see that Madonna's energy doesn't show any signs of dimming. In keeping with the new album's title, we were all given candy canes and lollipops on our way into the gig and Shanaz and I wave ours high in the air in approval. Madonna seems to be really enjoying performing her new songs, and a little earlier she said that it was a 'historical moment' for her to be appearing on the same mythical stage as music legends Edith Piaf, Juliette Greco and Marlene Dietrich, before adding jokily, 'But *they're* all dead.' The audience roared with laughter.

As she brings the song to its crescendo, I understand what it is I love so much about 'Give it 2 Me'; it encapsulates Madonna's incredible drive and determination to succeed. Just when I'm admiring her ability never to lose sight of her dream, I remember that the first time I saw her in concert I discovered mine; it was when watching her on stage in Leeds that I realized I wanted to be a writer. But I've hardly thought about that for years, at least not until I bumped into Mr Beveridge in The Star and Garter. I wonder whether now might be the time to resurrect my dream, whether I should take inspiration from Madonna one last time and rediscover it.

And then, all of a sudden, the show's over and Madonna disappears from the stage and once again exits my life. Except that this time she doesn't have to.

'Come on,' says Shanaz, 'let's go and meet her!'

On the train over here earlier today, Fuck-It Liz told us Madonna would be hosting a meet-and-greet after the show and promised to introduce us.

Shanaz's eyes are bulging with excitement. 'If our childhood selves could see us now,' she almost pants.

Looking around, it's clear that everyone else in our party is just as excited. Seconds after Madonna's disappeared from the stage, there's an indecorous scramble to be first through the entrance to the backstage area. I fiddle with my wristband and look over at the gathering queue. This is a moment I've wanted and fantasized about for nearly twenty-five years. But for some reason I find I don't want to go through with it. I've no idea where the feeling's come from but it's getting stronger and I can't shake it off.

I pull Shanaz to one side. 'What do you reckon?' I ask her. 'Shall we give it a miss?'

'You what?' she splutters. 'Are you *serious*?'

'Yeah, totally serious. I mean, I loved the show and everything but I'm not sure I'm actually that bothered about meeting her.'

She shakes her head. 'But Charlie, I don't understand. How can you say that after so many years of being such a big fan?'

'Well, that's just it, I *am* a big fan but I'm under no illusions anymore. Behind everything we've just seen on stage she has to be a normal person.'

'Yeah, but she's still Madonna!'

'I know, I know. But loving her music and her shows doesn't mean that if I met her we'd actually have anything to talk about. Or that we'd even like each other that much.'

'But Charlie, I always thought that meeting Madonna was your ultimate ambition.'

'Yeah, well, it was I suppose. And I still think she's amazing, don't get me wrong. But I guess I've discovered that *I'm* pretty amazing too – if that doesn't sound too cheesy. You know, I don't need someone like Madonna to look up to anymore. I mean, I'll still go and meet her if you want to but I'd probably rather go for a walk along the river and grab a hot chocolate somewhere. Just me and you – like in the old days.'

We both stop in silence for a moment and look at each other. At exactly the same time, smiles begin spreading across our faces.

'Come on,' she giggles, linking my arm, 'let's get out of here.'

And with that we skip out of the venue and onto the streets of Paris.

We stroll along the river, passing landmarks I remember from my weekend here with Christian. I'm pleased to be back now with my oldest friend, a friend who, despite everything, will always be the best I've ever had.

After a while we end up somewhere I've never been before but have always wanted to visit – Les Deux Magots, a café in Saint-Germain that has long been famous as the favourite hang-out of leading literary personalities. Sartre, de Beauvoir, Joyce, Verlaine, Rimbaud, Hemingway, Camus – they all came here at one time or another.

We order two hot chocolates from a waiter dressed in black tie with a white apron and take a seat on one of the red leather banquettes I recognize from photographs in tourist guides. Mounted high on the walls facing us are the famous statues of Chinese mandarins that gave the café its name. Shanaz begins to tell me about her plans to start a family soon and we chat at great length about what it'll be like to have a baby and how she'll cope as a mother. Then it's my turn to share with Shanaz something I've never told anyone before, something that I've hidden from myself for much of my life.

'I've been thinking about taking a break from telly soon,' I confide, tentatively.

'Really?' She narrows her eyes. 'What will you do instead?'

'Well, I thought I might try and write something.'

She takes a sip of her hot chocolate. 'Oh yeah? What kind of something?'

'I don't know, a novel. Yeah, actually, a novel.' There's a pause while the word hangs in the air between us. It suddenly strikes me just how much I've wanted to do this all along, even if I did hide it from myself. 'It seems like the simplest option,' I go on. 'I mean, I've read plenty of novels so I know how they're supposed to work. And I've no idea how to get published or anything but at least I can put pen to paper and get going.'

She nods. 'And why've you never mentioned any of this before?'

'Well, I guess you could say it's taken me a while to work it out for myself. Or should I say admit it to myself?'

'Well, I don't know why it took you so long. I think it sounds like a great idea.'

I smile. 'Thanks, Shanaz. I think part of the problem was that for a long time I wasn't sure what I'd actually write *about*. I mean, everybody says you should write about your own experiences and stick to what you know best. But for ages I had no idea what was special about my life or why anyone would want to read it.'

'And why's that suddenly changed?'

'I don't know, it just came to me tonight. I finally know what I'm going to write about. And I don't want to give too much away but I can't wait to get started.'

She claps her hands together. 'That's so exciting!'

'Yeah,' I agree. 'It is, isn't it?'

'Just think,' she rattles on, 'while you're writing you can work through your life and make sense of it all.'

'Yeah, I'm not sure how I feel about that.'

'Don't be daft; it'll be like therapy.'

'Exactly. It sounds terrifying!' But even as I say it I know that this time I won't give in to my fear.

'Hey and if you do tell your own story,' Shanaz goes on, 'you can rewrite reality here and there to make it funnier or sexier or more dramatic. I imagine that's the best part of writing a book – making stuff up.'

My mind begins to race with ideas. 'Oh, I can invent new characters – and make up whole scenes. I can tidy up the timeline and get rid of some of the boring stuff.'

She smiles at me. 'Too right you can. You can put right some of the mistakes you've made. You can even give yourself a fantastically happy ending.'

'Oooh that sounds good. With a lovely American called Justin!'

We look at each other and laugh.

Later, as we leave the café and re-emerge onto the streets of Paris, I can't stop thinking about the novel I'm going to write. The more I think about it, the more excited I feel – even more excited than I used to feel about the idea of meeting Madonna. My imagination begins swirling with ideas for the opening scene. Should I start the story at the very beginning in Bolton? Should I give the lead character my name or change it? And what should I call the book to best sum up what it's about?

As we spot our hotel and prepare to say goodnight to Paris, I realize that I may not have met Madonna on this trip but I'll be coming away from it with something much more important.

Twenty years ago Madonna gave me a dream. And now I'm finally ready to fulfil it.

Epilogue

The band begin playing the opening notes of the song and I jump to my feet excitedly. 'So come on then, are you going to dance with me or what?'

Justin screws up his face. 'Oh give me a break, you know I'm a lousy dancer.'

'Ah-ah! You *promised* me you'd get up to our song!'

He picks up his glass of apple juice and drains it dry. 'Oh all right then. Just go easy on me.'

'Course I will. You and me are a team now, remember?'

I take his hand and lead him to the dance floor.

A few hours ago, the two of us vowed to spend the rest of our lives together in the registry office of Bolton Town Hall. Civil partnerships between members of the same sex have been legal for a few years now and we were married by a registrar in front of our closest family and friends on a balcony looking out onto Victoria Square. Unusually for Bolton, it was a bright sunny afternoon and we were wearing pale blue suits to match the colour of the sky, with brilliant golden sunflowers pinned to our buttonholes. At the end of our vows, Justin gave me a crooked smile and his eyes sparkled at me in the sunlight. He leaned forward and hugged me and I was so happy that I could feel my knees giving way. As I looked down onto the square and saw the stone lions proudly standing guard on the steps of the town hall, I knew that I was especially happy to be getting married here in my hometown.

As soon as the ceremony was over, we all drove to my old primary school, where I've hired the main hall as our reception venue. It's the same hall where I performed Madonna's 'Dress You Up' more than twenty years ago but today it looks totally different. We've filled one half of the room with a bar area and dance floor, set up a buffet along the other side serving Lancashire hotpot and potato pie, and decorated the walls with photographs of me and Justin during the various chapters of our lives. We've also printed my favourite on the place mats and coasters; it shows the two of us standing arm in arm on the wooden bridge of St Christopher's College, on a day trip to Cambridge.

For our reception we used the stage in the hall for speeches and I was relieved to see that they went down far better than my youthful imitation of Madonna. I kicked things off by telling the story of how I first met Justin in the toilet roll section of my local supermarket, an anecdote that by this time I've worked up into something resembling a comedy sketch by Victoria Wood or Alan Bennett. Justin got up next and made several jokes about my bad taste in music and having to wean me off Madonna, which I noticed all the guests found particularly funny. His mum, who's flown over from the States especially for the occasion, drawled on about how she'd never heard of Bolton until Justin met me but now she's here she thinks it's 'charming', 'quaint' and 'just like *The Full Monty*'. And my best man Joe gave a touching speech in which he said how pleased he is to formally welcome Justin into the family and how proud he is to have a brother as special as me. As I joined in the applause I noticed that there were tears in my eyes but, rather than sniffing them back, I let them flow.

Now that the speeches are over, I've dried my eyes and the stage has been cleared so that the band we've booked can lead the dancing.

'This is going to be painful,' Justin jokes as we step onto the floor. 'You know I haven't danced in front of anyone for years.'

'Well, that's because it took you so long to meet me,' I sparkle back at him. 'Come on, partner, I'll lead the way . . .'

We spent ages trying to decide which song to choose for the traditional first dance. I obviously wanted something by Madonna and, as she's just released her Greatest Hits collection, *Celebration*, trawled through her body of work trying to pick one. This felt fitting as she's about to leave the record company that has released her music for twenty-five years and come to the end of an era in her life just as I'm starting a new one in mine. And not only that but, following her divorce from Guy Ritchie, she's leaving London to relocate to the US, for the first time moving further away from me rather than closer. But no matter how much I love so many of the songs, when it came down to it none of them quite summed up how Justin and I feel about each other.

The song we settled on in the end is the swing classic 'Beyond the Sea'; it has special significance for Justin and me as it was playing on the day that Justin proposed. The two of us were out walking on Hampstead Heath when it started throwing it down with rain and we had to sit huddled up under a tiny umbrella on a dirty old bench on Parliament Hill. As we snuggled together, shivering and gazing out over the view of the rain-drenched London skyline, Justin suddenly announced that he wanted to spend the rest of his life with me. Just as I told him that I felt the same way about him, the brass band who'd been carrying on playing under the cover of the bandstand launched into 'Beyond the Sea' – and Justin and I braved the rain to dance around to it in each other's arms.

Six months later we're dancing to it again on the day of our civil partnership, something we and everyone else are calling our wedding day. This time, though, I can tell that the audience watching are making Justin self-conscious. Several of his American friends and his colleagues from the zoo know how nervous he is and give him an encouraging cheer. He soldiers on and I can't help chuckling fondly at his ability to miss the beat with every move.

As the two of us judder around the dance floor I occasionally catch glimpses of faces in the crowd around us. It's wonderful to know that so many people who've been important in my life have travelled here to be with us.

Standing by the bar I can make out Auntie Jan showing off her false boobs to a fascinated Caroline Tits while Inappropriate Lee drunkenly reverts to his Cambridge ways and leers on at them from the sidelines. My Smint-popping Uncle Stan has also had too much to drink and is boring Uncle Les and Auntie Babs with his usual speech about England going down the pan and slurring his way through a list of reasons why they too should move to Tenerife. And my five-year-old nephew Frank has drunk so much Coke that he's having some kind of sugar rush and manically darting around the dance floor with his heavily pregnant mum Sarah in hot pursuit.

Just then Justin treads on my left foot and I have to make a real effort not to squeal out loud.

'Gee, I'm sorry,' he yelps.

'Oh don't worry about it,' I say. 'It's really not a problem.'

As we start up again, I catch sight of Shanaz over Justin's left shoulder. She's here with her husband Ravi and did a reading at the service, despite the fact that she too is expecting a baby any day now. Even though it'll probably mean we see each other less as she'll enter a world of sleepless nights and dirty nappies, I'm thrilled that Shanaz is going to be a mum.

My new husband treads on my other foot and I put my finger to his lips before he has time to apologize.

As we carry on dancing, I look over his right shoulder and spot Mr Beveridge. He's here with his new boyfriend Arthur, a much younger and rather handsome landscape gardener he met on that new dating app, Grindr. Arthur is trying to deflect the attentions of my twin cousins, who are now twelve years old but dress like they're sixteen, proudly sporting matching crop tops emblazoned with the word 'Slut'. Standing next to him, Mr Beveridge is bellowing with laughter as Mike revels in the retelling of some of his dirtiest stories.

'Honestly,' he gasps, 'I went down there and he had a full-on bush. I said to him, "If you've never heard of manscaping, I've never heard of a blow-job."'

I can't help smiling; while it's great that Mr Beveridge has found love, it doesn't look like Mike's showing any signs of settling down. But he seems happy and, even though he's responded to heartache differently to me, maybe his way works for him.

To my relief, by this stage Justin's looking less awkward than when he first took to the dance floor. He's still dancing out of time but his movements are less jerky and slightly more fluid.

'All right, partner?' he smirks. 'How am I doing?'

'Fantastically,' I gush. 'I'm really proud of you.'

As I sweep him across the floor, I'm pleased to see that all of our guests seem to be enjoying themselves. Standing by the buffet I spot a few Cambridge friends such as my old next-door neighbour Sally, who a few years ago interrupted her severe jolliness with an equally severe nervous breakdown, but has since settled into a more sustainable state of happiness somewhere between the two. She's here with Rent-a-leg, who a few years ago finally accepted she was an alcoholic, did her time in rehab, and has happily managed to abstain from drink ever since. The two of them are tucking into plates of potato pie and trying to console Adrian about all the rejection he's had for his poetry, arguing that he should use the experience to write something powerful about resilience and survival. I make a mental note to join in and back them up later.

Beside them is Amelia, looking blissfully happy as she snogs her boyfriend, a dashing Italian who works at the embassy in London and whose family run a high-class restaurant in Rome. The two of them have been together for a year now and are planning their wedding next spring at his farmhouse in Tuscany. Silver-haired Giovanni is in his forties and already divorced with children but Amelia's willingly adapted her dream of a traditional family unit and is looking forward to getting to know her stepchildren before having babies of her own. It's all happened very quickly and we're still struggling to get used to such a big change in Amelia's life – but she's happier than I've seen her for a long time.

Just a few feet away from Amelia stands Tash, who's lapping up the attention of a crowd of guests keen to chat to a real-life celebrity. Shortly after our holiday to Spain, Tash was cast in a TV commercial advertising a new brand of sanitary towels that claimed to 'set free the goddess within' and this was enough to lift her out of her career slump. Shortly afterwards she won the lead role in a major Britflick about a group of female gangsters taking revenge on the men who wronged them, and then she achieved her dream of starring in a West End play, causing a sensation in the process when she appeared nude in the opening scene. Unfortunately, none of this brought her any luck with men and she was recently dumped by a Spanish flamenco guitarist called Rodrigo, who had an excess of five o'clock shadow and long lank hair like an Afghan hound. But I was interested to see that the break-up didn't seem to bother her that much and she quickly recovered, saying that she always knew the relationship wouldn't last. For the first time since I've known her she's currently enjoying being single, as well as making the most of her fame and success. Right now she's in her element, frothing with delight as she poses for photos and signs autographs for an adoring public.

On the dance floor, Justin's losing his inhibitions and the two of us giggle as he takes my hand and clumsily twirls me around. As I whizz across the floor, I catch sight of Council House Jack in the distance, chatting up Fuck-It Liz and telling her all about abandoning Socialism to work as a city trader and the new Ferrari he's just bought. It's quite easy to lip-read her responses seeing as every single one of them begins with the letter F. Just next to them are a group of my former workmates who during the course of the party have somehow managed to gravitate towards each other. I spot Cathy and Mothertucker from *The Third Nipple* who are talking to Scramble and Bernie Baxter from *Dyke on a Bike* about my sudden departure from the world of TV. They were all stunned when I announced that I was packing in telly to try my hand at writing. But I've nearly finished my novel now and only have the last chapter to write.

I started by digging out the essay I wrote after seeing Madonna perform on the *Who's That Girl* tour; it was childishly written and embarrassing to read as an adult but I found it moving and quite stirring to reconnect with the boy I was all those years ago and to remember why it was I'd loved Madonna so much. This kick-started my creative process and I built up the rest of the novel from there. The closer I get to the end, the more I become convinced that I'm finally living my dream.

Back on the dance floor, Justin's confidence is starting to outstrip his ability. He rather cack-handedly attempts a complicated move I remember seeing on the latest series of *Strictly Come Dancing* but stumbles at the key moment and almost sends me crashing into a huge vat of hotpot. Just as I'm composing myself and reassuring him there's no harm done, I catch sight of Grandma, sitting in her wheelchair watching us with a faraway look in her eye. I guide Justin towards her so we can speak.

'Are you all right, Grandma?' I call out.

'Yeah,' she shouts back, 'this is smashin'. I was just thinking it's the best thing that's happened since our Jim died.'

'Do you really think so?'

'I do, cocker. It's like he's getting his own back on the world. It's like he's finally getting the life he deserved through you.'

'Oh yeah, I didn't think of it like that.'

'I'll tell you another thing an' all. I bet you any money he's looking down on us and smiling. And that makes me very happy.'

'In that case,' I say, 'it makes me happy too.'

Just as we're pulling away, the band comes to the end of the song and everyone applauds me and Justin. Despite his cheery face I know he'll be relieved he's done his duty and can retire from dancing.

'Right,' he breathes, 'I'm off to get an apple juice. I take it my husband would like a Pernod?'

I raise my eyebrow and give him a wry grin.

'One Pernod coming right up!'

My eyes mist over as I watch him leave.

'Bloomin' 'eck!' Mum's voice bursts through my thoughts. 'Talk about the look of love!'

I turn to her and frown. 'Sorry – is it a bit sickly?'

'Is it 'eck! It's nice to see, that's all. And I wish your dad were here to see it too.'

'Really? Do you think he'd have enjoyed today?'

'Enjoyed it? He would have *loved* it!'

'Honestly? You don't think he'd have been a bit embarrassed?'

'Charlie, what did I tell you? All he ever wanted was to see you happy. And believe me, if he could see how happy you are now then nothing else would have mattered.'

The two of us nudge shoulders and smile. If Grandma's right and Uncle Jim really is up there looking down on my wedding, then I like to think Dad's standing at his side. My dad proud of his lad.

'Now where's my grandson?' asks Mum. 'I'm hoping the little belter's going to give me a dance.'

I watch her move off and scoop little Frank up in her arms. She jigs him around on the dance floor in exactly the same way she did with me when I was that age. It's good to see Mum smiling again. As she commented to me recently, being a widow doesn't get any better but she's getting better at it.

Just then Justin reappears holding our drinks.

'Come here, partner,' I say. 'I'm taking you outside for a little walk.'

Before he has time to object, I grab him by the hand and guide him out through the door and along one of the corridors. It's been more than twenty years since I was last here but everything's still so familiar.

'Where are you taking me?' he asks.

'Oh you'll see.'

I lead him down a long corridor I remember well from my time as a schoolboy. On one side is a wall decorated with paintings by the current intake of children and I notice that in the corner of each, the artist has painted a bright sun shining; it's good to see that the children all view their world so positively, although I hope the sun's shining in their real lives and not just their imaginations. On the other side of the corridor are the classrooms in which all those years ago I sat cowering behind my desk, hoping no one would notice me and wishing I was somewhere far away. I picture the lonely, frightened boy I was and more than anything else wish I could hug that boy and tell him that one day everything will be all right, one day he'll be happy. I wonder what he'd say if he could see the person he'd become, a proud gay man who's just married a handsome American and is about to complete his first novel. I long to tell him that this will all be possible. But the boy's image fades from my mind and soon he's retreated to the past.

I squeeze Justin's hand and press on, guiding him past the staffroom that was always thick with cigarette smoke and the cupboard where the art materials were stored. I give Justin another tug and am just leading him past Miss Bleach's old office when we almost collide head-on with a middle-aged man I don't recognize.

'Hello, Charlie,' he says.

'Oh, hi, I . . .'

'You don't remember me, do you?'

'Urm, no, I'm really sorry – I don't.'

'It's Vince,' he says, nodding his head, 'Vince Hargreaves.'

Instinctively, I let go of Justin's hand, anxious to fend off an attack. After all these years can this really be Vince?

I take a good look and see that it really is. He's lost most of his hair, is wearing glasses so thick they distort his eyes, and has piled on so much weight that his belly comes bursting out from under his T-shirt. In fact, he looks uncannily like Matt Lucas's character Andy from *Little Britain*. But somewhere underneath it all I recognize the Vince Hargreaves who all those years ago terrorized me at school. And I can't help shrinking away.

'Vince,' I stammer, 'what are you doing here?'

'I'm the school caretaker now,' he explains. 'And I've come to clear up when you've all finished.'

'Oh right! Urm, I . . .' My voice trails away and I'm not sure what to say. Justin must sense something's wrong because he takes hold of my hand again. I suddenly remember my manners.

'Oh Vince, this is Justin,' I say. And then I feel a surge of defiance. 'Justin's my husband.'

'Yeah, I heard,' says Vince.

I'm suddenly outraged. '*I heard*?' Is that all he can manage, '*I heard*?' After all this time and everything he put me through? I tell myself not to let him get to me. I turn back to my husband. 'Justin,' I state matter-of-factly, 'Vince's someone I used to know at school.'

'Yeah,' sniffs Vince. 'And who'd have thought I'd still be here now?'

I shuffle my feet around in silence.

'Not like you, though,' Vince says. 'I hear you're doing really well down London.'

'Oh, you know,' I shrug. So much has happened since the last time I saw him, I wouldn't know where to start, even if I wanted to.

'Anyway, I won't keep you,' Vince goes on, 'I just wanted to say congratulations.'

'*Congratulations?*' Did I hear him right? Did Vince Hargreaves really just congratulate me on my gay wedding?

'Well, thanks very much,' Justin says, polite as ever.

'Yeah, thanks,' I mumble, knowing that now Justin's said it I have to follow suit. But I resent the word even as I force it out. What am I doing thanking Vince when he owes me an almighty apology?

There's a taut pause while the two of us stand looking at each other. I spot an old food stain on the T-shirt straining over his huge belly and that's when I realize; I don't need an apology from Vince. Seeing him right here where he started, looking so failed and pathetic and diminished, is all the apology I need.

'So . . . you look after yourself then,' he says, eventually. And he holds out his hand.

There's a moment's hesitation. I reach out and shake it. 'You too, Vince.'

I watch him waddle off into his room and can't help feeling a bit sorry for him.

'Nice to see you!' I call out after him.

'You too, Charlie!' he shouts back with a smile.

'Who was that then?' Justin asks as soon as he's out of earshot.

'Oh nobody,' I smile. 'Nobody important anyway. I'll fill you in later.'

I pull Justin's hand and lead him further along the corridor, through a doorway and around the corner to a quiet spot behind the caretaker's room. I tell him that this is where all the older kids at school used to come for a secret snog during playtime and he laughs. I try not to notice the smell of rubbish coming from the dustbins but look up at the vast indigo sky that's spreading out above us. It's a beautiful evening.

I move closer to my husband and give him a long, loving kiss.

'There,' I say, 'I've always wanted to do that here.'

'Good,' he replies, chuckling, 'I'm glad I could be of service.'

And then for a few minutes we just stand there smiling at each other.

'Are you happy, Charlie?' Justin asks after a while.

'I am,' I beam, 'I really really am.'

'Even though I'm a lousy dancer?'

'Oh don't be daft – that doesn't matter at all. I keep telling you we're a team now, remember? And I love you just the way you are.'

He looks down bashfully. 'I love you too, Charlie. I love everything about you.'

'What?' I tease. 'Even my obsession with Madonna?'

'*Even* your obsession with Madonna!'

He puts his arm around me and the two of us look up at the stars twinkling down at us. I breathe in slowly, happier than I ever thought I could be and keen to make this feeling last forever. I'm entranced by the starlight shimmering in the sky and find myself thinking of 'Lucky Star', the first Madonna song I ever heard.

As I do so, I swear one of the stars winks back at me.

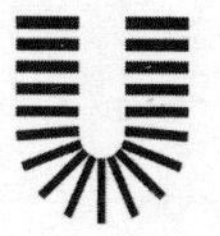

Unbound is the world's first crowdfunding publisher, established in 2011.

We believe that wonderful things can happen when you clear a path for people who share a passion. That's why we've built a platform that brings together readers and authors to crowdfund books they believe in – and give fresh ideas that don't fit the traditional mould the chance they deserve.

This book is in your hands because readers made it possible. Everyone who pledged their support is listed below. Join them by visiting unbound.com and supporting a book today.

With special thanks

Dorothy Byrne
Gordon Cain
Lynda Cain
Ruth Dunphy
Mark Gatiss
Franck Guillory
Jonathan Harvey
Robert Hastie
Omar Khwaja
Daniel Mallory
Waynne RC Meek
Tim Millward
Bianca Sainty
Francine Sheridan
SJ Watson
Aritha Wickramasinghe

Supporters

A Gay and A NonGay (Podcast)
Peter Acher
Jessica Adams
Lorraine Airley
Muna Al-Azzawi
Lara Alamad
Sue Almond
Tasos Anastasis
Bryan Anderson
Douglas Anderson
Jane Anderson
Jason Anderson
Kim Andersson
Anoush
George Ar
Liz Aragon
Christina Arestis
RJ Arkhipov
Eloise Armstrong
Rebecca Armstrong
Edward Arriens
Carl Ashworth
Kat Astley
Karen Attwood
Ben B
Gareth Bacon
Jimmy Baker
Anthony Barnes
Ruth Barrett
Tony Barton
Matthew Bates
Andrew Batmann
Lee Baxter
Rachael Beale
Richard Beaven
Kurt Beers
Ben

Eran Ben-Nathan
Simon Peter Bentley
Amy Berger
Tanya Bernard
Andrew Binns
KenKen Birdie
Fanny Blake
Simon Blake
Jamie Blowers
Remy Blumenfeld
Susanne Boldt
Christopher Bollinghaus
Becky Bolton
Emily Boocock
Alexander Borg
Ryan Boulton
Kris Bowes
James Boyce
Catherine McCarthy Bragg
Howard Bragman
Paul Brand
Emily Briggs
Carole Broadbent
John T Brock, Jr.
Daniel Brocklebank
Francesca Brown
Steve Brown
Claire Brydon
Mike Buckley
Wise Buddah
Kate Bulpitt
Leo Burley
Christine Burns
Chris Butler
Simon Button
Clare Cahill
Andrew Cain
Annie Cain
Charles Cain
Gordon and Lynda Cain
Harvey Cain
Jayden Cain
John Cain
Joseph Cain
Mia Cain
Neil Cain
Ron Cain
Ronnie Cain
Shirley Cain
Alex Call
Rubén Calvo
Bianca Campbell
Colin Campbell-Austin
Jimmy Canet
Tim Cashmore
Peter Chaivre
Chris Chalmers
Claire Chalmers
Angela Chan
Dennis Chang
Dominic Chapman
Ed Charles
KJ Charles
Yuen-Wei Chew
Kate Church
Keith Clapson
Jemima Clapton
Josephine Clapton
Laetitia Clapton
Nathan Clapton
Samuel Clapton
Kay Clark
Nick Clark
Adam Clarke
Mathew Clayton
Jonathan Clifton
Irene Clough
Ronnie Clough
Michael Coggin-Carr
Claire Coleman
Paul Coleman
Alexander Collum
Chris Colson
Rachel Congdon
Ed Connell
Martin Conroy-Edwards
Jude Cook
Owen Cook
Joe Cooney
Giles Cooper
Nigel Cooper
Scott Corbett
Nick Cordery
Jules Cornell
Isabel Costello
Marie Cowley
Jo Crellin
Martin Cremin
Jenny Crooks
Shannon Cullen
Martyn Daniel
Nicholas Daniel
Mark Davidson
Andrew Davies
Melissa Davies
Peter Davis
Mark Davison
Ian Dawe
Juno Dawson
Peter De Brauwer
Michael De La Torre
Remco de Ruig
Steven deLuque
Leigh Denault
Iain Dewar
Rachel Dove
Martin Dowd
Keith Dowling
Herman Duarte
Sandeep Dulai
Finlan Dunphy
Freddy Dunphy
Lucan Dunphy
Ruth Dunphy
Stuart Dunphy
Nancy Durrant
James Edgington
Lucy Edwards
Terrance Edwards
Josefine Ejebjork
George Ellenburg

Supporters

Mark Elliott
Gehrett Ellis
Janet Ellis
Sylvia Emmens
Abdi Estrella
Emma Eustace
Kate Evans
Martyn Evans
Gavin Eyers
Eiler Fagraklett
Stephen Fantinel
Maxine Featherstone
Julia Feld
Tayrina Ferguson
Fiona
Jamie Forshaw
Greg Fowler
Juergen Frankl
Jane Gage
Jen Gallagher
Martin Gallagher-Mitchell
Paul Gallimore
Jeremy Gelber
Dominic Geraghty
Tim Gething
KT Glitz
Katherine Godfrey
Douglas Goldschmidt
Caroline Goldsmith
Michele Gorman
Neale Goulding
Dayne Grant
John Greager
Garth Greenwell
Gillian Greenwood
James Gregory
Kath Grimshaw
Eli Grimson
Katy Guest
Diane Gunning
Michael Gunton
Claes Gylling
Joe Haining
Tony Hallam
Jamie Hammond
Janet Hampson
Darren Hampton
Rachel Handel
Jayne Hardcastle
Theo Hardy
Louise Hare
James Harknett
Emma Harris
Cheryl Harrison
Andy Hastings
Andrew Hatchell
Melanie Hawks
Andrew Hayden-Smith
David Headley
Lauren Milne Henderson
Bernard Henry
Julien Hernandez
Philip Hewitt
Rachel Heywood
Christopher Hilton
Matthew Hintzen
Keith Hirst
Alexia Hodgson
Stef Hoekman
Anne-Sophie Hoffmoen
Lisa Holdsworth
Chris Holliday
Jon Holmes
Stuart Honey
Ruth Hood
Andy Horn
Adam Horridge
Antony Howard
Joanna Howard
Colin Howe
Mark Howells
Lesley Hoyles
Lisa Hughes
Scott Hughes
Michale Hurstrom
Ali Huseyin
Simon Vogue Hutchinson
Katie Hutley
Asif Idsay
James Ingham
William Ivory
Angela Jackson
Diana Jackson
Kevin Jackson
Michael Jackson
Peter Jacobs
Simon James Green
Lisa Jenkins
Luke Jennings
Lisa Jewell
Cliff Joannou
John Johnson
Nick Jones
Simon Jones
Tracy Jones
Vic Jones
Timothy Junes
Chris Kerwin
Alexander Khalil
Tim Kidd
Dan Kieran
Patrick Kincaid
Charlie King
Ian Alexander Kirton
Julia Kite
Lotta Knutar
Marco Knuth
Kurt Koepfle
Alison Krafft
Seán Kretz
Bernard Krichefski
Lorne Kristofer
Morten Kvist
Pierre L'Allier
Karen Ladomery
Asifa Lahore
Klaus Laitinmäki
Kirstin Lamb
Nicola Lamb
Pieter-Jan Landsheer-Kock

Cameron Laux
Enrique Lavado
Emma Lawrence
Anthea Lawson
Gareth Leatham
Jodi Lehman
Derek Leitch
Rachael Levett
Lucy Leveugle
Kyle Lewis-McDonald
Axel Li-Mie
Eve Lizie
Morgan Lloyd Malcolm
Michael Loader
Angela Locke
Katrin Maack
Simon Macdonald-Smith
José Machado
Colin Mackenzie-Blackman
James Mackenzie-Blackman
Paul Madden
Claire Magowan
Rebecca Maguire
James Maker
Catherine Makin
Karen Makin
Lynne Makinson-Walsh
Chris Manby
Jayson Mansaray
Evelyn Marr
Gary Martin
Francisco Martínez
Tom Marx
Kate Marzillier
Rachel Mason
Stuart Mason
Lara Masters
Claire Matthews
Nigel May
Mark McAdam
Ruairí McAleese
Stuart McCaighy
Rebecca Mccann
Kate McCormack
Kevin McGoran
Jarlath McGrath
Clare McHale
Vicky Mcintyre
Tom McKay
James McKeon
Rob McManus
Ben McMechan
Ryan McMullan
Matthew McTague
Linda Medhurst
Erinna Mettler
Sarah Miller
Adrian Mills
Andrew Mills
Shane Mills
Lewis Mitchener
John Mitchinson
Jo Molloy
Monty Montgomery
Iain Moore
Joan Morgal
Yvonne Morris
Philip Mosley
GC Mosse
Kate Mosse
Nick Mowat
Gareth Mullan
Sean Patrick Mulroy
Emmalene Murphy
Sian Murphy
Nicky Napier
Jamie-Lee Nardone
Carlo Navato
Tim Neal
Andi Needham
Daniel Newman
Julie Newman
Nicki Newman
Robert Nguyen
David Nicholls
Claus Eschen Nielsen
Petra Nutting
Lucy O'Brien
Philip O'Ferrall
Owen O'kane
Jennifer O'Reilly
Kim O'connell
Simon Oliver
Krishna Omkar
Fernando Augusto Pacheco
Stefan Paetow
Alan Palmer
Siobhan Panayiotou
Cassa Pancho
Chris Park
Kathryn Parry
Wendy Pearson
Mike Pennell
Per-Olov Pettersson
Alana Phillips
Arlene Phillips
Robb Pickard
Peter Picton-Phillipps
Jennifer Pierce
David Pievsky
Sean Piggott
Arthur Pita
Ian Plenderleith
Ben Pollard
Justin Pollard
Nicholas Pollitt
Yvette Poskitt
Christopher Powell
Matthew Pratt
Zachary Preheim
Graham Price
Kate Price
Katie Price
Karen Prior
Gavin Pugh
Pino Pumilia
Marcin Radtke
Gavin Ralph
Ana Iris Ramgrab

Supporters

Martin Ramsdin
Dale Rawlinson
James Read
Martin Redfern
Matthias Reitzer
Marc Renwick
Matthew Rettenmund
Robert Reyner
Helen Reynolds
Amy Richards
Leo Richardson
Paige Richardson
Albert George Robinson
Billy Robinson
Enid Elizabeth Robinson
Frances Robinson
Ian Robinson
Joseph Robinson
Joyce Robinson
Juliet Robinson
Keith Robinson
Rosie Robinson
Stephen Robinson
NA Robinson Dunbar
Susan Roccelli
Susan Roccelli Belcher
Piotr Röllano
James Roman
Voravit Roonthiva
Andrew Rourke
Peter Row
AF Ruaud
Emillie Ruston
Martin Ryall
Amy Rynehart
Kristina Rynehart
Maia Rynehart
Josh Sabarra
Ed Sainty
Florence Sainty
Jack Sainty
Alejandro Salgado
Suki Sandhu
Andrés Santiago
Diane Scally
Elisa Schaeffer
Sabina Schiftar
James Seabright
Paolo Sgarbossa
Nicola Shaw (Beeson)
Bradford Shellhammer
Nigel Shipley
Ching Sian Sia
Hope Sills
Matilda Sills
Oscar Sills
Tomas Sills
Andrew Simmons
Mat Simon
Richard Sims
Nick Skinner
Hazel Slavin
Karen Smith
Kirsty Smith
MTA Smith
Ralph Smith
Ian Softley
Ste Softley
Eamon Somers
Sanjay Sood-Smith
Andrea Speed
Ethan Spibey
Kevin Stea
Zoe Stern
Jason Stevens
Paul Stevens
Emma Jane Stone
Frog Stone
Justin Strain
Darren Styles
Katy Sullivan
Christopher Sweeney
Ivona Swillo
Neil Symons
Scott Takenaka
Simon Tarrant
Peter Taysum
Jillian Tees
Jane Temple
Lucy Temple
Brett Templeton
The Society Club
Rob Thoday
David J Thomas
J.D. Thomas
Rob Thompson
Harriet Thorpe
Thomas Tillmon
Matthew Todd
Reza Tootoonchian
Eric Toribio
Christos Tsaprounis
Wayne Tulett-Wade
Michael Turner
Patricia Turner
Jani Turunen
Daniel Tye
Adrian Tyson
Jorge Ungo
Martin Vaessen
Sarah Valerkou
Sietske van Vugt
Emanuele Viviani
Angie Walker
Jane Walkinshaw
Robin Wall
Lee Wallace
David Walliams
Coenraad Walters
Louise Walters
Steve Wardlaw
Diane Wareing
Britt Warg
Gareth Watkins
Edward Watson
Gemma Watson
Graeme Watson
James Watts
Lynsey Weavers
Ian Webster
Juma Weeks
Gary Wells

James Wharton
Ricky Whatley
Louise Whitburn
Richard Whyte
Steven Whyte
Scott Wilkinson
Ross William
Christian Williams
Hannah Williams
Layton Williams
Simon Williams
Helen Williamson
Nigel Wilson
Paul Wilson
Victoria Wimpenny
Daniel Winterfeldt
Chris Wiseman
Chad Wong
Gary Wood
Susan Woodburn
Wendalynn Wordsmith
Alan Wright
Hugh Wright
Naomi Wright
Nicholas Yiannakou
Abed Zaid
Marco Zehe
Claire Zolkwer